ARCHANGEL

A MEDIEVAL ROMANCE
PART OF THE DE LOHR DYNASTY SERIES

BY KATHRYN LE VEQUE

© Copyright 2011 by Kathryn Le Veque Novels
Print Edition

Text by Kathryn Le Veque
Cover by Kathryn Le Veque

Reproduction of any kind except where it pertains to short quotes in relation to advertising or promotion is strictly prohibited.

All Rights Reserved.

KATHRYN LE VEQUE NOVELS

Medieval Romance:

The de Russe Legacy:
The White Lord of Wellesbourne
The Dark One: Dark Knight
Beast
Lord of War: Black Angel
The Iron Knight

The de Lohr Dynasty:
While Angels Slept (Lords of East Anglia)
Rise of the Defender
Steelheart
Spectre of the Sword
Archangel
Unending Love
Shadowmoor
Silversword

Great Lords of le Bec:
Great Protector
To the Lady Born (House of de Royans)
Lord of Winter (Lords of de Royans)

Lords of Eire:
The Darkland (Master Knights of Connaught)
Black Sword
Echoes of Ancient Dreams (time travel)

De Wolfe Pack Series:
The Wolfe
Serpent
Scorpion (Saxon Lords of Hage – Also related to The Questing)
The Lion of the North
Walls of Babylon
Dark Destroyer
Nighthawk
Warwolfe
ShadowWolfe

Ancient Kings of Anglecynn:
The Whispering Night
Netherworld

Battle Lords of de Velt:
The Dark Lord
Devil's Dominion

Reign of the House of de Winter:
Lespada
Swords and Shields (also related to The Questing, While Angels Slept)

De Reyne Domination:
Guardian of Darkness
The Fallen One (part of Dragonblade Series)
With Dreams Only of You

Unrelated characters or family groups:
The Gorgon (Also related to Lords of Thunder)
The Warrior Poet (St. John and de Gare)
Tender is the Knight (House of d'Vant)
Lord of Light
The Questing (related to The Dark Lord, Scorpion)
The Legend (House of Summerlin)

The Dragonblade Series: (Great Marcher Lords of de Lara)
Dragonblade
Island of Glass (House of St. Hever)
The Savage Curtain (Lords of Pembury)

The Fallen One (De Reyne Domination)
Fragments of Grace (House of St. Hever)
Lord of the Shadows
Queen of Lost Stars (House of St. Hever)

Lords of Thunder: The de Shera Brotherhood Trilogy
The Thunder Lord
The Thunder Warrior
The Thunder Knight

Highland Warriors of Munro:
The Red Lion
Deep Into Darkness

The House of Ashbourne:
Upon a Midnight Dream

The House of D'Aurilliac:
Valiant Chaos

The House of De Nerra:
The Falls of Erith
Vestiges of Valor

The House of De Dere:
Of Love and Legend

Time Travel Romance: (Saxon Lords of Hage)
The Crusader
Kingdom Come

Contemporary Romance:

Kathlyn Trent/Marcus Burton Series:
Valley of the Shadow
The Eden Factor
Canyon of the Sphinx

The American Heroes Series:
The Lucius Robe
Fires of Autumn
Evenshade
Sea of Dreams
Purgatory

Other Contemporary Romance:
Lady of Heaven
Darkling, I Listen
In the Dreaming Hour

Multi-author Collections/Anthologies:
Sirens of the Northern Seas (Viking romance)

Note: All Kathryn's novels are designed to be read as stand-alones, although many have cross-over characters or cross-over family groups. Novels that are grouped together have related characters or family groups.

Series are clearly marked. All series contain the same characters or family groups except the American Heroes Series, which is an anthology with unrelated characters.

There is NO particular chronological order for any of the novels because they can all be read as stand-alones, even the series.

For more information, find it in **A Reader's Guide to the Medieval World of Le Veque.**

Table of Contents

Chapter One 1
Chapter Two 12
Chapter Three 26
Chapter Four 39
Chapter Five 58
Chapter Six 69
Chapter Seven 86
Chapter Eight 98
Chapter Nine 107
Chapter Ten 119
Chapter Eleven 127
Chapter Twelve 139
Chapter Thirteen 146
Chapter Fourteen 154
Chapter Fifteen 164
Chapter Sixteen 177
Chapter Seventeen 190
Chapter Eighteen 203
Chapter Nineteen 214
Chapter Twenty 221
Chapter Twenty-One 236
Chapter Twenty-Two 242
Chapter Twenty-Three 246

Chapter Twenty-Four 257
Chapter Twenty-Five 271
Chapter Twenty-Six 290
Chapter Twenty-Seven 298
Chapter Twenty-Eight 310
Chapter Twenty-Nine 320
Epilogue 324
Author Note 330
Excerpt from Spectre of the Sword. 333
About Kathryn Le Veque 372

CHAPTER ONE

Year of Our Lord 1204 A.D.
The Month of May
Dunster Castle, Somerset

HE WAS SEEING ghosts.

It was true that he was weary after having spent the last seven days traveling from Kent to the shadowed edges of the Exmoor Forest. It was also true that the wilds of Somerset and Cornwall were said to breed wraiths and other netherworld creatures, and Dunster was right in the middle of dark and mysterious lands. But being a man of logic, Sir Gart Forbes wasn't one to believe in ghosts or phantoms or fairies. Still, he wasn't quite sure what he had seen.

He was standing in the darkened bailey of Dunster just after sunset. The castle was perched on the top of a hill, fortified and old even in Saxon times, and the battlements were lined with men standing guard, sentries with big dogs and big torches to keep away the night. Gazing up the wooden steps that led into the second floor of the enormous square keep, Gart swore he saw something at the top of the stairs that had just as quickly vanished.

All around him were sounds of the bailey as the men settled in for the night. He had brought one hundred men with him from Denstroude Castle in Kent, seat of Baron Thornden, Sir David de Lohr. Lord de Lohr was in the keep up in the third floor great hall and these wraiths, these wispy creatures, were between Gart and his liege. With a weary sigh, knowing he must have lost his mind somewhere back on the dusty road, Gart slowly mounted the steps.

The stairs were dark and old. Gart's enormous boots tested the weight of each plank as he made his way up and could hear the wood groan. Normally, he would have been focused on the meal awaiting him, but at this moment, he had to admit he was curious to see if the wraiths would make another appearance.

He didn't have long to wait. The moment he stepped inside the great Norman arch that embraced the entry, something small and white jumped into his path.

"Boo!"

Before Gart could open his mouth to speak, the phantom darted off and hid. It wasn't so much a phantom now that he had a closer look – it was a child, completely white from head to toe. Gart watched the child disappear into a darkened room, a solar that was directly off the entry to the right. His brow furrowed and he shook his head, undecided as to whether he was irritated or amused. He settled for amused until two more wraiths jumped out at him with sticks.

Gart was in armor so he didn't feel the blows, but his amusement quickly turned to irritation when one of the sticks landed a blow a little too close to his groin. He reached down to grab one of the children but his hand came away completely white. They were covered in something white and powdery.

Gart grabbed a stick that came flying at his groin again, yanking it out of the child's hand and tossing it out the door. He locked gazes with a boy no more than seven years of age and he would never forget the look of fury on the boy's face.

With a yell, the child charged him and tried to bite him, but all he came away with was mail to the mouth. Gart grabbed the child by the hair and the boy screamed.

"Let me go!" he howled. "I will have you arrested if you do not let me go!"

Gart's hand was bigger than the child's head as he gazed down at him. "Is that so?"

"It is!" The lad tried to kick him, struggling to dislodge the iron grip. "If you do not let me go, I… I will have you boiled! I will have you flogged! I will have you…!"

Gart put up a hand, cutting him off. "I understand your meaning," he said, noticing that the two other white-covered children were beating at his armored legs. He shoved one away by the head and kneed the other one across the floor. It wasn't a kick as much as it was a good push with his kneecap. Then he let go of the child in his grip.

"Let me pass and you can assault the next fool who walks in the door," he told them.

The three boys were not so easily dissuaded. They rushed back at him with their fists and sticks and Gart shoved them all away again, only to have them rush him once more as he tried to mount the stairs to the third level.

Irritation growing, he managed to grab all three of them, carry them over to the dark and empty solar, and shove them inside. Slamming the door closed, he noticed there was no exterior bolt as the boys beat at the door and yelled from the other side. Gart stood there as long as he could, holding the door shut as delicious smells taunted him from the hall above. He didn't have time for this foolishness. Daring to let go of the latch, he made a break for the stairs.

The solar door flew open and the three boys charged out, catching Gart as he was halfway up the spiral stone stairs. They grabbed at his feet and he kicked back, attempting to dislodge them. He didn't want to outright hurt them but they were annoying and beastly, so he finally kicked out and sent one boy crashing into the other two.

The whole lot of them slid down the stairs, leaving a trail of white powder as they went. They hit hard in a group, the older ones falling on the smaller one. The little lad at the bottom of the pile began to wail loudly and rub his head where he had smacked it.

Gart smirked at the screams, thinking now they would finally leave him alone. He hadn't taken two steps before he started to feel some remorse. They were just children, after all. He had been a child once, thirty years ago during times he could hardly remember. These children were just playing games. At least, he hoped so. Maybe they were really murderers in disguise. Taking another step, the cries prevented him from continuing.

With a heavy sigh he turned on the stairwell, peering down at the pile of boys at the bottom. The two older ones were attempting to pick the younger one up and convince him that he wasn't injured. Gart took a couple of steps down, watching the boys who seemed much less aggressive than they had been moments earlier.

"What are you three doing?" he demanded softly.

Three pairs of big blue eyes looked up at him as if startled by the question. He could see the hostility seep back into their expressions but, so far, not one of them had made a move against him. They seemed to be posturing an awful lot.

"Brendt hurt his head," the tallest child said angrily. "You did…."

Gart waved the boy off. "That is not what I meant," he took another step down. "What are you three doing attacking men who enter the keep?"

The tallest boy's brow furrowed. "Robbing them!"

Gart couldn't help it as his features screwed up in confusion. "*Robbing* them?"

"Aye," the boy insisted. "This is our castle. Whoever comes in this door belongs to us."

Gart stared at the lad a moment before finally shaking his head. Truth be told, he was fighting off a grin. The lad was deadly serious.

"Who are you?" he finally asked.

The boy stood tall. "Romney de Moyon," he announced. "These are my brothers, Orin and Brendt. Our father is Julian de Moyon, Baron Buckland, and this is our castle. Who are you?"

Gart came down the rest of the stairs and stood in front of them, massive fists resting on his hips. He avoided the question. "Why do you have white powder all over you?"

Romney looked at his brothers before returning his attention to Gart. "Because we are ghosts. You cannot see ghosts and it makes it easier to rob people."

Gart rubbed his hand over his chin and mouth so the boy would not see his grin. It was really quite dastardly and very humorous, he thought.

"I see you quite clearly," he ran a finger across Romney's chest, peering at the white powder. "What is this?"

"Dust from the stone," Romney told him. "Father is building a house for the soldiers and this is the dust from the white stone."

Gart inspected it a moment longer before wiping it on his tunic. His gaze moved to the youngest, who was no longer crying, but still rubbing his head.

"Had you not attacked me, you would not have hurt your head," he was looking at the smallest boy but lecturing all three. "Does your father know what you are doing?"

Romney lifted his shoulders, for the first time losing some of his confidence. "He does not care," he said. "Will you give me your money or will I have to fight you to the death?"

Gart bit his lip to keep his smile from breaking loose. "Are you sure you want to fight me to the death?"

"I am sure."

"I do not have any money on me."

Romney's fair brow furrowed and he looked to his brothers with uncertainty. "Well," he said reluctantly. "We will wait until you return for it. Come back with your money."

"I will not," Gart said flatly. "Why do you want my money, anyway?"

"Because," Romney said. "We want to buy nice things for my mother and sister."

Gart scratched his head. "Your mother and sister?" he repeated. "Surely they have enough nice things."

Romney shrugged. "It makes them happy. When Mother is crying, it will make her stop."

Gart scratched at his chin again, a little puzzled at the last sentence but he didn't pursue it.

"I see," he said. "I am afraid that I am going to disappoint you, your mother and your sister. You will have to get your ill-gotten gains somewhere else."

Romney didn't like that answer at all. It was clear he wasn't used to having his wishes denied. Gart eyed the children one more time before turning for the stairs and the three were on him in an instant with their fists and sticks. Gart rolled his eyes with frustration as he grabbed Romney by the arm and twisted it behind his back. Romney screamed and the other two lads stopped their onslaught.

"Oww!" Romney howled. "You are hurting me!"

Gart lifted an eyebrow. "I am getting tired of being attacked simply because I walked into this keep," he said in a low voice. "If you promise to cease your assault, I will let you go. Otherwise, I will bind all three of you and toss you into a closet."

Before the boy could reply, they heard a voice from the floor above. It was a female voice, soft and sweet, and soon the swish of a voluminous surcoat could be seen and heard. Great yards of crimson fabric descended the stairs, calling for Romney and Orin. As Gart stood there with Romney's arm twisted behind his back, a vision in red appeared.

"Romney!" the woman gasped. "What has happened? Are you injured?"

Gart stared at the woman in surprise, although his stone-like features did not give him away. He was actually stunned speechless for a moment as a vision from his past made an unexpected appearance. Although it had been years since he had last seen her, there was no mistaking the ethereal beauty. There wasn't anything like it anywhere else in England.

"Emberley?" he asked hesitantly. "Emberley de Russe?"

The Lady Emberley de Russe de Moyon came to a halt when she heard her name, staring at the enormous knight with shock and some fear. He had her son by the arm and the child was in obvious pain, but as she gazed at the man, he began to look vaguely familiar.

From the mists of her memories emerged the face as a very young man, someone her brother had been friends with. She had known that face well, long ago. Now he had grown into a strikingly handsome man. Her deep blue eyes lit up with recognition.

"Gart?" she asked.

Her voice was soft with uncertainty. Gart's green eyes glittered as he nodded his head, realizing he still had Romney by the arm and hastening to release the child. He tried not to feel guilty that this glorious creature had witnessed him roughing up the child.

"It is me." He just stared at her, a rather soft expression coming over his masculine features. "I have not seen you in years."

Emberley smiled broadly, a dimple on her chin and beautiful straight teeth. "It has been some time," she agreed. "I believe the last time I saw you was when I had just returned home from fostering at Chepstow Castle and you and my brother were newly knighted."

He nodded. "I recall," he said. "That was many years ago."

She warmed to the recognition. "Twelve years, at least," she agreed, cocking her head thoughtfully. "I also seem to remember that on the day I returned you and my brother tore through the outer ward on your chargers, slicing up anything that did not have a heartbeat. My mother yelled at you and my brother for an hour after it was over."

Gart was grinning, an unusual occurrence for him. The man had features of stone and cracking a smile was something that did not come easily. He was trying not to appear too embarrassed.

"We could not help ourselves," he admitted. "Erik had a new sword that your father had given him. We wanted to make sure that it worked properly."

Emberley laughed in remembrance. "My mother took it away for a week," she snorted. "Erik and my father were furious."

Gart's smile grew as he stared at the woman. His last memory of her was a slip of a girl barely past womanhood but to see her now, he could hardly believe the change. She was positively magnificent. His eyes moved over her luscious blond hair, arranged into a beautiful style that had it pulled off her face and trailing down her back. She had spectacular dark blue eyes, like sapphires, and ruby lips that were parted in a magnificent smile. The longer he looked at her, the more enamored he became.

"I was banned from visiting Morton Castle for a while," he said, wanting off the subject of his wild youth. "But that was long ago and now I find you at Dunster. Why are you here?"

Emberley lifted her hand as if to embrace the entire structure. "I live here," she replied. "You and my brother were in the Holy Land with Richard when I was betrothed to Julian de Moyon. Did you not hear of it?"

He shook his head. "I will confess, I did not," he said, somewhat regretfully. "My focus was on sand and battles until… well, until Erik was killed. Then I returned home to more battles and more intrigue."

Her smile faded, her dark blue eyes glimmering warmly at him. "I heard that you brought my brother home for burial," she said softly. "I never had the chance to thank you. It meant a great deal to my parents."

"Do they live still?"

She nodded. "Still," she said quietly. "They live at Morton Castle and have never gotten over the death of my brother. The fact that I have sons has eased their grief somewhat."

Gart gazed into her lovely eyes, the same color and shape as her brother's had been. He realized he missed his best friend very much, someone he'd not thought of in almost eight years. It was a sobering realization.

"Erik was a great knight," he said somberly. "He is missed."

Emberley smiled in agreement, in sympathy, knowing that her brother and Gabriel Forbes had been best friends since childhood. In fact, she had practically grown up knowing Forbes, a man known as Gart because he didn't like to be called Gabriel. To see him now brought her a great deal of emotional comfort in a life that knew little.

He was an enormous man, very tall, with a muscular body and long, muscular legs. He had sculpted cheekbones and a square jaw, and murky green eyes that were mysterious and intense. His hair, a dark shade of dark blond, had been practically shaved from his scalp but it did not detract from his virile, male handsomeness. The man was powerfully and painfully handsome.

Truth be told, Emberley had always been fond of Gart. As a young girl, she would dream of marrying him. But those days were long gone, as were her dreams. As she thought on the faded days of her childhood, she glanced at her boys and realized they were covered in white powder. Her brow furrowed.

"Why are my children dusty white?" she pointed at them.

Gart tore his eyes off her to look at the boys. "These are your children?"

She nodded. "Romney is my eldest," she smiled at the boy with pride. "He is an intelligent lad, sweet and loving. Orin is my middle son and Brendt is the youngest. Boys, why are you covered in white powder?"

She addressed her sons, who had a complete change of demeanor since her arrival and were now innocent little angels.

"We were playing, Mama," Orin insisted. "We were ghosts."

Emberley's delicate eyebrows lifted. "Ghosts? Why on earth are you ghosts?"

Romney took charge of the conversation before Orin blew their cover. "Because," he said simply, hoping that would be enough to satisfy his mother. "Mama, can we eat in the hall tonight? I want to see all of the knights!"

Emberley shook her head. "Nay," she told him. "You must eat in your chamber. Your father has business to attend to and does not want you underfoot." She looked at Gart. "Am I to understand that you have met my sons already?"

Gart wasn't sure how to answer. He looked at the boys, who all gazed back at him quite innocently. He didn't believe it for a moment. In fact, he was resisting the urge to scowl at them with disbelief.

"Aye," he said slowly, reluctantly. "I have just arrived and the boys were… that is to say, they were…."

"Mama," Romney latched on to his mother's arm. "We were going to show Sir Gart to the hall. May we do that, Mama? May we, please?"

"Of course, sweetheart," Emberley smiled at her eldest. "That is quite gracious of you."

Gart eyed the boys suspiciously as the youngest one reached out and took his big hand. "We will show you, Sir Gart," he said politely. "Come with us."

Gart didn't want to pull away from the child because he didn't want to offend Emberley. He stood there dumbly as the boy took his hand and Emberley smiled happily.

"'Tis so good to see you again, Gart," she said sincerely, her dark blue gaze drifting over his handsome features. "It has been a very long time. Much has happened since you and I last saw one another. I would like to know what you have been doing in the twelve years since I last saw you."

Gart could only nod. Realizing she was the baron's wife dampened his enthusiasm at their re-acquaintance and he was coming to think that he had been very, very stupid as a young man not to have realized her potential. True, she'd always been a lovely girl, but had he known she would have grown into such an exquisite creature, he might have vied for her hand. But that thought was tempered by the fact that she had apparently raised three hooligans who had her completely fooled. The woman was raising a pack of wild animals.

Emberley smiled at him and beckoned him to follow her back up the stairs. He did so willingly, gladly, but the moment she turned her back on the boys and headed up the stairs, the youngest one yanked his hand from Gart's fist and began smacking him on the leg.

Romney, too, waited until his mother's back was turned before shaking a fist at Gart, making horrible and threatening faces at him. Orin still had a stick and he whacked Gart on the back with it. Gart grabbed the stick and tossed it away but when Emberley turned around at the sounds coming from behind her, the four of them froze and smiled innocently at her. Emberley grinned and continued up the stairs.

The attack against Gart resumed and continued all the way into the great hall above.

CHAPTER TWO

"FORBES IS THE one they call 'Sach'."

Baron Buckland looked at the man who spoke. "What does that mean?"

Sir David de Lohr, Baron Thornden, wriggled his blond eyebrows, noticing that Forbes was entering the smelly, smoky hall in the company of a very beautiful woman.

De Lohr and Baron Buckland sat at the far end of the long, scrubbed table, enjoying the heat from the enormous hearth and the fine alcohol. Now their focus was on the pair approaching from the darkened entry.

"It is an abbreviated Celtic name," de Lohr told him quietly. "It means 'insane'."

Julian de Moyon, Baron Buckland, lifted his dark eyebrows. "Insane?" he repeated. "The man is mad?"

De Lohr shrugged vaguely, collecting his half-drained cup of tart port wine. "Not in the literal sense," he said, his voice lowering as Forbes drew near. "But there is no one fiercer on the field of battle or in the face of adversity. He is absolutely fearless and skilled beyond compare."

Julian's gaze moved between the enormous knight with the shaved head and chiseled features, and his wife as they approached the table.

"He is a giant," he commented quietly. "Look at the size of his hands."

De Lohr nodded slightly as he lifted his cup. "Those hands can rip a man's head from his body. I have seen it myself. I pity the man who truly enrages Forbes."

Julian looked at him, shocked, as Gart and Emberley reached the table. Emberley's warm smile turned into something forced as she focused on her husband.

"My lord," she addressed him. "This is Sir Gart Forbes, a man who was friends with my brother long ago. Gart and I knew each other when we were very young."

Julian eyed Gart, more focused on his wife. "Get out," he snapped. "The men have business to conduct."

Emberley's smile faded and her cheeks turned red, reflexive reaction to her husband's humiliation. He hadn't even acknowledged her polite introduction, which wasn't unusual. Still, she was embarrassed even though she should have been used to the treatment after all of these years.

"I will bid you gentlemen a good eve," she said politely to the table, turning to Gart one last time. "I hope to see you before you leave so we may finish our conversation."

Before Gart could reply, Julian slammed his fist against the table. "I told you to leave, woman. Go before I take my hand to you."

Gart eyed the baron, looking to Emberley and seeing how ashamed she was. He didn't like the way the man spoke to her. His first impression of the baron was not a good one. He smiled at Emberley, a gesture that those who knew him did not believe he was capable of. Gart Forbes was not a man who smiled, in any case.

"I will not leave before speaking with you, my lady," he said kindly. "Good eve to you."

Emberley's trembling smile turned real as she silently thanked him for his graciousness. Gathering her skirts, she fled the hall as Gart watched. His gaze lingered on the empty doorway a moment, thinking of Emberley and her three wild, beasty boys before returning his attention to the table. Seeing the baron and his crass manners, he was coming to see why the boys behaved as they did. He was coming not to like what he was seeing.

But he was a mere knight and his opinion was not of issue. He did what he was told to do and served whoever his liege directed. Without a word he sat down, collecting his cup and taking a large measure of wine only to realize that Julian was staring at him. Gart stared back, noting the small, dark-haired man with the bushy mustache.

"You are Forbes?" Julian confirmed.

Gart nodded shortly. "Aye, my lord."

"I have heard much of your abilities."

Gart simply nodded and Julian sat forward in his seat. He seemed to be taking a good deal of interest in studying him. The man was enormous, no doubt. Everything about him was big, from the top of his shaved head to the bottom of his massive feet. His voice was so deep that it seemed to bubble up from the ground. But it was his eyes that had Julian's attention – they had a sinister and calculating look about them.

As Julian gazed at the man, he could see why the soldiers had nicknamed him "Sach". From what he could see, it suited him.

"I understand you have been in Normandy for the past year, fighting on the king's behalf," Julian finally said.

Gart regarded the baron, his hand tightening around his cup. "I have, my lord," he replied.

"How did the battles fare?"

"My lord?"

"Were they well supplied and well commanded?"

Gart wasn't sure of the motivation behind the question but he nodded. "They were, my lord."

Julian digested the answer and, satisfied, moved on. "Am I to understand that you know my wife?"

"I do, my lord," Gart answered. "Her brother and I were the best of friends until his death in The Levant."

Julian snorted as he collected his wine cup. "Then you know she has always been a beautiful girl," he took a long drink of wine and smacked his lips. "She has provided me with three fine sons, perhaps the only thing that keeps her useful to me other than her obvious beauty."

Gart didn't react to the statement although he didn't like the way the man said it. Having nothing to say to him, he returned to his drink as Julian turned to the baron seated to his left.

"Does he know that you are sending him back to France?" he asked.

David glanced at Gart. "That has not been decided yet," he said evenly. "I am here to discuss the possibility. You and my brother are allies and he has asked me to come to Dunster to hear of your situation. I was told there was an issue with your lands in France."

Julian shook his head. "Not my lands," he said. "The queen's lands. Even as John fights to regain what he has lost in Normandy, his wife also has lands that are compromised. She needs protection and I have sworn to help her."

De Lohr wasn't too quick to support his claim. "What do you have to do with the queen?"

Julian smiled lazily, toying with his cup. "Have you not heard, my friend?" he flicked a careless wrist. "The queen and I are madly in love. She has my heart and I would do anything for her, including defending her lands against Philip Augustus. The French king envies her properties near Angouleme and I have sworn to keep them safe, which is why I need your assistance."

De Lohr sighed faintly. He had heard from his brother, the powerful Earl of Hereford and Worcester, that Baron Buckland was something of a political player and an opportunist. The man had rich lands, however, and a great deal of money and manpower, and spent a great deal of time in London soliciting the favor of the king. It seemed that he had garnered the favor of the queen instead.

"Surely she has enough troops," David said. "She cannot possibly need more men."

Julian poured himself more wine. "She is afraid," he said. "Afraid of the French king, afraid of her own mother who rules similar lands... the woman needs help and I have sworn to obtain it. Will you not supply me with men and knights for this purpose?"

It was evident that David was resistant. Gart stayed out of the conversation, listening to his liege and Buckland go back and forth on what was, and was not, appropriate support. Gart had served de Lohr for six years and knew the man and his family were rigidly opposed to John. They had been strong supporters of Richard until four years ago when the man was killed in France. Then, they had no choice but to support John as the rightful king. It was something that still left a bad taste in their mouths.

Gart sat at the table for quite some time listening to the arguing and pleading. He ate, he drank, and he generally grew weary of the bickering. Finally excusing himself just after midnight, he intended to return to the stables to collect his bags and then find a warm corner of Dunster to sleep in. He was exhausted and decided to let the barons do their bickering alone. He had no say in it, anyway.

Taking the spiral stairs down to the entry level, he could see remnants of white powder on the floor and steps. He half-expected the three little hooligans to come jumping out at him again and knew, reasonably, that they would be in bed and long asleep by now. Quitting the keep, he took the wooden stairs to the bailey and proceeded across the dark, dusty ward.

The moon was full overhead, casting the landscape in an eerie silver glow. Gart glanced up at the sky, seeing a million stars spread across the dark expanse. It was a beautiful night and unseasonably clear.

As he lowered his gaze in search of the stables, he could see the sentries upon the battlements as pinpoints of torch light moved through the darkness. Somewhere, a dog barked. Just as the stables came into view to the northeast section of the castle, his gaze fell upon a small and lone figure near the northeast tower.

He wouldn't have paid any attention except the figure turned and began to walk, and he noticed immediately that it wasn't a soldier. It was too small and too finely wrapped. Drawing closer, he realized he was gazing up at a woman as she walked the battlements.

Not only was it very late for a lone woman to be taking a nightly stroll, it was also unsafe. Only someone very comfortable with her position within the castle would show such confidence walking alone. Curious, he made his way to the northeast turret and took the stairs to the battlements.

The battlements were long and narrow, perched high on the walls of Dunster. There was a thirty-foot drop to the bailey below as he made his way along the narrow walkway. He could see the cloaked figure ahead of him, heading in the direction of the gatehouse. He picked up his pace, passing a couple of sentries, to catch up with her.

"My lady?" he said when he came to within a few feet of her.

Startled, Emberley spun around and nearly lost her balance. Gart quickly reached out to grab her so she wouldn't topple over the side. When he was sure she was steady, he immediately dropped his hands.

"God's Bones," Emberley cursed softly, patting her chest as if to restart her heart. "You frightened me."

He smiled, his strong feature shadowed in the moonlight. "My apologies," he said. "I did not mean to."

Emberley wasn't truly upset and she returned his smile to let him know. "I know you did not," she replied, studying him for a brief moment. Her gaze moved over his features in a warm, comforting manner. "I was lost in thought and did not hear you approach."

"Surely there are safer places to lose oneself in thought. Why are you on the battlements?"

She gazed across the wilds of Somerset beyond the castle walls. "I do not sleep well and walking helps me to relax," she told him. "Many are the nights I have spent upon this wall walk."

His eyes glimmered in understanding. "I know the feeling well," he said quietly. "I do not sleep well, either. Even now, I am exhausted from a week in the saddle but I do not know if I will be able to sleep."

Her smile grew. "Perhaps if you stay here any length of time, you and I will keep each other sorry company on nightly walks."

He flashed his teeth, big and straight and white. "There are worse things I can think of."

She laughed softly, leaning against the battlement wall as a night bird sang overhead. In the still of the night, it was calm and soothing. Emberley seemed to be staring at Gart quite intently. From the expression on her face, there seemed to be more on her mind than sleepless nights.

"May I ask you a question?" she finally asked.

"Of course."

"How much did my children steal from you?"

His smile faded and his eyebrows lifted. "Why would you ask that?"

She sighed heavily. "I know what they were doing in the entry earlier this eve," she said softly. "You do not have to pretend. I know they were robbing you."

He shook his head. "They did not rob me."

She cocked her head as if she didn't believe him. "Gart," she lowered her voice reprovingly. "Do not lie for them. I know what they do. They do it to everyone that enters the keep."

He chewed his lip thoughtfully and averted his gaze, leaning on the battlements just as she was. His eyes moved out over the shadowed land.

"How would you know this?"

She sighed with exasperation. "Because many visitors have told me this," she said. "They give them money simply to keep the peace. But I make the boys give it back. If they have stolen from you, please...."

He put up a hand to stop her, turning to look at her lovely face. She was a positively exquisite creature, made more beautiful by the haunting moonlight. As he gazed into her lovely eyes, her beauty nearly erased every thought in his head. It was a struggle to speak rationally.

"They did not steal from me because I did not have any money on my person," he told her. "Therefore, I am not lying to protect them. They did not rob me."

"But they tried."

He reluctantly nodded. "They did."

She held his gaze a moment longer before looking away and shaking her head. "Their motives are so complex," she said. "Romney believes that money will buy things to make Lacy and I happy."

"Lacy?"

"Their two-year-old sister," she explained softly. Then she started throwing her hands around as she spoke. "They rob anyone who enters the keep or, as Romney explains it, they exact a toll from visitors, and then the boys escape the castle and run off into town to purchase things. One time they purchased perfume for me and another time it was a belt, which I am sure they stole. Unless they robbed the king, they could not have afforded it. It terrifies me that they do this. I am afraid that one of these days, they will fall victim to bandits or wild animals. It is not safe for them outside of these walls."

"Nor is it safe for visitors inside of the walls with those three on the loose."

She looked at him and burst out in giggles. "This is serious," she chided him, although she was grinning. "I am nearly at my wits end with them. I apologize that they tried to rob you, Gart. You must think me horrible for raising such terrible children."

He looked at her, a smile playing on his full lips. "I think your children are bold and clever," he said, although it was not quite the truth. "Why do they feel the need to buy you nice things?"

Her smile faded and he could sense her manner becoming guarded. She looked away, off towards the forests to the east. The silence that followed was heavy as she thought on her answer.

"Things… things are not entirely pleasant here," she said, vaguely. "I suppose they think that gifts can make them better."

He watched her profile in the moonlight, a long and pregnant pause. "You are not happy."

It was a statement and not a question. Emberley shrugged. "I have four beautiful children," she said with feigned enthusiasm. "There is much to be thankful for."

He shifted, inadvertently moving closer to her in the process. "I did not question your gratitude," he said. "I questioned your happiness."

She shrugged again, still not meeting his eye. "It does not matter if I am happy or not. My children are healthy and we have much to be thankful for."

He sighed faintly, knowing he shouldn't involve himself in something that did not concern him, but unable to resist. He had known Emberley since childhood. He had seen her grow up for the most part. With Erik gone, he almost felt compelled to act in the man's place, to perhaps advise or console her. It was a foolish thought but he couldn't help himself.

"Does your husband always speak to you so rudely?" he asked quietly.

She looked at him as if startled by the question. "It is his way," she said rather lamely. "It is his right."

"I know what his rights are," Gart said. "I would suspect by the way he spoke to you that he does it quite regularly."

In the moonlight, Emberley's cheeks flushed dully. "It is his way," she repeated softly.

"Perhaps it is, but I do not like it," Gart said. "Based upon that observation, I will ask another question."

"What question is that?"

"Has he ever struck you?"

She hung her head, refusing to look at him. "Gart, I am sure you are asking out of concern, but it truly is none of your affair."

He watched her lowered head, her lovely profile, seeing tears pooling in her eyes. He suddenly felt very, very angry as he realized the truth. She didn't even have to tell him. He knew.

"So he takes his hands to you," he rumbled. "'Tis a vile, foul man that would strike a woman."

Emberley took a deep breath and wiped quickly at her eyes before the tears could fall. When she turned to look at him, he could read the anxiety on her face.

"I appreciate your concern," she whispered, laying a soft, white hand on his wrist. "I truly do. But you must not ask me any more questions. You would not like the answers and if Julian found out, he would not like that I have told you."

His jaw flexed. "Your husband was quite eager to announce to the men in the hall that he and the queen were lovers," he said. "Is this true?"

She yanked her hand away from his wrist and he would never forget the expression on her face. It was something between disgust and shame. Turning on her heel, she tried to rush away from him but he was on her in an instant, his colossal hands grasping her slender arms. She tried to shrug him off but he wouldn't budge.

"Leave me alone," she snapped. "I do not see where my husband's affairs are any business of yours."

He cooled, releasing her. She stepped away from him but she didn't run. She faced him defensively and he backed off.

"You are correct," he agreed calmly. "They are not my business. I suppose since your only brother was my best friend, perhaps I was showing interest on his behalf. It is simply that I look at you and see that young girl who used to follow Erik around and…forgive me. I should not have overstepped myself. I was only concerned."

Emberley gazed at the man, cooling significantly at his placating words. Then she sighed heavily as if all of the fight suddenly left her. Her defensive mechanism was always close to the surface, preparing to defend her tender heart from her cruel husband and his cruel words. She realized she need not be defensive with Gart. For as long as she'd known him, she'd never once heard of him showing women any manner of cruelty.

"You need not ask forgiveness," she said, remorseful. "It is I who must ask for your grace. I should not have snapped so. I know you are only asking out of concern."

He gazed steadily at her. "Great concern," he corrected gently. "Erik would ask this of me."

She smiled gratefully. "I know," she whispered. "I miss him very much."

"As do I."

"You are a good friend, Gart," she said. "When you were not upsetting my mother, I know she looked upon you as a son."

He gave her a lopsided grin. "I am thinking that Erik and I were much like your boys – into great mischief and mayhem in our youth."

She laughed softly. "Then perhaps you will not think me such a terrible mother that my boys rob anyone who enters the keep."

He was glad to see she was no longer tense and angry with him, thinking he would try yet again to get at the truth of the matter now that he seemed to have broken her defenses down.

"I never thought you a terrible mother," he said quietly. "But I would like to know the truth of your husband's treatment of you."

Her smile faded as she gazed up at him. "Why?" she lifted her shoulders. "There is nothing you can do. He is my husband and may do as he pleases."

Gart knew that and somehow, it hurt his heart. He knew it would have hurt Erik's. "Is he truly the queen's lover?" he asked quietly.

She nodded without emotion. "They have been lovers for almost a year," she replied. "I do not know what she sees in Julian other than his wealth. He is a terrible character and a horrible…."

She trailed off, embarrassed at divulging more information than she should, and Gart's expression grew serious.

"I am truly sorry," he said in his soft, deep voice. "You do not deserve such disrespect. The man is a fool."

Her smile returned, weakly. "You are very kind."

"Kindness has nothing to do with it. It is true."

Her smile grew, now modest. "I appreciate your concern. It has done my heart good to see you, Gart. You remind me of better days."

Her words, kind and sweet, softened him. His heart began to beat strangely in his chest as he reached out and took her small hand in his, bringing it to his lips for a gentle kiss.

"It has done my heart a world of good to see you," he said softly. "I see Erik in your eyes and it comforts me."

Gart's warm kiss on her hand made Emberley's breathing quicken. She was taken back to the days when he was a handsome, very young man and she was his adoring public. He had grown into such a magnificent man she could hardly believe it. She wondered how different her life would have been had she had not married Julian. If only Gart could have been her husband… *but no.* She chased the thought away as quickly as it came. It would do no good for her to long for a man she could never have. That opportunity was long gone.

"I am glad," she squeezed his hand and let it go. "Perhaps we will have more opportunity to speak in the next few days. Do you know when you are leaving?"

He shook his head, wishing she hadn't let go of his hand. Her touch had been magic.

"I do not," he told her. "My liege and your husband are debating that as we speak."

She pulled her cloak more tightly around her slender body. The evening was growing cool and damp in spite of the bright moonlight.

"Then perhaps tomorrow we may…."

She was cut off when something hit the wall just behind Gart. Startled, he jumped forward and threw his arms around her to protect her. But it was the wrong move. Standing several feet behind him was Julian. The arrow he held in his left hand, the second of two he had collected from the armory after spying his wife and Forbes upon the battlements, went sailing in Gart's direction. Gart put up an armored arm and easily deflected it.

Unwinding his arms from Emberley and turning to face Julian as the man approached, Gart could tell by his face that they were in for a good deal of trouble.

"Whore!" Julian screamed.

Gart remained cool, keeping Emberley protectively behind him. "My lord," he said evenly. "Your wife and I were discussing days past when we knew each other. We were discussing her dead brother."

Julian's thin face was livid. He approached Gart and slugged him in the chest, although with Gart's size and Julian's diminutive stature, Gart hardly felt the blow. Still, the implication was obvious.

"You are alone with my wife," he snarled. "You had your arms around her in a disgraceful embrace. How dare you violate my hospitality by taking my wife and… and wooing her."

Gart shook his head. "I did not violate anything, my lord," he was calm and steady. "Your wife and I knew each other as children and were discussing…."

Julian cut him off by shoving him back and reaching around to grab Emberley by the wrist. He pulled hard and she stumbled, nearly toppling over the side of the wall railing. Gart grabbed her to keep her from going over but Julian was wild with fury – he pounded on Gart's steadying arm even as he yanked at his wife.

Emberley didn't put up a fight but she was trying to keep her balance as he yanked. Sensing her hesitation as resistance, Julian slapped her hard across the face.

"I will deal with you, you treacherous whore," he snarled, lifting his hand to strike her again. "You are a…."

Before he could bring the hand down, Gart reached out and grabbed it. Julian turned to scream at him but was faced with an expression so tense, so deadly, that the words died in his throat.

De Lohr was suddenly on the battlements, as were several other de Lohr soldiers, and they were moving for Gart in a group, trying to pull him away from Buckland. Even Emberley, her right cheek stinging from the slap, reached out and grasped Gart by the arm.

"Gart, no," she whispered, begging. "Please let him go."

Gart heard her, as he also heard his liege behind him, firmly and quietly ordering him to let the baron's arm go. But at the moment, Gart could only see Buckland. From a man he had initially found distasteful and displeasureable, that displeasure had grown into full-blown loathing quickly. All he could see was a weak, bully of a man and he hated him for it.

"You will not strike her ever again," he growled. "Is that clear?"

Julian was torn between fear and outrage. "You cannot make demands of me!" he howled. "I will do as I please with my own wife!"

Emberley's soft voice infiltrated Gart's rage. "Please, Gart," she begged softly. "Please let him go."

Her sweet, pleading voice broke through his haze of rage and he tore his eyes away from Buckland long enough to look at her. She mouthed the world *"please"*, her big eyes beseeching him, and he reluctantly let the man's hand go. But Julian wasn't a smart man – he slugged Emberley in the jaw simply to demonstrate his power and Gart went straight for his neck.

Emberley screamed as she fell onto the wall walk, trapped beneath Julian as Gart tried to break the man's neck. But soldiers and knights were swarming over them and someone pulled her free of the fighting. Shaken, she looked up to see that it was de Lohr. His handsome face was taut as he made sure she was secure before diving into the fray.

Terrified for Gart, Emberley positioned herself back against the wall as she watched eight men pull Gart off her husband. He was such a big man and fed by such anger that his strength had been astounding. Julian was unhurt but he was furious, screaming threats at Gart. Knowing his wrath would eventually be turned against her, Emberley wisely fled the wall walk and raced for the keep, hearing the angry voices behind her filling the night with foul language and brutality.

Heart pounding, Emberley mounted the steps into the keep, running up the spiral stairs until she reached her children's chambers on the third floor. Scooping sleeping Lacy out of her bed, she fled into the boys' bower and closed the door, throwing the heavy bolt behind her. It would take an army to break the old door down and all of the pounding and screaming Julian would do could not breach it. She knew she was safe, at least for the moment.

With her daughter still sleeping heavily in her arms, Emberley sank to the floor and wept.

CHAPTER THREE

"THANKS TO YOU, I had to pledge men to Buckland's cause whether or not I agreed with it." De Lohr was rightfully seething. "What on earth possessed you to touch another man's wife?"

Gart stood in the dark, dusty stables, silently and stoically taking a verbal lashing from his liege. He deserved it, he knew, but he didn't regret his actions. Not one bit. De Lohr knew this, which was why he was so furious.

Gart Forbes was the best knight he had ever seen, and he had seen a lot of good men in his life. Many talented men had passed beneath his command or his brother's command at one time or another. But Forbes was different – they didn't call the man "Sach" without good reason. He was power, strength, cunning and brutality all rolled into one but, more than that, he was grossly unpredictable, as evidenced by the scene on the wall walk.

Gart could have easily snapped Buckland's neck but he hadn't – he just wanted to scare the man. Forbes had bouts of volatile fury but he was as cunning as a fox. He knew exactly what he was doing when he wrapped his hands around Buckland's throat.

"I did not touch her, at least not in the manner you are suggesting," Gart told him. "I swear upon my oath that we were simply talking."

David gazed at him a moment, trying to read the unreadable face, before letting out a heavy sigh.

"I believe you," he said, with less anger than he had been exhibiting earlier. "But Buckland has used this entire circumstance into blackmailing me for support."

"Blackmailing?"

De Lohr nodded with some disgust. "If I provide him with four hundred men, he will not have you thrown in jail," he said, throwing up his hands. "I have no choice. Unless I want to lose my best knight, then I must support him. I hope you liked France because you will be heading back there shortly."

The last sentence was spoken with some irony. Gart stared at de Lohr for a long moment before breaking down into a puzzled, disgusted expression. He just shook his head and turned away, pacing over to his charger. The beast was tethered in a far stall because he was so vicious, but with Gart, the black and white steed was as tame as a kitten. The animal nickered softly as Gart approached and began stroking the big neck, giving it an affectionate slap.

"My apologies, my lord," he finally said. "It was not my intention to put you in an awkward position."

De Lohr sighed with regret. "What were you doing with her alone up on the battlements? Did you not stop to think that it was a compromising position to say the least?"

Gart shook his head. "We were speaking," he reiterated. "I have not seen her in twelve years, this lovely young girl who was the sister of my best friend. Seeing her… it is as if I am seeing him again. I simply wanted to speak with her. Perhaps old memories are clouding my judgment but I do not believe so. We did nothing wrong."

De Lohr nodded his head in resignation. "Even so, you are not the one who will ultimately suffer in all of this. It will be her. Buckland is a vicious fool with a mean streak in him. She will be lucky if he does not beat her senseless for this."

Gart knew that but it didn't help the raging fury he felt, starting in his toes and rising up through his big body. By the time it reached his head, his face was red and he was sweating. De Lohr caught his expression and he put his hands up as if to stop the building tide. He knew that look well.

"There is nothing you can do about it," he told him sternly. "Your interference is what caused all of this in the first place. Had you simply walked away...."

"He struck her," Gart cut him off. "Could you have stood by while he did that?"

David rolled his eyes. "She is the man's wife, Gart. He can do with her as he pleases."

"Even assault her?"

"Aye, even assault her."

"You did not answer my question. Could you have stood by and watched him beat her?"

De Lohr eyed him, finally shaking his head after a moment. "Nay," he admitted, looking away. "But it is different with me. I am a man of rank and you are a mere knight. What you did, in most circles, would land you in the vault for the rest of your life."

Gart's jaw ticked dangerously. His face was still red and sweating, never a good sign. "I will not let him take out his anger on her. I cannot."

De Lohr threw up his hands. "You have no choice," he said. "Gart, I will send you home this night if you cannot control yourself. You are already in enough trouble. Any more from you and I may not be able to placate Buckland. He would throw you in jail and bury the key."

Gart didn't reply. Anything more out of his mouth would get him in deeper trouble. De Lohr was only trying to help him and he knew it.

There was a big pile of dry hay on the other side of his charger, stacked there by the grooms. He made his way over to the hay and plopped down into it, lying back against the clean, scratchy stuff. Folding his hands over his chest, he closed his eyes.

David watched him a moment, knowing that Gart was doing what he needed to do to calm down and stay on an even keel. Without another word, he quit the stable for his own quarters in the keep, a small room that Buckland had allocated to him.

Even as de Lohr made his way through the cold, bright night towards the distant keep, he knew that this was not the end of it. He could feel it. Gart felt as if he were protecting his best friend's sister and unable to process that the fact she was another man's wife took precedence.

David wondered what horrors awaited them come the dawn.

☙

GART AWOKE TO three little faces staring at him. Startled, he sat up, hay stuck to his back and arms. It was just growing light outside, the sky in shades of pinks and blues as the sun pierced the veil of night. It was cold in the stable as the animals began to stir, hungry for their morning meal. Gart rubbed the sleep from his eyes as Romney, Orin and Brendt gazed back at him.

"What are you doing here?" he asked them, shaking the sleep from his mind.

The boys were not particularly well dressed against the cold and Romney looked particularly pale, which concerned him. They all looked a little lost. Gart also noticed something else – without all of the white powder on him, Romney's ashen face bore a striking resemblance to his long-dead uncle. The mirror image was uncanny.

"We are sorry we tried to rob you yesterday," Romney said somberly.

Gart rested his arms on his up-bent knees. "You did not rob me. I did not have anything for you to steal."

Romney and Orin looked at each other, bewildered. "We tried to rob you," Romney looked back at Gart. "Mother told us to apologize."

Gart thought on that a moment, studying Romney. More and more, he could see Erik in the boy, even down to the expressions on the child's face. He couldn't help but think how thrilled Erik would have been with his three nephews.

"I see," he said. "Then your apology is accepted."

Romney cocked his head. "She said that you and Uncle Erik were friends."

Gart nodded. "We were," he said, eyeing the brown-haired, blue-eyed boy. "In fact, I was just thinking that you look a good deal like him. He was a great knight."

"Mother said he died in the Holy Land for Richard's damn crusade."

Gart fought of a smile. "She said that?"

Romney nodded solemnly. "She said it was damn foolish and damn stupid."

Gart bit his lip to keep from smiling. "Your uncle was a great knight on the crusade," he said. "We fought together for almost two years."

"How did he die?"

Gart didn't feel like smiling anymore and the grin faded from his lips. "A Saracen arrow pierced his helm," he said quietly. "It lodged in his eye and it killed him."

"Oh," Romney looked thoughtful, distressed. "Did it hurt?"

"I would imagine so."

Romney continued to look distressed as Orin and Brendt decided the charger was more worthy of their attention. Gart saw the boys moving towards it.

"Do not touch him," he admonished. "He will stomp you."

The boys drew back in fear, gravitating back towards their eldest brother. Romney was still looking at Gart.

"Since we are sorry that we robbed you, will you give us money anyway?" he asked.

Gart gazed steadily at the boy. "Why?"

"Because Mother needs a present."

"Why?"

"She is unhappy."

Gart's good humor faded completely. "Why is she unhappy?"

Romney seemed to lose some of his confidence. He looked at Orin and Brendt, who gazed back at him with wide eyes. Suddenly, Orin rushed Gart and grabbed the neck of his wrinkled tunic.

"Becausth," Orin had an extremely lazy tongue and a bad lisp. He yanked at Gart's tunic and began hitting him with his little fists. "He did thisth… and thisth… and she cries."

Gart put his hands on the lad to both steady him and pull him off. Even Romney moved forward to pull his violent brother away from the enormous knight. But Gart didn't miss the gist of what the boy said. In fact, he began to feel the familiar fury build in his feet again and start to work its way up. *She will be lucky if he does not beat her senseless for this.* He wondered if de Lohr's prophetic words had come true.

"Who?" he had Orin by the arms but he was looking at Romney. "Who made your mother cry?"

Romney wouldn't look at him. He was more interested in pulling Orin away from the man. "Father," he muttered. "He hits her and she cries."

The slow build of fury began to gain speed. Gart could feel the sweat popping out on his forehead and he struggled to control the brewing anger.

"Did he hit her last night?" he asked quietly.

Romney shook his head. "Nay," he replied, giving Orin a good yank and sending the boy off of Gart and onto his bum. "He did it this morning. She cried and cried."

The rage reached Gart's head and his cheeks began to turn red. "Where is your mother now?"

Romney shrugged, either losing interest with the conversation or afraid to say much more. He fidgeted uncomfortably. "In her bed," he said. "Father is leaving for London. Will you give us money now so we can buy her a present?"

Gart stared at the little boy, feeling a great many emotions in his heart that he was unfamiliar with. He'd spent most of his life allowing only one emotion to infiltrate his mind, and that emotion was fury. It worked well for his purposes. The soldiers didn't call him insane for no reason. They called him that because it was the truth.

But now he was feeling something more than fury. He was feeling great sadness and grief, feeling as if he had failed somehow. When he'd meant to protect Emberley, it seemed as if he'd only gotten her into more trouble. He had no reason to believe that the boys were lying to him and he muttered a silent prayer to Erik, begging the man's forgiveness for what he had done. It was a struggle to keep a rein on what he was feeling.

"Where is your father?" he asked, hoping he didn't sound as angry as he felt.

Romney shrugged. "In the hall," he said. "I heard him tell people that he was leaving for London today to see the queen."

Gart stood up from the hay pile, brushing pieces of hay off his arms and back as he went to the bags that were lodged against the wall next to his charger. The grooms began coming into the barn to feed and water the animals but he ignored them as he began to rummage through his bags. Although he wanted very much to go charging into the keep, he kept his cool. He knew that would only make the situation worse. He had to keep his wits about him. But he noticed as he dug through his bags, his hands were shaking.

As he rummaged through his possessions, he realized he had company. He glanced to either side and noticed that Romney was on one side of him while Orin and Brendt were on the other. They were watching him dig through his satchels with great interest. Surely the knight had many wonderful things in that dark and mysterious bag. Finally, they could stand it no longer.

Romney reached in and grabbed a strip of carefully rolled leather, pulling it out to look at it as Gart took it away. As he was distracted with Romney, Orin reached in and pulled out a very sharp razor. Gart snatched it before the boy could injure himself and told the boys not to stick their hands where they did not belong. As he packed away the razor and rolled up the leather strip, little Brendt literally climbed into the largest of his satchels.

He gleefully tried to bury himself in the clothing that had been carefully rolled up and packed. Gart removed the boy from his satchel but in doing so, it opened up the door for Orin to plunge head-first into another bag. Soon, Gart was occupied removing the boys from his bags rather than searching for clean clothes. He would remove one and another would take his place. He swore there were twelve children and not just three, so fast they moved. Finally, he stood up and spread his big arms.

"Cease," he roared softly, jabbing a finger at Brendt, who was back in his satchel and trying to pull one of Gart's enormous tunics over his head. "You – out. And stay out. All of you stay out."

Brendt started to weep and Romney turned his big, blue eyes to Gart. "He wants the tunic," he told him.

Gart waved his hands impatiently. "Fine," he snapped without force, lifting the boy out of his bag. "He can take the tunic. But you other two – get out and stay out. I do not have time for this foolery."

Dejected and scolded, Romney and Orin actually began to repack one of Gart's bags. He looked at their sad faces and began to feel like an ogre for scolding them. But he didn't apologize. He helped them replace what they had pulled out. With both bags repacked, he removed one carefully rolled-up tunic, removed his dirty tunic, put it back in his bag and then sealed everything up.

Meanwhile, Brendt had managed to pull the tunic he stole from Gart over his little blond head and was trying to walk with it. The tunic was far too long for him and he tripped, laughing as he wallowed in the dirt. Romney and Orin giggled at him and Gart couldn't help but crack a smile as the lad tried to get back to his feet without tripping again. He couldn't quite seem to manage it, which sent Romney and Orin howling with laughter. Even Gart was snorting, his gaze moving over the three boys. They were good boys even if they were mischievous. Erik would have been proud. Gart was starting to realize what Erik's mother and father must have gone through when Erik and Gart were into mayhem. Now, he understood.

Pulling the fresh tunic over his head, he proceeded to reclaim his armor. The boys watched with great interest as he pulled on his mail coat, his hauberk, and proceeded with pieces of plate armor that were still fairly rare. He wore great, well-crafted plate armor on both forearms that bore the crest of de Lohr. He also had a big piece that fit over his chest and back, hung from his shoulders by big leather straps. Romney inspected the piece curiously and even tried to lift it, but Gart discouraged him. It was an expensive piece and too heavy for the boy to play with. Leaving the chest piece in the stable next to his bags, Gart headed out into the dusty courtyard.

Dunster Castle was a massive place built in a long, rectangular configuration which positioned the stables on the far north side, away from the keep but near the kitchens and the well. There were two blocks of stables and as Gart emerged from the block that extended on the northeast wall, he could see that there was great activity from the block lodged against the north wall.

Two chargers and several other horses had been brought out and were being prepared, as well as a big wagon that was being loaded down with goods. The animals were excited and their breath puffed up in great clouds in the cold morning air. Gart's gaze lingered on the group, knowing it must be the baron's escort to London. Just as he passed from the stable yards into the big bailey beyond, he caught sight of de Lohr heading towards him.

Gart was surprisingly in control as he and David came together. Romney, Orin and Brendt were clustered around Gart, following him like puppies, something that didn't go unnoticed by de Lohr. He eyed the boys as he came upon Gart.

"Are you summoning your own army?" he asked.

Gart had no idea what he was talking about until he followed David's gaze and saw the boys standing around him. He grunted.

"Do not let their small size fool you," he told him. "They are brave beyond measure."

David lifted an eyebrow at Romney. "I know," he said. "They were unafraid to rob me yesterday when I entered the keep."

Gart lifted an eyebrow at Romney, who looked both fearful and defiant. "Mother only said we had to apologize to you. She did not say we had to apologize to everyone."

Gart just shook his head, resigned. "What did you steal from the baron?"

Romney's brow furrowed deeply. "Not much."

David fought off a grin. "I gave them a pence each to let me pass," he said. "I was afraid for my life."

Gart's eyes narrowed at Romney. "You will give him back his money. That is not a request."

Romney was deeply displeased. "It is upstairs."

"Go and get it. *Now*."

The boys darted off, scattering like frightened chickens at Gart's deep and growling tone. They weren't used to such commands but the instinct for survival bade them to obey it. David waited until they were well away before looking at Gart with a grin.

"Brave and bold boys," he commented. "I thought it was quite humorous."

"Did they hit you with a stick?"

"They tried. I paid them before they could whack me."

"Yet I did not," Gart wriggled his eyebrows. "They were not afraid to attack me when I would not pay their demands."

David snorted. "I would like to have seen that. The mighty Gart Forbes being set upon by three small bandits. Those children did what grown men are afraid to do."

Gart shrugged, his gaze trailing up to the enormous dark-stoned keep to the right. "Their mother interrupted what would have surely been a bloodbath," he said. "Speaking of their mother, I am told that the earl beat her this morning."

David's smile faded and he sighed heavily. "That is why I have come to find you," he said quietly. "Knowing how you feel, I wanted you to hear the news from me."

"Did he kill her?"

David shook his head sadly. "From what I can gather, she barricaded herself in her children's room last night after the incident on the wall to avoid her husband's wrath," he said quietly. "My chamber is on the floor below theirs and I could hear him banging at the door a good portion of the night. Then it faded away until dawn when, apparently, one of her sons unbolted the door and the earl was lying in wait. He locked the children out of the room, including the crying two-year-old girl, and proceeded to beat his wife. I could hear the woman screaming. By the time I reached the floor, I found four crying children staring back at me. Even the servants were crying. So I took everyone down to the hall, made sure the children were tended, before returning to the chamber. By the time I returned, all was silent and the earl was just emerging. He told me that if I wanted to remain a trusted ally, I would leave well enough alone."

By this time, Gart was the familiar shade of red. The veins on his neck and temple were standing out, throbbing. De Lohr knew that look. It was always the calm before the storm.

"Did you see Lady Emberley?" Gart asked through clenched teeth. "Is someone at least tending to her injuries?"

David shook his head. "The earl will not let anyone near her," he explained, sickened. "He says she must be punished. The servants are too afraid to go against his wishes and I cannot do it because he would not only break his alliance with my brother but more than likely accuse me the same way he accused you. The man has a warped and dangerous mind."

Gart couldn't stand it any longer. He began to walk towards the keep. David reached out and grabbed him.

"Wait," he snapped softly. "The earl is in the hall and if he sees you …."

Gart turned on him, his face red with rage. "I am going to see to Lady Emberley's health and well-being, and her husband be damned," he snarled. "Her brother was my best friend and I will not…."

De Lohr put up a silencing hand. "Listen to me," he cut him off. "I knew you would not be stopped but I also know that if Buckland sees you, there is no telling how volatile this situation will become. Do you not understand that your actions have brought this about? What do you think will happen if you do not understand your place and continue this behavior? It appears as if you are attempting to come between the baron and his wife."

Gart was so angry that he was sweating, his big hands working much in the same manner they did right before he plunged into battle. He was starting to reach the point that every man feared, the insanity that would soon overtake him. It was at that point that he would start ripping heads from bodies, Buckland's included, and to hell with the consequences.

"I am not trying to come between the baron and his wife," he said in a manner that suggested the whole idea ridiculous.

"It appears that way. Can you swear to me that there is nothing more to this than the concern of an old friend?"

"I can swear it."

De Lohr sighed softly. He wasn't sure if he believed him, given the fact that the man was acting in a way he had never seen before, but he would not dispute him. At least, not yet. "Very well," he said quietly. "But you must show restraint, Gart. This situation is delicate to say the least."

"I am going to see to her," Gart repeated, his jaw gnashing. "I must see what has happened. If you cannot understand that, then I cannot explain it to you any more than I already have."

David just shook his head, tightening his grip on Gart's arm. "I understand," he lowered his voice. "I also understand that whatever I say, you will do as you please."

"That is a fair assessment."

David sighed in resignation. "Then we must act carefully. You and I will enter the keep and I will distract the baron so you can slip to the upper floors to tend the lady. Meanwhile, I am going to tell Buckland that I have sent you away and hopefully that will appease him. But in doing so, you need to make every effort to stay out of the man's way until he leaves for London. If you hear him coming, hide or all will be lost, including his trust in me. Is that clear?"

Gart was agreeable with the plan for the most part. "It is," he replied. "My charger and possessions are still here, however. What if the earl sees them?"

David shook his head. "He would not know your possessions or charger from the next man's. He does not seem particularly bright or observant."

Satisfied, Gart could feel himself calming now that there was a plan, something that would enable him to see to Emberley. Taking a deep breath, he struggled to calm himself. "And once the baron has left Dunster? What then?"

David shrugged. "You can remain here if you wish, at least until I send for you. I suspect we will be mobilizing for France in the next three or four weeks, so be prepared. If you leave Dunster, go back to Denstroude because that is where I shall look for you."

Gart nodded, the dull, red tone of his face fading to a normal healthy color. David eyed the man one last time, just to make sure he was going to do as he was told, before finally nodding his head.

"Very well," he turned for the keep. "Let us make our move."

Gart was right behind him.

Chapter Four

Emberley's first awareness was of someone rolling her gently onto her back. She groaned in pain as her bruised and swollen body shifted, in particular the left side of her head. Julian had beaten her soundly about the head and shoulders and she had covered her face with her hands, trying to protect her mouth and nose. Consequently, her left ear was horribly swollen as was the entire left side of her head. Both hands were seriously battered from having defended herself.

Only half-conscious, she caught a glimpse of very large hands and she panicked. But the big hands grabbed her before she could move away.

"Easy, lady," a very soft, very deep voice whispered. "You are safe. Everything will be all right."

Emberley managed to open an eye, seeing Gart's unfocused face in her field of vision. She thought she might have been dreaming. "Gart?" she whispered.

He smiled gently at her. "It is me."

She was mildly incoherent, trying to push him away and get out of bed at the same time. "My children," she mumbled. "I must get to my children."

He gently, but firmly, eased her back onto the bed. "The children are fine," he assured her softly. "They are being tended."

Confused, she allowed him to push her back to the mattress simply because the pain in her head and neck was so great. It felt much better to lie down. "Where are they?"

"In the hall, eating their meal."

She looked up at him as if not quite understanding him. The dark blue eyes were struggling to concentrate. "What… what are you doing here?"

"I am here to help you."

It took her a moment to understand what he was telling her. As he watched, she burst into tears.

"Nay," she sobbed softly. "Please go, Gart. If Julian finds you here, he will kill us both."

Gart couldn't help it. He reached up a big hand to stroke her head simply to comfort her, but she yelped with pain when he touched her. Concerned, he moved to get a better look at the left side of her head and he could see that nearly the entire side of her head and scalp was bloodied. It was matted in her beautiful hair and dried blood filled her ear canal. He sighed with dismay, struggling to keep his anger at bay. He had only just quelled it and it threatened to surge again.

"He will not find me here," he said softly. "He is leaving for London. I have been given permission to remain behind to tend you."

Tears ran down her temples as she gazed up at him. "Who gave you permission?"

"My liege," Gart began to look around for water or anything else he could use to clean her up. She was a bloodied mess. "He has told your husband that I have already gone home. No one knows I am here."

Emberley watched him as he moved over to a table near the window and peered into a big pewter pitcher. He sniffed it and, determining it was rosewater, poured it into the earthenware basin that was next to it.

"He will kill you if he finds you here," she whispered. "Please go."

He looked at her. "I am not going anywhere," he said. "I am responsible for your misery. I must make amends."

Emberley was in too much pain to argue. She closed her eyes as Gart went in search of a rag or something he could use with the water, coming across great squares of linen that were neatly folded in the giant wardrobe. He pulled out an armful, dropping half of them on the floor as he made his way back to the bed. It was a children's room and the clean linen mingled with the clutter of toys and socks on the floor. He put the linen and the water next to the bed and took a knee.

Emberley felt him very gently begin to clean the blood from the left side of her head. She put up a bloodied hand and grasped his wrist, stopping him. Her dark blue eyes opened slowly and fixed on his intense green.

"Please," she whispered. "I want you to go. I want you to leave and forget you ever saw me here."

He gazed down at her, feeling something he couldn't describe began to blossom in his chest. It was as if an unseen hand were squeezing his heart, hurting him. He'd never felt such a thing in his entire life.

"I will not," he responded softly. "I will not leave and I will not forget you."

Her eyes began to tear up again. "Please," she begged softly. "Please go. I… I do not want you to see me like this. I do not want… you to remember me like this."

He smiled gently and resumed cleaning the dried blood from her chin and jaw, completely ignoring her request.

"Do you want to know what I remember of you?" he asked her. "I remember a little girl that looked like an angel with her long, blond hair and big, blue eyes. I remember how she used to follow Erik around and he would scold her to stop following him, but then she would pout and he would relent and let her come along with whatever he was doing. He could not refuse such a sweet little face."

Weak, Emberley lay there as he cleaned, remembering Erik through Gart's eyes. She remembered the brother with the dark, blond hair and blue eyes, the clouded memories of an adoring young girl of her only brother.

"It seems like an eternity ago," she murmured.

"Do you remember what he used to call you?" he asked softly.

She closed her eyes. "Kitten."

"Do you remember why?"

She smiled faintly. "Because I was never without a cat in my arms," she said softly. "They would breed in the barn and I would collect armfuls of them to play with. I have not heard that name in years."

He smiled as he focused on cleaning the blood off her ear. "It suits you. Do you still have cats?"

"Four."

He snorted softly. "I should have guessed."

She fell silent as he gently wiped at the dried blood, trying not to cause additional pain to her swollen ear. He thought she had fallen asleep, losing herself in blissful unconsciousness to remove her from her pain, but after several moments she stirred again.

"Gart," she whispered. "Will you do something for me?"

He stopped cleaning and looked at her. "Anything."

"Please leave. I do not want you here."

He lost some of his confidence. "I only want to help. Please let me."

She shook her head, closing her eyes. "Just… let me be."

"Why?"

Tears began to pour out of her closed eyes. "Because," she breathed. "If Julian finds you here, he will kill us both. That is enough of a reason."

Gart watched her struggle. "He will not kill you and he certainly will not kill me," he insisted softly. "I can adequately defend us both from your husband."

Her eyes opened and she looked at him. "Why?" she asked, almost angrily. "Gart, he is my husband. It is his right to do with me as he pleases and even though I appreciate your noble intentions, the fact remains that you have stirred up a good deal of trouble and I have suffered for it. You will leave here in a few days and I will be left with the consequences of your actions. You can easily leave the situation. I cannot. I must stay and bear Julian's wrath."

He stared at her, hurt and confused by her words. His chest began to constrict, knowing she was correct but still somehow trying to rationalize it. He set the bowl and rag on the floor and stood up, deeply troubled.

"Do you remember when you were about twelve years of age, you returned from Chepstow in the summertime?" he asked, crossing his enormous arms. "Erik and I were about twenty and one years old, newly knighted and very full of ourselves. We believed we were the greatest knights to have ever lived. Do recall that summer?"

Emberley nodded. "I do. It was the last time I saw you."

"Do you also remember that you and your silly friends went to swim at the lake one warm August day? What were their names? You know who I mean, the St. George girls."

In spite of herself, Emberley warmed to the remembrance. "Sorsha and Caroline."

He made a face. "Sorsha and Caroline," he muttered with exaggerated distaste. "Caroline wanted to marry me. That is all she would speak of. She followed me around so much that I had to hide to avoid her. One time, I was running from her and tripped into the well. Erik had to fish me out."

Emberley couldn't help but laugh, remembering that particularly humorous event. "You cannot fault the girl for her good taste."

He gave her a half-grin, pleased to see that his storytelling was having the desired effect. He had her interest and she was smiling. "If you want to know the truth," he said, pretending it was a great secret, "I would have much rather have had you."

The light of surprise came to Emberley's eyes. "Me?"

He nodded. "You were the prettiest girl in Shropshire."

She was flattered, bringing a flush to her pale cheeks. "You never told me. You never said a word about it."

"I was an idiot. Besides, Erik would have run me through for lusting after his sister."

She giggled softly. "Did you really lust after me?"

He winked at her. "Are you serious? How could I not?" When she continued to giggle, he continued with his story. "At any rate, you and your silly friends went to the lake to swim and you swam out too far.

Your legs became entangled in the underwater grass."

Emberley's smile faded. "I remember," she murmured. "I would have drowned had it not been for you and Erik. You two jumped into the lake and risked your lives to cut me free. I remember that you in particular spent a good deal of time under the water cutting my legs free. Once Erik brought me back to the shore, he had to practically drag you out of the water as well. You nearly killed yourself trying to save me."

Gart's green eyes were intense. "As I would do the same thing today," he said softly. "Never doubt for a moment that I would kill or die for you, my lady. I have been doing it since you were young. Therefore, your husband does not frighten me. Not in the least. I would willingly go to the vault or worse if it meant you would be safe and whole."

She sighed, understanding his point. Having known the man most of her life, he had proven his selflessness time and time again. As her brother had also been, Gart was a man of extremely good character and altruism, qualities that were very endearing.

"I understand and appreciate your chivalry," she said quietly. "But this situation is different. I am married and…."

He cut her off. "And your husband is a fool," he rumbled. "He does not deserve you, Emberley. Has he been treating you this way since you married him?"

She averted her gaze from his probing eyes. "Aye," she whispered. "We have been married for eight years. It has always been this way."

Gart shook his head, turning his gaze to the lancet window and the blue sky beyond. He could smell the sea wafting in on the breeze, as Dunster sat right on the coast. Seagulls cried as they rode the drafts and he watched them a moment, his thoughts lost and tumultuous. There was so much on his mind that it was difficult to isolate only one thought. But he did know one thing for certain.

"I am sorry," he finally muttered.

She watched his handsome profile, her gaze moving over his big body, long torso, and very long legs. "Why?"

"Because," he admitted, turning to face her. "I should have married you and saved you from all of this."

She smiled again. "You are being foolish,"

"Why?"

Her smile grew. "Must I answer that question?"

"If I want you to, you will."

She shook her head at him as if she truly thought he was foolish. "In the first place, you had no interest in me and in the second place, you and my brother were full of dreams of big wars and big glory. A wife did not fit into those plans. Moreover, it would have been as if I had married my own brother. You and Eric were too close."

He lifted an eyebrow. "Do you still feel that way?"

"What way?"

"That I am as your brother?"

Her smile faded. "Nay," she whispered. "I see you now as a very dear, very old friend. It has done my heart a world of good to see you and I shall miss you when you go."

"A few minutes ago, you were asking me to leave. Do you still want me to leave?"

She regarded him closely. After a moment, she weakly nodded her head. "Aye."

"You do?"

"Aye."

"Well, I am not going anywhere. I cannot leave you like this."

"But I wish it."

"I do not care. For once, I will not bow to your wishes."

"Even at the cost of Julian killing me should he discover you here with me?"

Gart's expression hardened and he made his way back over to the bed, going to his knees again and picking up the wet cloth. "He will not kill you," he replied. "I will kill him first."

Her beaten hand flew to his rough cheek and she forced him to look at her. When their eyes met, her deep, blue eyes were roiling with emotion.

"Gart, you cannot," she whispered firmly. "I will not let you do it. The penalty would be death and I could not live with that. I have already lost one brother. I could not lose you as well."

Gart stared at her, feeling unfamiliar emotions swamp him. True, he had known her the vast majority of his life but as he gazed at her, he was seeing an exceptionally beautiful and poised woman.

He felt himself warming to her as he had never warmed to anyone in his life. Something magnetic and wonderful was brewing in his heart, warm and powerful emotions he felt every time he looked at her. He had always known her on a youth level, as a boy to a girl. Now he was coming to know her as an adult, as a man to a woman. It was completely different than what he had known in the past. He couldn't explain it any other way.

Swiftly, he gripped her hand and kissed the palm that was on his cheek, twice, before setting her hand back down to her side. In silence, he picked up the rag and resumed cleaning the blood off her face.

He was afraid to say anything more to her as he cleaned her up, afraid that the odd, warm sensations filling his chest would cause him to say something he should not. Emberley lay still, her eyes closed, as he wiped off as much dried blood as he could manage. The left side of her scalp was still caked with blood but he didn't want to disturb her too much by washing it out of her hair, so he just left it alone for the time being. As he moved to her hands to inspect the wounds, the door to the chamber began to rattle.

Gart froze, eyes and ears alert, as the panel continued to clatter. Then, he could hear children's voices from the opposite side and realized it was the boys calling to their mother. Gart glanced at Emberley. She was dead asleep, exhausted from her injuries. Setting the bloodied rag aside, he stood up and made his way to the door.

Leaning his ear against the panel, he could hear the boys discussing what they should do because the door was locked. Silently, with great care, Gart unlocked the door and pressed himself back against the wall so that when the door opened, he would be concealed by the open panel.

Predictably, the door flew open when the boys realized it was unlatched and it slammed back, bumping against Gart. The three boys and one very little girl walked through, Orin holding on to his baby sister's hand. Gart eyed the little girl curiously from his position behind the door. He could see long, curly blond hair through the crack between the door and the wall but little else. But his master plan ultimately worked against him when Romney turned around to shut the door behind him and caught sight of Gart. The boy's mouth flew open.

"What are you doing here?" he demanded loudly.

Gart slammed the door and bolted it, turning to look at the four young faces gazing back at him with various degrees of astonishment. He considered Romney's question, locking the door before returning his attention to the children.

"Your mother is hurt," he said simply. "I was helping her."

Romney eyed him with some suspicion, turning to look at his mother passed out on the bed. His brow furrowed with confusion. "Did Father let you come?" he asked.

"Nay."

Romney was baffled but he wasn't sure what to do about it. In fact, he wasn't sure he wanted to do anything about it. For lack of a better response he lifted the bag in his right hand.

"Gerta sent us with this for Mother," he said.

Gart looked at the sack. "What is it? And who is Gerta?"

"Gerta is our nurse," Romney said, looking back to his mother as he lowered the sack in his hand. "She told us to bring this to mother. It will help her."

Gart stepped forward and took the sack, a rough thing sewn from crude plant fibers. Peering inside, he could see tied off bunches of herbs and weeds. Making his way over to the oak table near the bed that Emberley was lying upon, he began to pull the ingredients out and lay them on the table. He sniffed them one by one.

"Mint," he set down a green bunch and pulled out a few more, sniffing them in succession. "Lemongrass, and I'm not sure what this is. This looks like white willow."

The children were clustered around him, watching him remove the ingredients. "Gerta says we need to mash them up and put them on her hurts."

Gart asked the question even though he was fairly sure he knew the answer. "Why is Gerta not here to help?"

Romney looked sad. "Father told her she could not come."

"But he said you could come?"

"He did not tell us anything. We just came." He looked up at Gart, his expression somewhat fearful. "Does he know you are here?"

Gart shook his head. "Nay," he said seriously. "He does not know I am here. He must not ever know or else he might hurt your mother again. You must never tell him. Do you understand?"

He looked to all of the boys as he spoke and received two serious nods from Romney and Orin. Brendt had no idea what he was saying until Orin snapped at the little boy and he finally nodded his head. Little Lacy, a gorgeous child who looked just like her mother, stared up at Gart with a thumb in her mouth. She was too young to understand in any case, but after several moments of staring at Gart, she wandered over to her mother and climbed onto the bed next to her.

Gart watched the little girl snuggle down next to Emberley, who was in such a deep sleep that she didn't even stir. His gaze lingered on the pair a moment before he turned back to the herbs and began to pull them apart.

"Gerta said we must mash them up?" he asked Romney.

Romney helped him pull apart the mint. "She said to mash them and put them on Mother's hurts," he repeated. "It will make her feel better."

Gart looked around for a vessel to put the herbs in but could only come up with the bowl he had used to pour water in. Collecting it off the floor, he poured the water out and placed the herbs in the bottom of the bowl, mashing them all together with a little rosewater and the bottom of an earthenware cup he had found. Being that this was the children's chamber, it was full of clutter, both useful and garbage. It looked like a pack of wild animals lived there and not three little boys.

When the weeds were mush, he turned to Emberley. The three boys followed him and began jumping on the bed when they drew near their mother. Gart softly admonished them to stop jostling her around, so Brendt and Orin contritely climbed off. Lacy was lying next to her mother, sucking her thumb and looking up at Gart with big, blue eyes. Gart took the paste of herbs and began to smear it on Emberley's swollen ear.

"Can I help?" Romney wanted to know.

Gart held up the bowl and the boy put his fingers in it, very carefully putting it on the exterior of his mother's ear as Gart talked him through it. Orin and Brendt saw what they were doing and wanted to help, too, so Gart had them smear the stuff on her bruised hands. As the four of them carefully rubbed on the goo, Emberley began to stir.

Her dark blue eyes fluttered open and she quickly realized that there were more people in the room. Dazed, she began to move around but Gart put a big hand on her shoulder to steady her.

"Be still," he admonished. "You are being well tended."

Emberley blinked, catching sight of Lacy lying next to her and Orin's big grin, missing two front teeth. She couldn't help but smile weakly, reaching out a battered hand to touch Orin's cheek and realizing there was something smeared all over it. She blinked to clear her vision, looking at the green mess on her hands.

"What is this?" she asked weakly.

Gart stood over her, big hands on his hips as he gazed down at her. "Medicine," he said. "Your sons were eager to help."

Her blue eyes twinkled at him. "They are not such bad boys after all."

Gart smiled. "Nay, they are not," he agreed. "In fact, they are very helpful."

She returned his smile, prevented from speaking when Lacy suddenly sat up and put her arms around her mother's bruised neck. Emberley groaned as the little girl hugged her and kissed her cheek with sloppy, baby kisses. Gart instinctively moved to lift the little girl up so she wouldn't hurt her mother, but just as quickly he stopped himself, unsure what to do. Emberley looked up and saw his indecision, and her smile broadened.

"You have not yet met the Lady de Lacy Isadora de Moyon," she said. "My husband named her for his good friend, Walter de Lacy. She is not yet two years of age and you must be careful that you do not let her too close to you. She will hug you and kiss you until you pull her away."

Gart watched the little girl smother her mother in kisses, feeling those odd warm feelings swamping him again. In pain and injured, Emberley hugged her baby and let the girl deliver slobbery kisses. It was sweet and touching. Then he looked at Romney, the oldest, stoically putting green slime on his mother's injured ear while Orin and Brendt put it on the knuckles of her left hand. It tugged at his heart to watch these children, trying so hard to be brave and help their injured mother, strong and intelligent sons of a bastard who did not deserve them. It both deeply touched him and deeply angered him. Something inside him, deep down, was starting to transform.

He couldn't put his finger on what kind of transformation, but it was something he'd never felt before. He began to suspect it was jealousy but he largely ignored it, unsure how to handle it and not wanting to devote time and energy to it. He was jealous of what Buckland had. As he watched Emberley and the children, he realized it was more than simply taking Erik's place as an uncle and protector. He wanted this family for himself.

Someone pounded sharply on the chamber door, jolting him from his muddy thoughts. The children froze, terrified, and Emberley looked fearfully to the bolted panel. They could hear Julian yelling on the other side.

"Open this door!" he shouted. "Open it, I say!"

The children looked to Gart, terrified, as he put a calm finger to his lips to indicate silence. He was controlled, which helped the children in their reactions. His influence was calming. Motioning to Romney, he pulled the boy off the bed and leaned down to whisper in his ear.

"You will open the door," he murmured. "I will hide. Do not tell your father I am here. Is that clear?"

Romney nodded solemnly. "I will not," he whispered, turning sternly to the family on the bed. "No one tell Father that Sir Gart is here!"

As Orin and Brendt nodded fearfully, Gart patted Romney's head. "Good lad," he hissed. "Go and open the door."

Romney's big and anxious eyes were on Gart as he moved for the door. Gart, however, remained composed as he moved to stand next to the door as he had done earlier when the children had entered the room. He was such a big man that there was no other place for him to hide. He had to put himself behind the door when it opened and pray that was enough. As long as the door remained open, he had a chance.

He flattened himself against the wall as Romney put his hand on the latch. Gart nodded confidently to Romney and the boy unbolted the door and opened it. Julian was in the process of pounding again when the panel jerked open and Romney stood in the doorway.

He scowled at his son. "Why did you lock the door, boy?"

He didn't give Romney a chance to answer before he pushed into the cluttered chamber, his gaze falling on the mussed bed where Emberley and his other three children were. He didn't seem to notice their fearful expressions but if he did, he didn't care. His countenance was unrepentant as he stood over the bed, inspecting Emberley as she lay wounded. He looked her over and finally shook his head.

"I hope you have learned your lesson this time," he told her. "Were you not disobedient, I would not have to punish you."

Emberley would not look at him. She clutched Lacy up against her, knowing Julian wouldn't try to hurt her with the baby in her arms.

Julian could beat her from morning to night but, strangely, he wouldn't touch the children. Still, the tension in the room was palpable and the small family tensed, waiting for Julian to take notice of the enormous knight hiding behind the door panel and terrified of the consequences.

"Aye, Julian," she replied softly. "I understand."

Julian just stood there, eyeing her. He was finely dressed for his trip, wearing his standard colors of dark green, white and gray. When he seemed satisfied that his wife was adequately wounded from his thrashing, he began to pull on his fine leather gloves.

"I am leaving for London this morning," he told her. "The queen's requirements may keep me in London for quite some time, so I do not know when I will return. It could be months."

"*Bon voyage*, Julian," Emberley murmured.

He paused, irritated, still clutching one of his gloves in his hand. "Is that all you will say?"

She opened her eyes and looked at him, feeling the familiar fear at his tone. "We will look forward to your return, my lord."

That seemed to satisfy him. The man had no use for her but he wanted to feel appreciated and wanted, as if she were completely dependent upon him and longed for his return. The wrong words would result in another thrashing and Emberley was in no condition to receive another beating. She had to make him feel as if they loved him if there was any hope of her survival.

Julian lingered, eyeing her and the children, before turning on his heel and marching towards the door. Romney was standing there, holding it open for his father, and Julian paused in front of the boy, gazing down into his sweet little face.

"Perhaps I shall take you to London with me someday," he put his hand on his son's shoulder. "It is time you are introduced to Court. While I am there, I shall also make arrangements for you to foster. The time has come."

Romney looked up at him innocently, leaning back against the door and sandwiching Gart between the heavy oak panel and the wall.

"Aye, Papa," he said.

That was as far as Julian could go in showing his son attention. He went to put on his second glove but it fell from his hands, slipping on the floor and falling partially behind the panel. Emberley, watching the exchange between Julian and Romney, was seized with terror as Julian bent over to pick it up. It was very close to Gart's boot, the toe of which she could see a couple of inches from the glove in the shadow of the open door. But Romney was fast and he picked up the glove and handed it to his father before the man could make a reasonable effort.

"Here, Papa," he pushed the glove at the man. "Will it take you a long time to get to London?"

Sharp even at his young age, Romney was trying to divert his father's attention and get him out the door. The situation was becoming too uncomfortable for the young man and he knew what his father was capable of. He wasn't fearful for Gart as much as he was fearful for his mother. But Julian didn't know his son very well. He'd spent the majority of the boy's life ignoring him or in London or France, so he had no idea what was deep in the lad's heart and the fear he had for what his father was capable of.

At his son's words, Julian simply felt important as his son seemed eager to glean his knowledge. Now that the boy was getting older and more intelligent, Julian began to think that perhaps he was worthy of his attention.

"I will be gone at least a month, perhaps more," he told him. "It is a long journey to London."

"May I see you off, Papa?" Romney asked eagerly.

Julian slapped the boy on the shoulder as he quit the chamber. "Of course."

"Papa, why are you going to see the queen?"

Julian winked at him. "Because she is my very special friend, boy. We are linked, body and soul, and if she were to die, I would die as well. I will explain more to you when you grow older."

Julian went first through the door and Romney followed. The boy shut the door softly, leaving the room oddly still in his wake. Gart stood against the wall, listening to the fading sounds of Romney and his father descending the stairs before moving away from the wall and silently throwing the bolt to lock it. He listened until the distant voices fell silent before turning to Emberley.

She was looking at him from the bed, her dark blue eyes wide with apprehension. When she realized that Julian had come and gone from the room without discovering Gart, it was more than she could bear. She had been living the last few minutes in total terror, especially when Julian dropped his glove. She was sure her life was over at that moment. As Gart watched, her features crumpled and her head fell to the mattress. Frightened and relieved sobs filled the air.

Gart went over to the bed, his gaze moving over the children who were looking at their mother with confusion and fear. He put an enormous hand on Emberley's shoulder.

"Be at ease, kitten," he comforted. "He is gone, hopefully for a very long time. All is well."

She began wiping at her cheeks furiously, smearing green slime from the crushed herbs across her face. It took him a moment to realize the sobs had turned to weepy giggles.

"You called me kitten," she sniffled. "I have missed it."

He gave her a half-smile, looking around for the wet linen he had used to clean off her ear and using it to wipe the green smears on her cheek.

"I shall call you it often if it pleases you," he replied softly.

Emberley heard something in his tone, something that suggested other than brotherly concern, and it jolted her. She was wildly resistant and wildly thrilled at the same time. Muddled, confused, she thought perhaps she was reading too much into it. The man had literally been her shadow since their reunion yesterday and he had brought her a great deal of comfort, reminding her of times when she didn't live in daily fear of a brutal husband.

She didn't want to become dependent on Gart somehow, clinging to the vaporous memories of a dead brother, one who had always protected her. But even as she entertained those thoughts, she knew it wasn't true. Gart was different. He was a proud and powerful man.

Sickened by her thoughts, she simply smiled weakly in response to his statement.

"Would you please do something for me, Gart?" she asked softly.

He lifted an eyebrow at her. "Do not ask me to leave again because I will not."

Her weak smile turned genuine. "Nay," she chuckled softly. "I was not going to ask you to leave. I was going to ask you to take the children to Gerta. I wish to sleep and I cannot do that if they are here."

Gart looked around. "Is this not their room?" he asked. "Where is your chamber? I will take you there. You will be more comfortable."

"Perhaps later," she said softly. "Right now, I do not want to move."

He understood. There had been times in his life when he had been so badly thrashed that he didn't want to move, either. Nodding his head, he moved away from the bed and went to the lancet window, peering down at the bailey below.

The fog from the early morning had lifted and the day was dawning sunny. Everything smelled crisp and clean. He could see part of the bailey from where he stood, enough to see a portion of the gatehouse and the fact that Julian's escort to London was now congregated near the big oak and iron gates.

Men and servants were milling about, mounting horses and securing provisions, and he watched for quite some time until Julian came into view. He caught a glimpse of the man as he slipped out the front gates on his big, white horse, followed by several men-at-arms bearing the colors of Buckland. All were well-armed and seasoned. Following the horses were two wagons loaded down with provisions and trunks.

Gart could see a portion of the road outside of the walls and he watched as Baron Buckland's party faded into the horizon. Only then did he feel genuinely relieved that the man had departed, jolted from his position near the window when someone pounded on the chamber door. He moved to the panel, lifting the iron latch as Romney barged in. The young lad looked right at Gart.

"He is gone now," he assured him. "He will not come back for a long time. Mother will be well now."

Gart looked over at the bed where Emberley had fallen asleep beside her thumb-sucking daughter. Orin and Brendt were still on the bed, whispering between them, pointing at Emberley's head. Every once in a while they would grab at Lacy's feet and she would kick at them and whine. Now that Julian was gone, their source of terror, the relief was palpable. The children were acting like children, care-free, and Emberley was fast asleep. The tension, the terror, was over for now.

"Aye, she will," he told the boy. "She will be fine."

He moved over to the bed. Watching Emberley sleep stirred something deep inside him, an indefinable warmth that he tried to chase away but couldn't. He realized that whatever he was starting to feel wasn't healthy or normal, at least not for him, but the feelings were so strong that he couldn't seem to fight them off. They were wrong and he knew it, but he didn't particularly care.

He put his hand on Romney's shoulder. "Come along," he said quietly. "I told your mother I would take you and your siblings to Gerta. Where is she?"

Romney shrugged. "In the hall, I think. She was there the last time I saw her."

"Then let us go so that your mother may sleep uninterrupted."

He motioned Orin and Brendt off the bed, but Brendt got tangled in the coverlet, so he lifted the boy off and unwound his feet. Lacy, seeing that her brothers were leaving, suddenly stood up on the mattress and whined, lifting her arms to be picked up. Gart looked at the little girl, sweet like a little cherub, and waited for Romney to take her, but the oldest brother was already over by the door with his two younger brothers. Gart hesitantly reached out and picked the baby up, whereupon she promptly wrapped her fat, little arms around his neck and put a slobbery mouth on his cheek.

Gart didn't know what else to do but carry her over to the door. Little Lacy delivered a couple of very wet kisses to his rough cheek before hugging him tightly, her little face against his. Gart's momentary surprise, and perhaps disgust at the tongue-to-his-cheek kiss, was abated as Lacy hugged him. There was something inherently sweet and settling about the toddler in his arms, a gentle slice of life he had never before experienced. His intention to put her down once they reached the door changed. He hugged her back, smiling weakly when Romney and the other boys pointed at him and laughed.

"Mother told you not to get too close," Romney taunted. "She will kiss you until your whole face is wet."

Gart lifted an eyebrow as Lacy squeezed him enthusiastically. "Does she do this with everyone? Even strangers?"

Romney shrugged as they headed out the door. "Almost everyone," he said. "But she usually wants to be put down by now. She likes you."

As if to punctuate the statement, Lacy began to deliver open-mouth kisses against his jaw. She was babbling baby-talk the entire time, happy and chatty. Gart suffered through the baby's wet kisses in spite of everything, thinking it was rather sweet. Mildly repulsive, but sweet.

Romney had been correct. By the time they found Gerta in the great hall, Gart's entire face was wet with baby kisses.

CHAPTER FIVE

IT HAD BEEN two days since Julian's departure to London. David de Lohr had also departed during that time, heading back to Denstroude Castle to make arrangements for providing manpower to Baron Buckland for the conflict in France.

As soon as both barons departed, things at Dunster seemed to settle down and the entire castle moved back into their routine. Since the baron was gone from the castle more than he was in residence, the castle seemed to function much better without his presence. When he was away, Dunster was a lovely place of happiness and freedom, but when he was home, it turned into a place of uncertainty and fear.

Gart learned this in the three days he had spent at the castle. Emberley had slept in Romney's bed for two straight days, having only awoken twice to eat something and then falling back asleep again. Gart had spent most of his time sitting next to her, watching her sleep, reliving memories of the lovely young girl who grew up into a strikingly gorgeous woman.

He also relived memories of Erik, wondering what the man would be doing at this time had he lived. His father was a wealthy baron and Erik would have undoubtedly inherited the barony, but Gart wondered if Erik would have married and had a family. He wondered what course the man's life might have taken had it not been so tragically cut short.

On the fourth day of his arrival at Dunster, Gart was up before dawn, having slept in de Lohr's vacated chamber in the keep. He heard the children rise on the floor above him and their little feet as they scattered across the floor. Rising at the sounds of activity, he went to the basin of cold, stale water from the night before and went through his morning routine of shaving his face and head.

Although he had a full head of hair when he allowed it to grow, he found it more convenient and cleaner to simply shave himself almost bald. With his high cheekbones and intense green eyes, men seemed to be more frightened of him that way. He liked it.

This morning, he wasn't thinking about frightening men. He was thinking about Emberley and he looked at himself in the polished bronze mirror, trying to figure out exactly what he was feeling towards her. Whatever it was, he knew it was foolish, but it was growing stronger by the day, both frightening him and thrilling him. If he were a smart man, he would leave Dunster and return home as quickly as possible. But he just couldn't seem to force himself to do it.

He could hear the children making noise upstairs as he wiped the remaining water and soap off his face. Someone opened the chamber door loudly and it banged against the wall, rattling the entire keep. He set the linen towel down as he heard voices coming down the stairs to his level. Then there was great banging on his door.

Fighting off a grin, he made his way to the heavy oak panel, held together with pegs and iron. He was dressed in leather breeches, naked from the waist up, as he opened the door for the gaggle of children clamoring to get in. Just as he opened the panel, Brendt charged in with a squeal, running the length of the room with Orin and Romney on his heels. The boys chased each other madly around the room while Gart stood at the door, perplexed.

"What goes on?" he demanded.

Only Romney answered. "He has my shoes!"

Gart couldn't help the grin now, watching Brendt jump on his bed only to be captured by Orin. As Orin held tight, Romney began pulling off the small leather shoes on Brendt's feet which were, at closer inspection, too large for the boy. Brendt's giggles turned to sobs as Romney managed to get both shoes off of him. Brendt sat up on the bed and wept unhappily.

Gart went to the bed, standing over the crying boy as Romney pulled on his shoes. Orin saw Gart's bags against the wall and gravitated towards them, only to be warned off by Gart. He cocked a stern eyebrow at the boy, who pretended not to notice the rebuking expression. As Brendt wept, Gart went over to his bags and pulled out an old tunic.

It was threadbare and worn, normally used under heavy armor, and Gart took it over to the bed and draped it on Brendt's head. The sun immediately shined again as Brendt happily struggled to pull the tunic over his head. Gart stood with his hands on his hips, watching the commotion going on around him. The morning was starting out on a whirlwind.

"Boys!" Emberley was suddenly in the doorway with Lacy in her arms, her lovely face awash with chagrin. "I told you not to bother Sir Gart. What are you doing here?"

Gart turned to her. He'd not seen the woman out of bed in two days and now, here she was and looking absolutely exquisite. Dressed in a stunning yellow, silk surcoat with a neckline that emphasized her delicious figure to a fault, she looked rested and healthy. Gart noted that she had even washed her hair because it was still slightly damp, pulled back from her face with a comb in a very attractive style. Other than a slight bruise to her left cheek, she looked completely normal. He just stood there and stared at her, entranced, as Romney answered his mother's question.

"Brendt had my shoes," Romney told her. "He would not give them back."

He was pointing to his feet. Emberley gave Brendt her best motherly scowl, but the boy was having too much fun playing with Gart's tunic.

"Brendt," she scolded. "I told you that it is not nice to take things that do not belong to you. Are you listening to me?"

Brendt's blond head was peeking out from the arm of the tunic. He nodded seriously at his mother. Then he grinned brightly. "Ooo-nic,

Mama!"

Emberley shook her head in resignation. "You mean tunic, sweetheart," she said with a sigh. Then she turned to look at Gart for the first time since entering the room. She smiled at the man. "I am sorry if they disturbed you."

He returned her smile, feeling himself go weak and giddy.

"They did not disturb me," he said. "But I am sorry if they woke you up. I have spent the past two days trying to keep them from upsetting you."

Her smile broadened and the baby squirmed to be set down. As Lacy toddled over to the bed where Brendt was frolicking, Emberley focused on Gart.

"You have been an angel, Gart," she said softly, her dark blue eyes warm with appreciation. "Had it not been for you, I do not know what would have become of me and the children. I do not know how I can adequately thank you for spending your precious time with us."

Gart was caught up in a storm of warmth and excitement. He could feel the lightning flash every time their eyes met. He wanted to reach out and take her hand in the worst way but he held himself steady, reminding himself that it would not be appropriate. So he dipped his head gallantly in response to her statement.

"My time has never been so well spent," he told her, looking her over. "Are you sure you feel well enough?"

She nodded. "I feel fine," she said. "My ear is a little sore but for the most part, I feel very well thanks to your kind attention. You make a fine healer."

He wriggled his eyebrows. "Perhaps," he said modestly.

She gazed at his handsome face, realizing for the first time that he was without any clothes on from the waist up. She tried not to let her eyes drift to his naked chest but she couldn't help herself. The man was muscular and sculpted, with a broad chest, narrow waist and enormous arms. He was spectacular. The sight was enough to set her heart to racing somewhat and her cheeks to flush, and she struggled to overcome her reaction to him. She felt like that giddy young girl again, the one who used to follow Erik and Gart around with adoration in her eyes. She was feeling that adoration again and it frightened her.

"Will you be leaving us now?" she asked, not knowing what else to say and hoping he didn't notice her pink cheeks. "Surely you have pressing duties elsewhere."

Now that she was looking away from him, he took the opportunity to let his gaze drift over her body. Even though she had given birth to four children, the woman was magnificent. She had full breasts and a slender torso, and he could only imagine that what was covered by layers of fabric was just as luscious.

"I do not, at least at the moment," he said, his gaze moving back to her delicate profile. "In fact, I was hoping you could help me to that regard."

She turned to look at him. "How?"

He lifted his big shoulders, noticing from the corner of his eye that Orin was back over with his bags. Rather than scold the boy, he called to him.

"Orin," he said in his deep, bass voice. "Look down into the bag in front of you. There is a dark blue tunic. Can you please bring it to me?"

Orin gleefully did as he was told as Gart returned his attention to Emberley.

"According to my liege, your husband has commandeered four hundred of de Lohr's men to support his efforts for the queen in France," he said. "I am told that I will be heading to France at the head of this contingent in three or four weeks. I was hoping you would allow me to stay here and keep you company until that time. I have not seen you in twelve years and I would like to get reacquainted with my best friend's sister from long ago. Would that be acceptable?"

Emberley gazed steadily at him, feeling joy at his request that she couldn't begin to describe. She'd spent eight years with Julian in a hellish existence and the thought of kind, male attention was incredibly inviting. But she just as quickly knew that allowing him to stay might not be a wise decision in more ways than one. Not only would Julian become furious if he ever found out, but given the way she felt about Gart when she looked at him… nay, it would not be wise at all. Disappointment flooded her and she averted her gaze.

"I am not sure…," she started and then regrouped. "Surely we hold no particular interest for you. We live very ordinary lives, without excitement. You would become grossly bored within a week."

He gave her a half-grin. "With these children?" he looked to the group of them; two on the bed and two going through his bags. "You underestimate their entertainment value. I would like to get the chance to know Erik's nephews. Will you please allow me this privilege?"

"But…."

"I have nowhere else to go, Emberley."

She cocked her head, her expression somewhat curious. "Do you not have a home?"

He shook his head. "Only Denstroude Castle or Bellham Place in London, neither of which are my home. They are de Lohr's homes."

"But your father's brother is William de Fortibus, the Earl of Albemarle," she pointed out. "Surely your father…."

He shook his head, cutting her off. "If you remember anything about me, then you will also remember that my father and his brother had a disagreement long ago that severed all ties between them," he reminded her. "That is why my father changed his name from de Fortibus to Forbes. My father has been dead and buried for quite some time in the dark soil of Shropshire and left nothing for his only son."

She grew serious as the children around her began to play more loudly. Her gaze upon him was intense. "I remember," she murmured. "But it does not seem right, Gart. You are a great knight from a great family. Your uncle is an earl. Surely he is proud of his nephew and has provided for you."

His murky green eyes were riveted to her, ignoring the fact that Romney and Orin had emptied all three of his bags and were happily looking for valuables.

"The only thing my uncle ever did was ensure I fostered in a prestigious house," he said quietly. "I am sure you do not remember all of my past, as it was long ago when you and I last knew each other, but I have had to fight for everything I have accumulated. Fortunately, serving de Lohr has allowed me to build my fortune and someday, I will have a home of my own. But not yet."

Emberley watched his handsome face, sensing no distress and only determination. She shook her head sadly.

"It is not right that you should have to fight for everything when birthright alone should have dictated some manner of secure future," she sighed after a moment. "Perhaps you can marry well and that will seal your status. There must be a worthy bride for you somewhere."

He just looked at her, thinking of a thousand different replies and not one of them was appropriate. He couldn't say what he was thinking. *I should have married you.* After a moment, he smiled weakly.

"Perhaps." was all he would say. "Meanwhile, will you allow me to remain as your guest until I am called back to battle?"

Her expression grew serious. "I do not like the sound of that," she muttered, hardly noticing when Brendt climbed off the bed with the tunic over his head and began running around with Lacy toddling after him. "The last time I saw someone off to battle, he did not return. I should not like it if you did not return."

He smiled at her. "I would not want to disappoint you. May I stay, then?"

Against her better judgment, she reluctantly nodded. "Very well," she said softy. "I would like that."

His smile broadened in a warm gesture but he was cut short from replying when Brendt, still with the tunic over his head and running from his sister, bashed into his legs. He reached down to steady the boy.

"Orin?" he called over his shoulder. "Where is my tunic? Have you forgotten? And stop robbing my bags."

Orin popped up from the pile on the floor with a dark blue garment in his hand, running it over to Gart. Gart took the tunic, pulling it over his head as he turned to Romney and Orin and the complete mess they had made out of his saddlebags.

He sighed heavily at the sight, resting his giant fists on his hips as he surveyed the situation. Everything was all over the place.

"You two have made a mockery out of my possessions," he grumbled. "Start repacking those bags and if it is not neatly done, I will make you repack them again until you get it right."

Romney and Orin may have thought it great fun to go through Gart's possessions but they did not think it fun to repack everything. They scowled and made faces but did as they were told, trying to figure out where to start in the mess they had made. They looked a little lost. Gart pointed to the pile of tunics.

"Start there," he told them. "Roll them up neatly and pack them tightly together."

Romney sighed with displeasure and started to do what he was told but Gart suddenly grabbed the boy's arm and began frisking him. As Romney grumbled and tried to pull away, Gart began pulling all sorts of valuables out of Romney's pockets.

"My purse," he pulled out a heavy leather pouch from the front of Romney's tunic and tossed it into his bags. "What else of mine have you stolen?"

As Emberley stood by, mortified, Gart removed two small daggers, a pouch containing flint and stone, a couple of other small pouches, one of which contained white willow powder for the terrible headaches that Gart was prone to, and two spoons. He patted the boy down until he was sure there was nothing else of his that the boy had stolen before letting him go.

"Now," he pointed at his bags. "Pack. And if I find anything else of mine that you have stolen, you shall be very sorry."

Romney was defiant and contrite and the same time. "The money was not for me," he insisted. "It was for Mother."

Emberley rolled her eyes. "Romney de Russe de Moyon, you will not dare pull me into your thievery."

Romney turned his big, blue eyes to his mother. "But I was going to buy you a present," he told her. "I was going to buy you something nice."

Emberley sighed with exasperation. "I do not need for you to purchase anything for me with ill-gotten gains," she scolded. "Apologize to Sir Gart and finish packing his bags. We must break our fast."

Gart gazed down at the unhappy little heads and felt his stance soften as a thought occurred to him.

"Romney," he said. "I have a proposition for you. If you promise to stop stealing, we shall go into town after the morning meal and I will purchase something nice for your mother. How would you like that?"

Romney's expression cleared up immediately. "Can we buy sweets, too?"

Gart lifted his eyebrows. "I suppose so," he said. "Hurry, now. Pack my bags so we can go."

"Gart," Emberley grasped his arm gently. "Please… you do not have to purchase anything for us."

He turned to her, feeling her soft hand on his arm as one of the greatest sensations he had ever known. "I know that," he said. "I want to."

Her dark blue eyes were fearful, beseeching. "But… well, people in town know my husband," she whispered so the boys couldn't hear her. "They will see you and… and I am afraid that Julian might find out somehow. I am already risking much by allowing you to stay here simply because the entire castle will see you. It is quite possible that someone, at some point, will tell Julian."

He understood her concern and, for the first time, felt some doubt about staying on. If the baron did find out at some point, his wrath would fall on Emberley. Gart knew that. But it wasn't enough to convince him to leave because he very much wanted to stay. Against his better judgment, he very much wanted to enjoy Emberley's company. He simply couldn't help it.

"It is possible," he conceded quietly. "Do you think someone will run off to tell him?"

Emberley held his gaze a moment before finally shaking her head. "Nay," she admitted. "There is no great love for Julian at Dunster. If he were told, it would be by mistake."

He wasn't surprised to hear that Julian wasn't well liked. He had already seen in the few days he was here how much everyone at Dunster loved and admired Emberley. If there were loyalties, they were to her. He veered back to the subject of shopping.

"Where is the closest town to Dunster?" he asked.

Her delicate brow furrowed in thought. "Carhampton to the south and Minehead to the northwest, but...."

"Which one is larger?"

"Minehead."

"How far is it?"

"Perhaps a mile or less. It is not far. But...."

He put an enormous, warm hand over the small fingers on his wrist and squeezed. "Then we shall go to Minehead," he told her. "Please, kitten... do not refuse me the privilege that Erik has been denied. Let me do something nice for my best friend's sister and her children."

When he put it that way, she could not refuse him at all. With a faint sigh, this one of resignation, she nodded once and removed her hand from his arm.

"Very well," she said. "But let us break our fast before we go anywhere. I will take Lacy and Brendt with me if you will bring Orin and Romney when they have finished their task."

Gart nodded, watching her leave with the two youngest children, allowing his gaze to drift over her luscious backside. The woman had a round, healthy bottom that he could see beneath the fabric and it was extremely alluring. With thoughts of her round backside on his brain, he returned his attention to Romney and Orin. The pair was packing furiously and he lifted an eyebrow at them.

"What did I tell you?" he asked. "If you do not pack it to my liking, I will make you do it again."

Romney slowed down, gazing up at Gart. "But we are packing neatly."

Gart crouched down by the boys to show them what he meant. For a man who usually did not have an abundance of patience, nor did he normally associate with squires or pages in any fashion, he was showing a good deal of natural understanding with two small boys. For the two small boys who had rare interaction with their own father, the presence of the patient man they had tried to rob did them a world of good.

Two hours later, they were on the road to Minehead.

CHAPTER SIX

THE DAY WAS remarkably sunny and clear as the party from Dunster Castle traveled to the rather large village of Minehead, a little less than a mile to the northwest of the castle. The sounds of the ocean filled the air as Gart rode at the head of the party astride his vicious black and white charger, followed by a carriage that contained Emberley and the children. The carriage was surrounded by twenty men-at-arms personally sworn to Gart.

He had sixty retainers that traveled with him everywhere, men that were highly trained and carried the same sense of battle aggression that Gart did. They were a hard bunch, loyal to the core, intermingled with de Lohr ranks since David was Gart's liege. But on this trip, Gart's men alone had the escort duty.

Emberley sat in the carriage with Orin next to her and Lacy on her lap, smelling deeply the scent of the sea as they passed through the softly rolling hills that led to Minehead. She felt better than she had in days, her spirit renewed with the departure of Julian and the company of Gart, and her body healing quickly from the beating. She was actually happy, something she didn't normally feel, as she gazed off across the ocean and watched the seagulls ride the salty drafts.

Emberley could see Gart at the head of the column, riding strong and proud astride his black and white steed, and she realized that she had been watching him a good deal of the time. When she wasn't gazing at the sea, or the birds, she was watching his broad back. As Lacy fell asleep against her, sucking her thumb, Emberley settled back against the seat with her gaze still riveted to Gart.

Her mind began to wander to the days of her youth when she remembered her brother and Gart as young men of fifteen or sixteen years of age. It was right before she had gone to foster and she remembered that Gart was extremely tall for his age, a good-looking young man returned for the winter season from fostering at Kenilworth Castle. Erik, too, was fostering at Kenilworth and had come home to see his ailing mother. Gart had come with him simply because he had nowhere else to go. Emberley remembered the young man, so handsome and poised, until Erik, the ringleader, would whip them both into a frenzy and they would wreak good-natured havoc. She missed those days.

Although Gart had always been kind to her, she had never received the impression that it was anything more than polite concern. As she watched him ride ahead of the column, she could only surmise that in this situation, too, it was polite concern, but Gart's entire manner had changed over the past twelve years. He had grown up, acquired depth of character, and she would swear until the day he died that some of the exchanges between them had gone beyond polite concern. There was warmth to the man, a spark in his eye, and she had to admit she found it wildly attractive. She was sure that Julian had killed any ability she had to feel something for the opposite sex, but with the reintroduction of Gart Forbes, she was coming to think that she was not dead inside, after all.

In her arms, Lacy cuddled close in her sleep and Orin, sitting next to her, was leaning against his mother, dozing. Emberley's dark blue eyes drifted over her beautiful children. If only they were Gart's children. She realized, at that moment, that she would have sold her soul for that opportunity. Perhaps, for a time, she could just pretend they were. It would be a bright spot in an otherwise colorless life, her little secret to carry with her to her grave.

Lost to her thoughts as she watched Gart's proud posture, Minehead came into view and she was distracted from Gart by the sight of the sprawling village. It spread out over the softly rolling hills in little, brown bumps with dozens of tendrils of gray smoke trailing into the sky from cooking fires. Just as they crested the hill of the road that led down into the berg, Gart reined his charger about and made his way back to the carriage. Mud sprayed from his horse's hooves as he barked orders to his men. He flipped his visor up as he reached the carriage, a faint smile on his lips. Emberley smiled in return.

"We have arrived," he said, looking at Romney and Brendt as they hung over the side of the carriage to catch a glimpse. "Where shall we go first?"

Emberley stretched her neck, trying to get a look at the town without waking the children sleeping on her.

"There is a neighborhood with merchants over to the west," she told him. "There is the Street of the Farmers and next to that is the Street of the Merchants. This road will fork at the base of the hill and you will go left."

He nodded shortly, snapping more orders to the men around him, and the party took off again. They began the slow trek down the hill with Gart riding alongside the carriage astride his excitable charger. The animal danced about, switching his bound tail angrily, as Romney and Brendt tried to reach out and catch it. It made for quite a game until Gart moved the animal away to a safe distance.

"Since we have come to town to buy you something nice, where would you like to go?" he asked Emberley. "Surely there is something lovely or expensive that you would like."

She looked at him, shaking her head reprovingly, but there was a smile on her lips. "I told you that you do not have to buy me anything," she reiterated. "But I would like to purchase some durable fabric for the boys. There are merchants in town that carry such goods. The children seem to go through clothing so quickly."

He looked down his nose at her. "If you refuse me again, I shall become quite angry."

She lifted a defiant eyebrow in response. "Is that so?"

"It is."

She lifted her shoulders lazily. "There is nothing you can do about it so I suggest you focus your energies elsewhere."

He sighed heavily, with exaggeration. "You ungrateful woman. I will focus my energies on my palm to your backside if you do not show more cooperation."

She fought off a grin. "You would spank me if I do not let you buy me something?"

"That is the general idea."

By this time, Romney and Brendt were listening. Romney's young face was taut with rage and fear.

"You will not spank my mother," he put a hand out as if to shove Gart away. "I will not let you do it. I will kill you if you try."

Gart and Emberley lost all of their humor. "I was only jesting, Romney," Gart said evenly and sincerely. "I would never lay a hand on your mother. I would rather die than hurt her in any way. Surely you know that."

"Rom," Emberley reached out to her eldest child, gently, and pulled him against her. "You are such a brave young lad. But surely you know that Sir Gart would never, ever harm any of us. He is our friend."

Romney was angry but he eased up when his mother kissed his forehead. He eyed Gart, still suspicious.

"Well," he said reluctantly. "I guess he is."

Emberley hugged her boy. "Of course he is, sweetheart. He has been my friend for a very long time."

Next to the cab, Gart leaned down, bracing a massive arm against his thigh. He found that he wanted to soothe the confused, angry boy. "I will protect your mother, and you, always."

Romney cocked his head. "Like a guardian angel?"

Gart snorted softly and straightened in the saddle, a grin on his face. "Exactly like a guardian angel."

"You do not look like an angel."

Gart lifted an eyebrow. "Have you seen one?"

Romney shook his head. "Nay," he replied. "But the priests say that angels have a golden light around their head and carry harps. Your head is dark and you carry a sword."

Gart's lips twitched with a smile. "Archangels carry a sword. Perhaps I am the archangel Gabriel."

"I thought you did not like to be called Gabriel," Emberley whispered with a smile.

He wriggled his eyebrows at her. "That is because archangels do not wish to go around announcing themselves to everyone. Only to special people."

He winked at her and she giggled, shaking her head reproachfully at him. Romney fell silent, contemplating that particular bit of information, as they entered the outskirts of the village. It was the day before Sunday and the town was busy with people – travelers, customers and merchants. But what Emberley had completely forgotten was that it was the time of year for the annual *Obby Oss* festival, and the town was absolutely packed as they traveled deeper into the berg.

With all of the noise and bustle, Lacy and Orin woke up, and Emberley tried to get a better look at what was going on around them. The entire town was jammed.

Even Gart was impressed by the amount of people in town. He couldn't see all of the commotion from their vantage point on the road, only as they traveled deeper into the town. There were people everywhere.

"Is it always this busy?" he asked.

Emberley shook her head. "Nay," she replied. "I completely forgot that it is the time of year for the annual *Obby Oss* festival. These people must be here for the faire."

Gart looked at her. "*Obby Oss*? What is that?"

She grinned when Romney and Orin caught sight of mummers and began yelling. "They will parade a wooden horse around town and it is supposed to bring good fortune," she raised her voice over her children's screaming. "There will also be food and entertainment. Usually, they have a joust exhibition. It is quite exciting. With everything that has happened over the past few days, I completely forgot about it."

He could see the mummer that the children were yelling about. The man was dressed in colorful clothing with wooden shoes and a big, colorful cap. He had four white dogs around him doing tricks. Gart looked at the boys, nearly falling out of the carriage in their excitement, and he called a halt to the party in the middle of the busy street.

Climbing off his muzzled warhorse, he handed the animal off to one of his men and went to the carriage. He reached up and pulled Romney out, but Orin didn't want to wait so he practically jumped on Gart in his haste to get out. Gart lowered both boys to the muddy ground, telling them not to run off while he reached inside again and pulled out Brendt. Now all three boys were at his feet, dancing around with anticipation, as Gart opened the cab door to help Emberley out.

She handed him the baby, who latched on to his big neck and began kissing all over his helm because she couldn't get to his face. With Lacy in one arm, Gart reached out and took Emberley's hand, helping her down from the carriage.

"Mama!" Romney implored. "The *man*."

Emberley pointed to the mummer. "Go and see him," she said. "But do not run off. And pay attention to where...."

Unfortunately, she didn't get it out of her mouth fast enough. Romney and Orin tore off, immediately crashing into a well-dressed man who was emerging from the ointment broker's stall.

Emberley gasped as the boys bounced off the man, knocked the sack out of his hand, and continued running. The fat man with the big jowls teetered back, watching the boys run away. Brendt, who hadn't crashed into the man, zipped past and the outraged old man tried to grab him. Thankfully, Brendt went by untouched.

"See here," he scolded, turning to see Emberley and Gart standing a few feet away. "Are those your unruly children? You should teach them manners!"

Embarrassed, Emberley opened her mouth to apologize but Gart handed her the baby, pulled off his helm, and got in the man's face. He towered over the fat, old man, big and powerful and intimidating. Surely there were no more frightening things in life than an enraged knight, and Gart went over and above simply frightening. He was red in the face and terrifying.

"If I were you, I would watch who I gave advice to on the subject of child rearing," he growled. "Those boys are clever, brilliant and resourceful and perhaps next time, you should pay attention to where you are walking. And if you ever make a grab for one of those boys again, you will draw away a bloody stump. Is this in any way unclear?"

The old man paled dramatically, absolutely terrified. He could only nod his head before stumbling backwards, collecting his fallen sack, and shuffling off as fast as his tubby legs would carry him. Gart watched the man run off, his green eyes hard and furious, before returning his attention to Emberley. He gazed at her a moment and an apparent change came over him. He calmed dramatically and the fire went out of his eyes.

Without a word, he took his helm from her, tossed it into the carriage, and took Lacy from her arms. In silence, he carried the little girl over to the mummer where her brothers were being entertained.

Emberley watched him with astonishment. She had never in her life seen anyone defend her children, not even their father, so it was something of a shock to see Gart actually step into the role of protector. Even though he had declared his intentions to them all, to be their protector, to see him in action was something to behold.

But in the same breath, his defense of her children touched her like nothing she had ever known. It softened her, swelling her heart with gratitude and appreciation. It also broke down the barriers that were trying so hard to keep her infatuation at bay. The barriers were coming down and she could feel herself weakening, knowing how horribly wrong it was but not particularly caring. She had wished all her life for a man like Gart Forbes. It broke her heart to know that what she wished for could never be.

Silently, she went to where Gart and her children were standing, watching the mummer with his trained dogs. The group was watching one of the dogs walk on its front paws, laughing loudly at the antics. As she strolled up, Gart had to reach out a hand to pull Brendt away from the dog. The little boy very much wanted to pick it up. She stood next to Gart, watching her children laugh, when she began to feel his gaze upon her. She never even had to look at him. She just knew he was looking at her.

Without a word, she slipped her hand into the crook of his right elbow. She could make the excuse that she was only touching her daughter, cradled in the man's enormous right arm, but that wasn't the truth. The truth was that she just wanted to touch Gart. Greedily, secretly, she stood there and held him.

"Mama!" Orin suddenly turned to her. "Where are thweets?"

She smiled at her lazy-tongued son. "I am not sure," she said, looking around. "We will find some, not to worry. Are you finished watching the dogs?"

The boys all turned to her, nodding eagerly, and she finally dared to look up at Gart. His gaze was steady upon her, his smile faint but unmistakable. He turned to his men and ordered them to find someplace nearby to park the carriage. Ten men-at-arms broke off from the group and went in search of a rest area while Gart, Emberley, the children and another ten men-at-arms continued down the avenue.

The day was brilliant as they walked down the dirt street, avoiding piles of horse dung and pools of animal urine as they walked. Gart carried the baby, who had her arms wrapped tightly around his neck and her cheek hugged up against his. Emberley offered to take the little girl from him, twice, but he refused. He looked rather content so she didn't press. When she dropped her hand from the crook of his elbow, he switched Lacy to the opposite arm and reached out to take Emberley's hand with his free hand.

His enormous mitt closed in over her soft, warm fingers. Startled, feeling her chest swell with excitement at what could be considered an intimate action, she held his hand tightly. She was thrilled beyond measure, living greedily in her secret little world where Gart belonged to her and there was no Julian, no horrors of a brutal husband. But her secret dreams were shattered when Brendt took off running. Gart quickly handed Lacy to her mother and took off after the little boy.

Romney and Orin stopped before a woodworker as Gart chased Brendt down. The two older boys were fascinated with the wooden toys the man had on display – little carts and wooden horses, wooden shields and wooden swords. They were particularly in love with the swords and Emberley had to repeatedly tell them not to touch them. Unhappy, they began to beg and whine and she turned away from them, unwilling to give in to their demands. Across the avenue, she spied Gart approaching with Brendt tucked under one arm.

Brendt was squealing because Gart was carrying him sideways, like a parcel. The child was delighted, giggling, and Gart turned him upside down and pretended to plant his head in the mud once they reached his mother. Brendt giggled uncontrollably until Gart turned him right-side up and put him on his feet.

"No more running away," Gart wagged a stern finger in his face. "Do you hear me? If you run off again, I will not buy you any sweets."

Brendt's giggles were gone and he nodded seriously. Gart gave him a lingering look just for emphasis as he turned to Emberley.

She was smiling at him. "Where was he running to?" she asked.

He threw a thumb back over his shoulder. "There is a man over there with a goat that was dancing on its hind legs."

Emberley's features relaxed in understanding. "He loves goats," she sighed, then pointed to the woodworker where her three boys were now gleefully inspecting the goods. "I have a bigger problem now. This man makes little wooden swords and shields and I fear I shall not get the boys away from this stall without great drama."

Gart didn't think it was a problem at all. He purchased three little wooden shields and three little wooden swords over Emberley's protests. Thrilled to be well-armed knights, Romney, Orin and Brendt began attacking each other before Gart had fully paid for everything. Giving the woodworker a tidy sum for the little toys, Gart stilled the three combatants before the situation got out of hand. He could see that they were already far too enthusiastic about killing each other. When Brendt refused to stop, he pulled the toy sword away and held it out of his reach so he had the boy's attention.

"Now," he said firmly. "Along with these weapons comes responsibility. You must not hit each other in the head with them. You must not try to stab each other when them. Keep them away from your eyes. The first time someone gets hurt because of carelessness, I will take away everyone's toys and hold them until such time as I feel you are ready to accept the responsibility again. Is that clear?"

"How long would you keep them?" Romney demanded.

"Years."

Gart said it so seriously that Emberley bit off a smile, watching the distressed expressions on her sons' faces. Romney and Orin looked at each other apprehensively before returning their attention to the enormous knight.

"We will be careful," Romney said.

"Promith!" Orin piped up.

Gart cocked an eyebrow at them. "Very well," he handed the sword back to Brendt. "Behave yourselves."

Properly subdued, the boys took their toys and followed their mother and Gart down the avenue. Emberley let her grin burst forth when she knew the boys couldn't see her.

"You are very good with children," Emberley commented, eyeing her boys as they attempted not to hurt each other with their new toys. "You must have received experience somewhere."

Gart shook his head. "No experience."

"Is that so?"

"It is."

She looked up at him, a smile on her lips. "Then you have a natural talent for it and will make an excellent father," she said. "Your children will be very lucky."

He looked at her, feeling strangely sad at that statement. He'd only spent four days with Emberley and her children but it felt as if he'd spent an eternity with them. He fought down the familiar feeling of wishing they belonged to him, struggling against the sadness it provoked.

"Perhaps someday," he said quietly.

Emberley sensed his depressed mood but she wasn't sure why. She shifted the baby from one arm to the other as they walked.

"I always wondered if Erik would have married and had children," she said softly. "Do you not want to get married someday, Gart?"

He sighed with resignation, turning to glance at the boys when he heard wood against wood. The three of them froze when they saw that Gart's attention was on them and they tried to look very innocent. Gart eyes narrowed at them, although it was without force, before returning his attention to Emberley.

"To be truthful, I have not thought much about it," he replied. "My vocation makes marriage difficult at this time."

"But if the right woman presented herself, you would consider it, would you not?" she pressed. "You really should be married."

He looked at her. "Why does this concern you so much?"

She shrugged, trying to appear casual. "Because you are a good man and would make a wonderful husband. I do not want to see you waste the opportunity."

He didn't like this subject. It made him want to say things to her that were inappropriate and painful. He fully realized that the only woman he wanted was already married and it was a sickening awareness. He didn't want to talk about it.

"Look," he pointed to a merchant across the avenue, diverting her off the subject. "That merchant has piles of fabric. Did you not want to purchase some for the boys?"

Emberley knew he was shifting the subject. Either he hated the thought of marriage in general or he truly didn't care. So she allowed him to direct her towards the fabric merchant, making sure the boys were following her as she walked. Just as their group crossed the busy avenue, the fat man who had nearly crashed into the boys minutes earlier suddenly appeared. He had several soldiers with him, pointing to Gart and his group.

"Him!" he howled. "He threatened me. Punish him!"

People began screaming and running as Gart and his soldiers geared for a fight. As Gart's men began to strategically position themselves, Gart grabbed the three boys in one arm and Emberley in the other, and shoved them into the merchant stall that contained the material.

It was crowded and dark inside, smelling like damp wool. Emberley turned her frightened face to him but he cut her off before she had a chance to speak.

"Stay here," he commanded. "Do not come out until I tell you to."

Eyes filled with terror, Emberley barely had a chance to nod before he was unsheathing his broadsword and charging out into the street. Wisely, Emberley gathered the boys and herded them as far away from the door as she could because she didn't want them to get hurt should the fighting veer in their direction. They had never experienced a battle in their lives and she wanted to protect them as much as she could. Things like this never happened in their world. But as they stood there in a frightened huddle, Emberley's curiosity got the best of her. Handing Lacy over to Romney, she crept towards the open door as the sounds of metal upon metal filled the air.

Emberley spied Gart immediately. He was without his helm, as it was still in the carriage, his massive broadsword arcing in the morning sunshine like the sword of an avenging angel. The *Archangel Gabriel*, he had called himself. It was the only time she had ever heard him refer to himself by his given name. As she watched him aggressively go after his opponents, she began to see that it was the truth. He fought with the power of heaven, embattled now with two men. He was talented and strong, making short work of the men fighting against him.

Gart was precise in his actions. He held his sword with two hands, lunging at his opponents and then spinning away when they engaged him, turning a full circle and coming up behind the men and shoving them to the ground. One man he had been forced to kill when the man brought his sword up at Gart's head, but the second man surrendered, wounded, and rolled off to the side. Gart kicked the man far away to ensure he would not rise before returning his attention to the battle in the street.

He had an innate sense of a fight. He knew what his opponent was thinking and he counteracted accordingly. There was no wasted motion with the man. Every thrust and every parry had a purpose. He locked swords with one burly soldier, spun around and threw an armored elbow into the man's face, sending him crashing in an explosion of blood. It was a spectacular and brutal move.

Emberley continued to watch him, entranced at the power and skill of the man, when the fat, old man who had started the conflict suddenly appeared in the doorway. Before Emberley could move away, he grabbed her by the hair.

"I have her!" he shouted, pulling her out of the doorway. "I have your wife, knight! If you value your life, you will...."

Before he could finish, Romney and Orin rushed at the old man with their wooden swords. Orin poked the man in the thigh but Romney rammed his sword straight into the man's groin because it was at the young boy's arm-level. The old man howled and released Emberley, falling to the ground with his hands over his privates. Romney and Orin pounced, beating the man about the head with their wooden swords and shields.

"You cannot hurt my mother!" Romney was screaming as he hit the man in the face with his wooden shield. "You leave her alone!"

As Emberley caught her balance and went to grab her boys, an enormous body was suddenly in between her and her sons. Gart, bloody sword in one hand, reached down with his left arm and scooped both Romney and Orin up into his grasp. He whirled on Emberley and handed her the boys in one swift movement.

"Are you well?" he demanded as he deposited the boys against her. "Did he hurt you?"

Emberley shook her head fearfully. "I am fine."

His green eyes were in battle mode but she swore she saw them soften, just for a moment, as he gazed at her. Then he was back at the soldiers who were attacking him, kicking men away and using his enormous fists to punch them in the face.

Emberley stood in the doorway, holding the boys against her as she watched Gart dispatch at least six men personally. The others were put away by his soldiers and those that were left simply faded away. A pair of them reached down to collect the old man, still wallowing in the dirt, and dragged him away from the scene. As quickly as it started, the battle finished with an eerie and uncomfortable silence to follow.

For several long moments, no one spoke or moved. People began poking their heads out of stalls where they had run for cover, eventually emerging into the sunshine and staying clear of the four dead and wounded soldiers that lay in the muddy street. Gart whistled loudly between his teeth, sending his men into a defensive stance to ensure that no one else was left to fight as he went to Emberley and the children.

They were still huddled in the doorway of the fabric merchant, five pairs of big, blue eyes gazing up at him. Gart was in battle mode, taking a deep breath to calm himself, as he sheathed his broadsword. His focus was on the boys.

"You," he pointed at Romney. "That was a very brave thing you did to protect your mother but you could have gotten yourself killed. In the future, you will let me do the fighting since I am bigger than you are and presumably better prepared. Is that understood?"

Romney looked both confused and flattered. "I was very brave?"

Gart nodded, wiping the sweat from his brow. "Very," he concurred. "But you must know that it would upset me greatly if you were injured. You do not want to upset me, do you?"

Romney shook his head and Gart winked at him. "Good lad," he looked at Orin. "You, too, it would hurt me very much if you were injured. Although you are brave like your brother, you will not do that again. Is that clear?"

Orin, his eyes wide, nodded seriously. With that business settled, Gart finally turned his attention to Emberley.

She was gazing back at him with warmth and appreciation. Gart didn't even know what to say to her. It was the most wonderful expression he had ever seen. For lack of a better response, he simply cupped her face and kissed her gently on the cheek to assure her all was well. The smell of her filled his nostrils, the delicate scent of flowers and skin, but he would not let himself dwell on it. It hurt his heart knowing she could never be his.

Emberley didn't let him go so quickly. As he kissed her and pulled away, she grasped his face with both hands and planted a warm kiss right on his mouth. Their eyes met for a moment and sparks flew, lightning bolts that filled them both with indescribable sensations of excitement and attraction. Seized with the moment, Gart forgot himself and moved in for another kiss, but Emberley backed away as if suddenly realizing what she had done.

"Are... are you all right, Gart?" she asked, refusing to look at him. "You were not injured, were you?"

Heart thumping painfully against his ribs, Gart stood there and stared at her. "Nay," he said after a moment, licking his lips to see if he could still taste her. "I am not injured."

"Are you sure?"

"I am sure."

Lacy suddenly began to whine, holding her arms up to her mother, and Emberley picked the little girl up. She still wouldn't look at Gart.

"If you have no objections, then, I will look for fabric for the boys," she said, turning for the merchant's hut. "I will only be a moment."

Gart impulsively grabbed her arm before she could get away. "Em...," he began.

She turned to him, lifting her eyes, and he swore he could see emotions rolling through the dark blue depths. The lightning bolts were still there, rolling like distant thunder. He could feel them as he gazed into her sweet face.

"Aye?" she asked, somewhat reluctantly.

His gaze lingered on her a moment longer, realizing that four pairs of young eyes were gazing up at him. He didn't want to say anything unsuitable or make a fool of himself. But he swore, at that moment, that this wasn't the end of the lightning, not by a long shot. He wanted to feel it again.

"You…," he started, cleared his throat, and continued. "Are you sure you were not injured when he grabbed you?"

She smiled. "Nay," she said. "I am so sorry, Gart. We did not mean to cause trouble."

His eyebrows rose. "Cause trouble? Why would you say that?"

"Because the boys ran into that man," she explained haltingly, trying to voice her thoughts. "He was rightfully angry. The boys should have been more careful and I did not mean that we should cause trouble."

Gart looked down at the boys, all gazing up at him with something between open curiosity and abject admiration. He put an enormous hand on Romney's head.

"You did not cause trouble," he said softly, looking back at Emberley. "It was an accident and our fat friend reacted poorly. I would not worry overly."

"But you threatened him," she said softly.

He was unapologetic. "He deserved it."

Emberley started to reply but the man with the dancing goat suddenly walked by with the animal up on its hind legs and Brendt went mad. Emberley grabbed him before he could run but Gart put his big hand over hers.

"I will take him to see the goat," he nodded his head in the direction of the merchant's stall. "Go and inspect your fabric."

She resisted slightly. "Are you sure it is safe? There are no more soldiers intent to do us all harm?"

He looked around, at his men stationed along the street, and shook his head. "Not unless they are idiots," he assured her. "I seriously doubt there will be additional trouble. Rest your mind."

Emberley couldn't help but smile at him, struggling to resist the lightning that threatened again. It was starting to come too easily. As the minutes passed, the storm brewing between them was gaining strength. She knew it was as wrong as it could possibly be but she couldn't seem to resist.

She went to inspect material, alone, with warm thoughts of Gart Forbes on her mind.

CHAPTER SEVEN

THE DANCING GOAT had been a success, as had the puppet show down the street. Several children were gathered to watch two jester puppets beat each other up with Romney, Orin and Brendt front and center. They laughed with delight when a wooden puppet got its nose punched. Emberley and Gart stood to the rear of the crowd, Lacy cradled in Gart's big arms, and watched the spectacle.

Gart found it a rather interesting experience. He couldn't remember when he last took leisure time, something that didn't involve war or training or intrigue, so to stand on an open street in the midst of a festival, watching children enjoy a show was odd but not unpleasant.

He found himself watching the crowd of children, in particular Romney, Orin and Brendt, seeing such joy in their faces. He'd almost forgotten such things existed. It was a warm and wonderful realization.

The puppet show ended when the colorfully painted jester puppets began throwing candy made from honey and almonds at the children. It was hard candy, hitting more than one child in the head, but they all jumped up with open hands and screamed when it came flying out at them. Romney and Orin were on the front lines, grabbing more candy than they could hold. Romney tried to use his tunic to hold it like a basket but it kept falling to the ground. Finally, he raced back to his mother and shoved the horde of candy into her hands.

Before Emberley could stop him, he ran back to the front of the crowd to catch more candy. Emberley stood there, watching her greedy son, before looking to Gart with a slightly embarrassed expression. He burst into soft laughter.

"Do not look so surprised," he told her. "Romney is a lad who knows what he wants. He is aggressive and unyielding. He will make a fine knight someday."

She gave him a crooked smile, looking back to the crowd of children to see that Brendt was picking candy out of the mud and shoving it into his mouth.

"Brendt!" she called to him as she moved through the crowd of children. "Stop that. You will make yourself ill."

With a grin on his face, Gart watched her go to the boys and make them put the dirty candy back on the ground. She also made Romney share his additional booty with his brothers, which completely upset the lad. He wanted all of it.

Gart watched her sweet, gentle manner, his heart softening. She was such a lovely creature with grace, poise and wisdom. As he gazed at Emberley, spellbound, Lacy decided to squeeze his neck happily and give him wet, baby kisses on his left cheek. He let the little girl kiss him, even when she ended up hugging his head and not his neck. Her little arm was across his nose as she squeezed. He just stood there and took it because it was one of the sweetest things he had ever experienced. For a man who had known little emotion or affection his entire life, the introduction of the affectionate baby was both foreign and wonderful. He knew he could grow to love it.

With the candy situation ironed out, Emberley and the boys returned to Gart and Lacy. Lacy now had her little arms up around one of Gart's eyes and Emberley shook her head at the comical sight, reaching out to take the little girl from him. Gart resisted.

"She is fine where she is," he told her, his words partially muffled by a baby hand that was now on his mouth. "Leave her be."

Emberley bit her lip to keep from grinning. "But your face is all wet."

"It is of no matter."

She wouldn't argue with him. She began to look around the avenue at the variety of shops and people all around.

"Now that we have sweets and toys and fabric, I am not sure there is much of a need to stay here," she told him. "Perhaps we should return to Dunster."

He shook his head. "There is much more to see and much more to purchase," he told her. "Did you not say there was to be a joust exhibition?"

She nodded, shielding her eyes from the sun as she looked down the avenue. "Usually," she pointed down the street. "There is a large field to the west that is used for tournaments and games."

"Then that is where we shall go."

She looked at him. "Why? I have seen all of the swordplay I care to see for one day."

He fought off a grin. "Perhaps I wish to compete."

Before Emberley could reply, Romney piped up. "Will you fight for money?" he wanted to know.

Gart looked down at the excited faces around him. "Not only will I fight, I will win," he said confidently.

The boys began hooting and swinging the swords at each other, smacking them against the wooden shields. Emberley wasn't particularly enthusiastic about attending the exhibition but she could see how excited the boys were. She remained silent as they continued down the avenue, pondering the events of the day, when Gart nudged her.

"Look there," he pointed. "That man sells all manner of perfumes and soaps. Would you like to look?"

Emberley's head came up and she gazed at the stall across the dirt avenue, rather large as far as stalls go. The entire front of the stall was open and there were many types of goods on display. She could see beautiful fabrics, wooden boxes with soaps, and other feminine things. As she shrugged, Gart grasped her elbow and pulled her across the street to the alluring stall.

Given the way that they were starting to respond to each other, Emberley wasn't entirely sure about accepting a gift from the man. There was a large part of her that very much wanted to be spoiled and pampered, something she had never known from Julian.

Truth be told, her husband was just a man she had met only once before marrying him and in eight years of marriage, he had shown himself to be petty, self-centered and brutal. If she thought about it, he was still a stranger. He'd never made the effort to know her. Emberley didn't truly care that he and the queen were lovers. As far as she was concerned, the queen could have him. Julian held no part of her heart or mind. He was a provider, the man who fathered her children, the man who beat her brutally when the mood hit him, and nothing else.

"Here," Gart was holding up a gorgeous scarf with shades of gold and orange. "Do you like this?"

Shaken from her reflections, Emberley looked at the lovely piece and half-nodded, half-shrugged.

"It is beautiful," she lowered her voice as the boys swarmed around her, fingering the expensive goods. "Truly, Gart, you do not have to buy me anything. I would prefer that you did not."

His green eyes were steady on her. "Why not?"

She sighed regretfully, removing Brendt's hand from a box of undoubtedly expensive soap. "Because I will have to explain it to Julian," she whispered. "Already, I will have to explain these toys. I will have to lie or risk...."

She couldn't finish, averting her gaze when the conversation became embarrassing and painful. Gart watched her delicate features, knowing what she was going to say and feeling a surge of anger bolt through him. But he fought it, mostly because the boys were clamoring around him and Lacy had her hands on his face. He found he just couldn't get angry with the children around him, like water on a fire that quickly doused the flame. But along with the anger came the heartache, aching for Emberley in more ways than he could comprehend.

A man appeared in the door of the stall dressed in fine clothing and shoes with little silver bells on the toes. He swept from his shop and straight to Emberley, who was holding the box that she had taken from

Brendt. His smooth, round face lit up with delight.

"My lady," he bowed deeply, then did the same to Gart. "My lord, 'tis a pleasure to greet you on this fine day. How may I be of service?"

Emberley shook her head and set the box down when she realized the man was going to try very hard to sell them something. He had that air about him. She didn't dare look at Gart, who was now less confident about buying her something than he had been. As Gart moved the baby's hands from his mouth and attempted to reply, the man suddenly threw up his hands.

"Wait!" he exclaimed. "I have something wonderful for your wife. Wait!"

He bolted back into his shop, leaving the boys giggling and mimicking the noise that his shoes were making. They were dancing around and shaking their feet. Orin seemed particularly gleeful and he ran into the shop after the man, followed closely by Romney and Brendt.

"Oh… no," Emberley charged in after them. "Romney? Orin? Come back here, please. Do not touch anything and, for Heaven's sake, do not break anything!"

Gart followed with the baby in his arms, watching Emberley corral the boys and drag them back towards the entry. The stall was dark inside, cluttered to the rafters with treasures, and it was difficult to walk the narrow aisles and not hit something. As Emberley wrestled with the three, the merchant appeared from the rear of the stall with something in his hand. As he drew closer, they could see it was a beautifully painted box and he popped open the lid as he came to Emberley.

"I purchased these from a merchant who travels the roads of the Orient," he told her with some drama, as if he held a great treasure. "It is a soap that smells of flowers and oil that softens the skin. Would you smell it, my lady?"

It was all so beautifully packaged with a pretty box and pretty fabric that Emberley couldn't resist. She lifted out the phial of oil and removed the glass stopper, smelling the contents. It was lilac and violets.

By this time, Gart was inside the shop and standing next to her, stilling the wriggling boys with a snap of his fingers. Three pairs of blue eyes gazed up at him fearfully, terrified that they were going to get their toys taken away if they didn't listen to the man. So they stopped tussling and smiled hugely at him, very innocently, and Gart bit off a smile. He had to look away quickly before they saw it, otherwise, his dominance over them would be over.

He reached out and took the phial from Emberley, smelling deeply. She looked up at him and their eyes met, locked, smoldered. The thunder rolled and the lightening threatened. He smelled it again and a smile spread across his lips.

"We will take this," he told the merchant, his eyes riveted to Emberley. "If you have anything else decadent and sweet that she might like, bring it forth."

The merchant was delighted. "You have excellent taste, my lord." He was flustered as he ran about looking for more things to sell the man. "Your wife shall smell as beautiful as she looks. You are an extremely fortunate man."

Gart didn't even bother to correct the man. "Aye, I am. The most fortunate man in the world."

The merchant grinned at him. "I can tell you are content. Few married men I meet are half as proud of their wives as you are." He swept his arm in the direction of the boys. "She has given you three fine sons and a lovely daughter. What more could a man ask for?"

Gart just shook his head, slowly. "Nothing more. She is perfect."

Emberley felt as if she had been punched in the gut as she listened to the exchange. She would have sold her soul for it to be true. It was at that moment that she realized she was falling in love with the man and the knowledge cut her deeply. Gart Forbes, her brother's strong and compassionate best friend, had succeeded in stealing her heart. It was a horrible awareness. Blindly, with great anguish, she grabbed the boys and began shoving them out of the stall.

"Go," she pushed them. "Out, out. We must leave."

Brendt tripped in her haste and she picked the boy up, pushing them all out into the street. She felt someone bump up behind her and realized it was Gart. He had followed her from the stall. She caught a glimpse of Lacy in the big knight's arms and she reached out, grabbing her daughter away from the man and listening to her scream. She began to walk, very quickly, down the street.

Gart didn't let her get two steps before he was grabbing her by the arm, stopping her in her tracks.

"What is the matter?" he demanded softly. "Where are you going?"

She was pulling away from him, beginning to weep as Lacy cried loudly in her ear. "Please," she begged, whispering. "Let me go. Please let me go and let us return to Dunster."

He wouldn't let her go. "Why?" his voice was a pleading whisper.

She finally looked at him, the anxious look on his face, and she broke down into sobs. "Please, Gart," she wept. "I want to go home. I want to leave."

Gart had no idea what her trouble was but she was deeply upset and he would know why. He looked at the boys, who were gazing at their mother with some concern, realizing that her behavior was frightening the children. Lacy was already crying loudly. Looking over his shoulder, he saw a couple of his men standing back in the shadows and he whistled softly to them. They came forward immediately as Gart returned his attention to Emberley.

"Give me the baby," he pulled Lacy out of her arms before she could protest and handed her to Romney. Then he turned to his men. "Take the children, find them something to eat, and take them back to the carriage. I will meet you there."

When Emberley realized he was separating her from her children, she struggled strongly against him. "Nay," she snapped. "We are going home. You cannot…"

Gart shook her gently, forcing her to focus on him. "Still your tears," he commanded softly. "You have frightened your children with your behavior. Look at their faces. Is that what you want? To frighten them?"

She froze, tears on her face, as she looked down at her four children. Romney was holding Lacy, who was screaming unhappily in his ear, as Orin and Brendt looked rather frightened. She realized how she must be coming across to them. Her emotions had the better of her. Relaxing in Gart's grip, she struggled to compose herself.

"I am sorry," she murmured to her children, wiping at her face. "I am not upset with you. I… I suppose I am simply weary from all of the excitement of the day."

That seemed to soothe the boys but Lacy was still very unhappy. Gart bent over and kissed the little girl on her wet cheek and when she realized who it was, she stopped sobbing and lifted her arms to him. He kissed her little hands but stopped short of picking her up.

"Romney," he said, "these men serve me. They are going to find you something to eat while I speak with your mother. Please go with them."

Romney wasn't entirely convinced. He looked seriously at Gart. "You are not going to spank her, are you?"

Gart shook his head. "Nay."

As long as Gart wasn't going to touch her, Romney didn't argue but he cast his mother a lingering glance before doing as he was told. Orin and Brendt followed, subdued and no longer fighting each other with their swords. Gart watched as four of his men closed around the children and escorted them down the avenue. With the children taken care of, Gart turned to Emberley.

She was watching her children walk away as if he had just stolen them from her. A gentle sea breeze blew her hair across her face, making her appear forlorn and fragile. Gart gently cupped her face and forced her to look at him.

"What is wrong, kitten?" he asked softly. "What have I done to upset you so?"

She yanked her face away, slapping at his hand. "Do not call me that," she half-wept, half-hissed. "You let that man believe we were married and we are not. How could you do that?"

He stared at her, feeling unfamiliar emotion rolling in his chest, squeezing at his heart. He'd never felt so sad, so desperate, in his entire life. He'd never felt so confused.

"It was simpler to agree with him than to explain you did not belong to me," he said after a moment, his voice quiet. "I am sorry it upset you so."

She looked at him, her cheeks flushed pink with angst and turmoil. The tears were flowing faster than she could wipe them away.

"Do you think to toy with me, Gart?" she wanted to know. "If I was an unmarried maiden, I would take your behavior over the past few days to mean extreme interest in me. You have endeared yourself to me and to my children and have taken care of us as Julian never has. You have been kind and sweet and compassionate. You have made me feel things that I have never felt before and I hate you for it."

Her last words trailed off, mortified that she had spoken what was on her mind. Then she turned away from him and began to run, slipping in between two stalls and ending up in the small, dirty alleyway behind them. Gart was right behind her, throwing his big arms around her before she could get away. She tried to get her fists free to strike him but he held her fast.

"I am sorry," he said reassuringly, listening to her weep and struggle. "It was wrong of me, I know. But… Emberley, please believe me. I would never toy with you, not ever. I have a confession to make – I lied."

She was trying to break free of his iron grip. "I know you lied," she spat. "You lied to the merchant. I heard you. I am in enough trouble if Julian discovers you remained at Dunster without you spreading lies that I am your wife."

He sighed heavily. "That is not what I meant."

"What, then?" she managed to get an arm up and was trying to shove him away by the chest. "Let me *go*."

He ignored her demand. "I lied to de Lohr when I told him that my feelings towards you were nothing more than the concern of an old friend," he said softly. "I see in you the woman I should have married and I cannot help the emotions that have been growing since the day I arrived at Dunster. You are sweet and beautiful and everything I have ever wanted. I think I fell in love with those three hooligans you have raised the moment they tried to rob me, and that slobbery baby that just wants to be loved. Everything about them is perfect and wonderful and I want it. I want *you*."

She stopped fighting him, her dark blue eyes wide with shock as she gazed at him. The tears had stopped, replaced by unadulterated astonishment.

"You *what*?" she breathed.

He didn't back down. It was all coming out, anyway, so he figured he had nothing to lose. He felt like a fool but he didn't care. She had to know all of it.

"I want you," his voice softened. "I have since nearly the moment I saw you four days ago. I do not know how this has happened only that it has. It is wrong and immoral, and I understand that. But I cannot help what I feel when I look at you. You are married to a man who does not deserve you and it destroys me to see how he treats you. Please do not hate me for being weak enough to love you. I could not bear it."

Emberley stared at him, a thousand emotions rippling across her lovely face, before breaking into sobs. She fell forward, her forehead against his chest. Gart wrapped her up tightly in his arms.

"Oh, Gart," she wept against him. "I do not know what to say. I cannot give you encouragement where none exists. You love something that can never be and…."

She trailed off, shattered and sick. His cheek was against the top of her head, feeling the texture on his skin. "And… what?"

She lifted her head to look at him. "I want it, too," she whispered.

He pulled her closer, feeling her tense. "You do?"

She nodded her head, so hard that her careful hairstyle started to unravel. "But it can never be," she whispered, reaching up to touch his rough cheek. "You must leave Dunster today and never return. To remain would only cause us more pain."

He completely ignored her request, his eyes riveted to her. He held her tightly by the upper arms and his great head dipped low, kissing her gently on the cheek, the nose. He felt her shudder against him before planting his lips on her soft, warm mouth. He kissed her more powerfully than he had ever kissed a woman in his life, tasting everything about her, experiencing her scent in his nostrils and her warmth in his hands, and he knew at that moment that he would never leave her, not ever. He was fused to her somehow and it could not be undone.

"I love you," he murmured, his mouth against her. "Tell me you love me and I shall live on it the rest of my life."

The tears streamed down her face. "I love you," she whispered. "Oh, I do. You are my angel, Gart."

"And you are mine," he answered, kissing her chin. "Tell me that you want to be with me, forever."

Emberley couldn't stop herself from replying, feeling the bittersweet emotions exploding in her chest. "I want to be everything to you," she whispered, kissing his mouth when it came close. "But it is not possible."

"Anything is possible."

She stopped returning his kisses, struggling to come to her senses and processing what he was saying.

"But I am already married," she stated the obvious. "You and I cannot be together so long as Julian is my husband. What we feel… it is wrong."

"It is not wrong." Gart looked at her seriously. "True love is never wrong."

"We are violating God's law of marriage."

"Julian violated that the moment he took his hands to you." When she shook her head to dispute him, he continued strongly. "He took your marriage and stomped on it when he fornicated with the queen. Why would you be loyal to man who has only brought you pain and shame?"

She closed her eyes tightly and hung her head. "It is different and you know it," she said softly. "If... if I shame him, he will kill me."

Gart cooled. "He will not kill you because you will not return to him."

Emberley's expression tightened with confusion. "What do you mean I will not return to him?" she cocked her head, her hands on his face. "Gart, I have no choice. I am his wife and..."

"Nay," he barked softly, cutting off her words. "You will never say that in my presence again. You are not his wife. You are simply contracted to the man, chattel and nothing more. From this moment on, you belong to me. Do you hear me? You are mine. Someday you will be my wife and that is the only time I will hear that word from your lips. It will be the proudest moment of my life."

Emberley gazed at him, having no idea how to respond. Gart slanted his lips over hers, hungrily, tasting her deeply before pulling away. It wasn't that he was afraid someone would see them but more that he was rather conservative with public displays of affection. What he felt for her was something treasured and private. Now that they had spoken of their feelings, he could still hardly believe it. He needed time to reconcile himself to the situation because his mind was muddled. He'd never been so confused or so happy in his entire life.

"Come along," he kissed her gently again. "Let us find the children and eat with them."

Weak and weary from the emotional whirlwind, Emberley did as she was told. When Gart reached out to grasp her hand, she let him.

"And then what?" she asked softly.

He looked at her. "What do you mean?"

She fixed him in the eye. "What will happen when we return to Dunster?" she wanted to know. "What will become of us?"

Gart didn't know yet. But he was going to figure it out. Already, he knew it was going to be the fight of his life.

CHAPTER EIGHT

WITH THREE LITTLE boys with belly aches as the result of too much roast pork and sweets, the party from Dunster Castle returned home that afternoon.

Emberley rode in the carriage, her sleeping daughter cradled against her, as the cab bumped over the road back to the castle. The boys were around her in various stages of discomfort and she found herself holding Orin as well as her daughter as they headed home. She was quiet, subdued, her mind mulling over the situation with Gart. She was sickened by it, confused, but also thrilled beyond measure. It was too good to be true yet tragic at the same time. Gart rode at the head of the column and she rode in the center. He never said a word to her the entire trip back.

Once at the castle, Gart disbanded the escort and returned to the carriage for Emberley and the children. Romney and Brendt were at the cab door as he approached and he was surprised that they were not clamoring to get out. They just stood there, looking at him, until he opened the door and lowered them to the ground one by one. Tired and nauseous, they simply stood there at his feet. Orin, with the big belly ache, was next and cried softly as Gart set him on his feet. He wasn't happy in the least. Gerta, the fat old nurse with the thinning hair, was there to take charge of the children as Gart reached into the cab one last time to take the sleeping baby from Emberley.

Their eyes locked as he took the baby from her, bittersweet emotions passing between them even though no words were spoken. The air was heavy between them yet infinitely tender. Gart lowered his gaze as he collected the sleeping little girl against him, holding her carefully before passing her over to the nurse. Gerta took the little girl, kissed her sleeping head, and led the children back towards the keep.

Gart finally returned his attention to Emberley, still sitting in the cab. She had been watching him but when she realized it was just the two of them, she started collecting the booty around her. She was having difficulty meeting his eye, not knowing what to say to the man.

Her head was in turmoil at the moment. The boys had their toy swords and shields, but Gart had returned to the perfume and soap merchant and had purchased several different sets of soaps and oils for Emberley. There were several lovely painted boxes in the cab and she collected them, handing them over to Gart.

Gart took the six boxes in one hand and helped Emberley out with the other. In the sunshine of the lazy afternoon, he took her politely by the elbow and escorted her up the stairs into the dark, cool keep. It was quiet and still inside. Taking the stone spiral stairs to the third floor, they could hear the baby whining and the boys arguing as Gerta tried to settle them in for an afternoon nap. Emberley continued to the fourth floor and her big, sprawling chamber, and Gart followed silently with the boxes.

The master's chamber took up most of the fourth floor. There was an enormous bed in the center, lavished with expensive furs and coverlets, and two oak chairs with feather-stuffed cushions. Someone had banked the fire in the hearth and the coals glowed, providing a bit of warmth to stave off the cold in the room that the stone walls generated.

As soon as they entered the bower, Emberley turned to him and began taking the boxes. She took three and went over to her dressing table, a piece of furniture made from oak, polished, and painted with flowers on one side. There was a large mirror made from polished bronze but set in the middle of it was a much smaller mirror made from very precious polished glass. It gave a true reflection and Emberley set the boxes of oils and soaps down on the table, returning to Gart to take the rest from him.

"Thank you very much for these wonderful gifts," she said softly. "I am very grateful."

Gart stood in the doorway, watching her carefully organize the boxes. He didn't say a word but he shifted on his big legs, watching her. She pretended to be busy with her new items but he knew that her mind was on their situation just as his was. He couldn't think of anything else. It was like a fog that surrounded them in a confusing embrace. Very quietly, he closed the door.

Emberley heard the door close and thought he had left. She paused in her organization of the boxes, closing her eyes against the turmoil in her chest. Now that Gart's presence was no longer around to bewilder her, she could respond to the emotion she was feeling. Everything came out in a heavy sigh. She dropped her hands from the boxes and sat heavily on the stool next to the dressing table, dragging a weary hand over her face.

"What are you thinking, kitten?" Gart asked softly.

Emberley gasped with surprise, turning to see that he was standing just inside the door. She took a deep breath to steady herself.

"I… I do not know," she said honestly. "All I can feel is fear and joy. Thoughts of you make my heart sing and then just as quickly, I remember Julian and what he will do to me if he discovers us. He would kill me, Gart."

"We have not done anything wrong. Yet."

She heard the tone in his voice, feeling a bolt of excitement shoot through her body that just as quickly vanished. It was wrong of her to even entertain such thoughts and she angrily, sadly, pushed such ideas aside. She just couldn't….

"We cannot," she whispered. "Gart, please do not tempt me more than you already have. My life hangs in the balance – not yours."

He moved away from the door, heading towards her with slow, thoughtful steps. He sighed heavily.

"I know," he said in his soft, deep voice, sitting pensively at the foot of the bed. "I have thought of nothing else for quite some time. The only answer is to remove you and the children from Dunster."

She looked at him, surprised. "You would take us away?"

He nodded, still very much deep in thought. "I cannot involve Lord David in this situation, so it would have to be somewhere far away and...."

"But you cannot," she cut him off imploringly. "Think about what you are saying – you would take all of us from Dunster?"

"Aye."

She shook her head strongly. "You cannot steal another man's family, Gart. Julian would have you drawn and quartered."

He countered. "He would never find us. We would leave England and go far away."

He was deadly serious. She could read it in his face. "Then there is something else," she pointed out. "Romney is the heir to the Buckland barony. What of his inheritance? It is his right and you, as someone who was denied his strong family ties, should understand that. Is it fair to Romney to take all of that away from him?"

Gart gazed steadily at her. "Would you rather have a son who is unhappy yet will inherit a wealthy barony or a son who is extremely happy but will not inherit a fraction of his due?"

She returned his gaze, seriously, so many thoughts and feelings rolling through her mind. "What are you saying?"

He lifted his eyebrows. "I am saying that I am offering to provide you and your children with a happy home. I would live like a pauper so long as you are with me, kitten. Money does not buy happiness, as you are well aware. But I swear to you that you would be rich in love, and I would love you and only you until the day I died."

He had a valid point but she was still overwhelmed, confused. Wearily, she rose from the stool and went to the bed, plopping down beside him. She was despondent and depressed.

"It is a dream," she murmured.

He stood up from the mattress, increasingly agitated as he paced away from her, hand to his head as if it would help him think more clearly.

"It is not a dream," he told her firmly. "It is as real as flesh and blood and bone. We will leave tonight and never look back."

He was speaking passionately and she exhaled lightly, rising from the bed and putting a hand on his arm to quiet him.

"For arguments sake, let us pretend that we will leave Dunster and never return," she said softly. "You and I could never legally marry, Gart. Any children you and I had would be bastards. Please know that I would run with you this very moment if it was just me but I must think of my children. I do not know if it is fair to them to make such a decision affecting their future. We would be selfish to think only of ourselves."

He gently took her hand and brought it to his lips for a sweet kiss. "I am a selfish man," he admitted quietly. "If I want something, I take it."

"In this case, it is not that simple."

He appeared downcast, his lips against her fingers. "I realize that," he murmured. "But I am offering happiness and love for the rest of your life. You would never know fear from me, only protection and security. Does that not outweigh the lure of Julian and his empire?"

She watched him kiss her hand, feeling the excitement his warmth brought. The only kiss she had ever known was Julian's, and that didn't compare to what Gart was doing. The bolts of lightning were tearing through her. Now, she was coming to understand what a kiss really meant. Gart had shown her that.

"As I said, if there was only myself to think about, there would be no question," she whispered. "I would go with you this very moment. But we must think of the children."

"I *am* thinking of the children. They cannot live their lives in fear of their father. Who is to say that when they grow older, Julian will not beat them also? Is Romney's inheritance worth that risk?"

She knew he meant well but it wasn't as simple as he pretended it was. She also knew that, deep down, he understood that. Right now, Gart was only thinking of what he wanted and little else. Without an argument, Emberley laid her head against his armored shoulder, swamped and overwhelmed with a situation she had never believed she would ever face. It was exhausting.

"Let us speak no more of it today," she said softly. "I think we both need some time to understand what has happened."

He looked at her blond head against his arm. Then he shifted, winding his big arms around her and gazing into her deep, blue eyes. He took a moment simply to gaze at her, to acquaint himself with the feel of her in his arms. It was the most wonderful feeling in the world.

"I already understand what has happened," he said quietly. "I have finally found what I have been looking for all of these years and I will have her. I am not sure how yet, but I will. Mark my words."

Emberley gazed up into his eyes, the features so strong and handsome. "I still cannot believe it," she admitted. Then she lifted an eyebrow at him. "It would have saved us a good deal of trouble if you had declared your intentions about eight years ago."

He laughed softly. "I do not think I could have," he told her. "Erik would have run me through. As it is, he still might rise from the grave and come after me."

She giggled. "I think he would have been very grateful."

"For what?"

"For trying to save his sister from hell."

Gart's smile faded as he gazed into her lovely face. He didn't have anything to say to that. Closing his eyes, his lips slanted gently over hers.

The first few seconds of the kiss were soft, gentle, tantalizing. But soon enough, he was intoxicated with the feel and smell of her and his senses overwhelmed him. The lightning flashed again, this time swamping them both, and he pulled her into a crushing embrace, his tongue invading her sweet mouth. But it still wasn't enough. He had to have more.

Emberley had never been kissed with such passion. At first, Gart frightened her with his onslaught and she tried to pull away, but very quickly, she realized that she wasn't frightened at all. Gart was powerful and manly, and she realized that she craved him more than she had realized. As his mouth left hers and blazed a heated trail down her neck, all self-control left her. She could no longer resist him. She'd never known such heat or lust in her life and, with a gentle growl, she snaked her hands underneath his mail and tunic to make contact with his muscular body.

Her heated hands caressed his tight abdomen, flesh against flesh. Gart went mad. He ripped his mail off, then his tunic, and didn't remember doing either. All he remembered was the feel and taste of Emberley. Her fine surcoat disintegrated beneath his hands, the sounds of material ripping filling the chamber. Before either of them realized it, she was nude but for the hose tied to each leg with a silk ribbon. When Gart realized her state of dress, it threw him over the edge. He latched on to her mouth and picked her up in his big arms.

Emberley wrapped her legs around his waist, as a child would, her arms around his neck as he carried her to the bed and carefully laid her down on the coverlet. He suckled on a delicate earlobe but she turned the tables on him, latching on to his shoulder and suckling his smooth flesh. He groaned as she moved to a nipple, hissing when she latched onto the peaked flesh and suckled hard. It was driving him out of his mind. With his last shred of sanity, he released his breeches and they collapsed around his knees.

Grabbing Emberley by the hair, he pulled her off of his chest and settled himself between her legs, his hands moving to her ripe, full breasts and loving the feel of them. She was round and lush. His heated mouth suckled her tender nipples, first one breast and then the other, and Emberley whimpered softly as he lapped and drew at them. His hands were everywhere, caressing her, acquainting himself with her body, before moving to the fluff of dark curls between her legs.

He could feel the moist heat against his fingers as he stroked her.

Being that Emberley was not a virgin, she didn't flinch from his touch. Although sex with Julian had been a duty, she still knew something about it. Julian had made sure to educate his naïve wife.

Emberley grasped Gart's hand and pushed it up against her pink folds and Gart took the hint. He stroked her intimately, invading her responsive body with his big fingers and listening to her weep softly with joy. His mouth was on her breasts, her ribcage, nibbling along the curve of her torso as his fingers stroked in and out of her. Finally, when he could stand no more, Gart lifted himself up and thrust firmly into her slick, heated body.

Emberley cried out softly as he drove into her, lifting her pelvis to his, wrapping her slender legs around his hips and drawing him in deeper with every stroke. She held him tightly with her legs as her hands wandered to his buttocks, her fingers invading the crease between his hard cheeks, touching deeply intimate places.

Gart was so highly aroused that he groaned as he felt her little fingers, seeking his private crevices, and he gently removed her probing fingers. He knew if she continued that he would spill himself too soon, so he took both hands and stretched them sensually over her head, tenderly trapping her as his great manhood thrust deeply into her.

Emberley was lost in a haze of delirious desire. She could feel every one of Gart's thrusts deep inside her, touching her womb, feeling her tremors of pleasure begin. As his mouth moved down her neck to her breasts, a powerful climax came over her, followed by another. Gart was merciless as he felt her walls tighten around him, wanting to prolong her pleasure and his own.

Eventually, he could no longer hold his concentration and he spilled his hot seed deep into her beautiful body, feeling every last tremor with the greatest of pleasure. But even as he went through the throes of his release, he could feel her climax yet again and he continued to move deep within her, not wanting the experience of their first coupling to end. It had been the most powerful personal experience of his life.

When their sweating, heated bodies slowed to a halt, Gart found himself looking Emberley in the eye. He was still buried deep within the soft, moist haven of her sweet body. They just stared at each other, shocked at the power of their mating. It was more than either one of them could have imagined, an experience that went above and beyond simple passion and emotion. It delved into the realm of the soul. Gart leaned forward and very gently, very sweetly, kissed her on the lips.

"I love you," he murmured against her mouth. "For all time, I will love you and only you."

Emberley burst into body-wracking sobs.

CHAPTER NINE

"FIGHT ME, YOU coward!" Romney challenged Brendt, who went running in the opposite direction as Romney brandished his great, wooden sword and shield. Romney was undeterred, ignoring the scolding by Gerta as he and his siblings played in the late morning sun. Romney wanted to fight but no one would engage him. He was now a mighty knight with his new sword.

Shielding his eyes, Romney could see Gart upon the battlements. The man was seeing to the posts, now staffed with his own men since the baron took most of his troops with him. His little face lit with mischievous excitement.

"You!" he hollered at the battlements, pointing to Gart as the man spoke with a couple of soldiers. "Come here and fight me or else!"

Gart heard the yelling, glancing down in the midst of his conversation to see Romney pointing a sword at him. With a smirk, he finished his conversation and sent the soldiers away.

"Or else what?" he called down to the boy.

Romney was as frisky as a Billy goat. He pawed the ground with a foot. "Or… or else you will be sorry!"

Gart lifted his eyebrows. "Is that the best you can do?"

Romney growled like a bear and began swinging his sword around, barely missing Orin when the child came too close. Realizing he almost hit his brother, Romney paused to see if Gart had seen it. He had, still watching the boy from the battlements. Romney smiled apologetically but Gart shook his head reproachfully and began to make his way towards the turret stairs. Romney watched with apprehension as Gart disappeared into the turret. He knew the man was coming to take his toys away.

"Romney?" Emberley appeared next to her son. "What are you doing, sweetheart?"

Startled, Romney looked up into his mother's face. He hadn't seen her all morning. In fact, he hadn't seen her since they returned from Minehead yesterday. Gart said she wasn't feeling well, so it was something of a surprise to see her standing next to him.

"Are you well, Mama?" he asked, concerned.

She nodded. "Of course," she replied, looking around. "Where are your brothers?"

Romney pointed back over towards the kitchens. "Gerta went back there. She went to get milk for Lacy."

Emberley shielded her eyes from the sun as she gazed over towards the kitchens. She could see Orin running around, being chased by Brendt. Gerta appeared, carrying Lacy, and the old woman urged the boys away from the kitchen yard where they might hurt themselves on any variety of implements. As Emberley watched her children head back in her direction, she felt a body stand next to her.

She could feel the heat, the power, knowing it was Gart before she even looked. Already, her heart was thumping madly against her ribs and her breathing was beginning to come in swifter gasps. But she stilled herself, dropping the hand from her eyes as she turned to look at him.

Gart's intense eyes greeted her, warmth and emotion radiating from him. Emberley smiled faintly.

"Good day to you, Gart," she said softly.

He smiled, looking far more relaxed and content than she had ever seen the man. Usually, he had some manner of hardness or professionalism about him. But not today, he actually appeared happy.

"My lady," he greeted evenly. "You are looking exceptionally well."

Her smile broadened. "Thank you," she replied. "As are you."

Orin and Brendt began clamoring around their mother and Emberley's attention was momentarily diverted. Gart took the opportunity to study her as she dealt with her boys. He hadn't seen her since yesterday afternoon, after they had made love and she had wept painfully. She had fallen into a fitful sleep after that and he had stayed with her, if only just to hold her. He had never loved anything in his life as much as he was coming to love her and the passion of their lovemaking, the depths of the emotion they were coming to feel for one another, had his insides tearing themselves apart. He was struggling to think clearly about it.

He'd left her sleeping in her big bed towards dusk, heading down to the great hall to find all four children at the table eating like pigs. He had taken the meal with them and a few of his senior soldiers, telling the children that their mother wasn't feeling well, which wasn't anything new in their world. They were used to that. Gart returned to check on Emberley after dinner but she was still sleeping heavily. He'd ended up taking the night watch, checking on her every couple of hours throughout the night and watching her sleep. When dawn broke, he'd stolen a couple of hours of sleep himself only to rise, more exhausted than he had been when he had gone to bed, when one of his soldiers had roused him.

So he forced himself to awaken and get to business. His first action after shaving and washing had been to check on Emberley again, who was still in an exhausted sleep. Gart had broken his fast with a very sleepy Romney and proceeded out to the grounds. Julian had taken most of his army with him and there were no more than fifty men-at-arms left behind, not a particularly wise move with a castle the size of Dunster. On the edge of the moors at the gates to Cornwall, a castle like Dunster needed to be more heavily manned against the wilds that plagued the area.

Gart had spent his morning putting his own men on the walls. Then he had been challenged by Romney, only to come face to face with Romney's beautiful mother. Now, all he could do was stare at her, feeling as if he was on brittle ground. The mood between them was uncertain given the events of the previous day and he was unsure how to act or even what to say. Eventually, Orin and Brendt resumed fighting with their wooden swords as Lacy, set to her feet by Gerta, took off running. As the fat nurse followed the baby, Romney faced off against Gart.

"Well?" he demanded. "Are you ready to fight me?"

"Romney," Emberley admonished softly. "Enough with your impertinence. You do not make demands of Gart."

Gart gave her a half-grin, holding up a hand to let her know it was all right. He faced the boy. "Are you sure you want to fight me?"

Romney nodded, holding his sword defensively. "I am."

Gart cocked an eyebrow at the lad. "Not the way you are holding that sword. Look at the way you are gripping the hilt. You are going to get your fingers chopped off if you hold it like that."

Romney looked seriously at his hands. "I am?" he frowned. "I need my gloves."

Gart gestured in the general direction of the keep. "Go and get them."

"Will you fight me then?"

"If you are sure you want to take me on."

Romney flashed a bright grin and was gone, rushing across the courtyard towards the keep. Gart and Emberley watched him go, realizing they were now alone. The silence grew odd. Gart kept stealing glances at Emberley out of the corner of his eye. She was watching her boys as they smacked each other with their swords. He cleared his throat softly.

"How are you feeling this morning?" he asked softly.

Emberley sighed, her gaze still on her boys in the distance. "Well enough."

Gart looked at her, then. She seemed distant. "Please," he said quietly. "Do not shut me out. Please tell me what you are feeling. You were very distraught yesterday and… well, I just…."

He trailed off, unable to continue, and Emberley looked at him. She knew what he meant and she could feel her stiff stance relenting.

"In truth, I do not know what I am feeling," she said seriously. "All I know is that I am deliriously happy, more than I have ever been in my life. I look at you and I see a man I have loved most of my life. I know you, Gart, and everything about you. You are a true and strong man. I feel like the most fortunate woman in the world to have your love. But the reality is that we have a very serious problem and I do not know what to do about it. It sickens me to think that the love we know now may soon be gone."

His gaze was intense. "Why do you say that?"

"Because Julian is my husband. My children belong to him, and I will not leave my children behind no matter how much I love you."

"I never asked you to."

He was right. With nothing more to say, Emberley simply averted her gaze, watching Orin and Brendt in the distance. Gart never took his eyes off her as he took a few casual steps in her direction, ending up standing very close to her. He could feel the warmth radiating off her body, making his palms sweat and his heart race.

"I have been thinking on our situation with every waking moment," he confessed. "I have never in my life thought of something more seriously and I believe I have come up with a plan. Will you hear it?"

She sighed again, wanting to, yet not wanting to. "Please, Gart...."

He cut her off softly. "I beg you, kitten. Please hear me out."

She looked miserable but nodded. Gart collected his thoughts, looking over at the boys when Brendt yelled because Orin shoved him into the dirt. Brendt swiped at Orin's legs, knocking his brother down, and they began scuffling in the dirt.

"When my father and his brother stopped speaking, my father essentially separated himself from the family," he said softly. "The truth is that my father was titled. He carried the title Viscount Tenbury, heir presumptive to the Earldom of Albemarle. But when he and my uncle had their disagreement, my father disregarded his titles and trappings. He did not want anything to do with my uncle ever again. That is not the case with me. The title of Viscount Tenbury is mine by birthright and I want it."

She turned to look at him, somewhat started at the information. "Tenbury is your inheritance?"

"It is."

"And you have never gone to your uncle before now to demand it?"

"Nay."

She was both puzzled and astonished by his answer. "What are you going to do about it?"

He shrugged. "Seek audience with my uncle. Along with the titles, the property of Bridgnorth Castle in Shropshire comes with it. When my father left the family, my uncle had the castle garrisoned for Albemarle. I will demand it returned, as my right."

Emberley was stunned. "All of that belongs to you?"

He nodded. "All that and more," he said. "My mother was a de Belléme, from the family of the great Robert de Montgomery, hereditary heirs to the Earldom of Shrewsbury. My mother's father descends from Roger de Montgomery, William the Conqueror's chancellor. Her family is very powerful and I believe my mother inherited property from them."

Emberley was listening intently. "What do you intend to do about it?"

"Find out what is my due."

Emberley stared at him. "Five days ago, you told me that you have had to earn your fortune," she said. "You said you inherited nothing from your father and have had to make your own way."

He nodded. "That is true for the most part. I did not inherit anything from my father but there is much that, by birthright, is mine. There is much on my mother's side as well but I have not given it much thought simply because I like my life. I enjoy my vocation and the travels and adventure of it. I did not want to be saddled with the responsibilities of title. But the situation has changed markedly in the past few days."

"What do you mean?"

He looked at her. "You speak of taking Romney and the children from their inheritance. I will provide them with mine."

Emberley's eyes widened. "But... but it is not their right," she whispered urgently. "It will belong to any child you will have, a child that will bear your name."

His eyes were intense. "You will bear any child I have," he murmured. "My inheritance will belong to all of our children, whether I fathered them or not."

She stared at him, overwhelmed at his declaration. "But it is not their due," was all she could think to say. "Romney... he is Buckland's heir and... what is yours does not belong to him."

Gart could see how off-balance she was. Frankly, he was off-balance as well. He simply didn't show it as she did. He grasped her gently by the elbow.

"Walk with me," he said softly.

Dumbly, she followed. They began to walk towards the main bailey of Dunster, a great dusty mess of men and animals. Smithy shacks lodged against the outer wall and one smithy was shoeing a particularly unhappy horse. Overhead, puffy gray clouds were blowing in from the sea, indicative that a storm was approaching. Emberley glanced up, watching the clouds skip across the crystal blue sky.

"Gart?" she asked softly.

He didn't look at her. "Aye, kitten?"

She sighed, taking her eyes off the sky and gazing over the busy bailey.

"You said that you did not want to be burdened by the responsibilities of title because you enjoyed the travel and adventure of your profession." She stopped walking and faced him. "The responsibility of a family is much greater than those of any title. Do you realize what you are wishing for when you say that you want me and the children?"

"I believe I do."

She shook her head. "And I am not entirely sure you do," she said pointedly. "You have never had a wife or children dependent upon you. Perhaps you love the lust of the moment, the humor of the children when they...."

He cut her off, his eyes blazing. "I realize that you and I have not seen each other in many years and I further realize that you still may see me as that young and perhaps foolish knight from days gone by, but I assure you that I have matured into what I would consider a stable man. I do not say anything I do not mean and I do not act upon a whim. When I told you I loved you, I meant it. When I told you I wanted you and your wild children, I did not say it on impulse. I said it because I meant every word."

She gazed up at him, sadly, wanting to believe him but deeply torn. "When you tell me you love the travel and adventure of being a knight, I would believe that more."

He felt slandered, hurt by her doubt. "How can I prove to you that my intentions are sincere?"

Her gaze held steady as she studied his face. "I am not sure. Quite honestly, I am still not entirely sure that any of this is real."

His jaw ticked as he gazed down at her. "Shall I ride to Albemarle today and demand my inheritance returned?" he asked. "I will do it if it would prove to you my sincerity. I will also ride to Arques-la-Bataille Castle in Normandy and demand my inheritance from my mother's family. I will do this and I will not return until I have secured a solid future for the children. Would this convince you I am true?"

Impulsively, she reached out and took his hand, simply because he was becoming agitated. She did it to calm his manner.

"You do not have to do that," she said softly, firmly. "Perhaps… perhaps this is something only time can settle for me. I still cannot believe… it is difficult to comprehend everything. You must give me time to come to terms with it."

He watched her carefully. "And if you do not?"

She let go of his hand. "Will you abide by my wishes, whatever they may be?"

His jaw started ticking again and he hung his head after a moment. "I will have little choice. I would not want to make you miserable no matter what my feelings in the matter."

She stood there and looked at him. He had moved from staring at the ground to gazing over the bailey, anything to keep from looking her in the eye. Emberley could see how distraught he was at the mere mention that nothing might ever happen between them, of a rare and precious love that would be pushed aside for a variety of complex reasons.

The truth was that it was killing her as well. The more she thought on the man she had always wanted versus the husband she hated, it was becoming easier to ignore the morality of it. It was becoming easier to ignore Julian. God, how she wished Julian would simply fade away forever.

"Gart," she said softly.

"Aye?" he was looking off towards the stables.

"Look at me."

He did, the green eyes wrought with turmoil. She smiled at him. "Do not worry," she whispered. "All will be well."

His expression loosened. "Can you swear it?"

"I can," she murmured. "I love you, Gart. I have always loved you. But it surely would have made things considerably easier had you not been afraid of my brother eight years ago and married me before you went to The Levant."

He fought off a grin. "I was not afraid of him. Well, not much."

She laughed softly, sobering. "You mentioned that you would take us away," she said. "Where would you take us so that we would be safe from Julian's wrath?"

Gart took her question seriously. "I have many friends in England and Wales but they are knights, fighting men, and not well-propertied. I do know one man, however, who has the means to accommodate us. He lives far to the north at Prudhoe Castle."

"Will we go there?"

"Prudhoe is a well-fortified castle and very far north," he said. "Julian would never find us there and it would allow me time to do what I must, knowing you were safe."

She thought on that a moment. "But what of your liege?" she wanted to know. "You have a great deal of respect for de Lohr. Will you abandon your oath to him?"

For the first time, Gart seemed to show some distress. "David has been extremely good to me," he said quietly. "I will not abandon my oath to him but I will ask to be released from it."

Emberley was thinking seriously on their future. "And then what? You must serve someone, Gart, or do you intend we should live in the wilds, isolated from all contact, simply so that Julian will not find us?" she shook her head. "Julian is the queen's lover. He is very prominent in political circles. If we stay in England, we cannot escape the man no manner how hard we try."

He was coming to see her logic with sickening realization. Even if he was to take them far away and provide them with his inheritance, the fact remained that Julian would always be a threat. He was Emberley's husband and the father of her children. As long as he lived, Gart and Emberley would never be safe.

Gart was a knight. He had better fighting instincts than most men and had built an astounding reputation. But the truth was that he wasn't a great intellect or scholar. He tended to act on emotion or instinct more than he actually reasoned a situation through in his mind. He was coming to think that there might not be a solution to the situation that wouldn't somehow be detrimental to them all. But he gave it one last try.

"Is Julian a greedy man?" he asked quietly.

Emberley looked strangely at him. "No more than most, I suppose," she replied. "Why do you ask?"

Gart drew in a long, thoughtful breath, "As much as I do not want to admit that running may not be the answer to our problems, I am beginning to suspect it would not be the perfect solution," he looked at her. "I will still go to my uncle and my mother's family and demand all that is due to me. It would be a great deal. Do… do you suppose that if I offer it all to Julian in exchange for you and the children, he might accept my offer?"

Emberley couldn't help it, her jaw dropped. Hysterical tears began to bubble up and she put her hands over her mouth, trying to block out the noise.

"You cannot do that," she gasped. "Gart, you cannot give him everything you have. I will not let you do it."

He put his hands on her shoulders to calm her down. "No need to become upset, kitten," he said soothingly. "I simply asked a question. Do you think he would take it?"

She was struggling against the tears, resisting his question but finding it oddly intriguing. "I will not hear you. I cannot."

He made sure no one was watching before kissing her hands swiftly, sweetly, before letting them go. "Easy, lady," he murmured. "No need to upset yourself. It was simply a question."

Emberley wiped at her eyes, taking a few deep breaths to calm herself. She simply couldn't believe that Gart would give up everything just for her. "If you gave him all that you had, then what would be left to live on?" she asked softly, urgently. "We would be destitute. Do you think that would make us happy? You would come to resent us."

Gart shook his head. "Nay, I would not," he insisted softly, interrupted her gently when she opened her mouth to argue. "Kitten, you swore to me that all would be well. I will hold you to that. But it is apparent that this is a situation with no simple answer. I need time to think of a resolution that is best for all of us."

Emberley took another deep breath, calming further. She nodded in agreement. "As you say," she said softly, turning when she heard her daughter scream in the yard. "I will trust that you will do what is right."

He very much wanted to take her in his arms. He was fairly aching to hold her. But he took a step back instead, fearful that his control would snap if she was too close to him. As he stepped back, Lacy suddenly came toddling their way as fast as her baby legs would carry her. Brendt was hot on her heels, telling her that he was going to capture her, and the little girl was screaming in delight. Gerta brought up the rear several feet back, the old nurse huffing to keep up with the pair.

Gart reached down and scooped the little girl up as she passed by, growling like a bear against the side of her head and nibbling at her ear. Lacy giggled uncontrollably as Gart snarled and tickled. Brendt, standing at the man's feet, whacked him with his wooden sword to get his attention. When Gart looked down at the boy, he heard Romney's battle cry.

"He has captured her!" the child shouted. "Get him!"

Emberley tried to stop the out and out assault, but she ended up stepping out of the way and letting Gart handle it. He didn't seem to mind. As she stood there and watched, she began to think that perhaps they could live without anything to their name as long as they were all together. Already, her children showed Gart more attention and affection than they had ever shown Julian. But Gart had opened that door the moment they had met him. They had tried to rob the man and he hadn't truly punished them. He had been kind and understanding of their games, for the most part. He loved them.

It warmed her heart to watch Gart fight off her boys, grabbing Brendt so the child hung upside down in his arms and using his knees to shove Romney and Orin away. Lacy had her arms around his neck and was giving him big, sloppy kisses even as he wrestled with the boys. The enormous knight that grown men were afraid of was enjoying every minute of it. He had four very young and very adoring admirers.

And one woman who loved him deeply.

CHAPTER TEN

Early July, 1204 A.D.

"MY LADY?" GART addressed Emberley as he entered the great hall of Dunster. "You should come to the kitchens and see the impressive buck that your sons killed."

The afternoon was warm, lazy, with a stiff sea breeze blowing off the ocean. It made the outside air sticky with moisture and salt. The great hall of Dunster was a nice cool spot, dry, smelling of smoke and old rushes. It had been quiet and peaceful until Gart and the boys had broken the spell.

Emberley smiled at Romney and Orin, who were flanking Gart with faces full of pride. She set down the sewing in her hand, a lovely little dress that she was making for Lacy. It was blue with embroidered flowers around the neck. Spread out all over the table were her sewing things as she mended breeches and sewed little dresses. Although the servants could do the work, she enjoyed it.

"A buck?" she lifted her eyebrows at her boys, then Gart. "I thought you were teaching them to ride. You said nothing about hunting."

Gart nodded. "I was teaching them to ride, but we were interrupted by a three point buck. Rom and Orin are very good with a crossbow."

She tried to keep the shock from her expression. "Crossbow?" she repeated. "Those weapons are bigger than they are."

"I held it and they pulled the trigger."

The boys were nodding proudly throughout Gart and Emberley's exchange. They seemed so genuinely happy that Emberley didn't have the heart to scold Gart for allowing her sons around something as dangerous as a hair-trigger crossbow.

"Come and see our buck, Mama," Romney reached out and grabbed her hand. "We will feed everyone with it and Gart said he will have a man make shoes from the hide."

Emberley let Romney pull her from the great hall. Orin was running on ahead, jumping up and down and shouting about the buck. Gart brought up the rear, a lazy smile on his face as he watched the boys dance around, yanking on Emberley's arm.

She looked over her shoulder to make sure he was following, smiling when their eyes met. Gart's smile broadened and he winked at her. It made his heart swell simply to look at her. The past seven weeks at Dunster had been just like heaven. Tucked away in their own little world, he could pretend that Emberley and the children belonged to him. They played together every day and at night after the children went to bed, Gart would sneak into Emberley's bower and make love to her most of the night. He couldn't ever remember being happier, safely shielded in this little corner of paradise with a woman he deeply adored.

Days like today had become commonplace. He would spend his time with the boys during the day, teaching them about riding or battle, schooling them as he had often schooled pages and squires in the past. All three boys were fast learners, eager, and they had all become quite attached to each other. Gart always made sure he returned to his own bedchamber before the children woke up because every morning at dawn, three eager little boys woke him up. It was the best thing he could wake up to, this part of life he had never known existed.

As Gart thought of the joys of the past several weeks, watching Emberley's shapely backside in the process, the group rounded the corner of the towering keep and entered the kitchen yard. The big buck was lying in the middle of the yard, surrounded by a couple of male servants and the cook as they figured out the best way to go about butchering it. Romney made sure to tell the cook that he killed the buck and the fat woman was very proud of him.

"Good heavens," Emberley exclaimed softly. "That is a very big deer. We will have lots of meat from him."

Romney and Orin were nearly bursting with satisfaction. "Gart said we could kill another one the next time, too," Romney said. "Can I have my own crossbow, Mama?"

Emberley shook her head. "You may not," she said. "It is not that I do not trust you, but a seven-year-old boy simply does not need a weapon like that."

"But I will be able to feed the castle," Romney insisted, looking at Gart. "Do you think I am big enough to have one?"

Gart didn't want to get in the middle of the debate. "If your mother says you must wait, then you will listen to her," he told the boy. "Her decision is the one we will abide by."

Romney didn't seem pleased but he kept his mouth shut. Not wanting to crush her son's spirit, Emberley hastened to reassure him.

"You did a fine job, sweetheart," she told him. "I am very proud of you. Go find Gerta now and I will meet you in the hall for the nooning meal."

Romney obeyed his mother, taking Orin with him. As Emberley eyed the big buck, Gart noticed that the cook and the two servants had moved back into the kitchens to find a knife big enough to cut the buck with. It was just him and Emberley left in the yard as he faced her.

"Did I do a fine job, also?" he asked softly.

She looked at him, a smile playing on her lips. "You did, sweetheart. I am proud of you as well."

He smiled at her. "Just so you are aware, I had a crossbow when I was Rom's age. My father commissioned it for me."

Her smile left her and she flattened her lips irritably. "Did Rom coerce you into begging on his behalf?"

Gart laughed. "He did not. I am begging of my own accord. Boys must be allowed to become men."

Her eyebrows lifted. "At seven years of age he must become a man?" she shook her head. "That is ridiculous. He is still a child."

"He wants very much to be a man. You must let him."

She cocked her head "If he was your flesh and blood child whom you had raised from birth, I wonder if you would be so eager to see him grow up?"

"I suppose we shall find out one day if God is merciful."

Her smile abruptly faded and she turned away from him, hoping he would not see her change in expression. But Gart was extremely observant and noticed immediately. He also noticed she was trying to hide it from him.

"What is wrong?" he asked softly. "Why do you look that way?"

She shook her head but he wouldn't let her get away so easily. When she tried to move away, he blocked her path.

"Tell me what is wrong," he begged softly.

She grew frustrated and stepped back from him, still not meeting his eye. "Do you have any idea what you ask for?"

"What do you mean?"

She looked at him then. "You pray for a child of your flesh and mine."

"I realize that."

"It will be a bastard!"

She lifted her voice and he shushed her softly. "It will not be that way forever."

She rolled her eyes miserably. "You do not know that for certain."

"Aye, I do."

She burst into quiet tears. Unsure why she was so emotional, Gart looked around quickly, spying the buttery in the corner of the kitchen yard. It was a little stone shack where cold dairy products were stored. It was also sturdy and private. Not wanting Emberley's tears to be seen by everyone, he took her by the elbow and gently pulled her into the buttery. She followed without a fight.

He shut the door behind them. It was cool and dark inside, a small window near the roof allowing for ventilation and a small amount of light. Gart pulled her into his arms now that they had some privacy, rocking her gently.

"What is the matter, my love?" he asked, his lips against her head. "Why do you weep?"

She sobbed miserably. "We are in trouble."

Other than the obvious, he had no idea what she meant. "Why?"

She was sobbing so much that it was difficult for him to understand her. "Since… since Julian and the queen have been lovers, he has not… not… touched me. He said that it would not be right."

Gart digested that statement, the ridiculousness of it, feeling a great deal of happiness in the declaration. But he was still confused.

"I see," he wasn't sure what more to say. "What does that have to do with anything?"

She pulled back, gazing up at him with a harried, frightened expression. "Because he will know he is not the father."

Gart still wasn't quite following her. "What do you mean?"

She struggled to calm herself, gazing into his handsome face and laboring to bring forth the words. "The baby," she said softly. "He will know it is not his."

"What…?"

"I am pregnant, Gart," she interrupted him softly. "You have your wish. But Julian will know the baby is not his."

Gart stared at her, such shock invading his features that, for a moment, it looked as if the man were about to blow the top of his head off. He was stunned. Genuinely speechless, he pulled her into a crushing embrace.

"My sweet, sweet girl," he breathed, holding her tightly. "How do you… are you certain of this?"

Emberley was tucked up against him, protected and safe. She wanted to stay there for the rest of her life. At the moment, she didn't feel nearly the fear she had been feeling seconds earlier. Gart seemed to have the ability to suck the fear right out of her.

"I have had four children, Gart," she said with some irony. "I know when I am with child."

He suddenly held her at arm's length, looking her over. There was a quiver to his movements, as if everything were all bottled up inside of him and waiting to come bursting forth. Even his hands were shaking as he gripped her.

"But... how?" he asked, correcting himself when he realized how stupid that sounded. "What I mean to say is why did you not tell me before now?"

She couldn't tell if he was upset or thrilled. She wiped at the tears on her face, composing herself.

"I am only now certain," she said. "I was not going to tell you my suspicions until I was certain. There was no need to upset you."

His eyebrows flew up. "*Upset* me?" he repeated, almost outraged. "Did you truly believe this news would upset me?"

She shrugged weakly. "I was not sure," she said honestly. "In fact, while you were out shooting the buck, I was sitting at the table trying to determine just how I should tell you. It is not as if we do not have enough worries on our minds."

He knew she was right. It was both joyous and terrible news. With a heavy sigh, he pulled her back into his powerful embrace, feeling her soft warmth against him. He leaned back against the cold stone, holding her as his mind wandered to the new scenario now presented. Now, things had changed dramatically.

"It is not as if we did not know this could happen," he said softly. "We have been with each other nightly. I did not have to spill my seed inside of you but... I was selfish. I wanted to. To lose that joy and that expression of my feelings for you somehow made the act itself seem trite and incomplete."

Her head was against his chest, listening to the steady beating of his heart. "I became pregnant very quickly with my children," she confessed. "In fact, Julian has truly only touched me a handful of times since we have been married, and only then he did it until I conceived, which was mercifully quick. I seem to be very fertile. I knew this could happen but it did not discourage me. You belong to me, Gart, as I belong to you. Conceiving a child in such love does not seem wrong."

He grunted in agreement. "Nay, it does not," he whispered. "But the fact remains that the situation has changed considerably. We must make some hard decisions and make them quickly."

She was coming to feel afraid again. "I told you once that I will trust you to do what is right. I still trust you, more than ever. What shall we do?"

Gart had been thinking on that subject for more than seven weeks. There were times he would wake up in the middle of the night, unable to go back to sleep because his mind was whirling with thought. He would lay there with Emberley in his arms, staring at the ceiling and wondering what in the world he was going to do. As much as he loved living a fantasy life at Dunster, the truth was that he could not do that any longer. He had to make a decision and follow that path through to completion or the consequences could be deadly.

But he needed time to clear his thoughts. A pending child had changed everything. He put his enormous hands on Emberley's face, kissing her sweetly in the dim light of the buttery.

"Go inside and take the nooning meal with the children," he told her. "I will see you later and we will make plans."

She nodded. "As you say," she replied. "Will you not take the meal with us?"

"Nay. I will see you later."

"Where are you going?"

He paused. "To see a priest."

She blinked. "Priest?" she repeated. "What about?"

He grinned. "Can I not keep any secrets from you?"

She returned his smile, reluctantly. "I did not mean to pry, but if you are going to confession, do not go to the church in town or in Minehead. Those priests are loyal to Julian and they would not hesitate to tell him your confession."

Gart nodded, his smile fading. "I understand. Thank you for the warning. But I did not intend to go to confession."

"May I ask what you intend to do?"

"I want to know what the church would consider grounds for a divorce."

She looked at the man as if he had lost his mind. Gart quietly opened the door, peering out into the kitchen yard to see that the cook and the two male servants had returned to butcher the buck. They were far enough away that Gart and Emberley were able to slip from the buttery unseen. Gart touched her hand sweetly before moving off towards the stables while Emberley continued on to the keep.

Lost in thoughts of a divorce, Emberley rounded the corner of the keep from the stables and kitchen yard area into the main body of the bailey. She could hear soldiers on the wall, shouting to one another, but she was used to the commotion and didn't give it much thought. Life went on around her, dogs and men and horses, but she ignored it as she pondered her future. She was afraid, but she was also hopeful. At the moment, she couldn't really decide what she was feeling because it was all so surreal. Like Gart, she needed time to sort her thoughts out as well.

Mounting the stairs, she noticed that there seemed to be a good deal of activity on the walls, enough that it jarred her from her thoughts. Glancing up, Emberley could see that Gart had mounted the walls and his men were talking to him, pointing out into the countryside beyond. Curious but not overly so, Emberley continued into the keep where her children were taking their meal.

CHAPTER ELEVEN

Gart caught a glimpse of Emberley disappearing into the enormous keep as his men described the rider that had been sighted a mile from Dunster. But he shifted his focus from Emberley to the approaching rider, curious and nothing more. A lone rider was not much of a threat so he climbed down off the wall and went to the gatehouse. He ordered his men to lower the portcullis to half-staff, which would discourage the rider from charging into the bailey yet not give off a completely unfriendly appearance from Dunster. It was a precautionary measure.

Gart stood back in the shadows because if the rider was someone familiar to Julian, he didn't want to be seen. He wasn't supposed to be here. Crossing his big arms, he waited expectantly for the mysterious rider to appear.

The man wasn't long in showing himself. Hooves pounded and mail armor creaked as the rider slowed, approaching the gatehouse. A big, brown charger with hairy white feet came into view and Gart recognized the horse immediately. He'd seen that snappish beast before.

"Open the portcullis," he commanded, moving forward as the horse slowed and began to move through the low-ceilinged gatehouse. "If he makes a wrong move, use him for target practice."

The knight on horseback heard him, grinning as he raised his visor. Gart met him halfway through the cool passage of the gatehouse, a smirk on his lips.

"And so you have found me," he said. "Even at the ends of the earth, you have tracked me down."

The knight nodded, leaning wearily against his saddle. "De Lohr said you might be here," he replied, his blue eyes twinkling. "I must say, I am rather surprised."

"Why?"

"Because you are not usually one to keep yourself in the wilds and out of the action."

Gart wriggled his eyebrows. "Did you come to tell me about the action I am missing?"

The knight shook his head. "Nay," he replied. "But I do bring a message for you."

Some of Gart's humor left him. He motioned the knight forward, following him as he brought his charger into the bailey and laboriously dismounted. The animal was sweaty and foaming, and the knight was nearly doing the same. Both were exhausted. Gart noticed the sheer fatigue and it concerned him. Why was the man so strung out from his ride? What was so important that he was forced to ride so hard? He faced the man with more composure than he felt.

"How long have you been in the saddle?" he asked, making small talk as the weary knight removed his helm.

"Do you mean to ask if I have slept over the past week?" the knight's dark eyebrows lifted with some irony. "The answer is I have not. I left Bellham Place six days ago and was told to make all haste for Dunster to see if you were still here."

Gart eyed the knight. He had known Sir Kevin de Lara for several years, a rather short knight with the strength of Samson. He was young, very handsome, with blue eyes, a square jaw and a bright smile. Moreover, he had a good deal of charisma and was brilliant and honest to a fault. They had served de Lohr together for three years, having spent a full year in France on behalf of the king. They had seen many adventures, and many battles, together. Consequently, Gart respected and trusted the man more than most. He considered him a friend.

"What is the message?" he asked with some trepidation.

Kevin looked around to make sure there wasn't anyone within earshot. He looked at Gart as he began to pull off his gauntlets. "Do you want me to tell you now or do you wish to go someplace more private?"

"Tell me now. What is the message?"

Kevin tucked his gloves into his saddle before facing Gart. He exhaled wearily, running a hand over his face.

"De Lohr says to tell you that Buckland is sending an escort to Dunster," he lowered his voice. "The man wants his family with him in London. David says to tell you that if you are still here, then to get out in a hurry. Buckland's men can't be more than an hour or two behind me. I had to ride like the wind to avoid them."

Gart stared at him. "Buckland wants his family with him in London?"

"That is my understanding."

"Why, in God's name?"

Kevin shook his head. "This I cannot know." He eyed Gart, his good friend. "Do I want to know why you are here and why de Lohr has sent me with this message?"

"What did de Lohr tell you?"

"To help you if you need it."

Gart gazed steadily at the man, finally emitting a weary sigh and turning away. He thought on the irony of Kevin's statement. *To help you if you need it.* At the moment, he needed help. He'd never needed it more in his life.

"Is that all he told you?"

Kevin nodded, starting to feel great curiosity along with his fatigue. "Gart, what goes on?" he demanded softly. "Why are you here? Why was I told to make all haste to Dunster so I could warn you off of Buckland's approach?"

Gart looked at him. "You would not believe me if I told you."

"Tell me."

Gart's jaw ticked and he hung his head, running his hand across his stubbled, bald head, trying to think of a way to phrase what he had been feeling for the past seven weeks. So much had happened. He suddenly felt like a fool because only fools got themselves into this kind of trouble. He was about to confess his biggest weakness to a fellow knight. But, on the other hand, he had never felt more strong or whole. It was an odd combination.

"You and I have been through much together, have we not?" he finally asked, looking up at his friend.

Kevin nodded. "I would trust my life to you a thousand times over."

"And I to you." Gart paused to collect his thoughts. "De Lohr and I came to Dunster two months ago because Buckland had requested de Lohr's assistance in protecting the queen's lands in France."

Kevin nodded. "I know," he replied. "We are preparing to sail in three weeks, which I am also supposed to tell you. De Lohr wants you in London as soon as possible."

A second blow in as many minutes. Gart struggled to stay on an even keel as he took a deep breath, digesting the news. After a moment, he snorted ironically and stared up at the sky as if beseeching God for strength to do as he must.

"Buckland's wife is the sister of Erik de Russe," he took his eyes off the sky and looked at de Lara. "You remember de Russe, do you not?"

Kevin's brow furrowed in distant remembrance. "Of course," he said. "We fostered together. As I recall, you and de Russe were as thick as thieves. So his sister is married to de Moyon?"

Gart nodded. "I have known Lady Emberley since she was a young girl," he said quietly. "I had not seen her in years until two months ago."

Kevin's brow furrowed, appearing quite serious. "De Moyon is the queen's lover," he lowered his voice. "The man is spouting it all over London."

"I know," Gart replied. "Which is why it makes no sense that he should want his family with him in London. Surely they will only be a burden to him and interfere with his affair with Isabella. Have you heard anything about Buckland other than what de Lohr told you?"

Kevin shook his head. "Nothing other than the fact that the man is a pompous idiot," he said, his serious gaze moving over Gart's tight features. "What is this all about, Gart? You still have not told me why you are here."

Gart looked at him, feeling as if he needed to confide in the man. He'd never felt like that in his life and the walls of self-protection began to crumble.

"What I tell you must not leave your lips," he muttered. "If it does, many people will suffer."

Kevin grew intent. "The information will die with me, I swear it."

"I believe you," Gart said, taking a deep breath for courage. "I told you that I have known Buckland's wife since she was a child."

"You did."

"I love her," his voice was a whisper, full of pain. "I am here because I love the woman and she loves me. I intend to take her and the children out of this hellish place where Buckland can never find them."

Kevin, surprisingly, didn't react overly. He remained intent, serious. "You… you intend to abduct her?"

"I will not abduct her."

"She is agreeable to this, then?"

"She is."

Kevin fell silent as he processed the news. Then he said the first thing that came to mind, the obvious. "But she is married to Buckland," he lifted an eyebrow, his reaction becoming evident. "You cannot simply take his wife."

"I am not taking anything. We love each other and will be together."

"But he can have you charged with thievery for stealing his family if you truly intend to do this. Stealing another man's wife, particularly a nobleman's wife, is very serious."

Gart didn't back down. "I realize that," he said steadily. "But he has been beating Emberley since the day they married. When I first arrived here, he beat her so badly that she could not rise from bed for two days.

The man is vile and horrible and treats her no better than an animal. Do you have any idea how it feels knowing that the woman you love is married to man who brutalizes her? You cannot comprehend the fury and pain I feel every time I think about it."

De Lara's expression darkened. "Nay, I cannot," he agreed. "But the fact remains that she is Buckland's wife and…."

"She carries my child."

So much for composure. De Lara's eyes widened and his jaw popped open. He stared at Gart for a long, painful moment.

"Are you serious?"

"I would not lie."

"Then if what you say about Buckland is true, he will kill her when he finds out," Kevin hissed. "He will also kill you."

"I know."

De Lara grabbed him by the arm and began yanking him towards the keep. "We stand here chewing words as if we have all the time in the world when the truth is that time is slipping through our fingers," he said urgently. "You must leave immediately and take your lady with you. There is no time to waste with Buckland's men on my tail. No wonder de Lohr sent me ahead to warn you."

Gart let him pull. "We have nowhere to go."

"Ridiculous," de Lara spat. "You will go to my father in Wales until you decide what needs to be done. You will be safe there."

Gart was greatly relieved yet greatly concerned. "You should not involve yourself in this, Kevin. If you send me to your father, you involve him as well."

Kevin didn't seem particularly concerned. "My father hates John, Isabella and everything about them," he said. "He is an old man with a good deal of power. He will consider assisting you a victory against the king and his vile queen. You have heard of the Trinity Castles on the Welsh Marches, have you not?"

Gart nodded as they mounted the steps to the keep. "Trelystan, Hyssington and Caradoc Castles. They are great Marcher castles."

"They are my father's holdings as Viscount Trelystan."

"I recall," Gart said thoughtfully. "But I had nearly forgotten. You do not speak much of your father."

Kevin shrugged. "I do not speak much of my family in general," he replied as he pulled Gart to the top of the stairs. "Gather the lady and your possessions. Meet me in the bailey as quickly as you can."

Gart just stared at him, having one of the weakest and most indecisive moments of his life. He was so grateful for the help but he didn't want to involve Kevin and his family in something so serious. The consequences, for the de Laras, could be as bad as the consequences for Gart. He looked helplessly at his friend. It was clear he didn't know what to say.

"And then what?" he asked quietly. "It will not end there, Kevin. I must still...."

Kevin waved a big hand towards the keep. "It will end right here if you do not get moving," he told him. "You can make decisions once you reach my father's castle, but until then, you can...."

He was cut off by a shout from the wall. Both Kevin and Gart strained to catch a glimpse of what the sentries were pointing at. From their vantage point at the top of the stairs, they could see some of the countryside beyond the walls but not much. Gart shouted up to the battlement.

"What do you see?"

One of his men answered. "Buckland colors, my lord!"

Gart and Kevin looked at each other, stricken. "He is already here," Kevin hissed. "You must go now if there is any hope for survival. Go to Trelystan Castle near Welshpool and I will meet you there."

Gart didn't waste any time. He raced into the keep and on into the great hall, watching as Emberley and the children looked up from their meal at him. He was barreling at frightening speed and Emberley shot to her feet, immediately on her guard.

"What is wrong?" she asked. "Why are you...?"

He grabbed her by the arms, pulling her away from the table so the children couldn't hear him. But the children were sharp and they could see his agitated manner. Gart was a man always in control, especially around them, and his demeanor roused their concern. Gart didn't look at the children as he focused on Emberley, taking a deep breath and struggling for calm.

"Buckland has come to escort you to London," he told her quietly, quickly. "We must escape now or all will be lost."

Emberley's eyes widened with shock. "Julian is here?"

He shook his head. There was no time for explanations. "Please," he begged softly. "Just do as I say. We must escape. You know this castle – how may we escape unseen?"

Emberley's big eyes filled with tears, overflowing as he watched. She was struggling not to fly into full-blown panic. "There… there is a postern gate by the kitchen yard."

"Is it locked?"

She shook her head. "During the day it remains unlocked for those who would pass through to do business with the cook."

"Is that the only way out?"

"Other than the gatehouse, it is the only gate in the wall."

Gart nodded swiftly. "Then we take the gate," he went to the table, scooping Lacy into his arms. The little girl threw his head in a bear hug and began to slobber on his cheek. "Get the boys and follow me."

Terrified, Emberley did as she was told, grabbing little hands and pulling them along. But the boys didn't understand and they began whining for their toy swords. Just as Gart reached the narrow stairs that led down to the kitchen on the floor below them, Kevin darted in through the keep entry. Gart threw open the door to the stairs as Kevin raced into the great hall.

"Gart," he was trying not to shout. "Buckland's men are upon us, at least sixty or seventy of them. They are spreading out around the fortress wall as a small party approaches the gate. You cannot make it out of here in time with all of this baggage."

He was referring to the children, who were already dragging their feet and complaining loudly. Emberley looked at the strange knight, confused by his appearance, and then to Gart with such fear that he could physically feel it like knives stabbing his heart. He didn't want to acknowledge that de Lara was right but he knew, deep down, that the man had a point. They could not escape with four screaming children. They would be a target, and a very slow one at that.

"If they find you here, they will kill you," Emberley whispered, tears filling her eyes. "Those men are loyal to Julian and if they see you...."

He cut her off, his face a mask of anguish. "I will not let them take you to London."

She grabbed his arm. "And I cannot stand by while they kill you," she begged, tears streaming down her face. "Please, Gart. Hide somewhere. I have faith that you will come for us but for now, my priority is keeping you safe from Julian's men. Please."

He stared at her, torn and in agony, as Kevin agreed with Emberley. "She is right, Gart," he told him. "You must hide. Let the escort take her out of here and we will follow. It will be a simple thing to steal them once they are upon the road."

Gart sighed heavily, raggedly. "What about my men? They are on the walls."

"I have already told them to scatter and regroup in the town," he told them. "They are clearing out and so should we."

"And what about you?"

"I am a visitor passing through on my way to London. They will not know or care who I am, but they will care about you."

"Go," Emberley reached up to pull Lacy from his arms and the little girl screamed unhappily. "Please go, Gart. We will wait for you to come for us before we reach London. I have faith in you."

Gart stared at her, truly concerned that he was going to burst into tears. He'd never felt so much pain in his life. There wasn't time to argue. He threw his arms around her, kissing both her and the unhappy baby.

"I love you," he murmured. "I will see you all again, very soon."

"Gart?" Romney was pulling on his leg. "Can I come with you? I can help you."

Gart felt more pain at the boy's brave offer. He touched the lad on the head affectionately. "I know you can," he said quietly. "But it is more important that you stay with your mother. She will need your protection."

"She has Orin and Brendt. She does not need me, but you do. Who will help you?"

Gart sighed faintly, so deeply touched by the boy's earnest question. Before he could answer, Kevin spoke.

"I will help him, lad," he gave Gart a tug, hissing at him. "We must leave. *Now*."

Romney eyed Gart before looking to his mother, seeing her eyes full of tears and her lower lip trembling. As young as he was, he wasn't stupid. He could see that something was happening between his mother and the knight. He'd seen Gart steal kisses from her and since his father had left for London, he'd never seen his mother smile so much. She was happy and he didn't have to buy her any more gifts to please her. Gart made her happy and made her smile. But he also knew that his father must never know how happy Gart had made his mother or terrible things would happen. Gart had to leave. He slipped his hand into his mother's elbow.

"Come on, Mama," he pulled at her. "Gart must go before Father's men come."

Romney's gentle encouragement was all Emberley needed to hear for her composure to leave her. She broke down into soft sobs as Gart kissed her again, murmuring of his love for her, before being pulled away by Kevin. It was a painful parting. Emberley's last glimpse of Gart was as he and Kevin disappeared down the stairs to the kitchen, her heart breaking into a million pieces when he vanished from sight. Next to her, Romney was pulling on his mother insistently.

"Come along, Mama," he told her. "Sit down."

Weeping pitifully, something Gart had said to her suddenly rang true in her head. *He wants so much to be a man.* She looked at Romney's serious face and already, she could see Gart's influence on the boy. He'd grown up sometime during the past seven weeks and she hadn't even noticed. Her tears ran fresh.

"You are a good boy, Rom," she kissed his forehead. "You will be a fine man someday. I am very proud of you."

Romney regarded his mother a moment. "Why did Father send his men from London?"

Emberley wiped at her eyes. "Because... because it would seem that he wants us to go to him in London."

"I do not want to go."

"We do not have a choice."

Romney wasn't quite sure how he felt about that. He was proud that his mother recognized his strength but very concerned that Gart had fled and his father's men were about the castle. He liked Gart a great deal, feeling guilty because he liked him more than his father. He didn't want anything to happen to him. Romney looked at Orin, who was standing with Brendt, wide-eyed as they watched the situation unfold.

"Get Mama some wine," he told Orin. "Hurry up. And do not spill it."

Orin nodded his blond head emphatically and rushed to the alcove of the hall where the wine and ale were usually stored. Brendt came to sit next to his mother on the bench, gazing up at her with frightened, blue eyes, and Emberley put an arm around her son's shoulder and hugged him gently.

"Everything will be all right," she promised softly. "But we must never mention Gart to Father or to his men, ever. It is a serious secret we must keep or else your father will become very angry. Do you understand?"

Romney and Brendt nodded seriously as Orin returned with a full cup of wine, struggling not to spill a drop. He carefully extended it to his mother, who smiled as she took it from him. She wiped the remaining moisture from her eyes, trying not to think about Gart and his safety as she took a healthy swallow of the tart, red wine. To dwell on Gart would only drive her mad.

She could hear men outside, shouting in the bailey. She knew that Julian had left behind a few men to man the walls and they would undoubtedly speak of Gart Forbes' men. It was something she couldn't get around, but she wasn't particularly concerned for herself at the moment. She could make up an excuse and say they were de Lohr's men. Gart was out there, somewhere, trying to find a safe haven to hide from Buckland's party. The more she thought on it, the more fearful she became. She was compelled to do something to help him.

"Rom," she set the wine down on the well-scrubbed table surface. "Follow the path that Gart took down the stairs and into the kitchen. Find him and help him find a place to hide. We know this place better than he does, do we not? Make sure you keep him out of sight. I will distract your father's men as much as I can, but you must help Gart. If they find him, they will kill him. Do you understand?"

Romney nodded seriously. "Aye, Mama."

Emberley touched his cheek sweetly. "Good lad," she whispered. "Hurry, now. Find him and help him."

Romney was off, sprinting to the stairs that led down to the kitchen as Emberley rose from the bench and set the baby to her feet. She smoothed her surcoat, composing herself, preparing to do what she must to keep both her and Gart alive. She knew all of Julian's men on sight and was preparing what she would say to them. They had come to take her to London and she would know why.

She was quite concerned, in truth, because any reason she could come up with was not a good one. With Brendt in one hand and Orin carrying Lacy, she made her way to the keep entry just in time to see one of Julian's senior sergeants mount the stairs.

She couldn't keep the dread from her heart as she watched the man approach.

CHAPTER TWELVE

AFTER HIDING OUT in the buttery until Romney was able to safely smuggle Gart through the postern gate, Gart fled to the forest south of Dunster sometime in the late afternoon. It was perfect cover in the heavily foliaged area. Shielded by the big oaks, he found a good vantage point from where he could watch the castle and spent the rest of the daylight watching the activity.

Everything at the fortress seemed normal. There were no groups of scouts running about and no real activity on the wall to speak of. Satisfied that no alarm had been raised by either his presence or escape, he was fairly convinced that Julian's party would depart sometime the next morning. Leaving the shelter of the trees, Gart regrouped with his men in town just after sunset. The town of Carhampton had several hostel establishments and they found a moderately large tavern and settled in.

Morose and moody, Gart drowned himself in cup after cup of ale while his men ate and played games of dice. Gart sat in the corner, watching his men, thinking on Emberley and the children and growing increasingly despondent. He had been living such a fool's dream for the past seven weeks, hidden away from the world. But reality had come fast and heavy, and he was still reeling. He wasn't ready to face it yet. He was so depressed he could hardly function.

The evening rolled on, people came and went from the smoky, smelly inn. Whores in the guise of serving wenches came by his table, offering him more drink and a suggestion of nocturnal activities, but Gart chased them away with his stony expression and disinterested manner. He couldn't stop thinking of Emberley's sweet body, of her smile, her gentle wit. Watching his men retreat from the inn with whores in their arms only fueled his loneliness. He missed Emberley desperately.

By midnight, he had imbibed copious amounts of alcohol and was fairly drunk but he didn't particularly care. He hoped it would make him pass out long enough to forget the torment in his heart. As midnight came and went, the inhabitants of the inn grew drunker around him and a few fights ensued. At one point, a pair of combatants came near his table and Gart lashed out an enormous boot, sending the pair flying. Once they regained their balance, they turned on him but one look at the enormous, drunk knight and they decided a counterattack would not be wise. They moved on to easier targets.

Finishing off his fourth large pitcher of ale, Gart finally sat with an empty cup, staring off into the room and wondering if he should try to get some sleep. He hadn't passed out yet and that disturbed him. Several of his men were still involved in a heated game of dice near the hearth and he listened to their cheers and jeers, bored and miserable. As he was summoning the will to find the innkeeper and secure a room for the night, the front door to the inn flew open, slamming back on its hinges.

Gart looked over, disinterested, until he saw that it was Kevin. Startled, he sat forward in his chair, his eyes wide on the man. Kevin caught the movement out of the corner of his eye, turning to catch sight of Gart. Before Gart could say a word, Kevin abruptly quit the inn and the door slammed shut behind him. Greatly puzzled and deeply concerned, Gart rose on unsteady legs and began to make his way over to the door. He hadn't quite reached the panel when it flew open again. Kevin was there, followed by Emberley and the children.

Shocked, Gart's reaction was to throw his arms around Emberley, who was carrying the sleeping Lacy. Emberley returned his furious kisses, tasting the ale on his lips.

"Gart!" she gasped as he smothered her face with kisses. "Are you well?"

He was very drunk and very emotional. An enormous hand went to her face, cupping it, while the other affectionately grasped Orin and Brendt.

"I am fine," he kissed her again. "What are you doing here? How did you escape Buckland's escort?"

Emberley could see how drunk he was. She was exhausted, frightened and more than shocked to see Gart's physical state. She had been looking for a rock to cling to at the end of her harrowing flight from Dunster and was stunned to see that Gart was less than strong. She passed a long glance at Kevin before replying.

"It was not difficult considering they are all asleep from their long ride from London," she gestured at Kevin. "Sir Kevin came to me with a plan this afternoon and we plotted our escape. We slipped from the postern gate an hour ago. The trouble was in finding you – we have been to four inns tonight already. We did not know where you had gone but we knew you would not have gone far."

He kissed her cheeks, her lips. "I could not go far away from you, not ever," he breathed, then looked at Kevin. "I can never thank you enough for risking yourself for me. I am deeply indebted to you."

Kevin's eyes glimmered impishly. "Aye, you are, and someday you will repay me handsomely."

Gart grinned at the man, both of them knowing that Gart would indeed pay his debt and then some. The bond of a knight was strong that way. Gart's attention moved back to Emberley when a strong, chill breeze gusted in through the open door.

"Bring the children inside by the fire, kitten," he told her. "It is too cold here by the door."

He started herding the sleepy children over to the hearth but Kevin stopped him. "We need to get clear of Dunster," he told him. "Buckland's men are asleep and that will buy us time until morning. We must leave immediately."

Gart was struggling with his inebriation. He wasn't thinking particularly clearly. "But the children need to sleep. Surely they are allowed a few hours of rest before we whisk them off to the Marches."

Kevin could see that Gart was fairly far gone with alcohol. "They can sleep on the road," he told him. "I brought your charger and mine but little else. We must ride for the Marches tonight."

"How did you remove my charger from the stables? He bites anything that moves."

Kevin kept looking around the room nervously. He was still in escape mode and feeling frustrated that Gart didn't feel his sense of urgency.

"It was not easy but I managed it," he told him. "I loaded all of your possessions, at least what we could find in your chamber. But there is no more time to delay, Gart. We must leave this moment. Do you understand me?"

Gart rubbed at his eyes, struggling to focus. When he opened his red-rimmed orbs, he could see the expression on Emberley's face. There was fear and disillusionment there. He'd never seen that expression before and knew he didn't like it. He suddenly felt very self-conscious and weak, and it was enough to shock him into a semblance of sobriety. He didn't like the look of disappointment in her eyes. He never wanted to see it again.

"I do," he nodded his head, rubbing his eyes again and focusing on Emberley. "Forgive me. You have found me doing the cowardly thing by drowning my sorrows in ale. I was so distressed after leaving this afternoon that… well, suffice it to say that I was attempting to ease my pain. Forgive me, kitten. I did not mean to disappoint you."

Emberley softened, sighing faintly as she put a hand to his cheek, which he kissed fervently. "You did not," she said. "But I am rather surprised to see you so drunk."

Gart lifted a lazy eyebrow in agreement. "Had I known you and de Lara would plan an escape, I would not have consumed every bit of ale in this place. I think I drank enough to fill a pond."

At his feet, Romney giggled. He looked at the boy, his eyes half-lidded, weaving dangerously. "Do you find that humorous, little man?"

Romney nodded firmly. "Can I get drunk, too?"

Gart made a face at him. "You may not," he rumbled, returning his attention to Emberley. "Already, I can feel my head pounding and it is not even the morrow. Let us ride before it grows any worse and my head falls off completely."

In spite of everything, Kevin had to grin at the man. "Are you sure you feel up to it?"

"We have no choice."

"True, but it would not do for you to fall off and crack your skull."

Gart snorted. "I swear that I will not fall off." He picked up Brendt when the child leaned against his leg, whining and rubbing his eyes sleepily. "Let us leave this place and never look back."

With that, he turned to a few of his men standing on the outskirts of the room and ordered them to gather the rest and meet at the southeast edge of town. As his men began to collect, he and Kevin took Emberley and the children out into the night.

It was cold and damp outside, a soft sea breeze wafting in the air. With Brendt now sleeping on his big shoulder, Gart listened to Kevin as the man ran through the list of what he was able to slip from Dunster – Gart's saddlebags, weapon, and most of his armor. Emberley had packed two large bags with items for her and the children, everything she could squeeze into the two satchels. Kevin also had a saddlebag that contained foodstuffs and other assorted items, as did Gart, but they realized that they were going to have to purchase a wagon or other means of transportation by the time they reached a safe distance. Right now, they were fleeing with what they could carry. It had to be swift and light.

Kevin mounted his blond charger and Gart handed him Romney and Orin – Orin sat to the front and Romney sat to the back. The boys both thought it was great fun riding on a charger and Gart even heard Romney try to coerce a dirk off of the knight just in case they needed to fight their way out of the village. It was just a ruse because Orin started rifling through one of the bags thrown across the front of the saddle.

Drunk or not, Gart saw what they were up to and snapped his fingers at the boys. They immediately ceased all covert activities at the sharp noise, eyes wide with feigned innocence. As Gart cast a lingering glare at Romney, Kevin puffed out his cheeks.

"They tried to rob me this afternoon when I entered the keep to speak with their mother," he said casually.

Gart sighed heavily. "Did they succeed?"

Romney interrupted, afraid that Gart would become angry with him. "We gave it back," he insisted. "Mother made us."

Gart pointed a finger at him. "I told you no more robbing," he said sternly. "You and I will have words about this later."

"Gart?" Orin called.

Gart looked at him. "What is it, Orin?"

"We will not do it again, I promisth."

Kevin fought off a smirk as both boys appeared contrite, fearful and defiant at the same time. Orin even gave Gart an innocent smile with his missing two front teeth but Gart didn't believe him for a minute. Casting the boys a final intimidating glance, he took Lacy from Emberley, who mounted Gart's black and white charger on her own since Gart had two sleeping toddlers on his shoulders. She took Lacy once she settled herself in the saddle and Gart handed Brendt up to her as well. Then he mounted, settling in behind her and wrapping a big arm around her as she held the sleeping babies.

Gart was feeling the sense of urgency now, struggling to shake off the alcohol. He had what he wanted and he would get them all clear of Dunster or die trying. He managed to pull an oilcloth from his saddlebags, one he usually used when it rained, and covered up Emberley and the sleeping children. Only Emberley's head remained above the cloth. Properly covered and secure, Kevin and Gart spurred their chargers towards the southeast end of town where they would meet up with the rest of Gart's men.

The die was now cast and there was no turning back. The moment

Gart mounted Emberley and the children, he had chosen his path in life and it would not be an easy one. Whatever was to come, he was prepared to face it. He would lie, kill, cheat or steal if it meant keeping Emberley and the children safe. All that mattered was they were together, come what may. He wondered if Erik would have seen it the same way.

Swords at the ready and the men on high alert, they embarked into the dark and misty night, heading for the dangerous Welsh Marches.

Chapter Thirteen

London

BELLHAM PLACE WAS a stone and mortar fortified manse approximately two miles from the heart of London situated along the River Thames. It had been in the de Lohr family for almost a century as a place of residence when the de Lohrs visited London. Surrounded by a well-designed garden that included every thorny bush or vine in existence, the prickly foliage was more of a deterrent to invasion or thieves than the enormous walls themselves. Huge strains of bougainvillea, blooming in brilliant colors of pink and purple, grew all over the house. The thorns on the plants were more than an inch long, sharp like a dagger. All of the de Lohr offspring had met with a run-in on those plants at one time or another. They all had war wounds from having done battle with Bellham's plants.

In spite of the prickly exterior, the interior was lush and comfortable. David had been in a sunny, upstairs study, reading a missive from his brother, when he heard the sounds of a charger in the yard. Rising from the desk, he peered outside into the courtyard to see Kevin de Lara on the approach. The missive ended up tossed back onto the desk as David made haste from the study. He was descending the stairs when a sweet female voice stopped him.

"David?" she called. "Sweetheart, where are you going?"

David paused on the bottom step as his wife, the Lady Emilie Hampton de Lohr, emerged from one of the upstairs bedrooms where she had been attempting to lull their two-year-old daughter, Christina, to sleep. Blond and beautiful, with big, brown eyes, Emilie smiled at her husband. David returned the gesture.

"I am stepping outside, love," he told her. "Not to worry. I am not going anywhere."

"I heard a horse," Emilie was coming towards the stairs. "Who has arrived?"

David could see Kevin dismounting his steed through the window. "De Lara," he told her. "I shall be outside if you need me."

Emilie descended the stairs, coming upon her husband and winding her soft hand into his. David kissed her on the cheek.

"May I come with you?" she asked softly. "It is such a lovely day outside."

David sighed agreeably. Emilie was the sweetest, most genuinely kind person he had ever met. She had such a soft manner about her, gentle and compassionate, without an ounce of disobedience or rancor in her personality. She was the most perfect person he knew and, consequently, he could never deny her anything, not even the slightest little question. He was a weakling and he knew it, but he didn't much care. He adored her.

"Very well," he kissed her hand, pulling her off the stairs with him. "I am anxious to hear what de Lara has to say."

Emilie followed him to the enormous front door. "Why?"

David shrugged. "To see if he was able to locate Gart, first and foremost. My men are due to sail for France in ten days and I want Gart at the head of the command."

Emilie shaded her eyes from the sun when David opened the door. "Gart would never disappoint you," she said. "He is your best knight. You have said so yourself."

David had no reason to dispute her statement, nor did he have any reason to be on his guard as de Lara approached him. He was looking forward to positive news in spite of the fact that he had sent Kevin to find Gart specifically to warn him of Buckland's return to Dunster. He assumed all had happened as it should because his knights had never failed him. Kevin saluted David sharply.

"My lord," he greeted, looking to Emilie and smiling at her. "Lady de Lohr, it is a pleasure to see you again."

David looked the man over. He looked particularly exhausted, having been gone from London almost a month. He appeared as if he had been riding every day of his travels. It was a disheveled state that forged the first blooms of concern in David's chest.

"You look weary and haggard, de Lara," he commented. "Were you able to find Forbes?"

Kevin took a deep breath, nodding. "He was at Dunster Castle as you had suspected, my lord."

The knight began to look uncomfortable, glancing at Emilie as if afraid to say anything more in her presence. David didn't like the hesitation at all and his concern mounted.

"And?" he pushed de Lara. "What happened? Did you warn him of Buckland's escort?"

Kevin took another deep breath, reasoning that he might as well tell his liege all of it. There was no point in holding back, for it would only enrage de Lohr. It wasn't as if he had a choice in the face of a direct question.

"I arrived less than an hour before Buckland's escort for Lady Emberley," he told him. "Gart was there, as you had suspected, and I relayed your messages. But… well, there is a problem, my lord."

David's eyebrows lifted. "What problem?"

Kevin hesitated. "It would seem that Gart… there is no simple way to tell you this so I will come out with it. Gart and the Lady Emberley de Moyon are in love. Gart would not permit Buckland's escort to take Lady Emberley and her children to London so I helped them to escape."

David stared at him. The shock in his expression was evident. "But…," he faltered and started again. "Gart swore to me that there was nothing more than casual concern towards the lady, as the sister of his best friend. He looked me in the eye and swore to me that he was not attempting to come between Buckland and his wife."

Kevin sighed in frustration. "Having spent the past few weeks with

Gart and Emberley, he had come to see the love between them and was naturally defensive of the pair, right or wrong.

"All I can tell you is this," he said quietly. "I have spent the better part of three weeks with Gart, the lady and her children. It is vastly apparent that Gart and the lady love each other a great deal and from what I have been told, Buckland is abusive and horrible to the woman. Moreover, Buckland has announced to all of England that he and the queen are lovers. Lady Emberley does not deserve such shame, my lord."

David's shock was turning to anger. "It is not your right or duty to decide such matters, Kevin," he said. "Gart is in a world of trouble and you along with him. How on earth could you assist him in this... this madness?"

Kevin wouldn't back down. "Because, quite simply, Buckland will kill him if he finds out. Gart is my friend. I cannot let that happen."

David was normally quick to temper, a reputation that was not in danger of dying this day. With a growl, he smacked his fist against his open palm, pacing away from his wife and Kevin to blow off the building steam. He whirled on Kevin, jabbing a finger at the man.

"Gart knows what trouble this will bring him," he hissed. "He swore to me that there was nothing between him and the lady. And now I find out he lied."

Kevin shook his head. "From what I was told, he did not lie to you. What he felt for the lady came well after you had left."

"He told you this?"

"He did. We discussed it."

"It does not matter," David threw up his hands. "He lied to me and now he is on the run with Baron Buckland's wife and children. Gart Forbes has never been a fool, not in the entire time I have known him, so for him to commit something so utterly stupid and deadly is beyond my comprehension. What in the hell is the man thinking?"

Kevin remained calm. "He had to take her into hiding, my lord," he said quietly. "She carries his child. If Buckland discovers this, he will kill her as well."

David's ranting came to an abrupt halt and he stared at Kevin, wide-eyed. "Sweet Jesus," he breathed. "Is this true?"

Kevin nodded, reaching up to remove his helm. His dark blond hair was matted with sweat and filth, and he ran a gloved hand across it to scratch at his scalp.

"While we traveled to Wales, Gart told me the entire story of his acquaintance with Lady Emberley. I was told that you were there on the last occasion that Buckland beat her," he said softly. "Gart said you tried to help but Buckland threatened you."

Some of David's anger left him. He sighed heavily. "I was there," he admitted sourly. "It is cruel and brutal, and something I would never engage in, but a husband has every right to beat his wife so long as he does not kill her."

This time, Emilie gasped. She had been listening to the entire story, wide-eyed and silent, but her husband's comments compelled her to speak.

"David," she said reproachfully. "That is a terrible thing to say."

David looked at his wife and lifted his shoulders. "It is true," he said. "As weak and foolish as it sounds, it is true. I should have known Gart was feeling more for Lady Emberley than he let on simply by the way he was acting towards her. He almost killed Buckland the night we arrived because Buckland struck his wife in Gart's presence. I should have… known."

He shook his head and averted his gaze, truly at a loss with the situation. With his fury abating, now he was feeling despondent and apprehensive. Sensing this, Emilie turned to Kevin.

"Where did Gart go?" she asked gently. "You said that you helped him to escape. Where is he?"

Kevin passed a glance at David before speaking, hesitantly, but knowing he had to answer her question. "To the Welsh Marches. He is with my father."

David looked sharply at him. "Viscount Trelystan?"

Kevin nodded. "My father was more than happy to house a fugitive of the king's ally."

David looked sick, making a face and rolling his eyes miserably. "This is my fault," he grunted. "I should not have allowed Gart to remain behind with Lady Emberley. He said he simply wanted to get reacquainted with his dead friend's sister but I should have known there was more to it. Buckland is going to come down around me now, for everything."

Kevin shook his head. "Buckland's escort never, at any point, saw Gart," he told him. "I made sure of that. For all they know, the lady and her children simply fled the castle during the night. Gart's name was never mentioned nor was he sighted."

David waved him off irritably. "It does not matter," he said. "Buckland will remember what happened when Gart was at Dunster and will assume, correctly, that the man is somehow involved in his wife's disappearance. Do you know why de Moyon sent for his wife and children to join him in London? Did you hear the foulest of reasons before you left?"

Kevin shook his head and David continued, disgust in his tone. "He sent for them because, as rumor has it, the queen has set her sights on another lover and Buckland hopes to make her jealous. He assumes having his wife at his side will accomplish that. But now she is missing and Buckland will remember how Forbes acted towards the woman. He will presume the man is responsible for her disappearance and that presumption will bring him to me."

Emilie could see how torn her husband was and she went to him, putting a soft hand on his arm. "I have heard the same thing," she said gently. "Isabella has made it clear that her interest is in a French mercenary, a friend of her father's. It is all the gossip mills can speak of. Buckland is falling out of favor."

David sighed heavily. "It will only make de Moyon bent on blood," he said quietly. "He will be shamed by his wife's disappearance and his vengeance will know no limits."

Emilie stroked his blond head. "When he comes to you, you will tell him that you do not know where Gart is," she said firmly. "You were not involved in this and it is not your fault."

Kevin interrupted. "My lord, if I may," he said, watching David and Emilie look at him. "Gart is coming to London as we speak. He wanted to settle Emberley and the children first before leaving them, but he is coming to see you. He is coming to tell you everything himself."

David rolled his eyes again. "Dear God," he muttered. "He is going to get himself killed. Buckland will have him arrested the moment he sets foot in the city."

"Buckland will not know he has anything to do with his wife's disappearance."

De Lohr looked at the man as if he were an idiot. "Are you serious? After everything I just told you, you do not believe that de Moyon will be intelligent enough to figure out what has happened? Either you are a massive fool or I am."

Kevin didn't take offense. He propped his helm up on the saddle as a groom approached to take his charger away, feeling increasingly weary. The entire venture had him physically as well as emotionally drained.

"I will not tell you any more than I already have, my lord," he said quietly. "That way, when Buckland asks you what you know of the situation, you can be truthful and tell him that you do not know where Gart has gone. But I will tell you this, Lady Emberley is a sweet and wonderful woman, and the stories I have heard about Buckland's treatment of her makes me want to kill him myself. I will die before I tell Buckland anything about Gart or the lady."

David knew he would, too. De Lara was a man of great honor, honesty and strength. He waved the man off.

"It will not come to that," he said, all of the fire and agitation gone out of him. Then he looked at Kevin. "Did you tell Gart that he is due to leave for France next week?"

"I did, my lord. That is why he is coming to see you."

David thought on the great implications of that visit, none of which he was particularly thrilled to entertain. He couldn't see Gart wanting to leave the lady and her children, especially to fight for the lady's husband's lover. He shook his head in resignation. The situation grew more complicated by the minute. Emilie, seeing that her husband was mentally spent after such devastating news and that de Lara was so exhausted that he was about to collapse, intervened.

"Kevin, go and gain some respite," she told him. "You look as if you are utterly spent. We will speak more of this later."

Kevin nodded gratefully and turned for the rear of the manse, the back entrance used by servants and soldiers. There was a kitchen back there and cool, comfortable rooms with fluffy beds. He was dreaming of one now. As the knight wandered away, Emilie turned to her husband.

"I will say this to you, husband," she murmured, moving to the man and winding her hands around his arm. "You and I know what it is like to truly love someone. If Gart has found true love in the arms of an abused woman, then we cannot fault him. Look at the situation in his terms – what if I was married to another who beat me terribly? How would you feel? Would you walk away or would you do something about it? Gart apparently has the courage to do something about it and I find that sweet and admirable."

David looked at her a moment before kissing her soft cheek. "I do not fault the man true love," he responded. "But facts are facts – Lady Emberley is married to Baron Buckland. Gart, at the very least, could be tried for thievery if this situation gets out of control. But I suppose we shall hear the whole story when he arrives so there is nothing to do but wait."

Emilie knew he was right, but she was more than curious to hear the tale. She had known Gart Forbes for four years and the man was the consummate knight, always in control and always professional. He was big, strong and frightening. To hear that he fell in love with a married woman was something of a shock. She would have never guessed the man capable of such emotion.

For Gart's sake, as well as her husband's, she truly hoped Buckland never discovered the truth of it.

CHAPTER FOURTEEN

"Why can I not go with you?" Romney was on the verge of a full-blown tantrum. "I can be your squire."

Gart was patiently packing his bags. "I do not need a squire."

"I can tend your horse, then. I will not eat much, I swear it." Romney, his wooden sword in hand, went to Gart and put his face between Gart and the bag the man was packing. When Gart looked down, all he could see were big, blue eyes staring up at him. "Can I please come with you? *Please?*"

Gart sighed. "If you go with me, who will take care of your mother?" he ran a big hand over the boy's brown hair. "If I am gone, there is only one man I would trust with her protection and that is you. Would you disappoint me so?"

Romney's face screwed up in a terrible frown. As he was thinking of a serious reply, Emberley entered the chamber with her arms laden with freshly washed garments. She went to the big bed in the center of the room where Gart was packing his bag and carefully laid them out across the heavy wool coverlet.

"These are dry," she told Gart as she peeled the top layer off, a tunic, and began to carefully roll it up. "I have six of them. There are four more drying in the sun."

Gart glanced over at the stack. "Is my padded tunic in that group?"

She nodded. "It is at the bottom. It was very dirty and required more cleaning than the others. Have you never cleaned it, Gart?"

"Never. It has years of sweat and blood on it."

She made a disgusted face as Gart moved around the side of the bed, around the pouting Romney, and fingered the padded tunic at the bottom of the pile.

"It is soft," he looked at her, surprised. "How did you accomplish that?"

She smiled. "You mean it does not feel like a prickly patch? I must have cleaned it incorrectly."

He grinned at her and carefully pulled the tunic out from underneath the pile. As he inspected the seams and wear of the tunic, Brendt and Orin rushed into the room and dove onto the bed. The neat pile of clean tunics scattered as the boys jumped about and Emberley screeched.

"Orin!" she grabbed the boy by the arm and pulled him off the bed. "Brendt, get down. Go play in your chamber."

Brendt was gleefully bouncing on the scattered tunics until Gart grasped him around the waist and put him on the floor. Then he was unhappy and started swatting Romney with his wooden sword. Romney, upset because Gart would not take him along on his impending trip to London, grabbed his youngest brother by the collar.

"Stop hitting me," he told him. "Come on – let us go somewhere else."

"Where?" Orin wanted to know.

Romney was leading his brothers from the room, whispering to them as he went. Gart's ears were peaked to their clandestine hisses even as he and Emberley straightened out the pile of mussed tunics. He turned to the boys as they neared the chamber door.

"I told you what would happen should you engage in robbery again," he said pointedly, cocking an eyebrow at the three brothers when they paused in the doorway to look at him. "You have already tried to rob Lord Stephan, twice, in his own keep. One more infraction and I will blister your backsides. Is this in any way unclear?"

Romney sighed, extremely unhappy with the way the day was panning out. "We did not rob him."

"Rom, I have warned you about lying."

"I am not lying," Romney insisted. "We were playing and accidentally poked him with our swords. We did not rob him."

Gart wasn't falling for it. "I suppose the fact that you tried to cut his purse from his belt was an accident, too," he shook his head. "If you ever want to be a knight, you will cease this behavior. Knights are not thieves and they are not liars."

Unhappy, confused and defiant, the three of them quit the chamber and crossed the hall to the chamber on the opposite side of the landing. It was their bedchamber and their playroom combined. Stephan de Lara, Viscount Trelystan and Lord de Lara, had gladly given the chamber to the four de Moyon children. It was the same chamber his two boys, Sean and Kevin, had occupied in their youth. The old man was thrilled to hear the laughter and clamor within the old walls of Trelystan Castle again, even when three of his young guests had tried to rob him.

Emberley and Gart could hear the boys playing in the other room, listening to battle cries and mysterious items crashing to the floor. Twice, they heard something fall as the boys wrestled and twice, Gart looked to Emberley to see if they should go check on them, but she merely shook her head and continued rolling tunics. He assumed that if she wasn't worried, he shouldn't be either. Besides, there was no screaming so all must be well. He was still getting used to having three lively boys around. He admired her calm and acquired patience.

They had arrived at the enormous border castle of Trelystan Castle four days prior after the harrowing five day flight from Dunster. They had arrived exhausted and hungry, and after Kevin explained the situation to his father, the old man was more than happy to provide Gart and Emberley safe haven. He hated the king, his queen, and everything about the throne so as Kevin predicted, he was quite happy to have the refugees. Their reasons for their arrival didn't matter to him in the least. He seemed more than eager to have guests.

Gart began to see at the onset that Stephan was an old and lonely man, which partially accounted for the fact that the man was so happy to have visitors. He lived rather sparingly, with only a few servants in the keep, but a mountain of soldiers at the castle. Gart guessed around eight hundred and he was told there were just a little over nine hundred men. The other two castles, Caradoc and Hyssington, carried slightly more. In all, Viscount Trelystan had nearly three thousand men at his disposal, all along the Welsh border where things could be moody and volatile. It was an impressive show of power and Gart began to feel some safety at the sheer numbers. Not even Buckland carried that many men.

With their arrival at Trelystan, he now had time to breathe and think. Before he could get involved in too much reflection, however, Kevin reminded him that he was expected in London in about two weeks to lead de Lohr's men into France. Gart found it fairly ironic that he was expected to support a man whose wife he had essentially stolen, but he didn't linger on life's little ironies. Buckland deserved worse.

Gart hadn't said much to Emberley about the duties expected of him as one of de Lohr's commanders, mostly because he didn't want to upset her after such a strenuous trip from Dunster. He had spoken of his orders once before so he knew that she was aware of them, but she'd never said a word about it. Even so, he knew he could not delay too much longer before heading to London. He also knew he had to make things clear with her about what was to happen and the future of their life together.

When the subject eventually came up, he again mentioned his need to leave for London, casually, specifically designed so Emberley would not be overly worried about it. He only mentioned his need to speak with de Lohr face to face and naught much else. His plan to keep her calm had so far worked and Emberley had even offered to help him pack for his trip. They found themselves in the big chamber that they shared, packing up his clothing and other items to take with him on his trip. As the boys banged about in the other chamber, he tucked his padded tunic into his saddlebag and sat on the bed.

He watched Emberley as she carefully rolled his clean tunics, packing them into his saddlebags. She was so graceful and fluid in her movements that he simply liked to watch her. She was enchanting.

"I should take the remaining tunics," he said softly. "I tend to change frequently."

She didn't look at him as she neatly packed in the garments. "I know," she said. "I have never seen a man change his clothing so much."

"I do not like to wear clothes that are too soiled."

She lifted an eyebrow at him. "Yet your padded tunic, the one you wear beneath your armor, has not been washed in ages until today. Why is that?"

"Do you really want to know?"

"I do."

"I do not think you will like the answer."

"Tell me."

He sighed faintly, reaching out to take her hand. "Because…," he paused, playing with her fingers. "Because it was the tunic I was wearing when Eric perished. It still had his blood on it."

Emberley's expression turned to one of horror. Her hands flew to her mouth and tears immediately began to pop out of her eyes. "And you let me wash it?" she was deeply upset. "Why did you not tell me? I would not have touched it."

He reached up, calmly soothing her. He eased her onto his lap, his big arms wrapping around her.

"It is time," he acknowledged, hugging her gently. "I clung to it to remind me that we are mortal and life can end tomorrow. It was a superstitious, bitter reminder. But with you… you show me that life is worth living and infinite in its joy. I wanted you to wash it because I wanted you to touch it. Now it has your scent on it and not your brother's. It comforts me. Does that make sense?"

She wiped at her face, calmed by his words. "It does," she looked at him with her big, blue eyes. "Are you sure?"

He smiled, kissing her damp cheek. "Of course," he said. "Now, we must have a serious talk about what the next few weeks will bring."

She nodded her head, wiping away the last of the tears. "You are going to London to see de Lohr. What will you tell him about what has happened?"

Gart took a deep, thoughtful breath. "Kevin has gone on ahead of me and has already broken the news, I am sure, so my visit is simply to confirm it. More than that, you are aware that my original visit to Dunster was because Buckland was trying to coerce de Lohr into providing support for Isabella's lands in France." He looked up at her, his chin resting on her arm. "When Kevin came to Dunster to warn me off of Buckland's escort, he also told me that I am still expected to head up de Lohr's contingent to France."

Emberley was calm. "I know."

"How do you know?"

"Kevin told me."

Gart lifted an eyebrow. "He did?" he said. "When did he do this?"

"We had time to talk on the journey here."

Gart frowned. "You did? Where was I when you were talking to him?"

She could sense jealousy and she grinned. "Playing with the boys, mostly, and loving every minute of it. De Lara was simply making conversation with a lonely woman while you were off rough-housing."

Gart gave her a lingering glare, much like he did with the boys when he doubted their sincerity. But her grin broadened and he gave up, shrugging his big shoulders.

"Well," he said. "I suppose there is nothing else I can tell you, then. De Lara seems to have told you everything."

She shifted, wrapping her arms around his big neck. "You can tell me what you plan to do once you reach London."

He wrapped his arms around her waist, gazing into her beautiful eyes. He kissed the tip of her nose.

"I will ask to be released from my oath," he said quietly. "And then I will ride to Albemarle and demand my inheritance. I have already spoken to the viscount and he has agreed to allow you and the children to remain here, well protected, until I return."

Emberley was trying to be brave, trying not to think about all of the obstacles facing them, but it was a struggle. "When do you suppose that will be?"

"It is difficult to say," he replied honestly. "But it will not be any longer than absolutely necessary. I will return for you, kitten, I swear it."

She gazed at him and he could see the thoughts rolling through her mind. In spite of his effort to keep the conversation light, he could sense the emotions rolling in like a fog. The feelings covered them, bound them, creating anxiety at what they were about to face and a sense of longing at being separated.

"I do not doubt that you will," she said softly. "But I fear what will happen if de Lohr will not release you from your oath."

"He will not have a choice."

She shook her head at him. "Gart, you have worked many years to achieve your post. David de Lohr is a powerful baron whose brother is the Earl of Hereford and Worcester. You are part of the de Lohr battle machine and that is not something to be taken lightly. If you walk away from that without permission, your reputation will be damaged forever."

He wasn't surprised that she understood a good deal about the knighthood and politics. She was a bright woman. He gave her a gentle squeeze.

"I do not see any reason why de Lohr would deny me," he replied quietly. "As much as he has done for me, I have done equal for him."

"What do you mean?"

He shrugged, looking down to her hands cradled in her lap and reaching to collect one. He brought it to his lips as he spoke.

"I have served de Lohr for six years and before that, I served William d'Aubigney of Belvoir," he said. "D'Aubigney was a supporter of the Archbishop of Canterbury, who was battling for Potigny Castle in

Burgundy. I served in France for a year and was subsequently joined by David de Lohr for a time, at one point, saving his life from assassins sent by the king. It is a complicated tale but suffice it to say that David asked for my fealty and rewarded me handsomely for saving his life. Since then, I have been his top commander. I have served him well."

"He will not want to let you go."

"I am sure he will not. But he is not unreasonable."

She watched him as he kissed her fingers. "What if he wants you to go to France before he releases you?"

He sighed. "He will not."

"But what if he does?"

He cupped her face in his two enormous hands, kissing her cheek. "Kitten, you worry overly," he smiled at her. "Trust me that I will do what is necessary in order to return to you."

She couldn't return his smile. There was too much apprehension in her heart. "What about Julian?" she whispered, succumbing to her fears. "Surely the escort has returned to London by now to tell him that I have disappeared. He will...."

He cut her off, kissing her soft mouth. "I do not want you to worry about that," he told her firmly. "You will let me worry about Buckland. I will do what needs to be done in order that you and I should enjoy a safe and comfortable life."

She eyed him, thinking on the Gart she knew, had known, of her brother and the adventures the two used to have. She had heard stories as a girl, from her parents, though Erik or Gart would not confirm them. She cocked her head after a moment, thoughtfully.

"I seem to remember that even newly knighted, you and Eric had seen battle against Prince John twelve years ago," she said. "It was in the fall sometime, I think. I had only seen you and Erik for a couple of months after returning from Chepstow until you were off again."

Gart nodded faintly. "We fostered at Kenilworth and the bishop called us into service in a skirmish against John," he remembered that battle with a smile. "It was near Oxford and the first true battle that Erik and I fought together. We were a fearsome sight."

She smiled because he was. "I remember when you both came back to Morton," she said. "The first night back, Erik made my mother ill with tales of your battle prowess, as I recall, telling her of a man whose head you tore clean from his body."

Gart just looked at her and smiled and Emberley's hand trailed down his right arm and lifted his hand. His fist was nearly as large as her head and she inspected the scarred knuckles, the calloused palms. They were powerful, skilled hands.

"He told the truth, did he not?" she asked softly.

He bit off his smile, modestly. "Does it matter?"

She looked at him. "Tell me the truth."

He sighed, smile fading as he met her gaze. "It is one of many skills I have."

She gazed deeply into his eyes, her expression intense. "Gart, I want you to swear to me that you will not kill Julian unless it is in self-defense. No matter how much I hate the man, he is not worth the risk."

His smile was gone. "What risk?"

She lifted her eyebrows at him as if he were daft. "If you were found out, you would be executed for such a thing and Julian would yet again ruin my life. He would take you from me and I could not live with that."

Gart wasn't pleased by her statement but, deep down, he knew she was right. Eventually, it would get around that Gart Forbes had absconded with Baron Buckland's wife and if Julian turned up dead, all fingers would point to him. He wanted to live a safe and healthy life with Emberley and the children, without Julian hanging over their shoulders, but killing the man would only exacerbate the issue.

Truth be told, he was actually considering killing the man to be rid of him. He was vile and evil and deserved nothing less for the way he had treated Emberley. His thought had nothing to do with ridding himself of a rival. He was eliminating something that caused pain and horror to Emberley. But her soft plea had him reconsidering.

He pulled her into a warm, soft embrace, his face tucked into the crook of her neck. "Do not worry, kitten," he whispered, kissing her neck. "I will do what is best for all of us. You must trust me."

"I do. I always have. But I am understandably worried."

"No need," he nuzzled her. "All will work out as it should, I swear it."

She sighed with resignation, her arms tightening around him. "I love you, Gart."

"And I love you, deeply and for always. When I return, it will be to marry you."

Emberley didn't know how to respond to that. With Julian still alive, she had no idea how he would accomplish such a thing even though she wished for it, as he did, with all her heart. But Gart seemed confident that everything would work out in their favor so she did not dispute him. To do so would have been to doubt his word.

All she could do now was hug him tightly and pray.

CHAPTER FIFTEEN

Two weeks later
Bellham Place, London

EMILIE WAS SEATED in the lavish reception hall of Bellham, enjoying the bright sunlight that streamed in through the great Norman arched windows. She was working on embroidery for a dress for her daughter as the Lady Christina Louisa Amalia de Lohr played on the floor at her feet with a fat, orange cat. The cat was also enjoying the warmth beaming in through the windows, its tail snapping back and forth as the baby tried to grab it. The blond-haired, blue-eyed cherub would squeal with delight when she captured the tail and the cat would narrow its eyes irritably. But the fat, dumb cat wouldn't move. Then the tail would snap free and the game would begin again.

Emilie grinned as she alternately watched her daughter and paid attention to her sewing. It was a peaceful, brilliant morning when she began to hear the thunder of hooves approaching from the road. She wasn't close enough to the window to look and she wasn't particularly curious about who the visitors were so she stayed focused on her sewing. The horses drew closer and she could hear male voices in the courtyard. Continuing on with the red ladybug she was stitching, she stabbed herself in the finger when someone pounded loud enough on the front door to startle her right out of the chair.

The cat scattered and her daughter jumped, frightened, and started to cry. Emilie swooped down on her daughter and picked the little girl up, comforting her, as David suddenly appeared from a neighboring solar. He held out a hand to his wife, indicating she remain in the reception room and away from the door. Emilie sank back, comforting her sobbing child, as David opened the heavy oak door.

"Where is Forbes?" Julian boomed.

David wasn't surprised to see Buckland standing on his doorstep with several heavily armed men. In fact, he wondered what had taken the man so long to come. Kevin, having been in the solar with David discussing the logistics for the troop movement to France, suddenly appeared with his broadsword in his hand, positioning himself next to his liege protectively. But Julian ignored the armed knight. He was focused on de Lohr.

"Tell me where Forbes is!" he screamed.

David was calm. "Welcome to Bellham, Julian. Why do you want Gart Forbes?"

Julian's teeth were clenched like a maniac. "Give him to me, do you hear? I will tear this place apart looking for him if you do not present him to me!"

David was starting to lose his humor. "You do not come to my home and make demands," he growled. "If you cannot remember your manners, then I shall throw you bodily from my property and you can return at such time when you are better behaved."

Julian's small, brown eyes bugged crazily. "You are aiding a criminal?"

David's expression was droll. "I am aiding no one," he said. "If you calmed down and told me what the trouble was, perhaps I would know what you were asking. As it is, I have a madman on my doorstep screaming incoherently."

Julian was so angry that he was sweating. Veins bulged and teeth gnashed. With a growl, he grabbed one of the men standing slightly behind him, thrusting him forward.

"Tell him what you told me," Julian demanded. "Tell him!"

The soldier looked uncertain and exhausted. He was clad in Buckland's colors of brown and yellow with well-made mail. He was older, seasoned, as he gazed steadily at de Lohr.

"My lord," he said calmly. "I have just returned from Dunster Castle. I was sent to escort Lord de Moyon's wife and children to London, but after we arrived, they disappeared without a trace. In fact…," he caught sight of Kevin standing next to de Lohr. "That knight was at Dunster. I saw him the day we arrived but he, too, disappeared."

David didn't outwardly react but inside, he was cursing up a storm. He turned to Kevin, quite casually, knowing that Kevin must surely be kicking himself to have been sighted by one of the only people who had seen him at Dunster. Yet, he could not have known. Neither one of them could have. There was nothing left to do now but try to keep from digging themselves into a hole and incriminating Gart.

"My knight was traveling and since Buckland is an ally, he stopped at Dunster for respite," he said evenly, then spoke to Kevin. "De Lara, did you see Lady de Moyon?"

Kevin nodded without hesitation. "I did, my lord."

Julian was shrieking. "Where is my wife?"

Kevin looked him in the eye. "I do not have her, my lord. But I did see her at Dunster."

"Did you speak with her? Did she say anything about Gart Forbes?"

"Why would she say anything to me about Forbes?" Kevin countered. "I saw the woman once in the hall, my lord." *And once in the bailey, and once fleeing the postern gate….*

Kevin was walking a very fine line, not wanting to outright lie to the baron but compelled to answer the man's questions. Julian had stepped inside the door and was now practically in his face.

"Did you see Gart Forbes at Dunster?" he demanded.

Kevin met his gaze steadily, wondering how he was going to get around a direct question with no good answer. Before he could answer, David intervened.

"I told you that I ordered Gart back to Denstroude Castle," he said, not entirely a fabrication. He *had* ordered the man back to Denstroude when he finished his business at Dunster. "Why are you so certain he is responsible for your wife's disappearance, anyway? Perhaps the woman simply ran off? It is not unheard of."

Julian was so furious that spittle sprayed from his mouth. "Because Forbes tried to seduce her the night he arrived at Dunster," he accused. "He tried to kill me when I attempted to protect what was mine. You were there, de Lohr. You saw him try to tear my head off. The man is truly insane."

David was struggling not to lose his patience at Julian's ridiculous twist on the story. The man was self-serving and pleased to be made the victim in all of this. David couldn't help the anger rising in his chest.

"What I saw was a chivalrous knight protecting a lady from your brutality," David stepped close to Julian when the man's mouth flew open in outrage, bumping into him and pushing him in the direction of the door. "You hit the lady twice in our presence and had I been faster, I would have been the one to punish you. It is a weak and foolish man that beats his wife, Buckland. Gart did nothing but champion the sister of his long dead friend and if I were you, I would stop looking to blame someone for your wife's disappearance. You are the only person to blame for the way you have treated her. Perhaps she ran off because she could no longer stand the thought of being with a husband who openly cavorts with his lover."

Julian was verging on a hysteria attack. "You have no right to judge me, de Lohr," he hissed. "You and your pious brother are nothing but rebels in disguise. You served Richard against John and...."

"And you are having conjugal relations with the king's wife. Perhaps I should hold you here and send for the king. I am sure he would be very interested to speak with you."

Julian exploded, lifting a hand to strike David, but David was faster. He slugged Julian in the mouth, sending the man reeling into the wall. Julian's men began to unsheathe their swords and Kevin leapt forward, slamming the door and bolting it before they could rush forward. Meanwhile, David moved to Julian and yanked the man off the floor by his tunic. David's sky blue eyes were blazing.

"If you ever make an attempt to strike me again, I will kill you," he seethed. "Listen to me and listen well, leave Gart Forbes alone. He did nothing more than befriend a lonely, brutalized woman. If your wife is missing, then it is your own damnable fault for being such a reprehensible husband. Go back to your queen and look elsewhere for support for her lands in France, for I am officially withdrawing my support and the support of my brother. I would rather have an enemy of you than an ally because I do not associate with filth, de Moyon. And you are most definitely filth."

Julian was missing two teeth, bleeding profusely from the mouth. He snarled and spit at David, trying to scratch him, but David slammed him up against the wall and nearly knocked him unconscious.

"Do you hear me?" David growled. "You are no longer my ally. If I hear that you have attempted any transgression against me or Gart Forbes, or any other ally or man under my command, I will come for you personally."

Julian clawed at the fist that held him. "You will regret this, de Lohr," he spat, blood flying onto David's hand. "You will regret everything."

David wasn't going to respond to his madness. He pulled him to the door, unbolted it, and opened wide the panel. He tossed Julian out onto his men.

"Get him out of my sight," he barked. "Leave my property before I have my army down around you."

With that, David slammed the door and sent Kevin out the back entrance, going for the outbuildings were David housed his soldiers. There where at least one hundred men on the grounds and he wanted them on alert. David stood at the door, listening to Julian rage, intermingled with the softer voices of his soldiers. From what he could tell, the voices were fading away.

He caught a glimpse of yellow from the corner of his eye, turning to see Emilie standing in the reception room doorway with Christina clutched against her. Emilie's eyes were wide with shock at what had happened and David left the door to go to her, pulling her and the baby into his arms.

"All is well, love," he kissed her forehead. "He is leaving."

Emilie was shaken, verging on tears. "That terrible, terrible man," she sniffed. "What are you going to do?"

David smiled at his daughter when she reached up and grabbed at his nose. He kissed the little fingers.

"Not to worry," he told his wife vaguely, mostly because he didn't have an answer for her. "Men like Julian are an annoyance and little more."

"But he did what you said he would do," she persisted. "He has come to blame you for his wife's disappearance."

David could only nod in agreement, thinking on the trouble they would now be in for. His brother was due to visit London in a few days and he had to apprise the man of the situation immediately. Kissing Emilie one last time, he gently released her and went to one of the long lancet windows to see the activity outside. He could see Julian and his men mounting their horses, and Kevin and several de Lohr men ensuring they rode for the gates. He could hear Julian screaming threats as his party thundered away from the manse.

The group passed out of David's line of sight but he continued to stand at the window, watching Kevin and his soldiers as they formed a defensive line around the front of the manse. There were at least seventy men now, protecting the house from Julian and his madness, waiting for the man to clear the main gates. Another twenty men were running after Julian's party to close the gates when he left.

David breathed a sigh of relief and turned from the window. He was wondering how he was going to explain all of this to his brother, the extremely powerful Earl of Hereford and Worcester. Christopher de Lohr had served Richard the Lionheart during the Crusade to The Levant and had quickly established himself as the king's mightiest warrior. He had even earned himself a nickname, *the Lion's Claw*. A lion, even a Lionheart, was only as deadly as his claws, and Christopher had been exceedingly deadly. He still was.

His brother was, even now, on his way from his seat of Lioncross Abbey to Bellham, bringing troops that would reinforce Buckland's numbers in France. David had sent word to his brother when he had left Dunster to send men and material for Buckland's cause. Now, David didn't relish the thought of telling him what had become of his alliance with Baron Buckland. He knew his brother would not be pleased.

David's thoughts were interrupted by a shout from the courtyard. He returned to the window, quickly, to see his men bolting from their strategic positions at the front of the manse. They were running towards the front gates as fast as they could. Concerned, David made haste to the front door.

"Where are you going?"

Emilie, having recently regained her seat and her sewing, was frightened anew at the sight of her husband running to the front door. David waved her off.

"Stay here and bolt the door," he told her. "Do not open it for anyone but me or Kevin. Is that clear?"

Emilie nodded fearfully and David threw open the front door, noting quickly that there was some kind of skirmish going on at his front gate. He raced into the solar and collected a sword from the small armory closet that was there. Running back at the front door, he passed by his fearful wife as he quit the manse. He heard her slam the door and throw the bolt behind him.

As David raced to the front gates, he truly had no idea what he would find. All he knew was that there was some kind of battle going on. He could hear shouts and see men pounding one another. Fast as lightning and fearless, David plunged into the fray, having no idea what he was fighting for. He tended to fight first, ask questions later. But the sight of a snapping, kicking charger, riderless, caught his attention. He recognized the beast as someone tried to corral it. In a panic, he began looking around for the horse's rider.

It was Gart's charger.

IT HAD BEEN a long ride to Bellham Place, the de Lohr residence in London. The weather from the Marches had been terrible and he had ridden through driving rainstorms for three solid days. Mud was his daily companion, up to his horse's knees in the black and mucky stuff. He had stopped only to rest the horse and eat, plowing through the wet, green plains north of Salisbury and on across the softly rolling hills as he approached London.

He'd stopped the night before arriving in London at a livery he had patronized before, a big place with lots of fresh straw and comfortable for the horses. He'd put his big charger in an end stall and stretched out on a pile of hay in the corner of the stall, lulled to sleep by the sound of his horse chomping on grain and grass.

When he awoke a few hours later, the horse was still eating and he had to grin at the beast. The horse would eat until it exploded so he got up, brushed down his horse, put the saddle back on, and was along his way.

He calculated that he would arrive in Bellham around noon and he was precise in his estimate. It was just the nooning hour as he trekked down the shady, tree-lined road that led to the great gates of Bellham, the sounds of birds and the soft clip-clop of his horse the only sounds in his ears. Then he noticed a group of men leaving Bellham, soldiers, with one man leading the pack. The man was bellowing unintelligible words.

Gart couldn't tell what was happening until he was nearly upon the group and then, with a jolt of shock, he recognized Julian. It was Julian who had been doing the screaming and Gart didn't have to guess why. He also didn't have to guess at the man's presence at Bellham. Frankly, he was a little shocked to cross paths with the man but the truth was that, at some point, he had expected it. He had planned for it. Just not so soon.

Gart's helm was on but his visor was up. It was too late to slam it down because Julian, unfortunately, had already noticed him. He was screaming something about making de Lohr pay and hurling curses. Gart reined his charger as far to the right as he could, trying to stay out of Julian's way because the man was all over the road. His poor horse was frothy and excited. But Julian fixed Gart in the eye and the man's jaw dropped. The disbelief in his expression was evident, a stroke of luck in the most unexpected of places. He began hollering at the top of his lungs, pointing in Gart's direction.

"It is him!" he screamed, his voice cracking. "Forbes is here! He is here!"

Gart quickly assessed the escort with Julian. There were at least ten men, perhaps more. They were all scrambling and it was difficult to gauge an exact count. Gart didn't stop to try and talk with Julian because he knew it would do no good. There was nothing to do but face the man head on. Unsheathing his broadsword, he was focused on the two men rushing him on horseback when something hit him from his blind side. Knocked squarely in the head, he lost his balance and toppled onto the ground.

Bordering on unconsciousness, Gart could hear weapons being drawn around him. He could hear men snapping, shouting, and somewhere in the middle of it was Julian's shrill voice. He realized he still had his broadsword in his hand and he brought it up, slashing at men near him. He struggled to get to his knees, shaking off the buzzing in his head as he labored to defend himself.

Men were kicking him and pummeling him. His slashing broadsword made contact with someone because he felt the strike followed by a scream. He tried to get to his knees but there were too many around him, overwhelming him.

Since he was covered in armor, the blows weren't doing any real damage but the initial strike to the head still had him reeling. He was starting to feel some rage at having been attacked, building as he realized it was him against a dozen armed men, and the *sach*, the madman, began to make an appearance. The rage began to grow, rising up through his legs to his chest until it reached his head. It was insanity unleashed.

He grabbed the leg nearest his head and he twisted the man's leg brutally, flipping him onto the dirt. As the soldier screamed in pain, Gart dropped his broadsword to the ground and rolled to his knees. Massive fists began striking men in the vulnerable pelvic area and he sent at least two men down with blows to the groin. Staggering to his feet, he took out another two soldiers with savage blows to the face.

The heat of fury was rolling through him. His face was red and sweaty. One soldier ran at him and he grabbed the man around the neck with one hand, using his other to twist his head so hard that his neck snapped. Bones crumbled in Gart's iron grip and he dropped the dead soldier, moving in for another.

Buckland's men began to see that Gart was bent on murder and they withdrew every weapon in their arsenal, daggers and broadswords, moving towards Gart with the intention of killing him. It was no longer a case of simply beating the man senseless. Gart saw the weapons and knew the battle was about to get even more lethal. He spied his broadsword on the ground several feet away and made haste in its direction.

Before he could retrieve his weapon, Kevin was suddenly in his midst, intercepting Buckland's soldiers. Several de Lohr soldiers also appeared and soon there was a vicious brawl going on. Gart watched David jump feet-first into the fracas, broadsword swinging. David wasn't the biggest man in a fight, or even the strongest, but he was definitely the fastest. His speed was truly something to behold. As Buckland's soldiers found themselves swarmed with de Lohr men, Gart searched for Julian.

He saw him on the edge of the fight, screaming at his men. His words weren't even intelligible. They were simply screams and shrieks. Gart gazed at the man, envisioning the brutal bastard who had beat Emberley senseless, and it was all he could think of. The rage he felt only increased and murder filled his heart. With his massive broadsword in his hand, he began to make his way towards Julian.

Gart wanted to snap Julian's neck. He really did. But as he approached the man, he remembered Emberley's words – *please do not kill Julian unless it is in self-defense*. This was a situation that warranted it. Julian had attacked him, after all. He was simply defending himself.

But as he approached Julian, another thought occurred to him. He wasn't sure how he could explain to Romney, Orin and Brendt that he had killed their father. He began to wonder if that kind of cloud hanging over his head would somehow scar his relationship with the children, boys he had come to love as his own. Perhaps not now, while they were young, but as the boys grew into men, he wondered how they would view the man who had killed their father, even under the pretense of self-defense. He didn't think he could take it if they grew up to mistrust or even hate him.

Not that they had any love for their father, but still, the death of Julian at Gart's hands would speak volumes of what Gart was capable of. He was a knight, sworn to chivalry and a moral code. Killing the husband of his lover, no matter how vile the man was, would tarnish that reputation. It would be viewed as dishonorable.

So he forced himself to take a deep breath and rethink his plans, trying to remove the emotion and passion from his view of the situation. He approached Julian, lowering his broadsword. Julian spied him on the approach, however, and backed off, holding his sword defensively as Gart closed in. There was great fear in his expression.

Gart's eyes were intense as he focused in on Julian, yet he made no provocative action against the man. The terror in the air was palpable.

"Gart!" David saw what was happening and he made haste out of the mêlée, heading for Gart. "Stop! Go no further!"

Gart held up a hand to his liege, a calming gesture. "I am not going to kill him," he said. "I am going to ask him a question."

David reached Gart by this time, putting himself between Julian and Gart. David put a hand on Gart's chest to prevent him from advancing.

"Go inside," he jerked his head in the direction of the manse. "Get your horse and go inside. I will take care of Buckland."

Gart was quite a bit larger than his liege, towering over David as the man tried to stop Gart's onslaught. But in truth there was no onslaught. Gart was oddly calm for a man facing his lover's vile husband – still, David didn't trust him. He knew only too well what the man was capable of.

"I simply want to ask Buckland a question," Gart said calmly.

David shoved him back by the chest. "You are not going to ask him anything," he told him. "Get out of here. That is not a request."

"You – Forbes!" Julian came alive, feeling safe now that David was between him and Gart. "What have you done with my wife? Where is she?"

David interrupted. "Do not say a word," he told Gart. "If you value your life, you will keep your mouth shut."

"Let him speak," Julian was feeling braver. "I asked him a question and I expect an answer."

David opened his mouth but Gart spoke first. "Clearly, I do not have her," he said. "I am quite alone."

Julian was quickly approaching a shrill tone again. "You took her from Dunster!"

"How would you know that?"

"Because she is not there!"

"And what proof do you have that I am responsible for her disappearance?"

Julian began gnashing around, swinging his sword. "You tried to seduce her, you bastard!" he screamed. "I know you have her. Where is she?"

Gart's gaze held steadily on the man, someone he hated more than he could comprehend, and eventually he broke out in a smirk. Julian was just too ridiculous to believe.

"If it is true that she is gone from Dunster, why would you seek to blame someone other than yourself?" he asked. "Perhaps she could no longer take your abuse and fled of her own accord."

Julian screamed and charged him, only to be shoved to the ground by David. David and Gart stood over Julian, quite calmly, while Julian writhed on the ground.

"I told you to get off my property," David growled. "If you and your men do not clear out of here immediately, I will call out my entire army to escort you off and their orders will be to do it by any means necessary, including deadly force. Is that clear?"

Julian was far gone with madness, rolling around in the dirt until he managed to get to his knees.

"You will regret this, de Lohr," he howled. "I have the ear of the queen and she will punish you. Do you hear me? *She will punish you!*"

David merely lifted an eyebrow at the threat, watching as Julian spat and cursed, gathering his men and collecting their horses. De Lohr's soldiers began to break off, allowing Buckland to pull out his men and retreat.

The dust of the road flared up, filling nostrils and coating skin as the two sides settled apart. Gart and David watched the man race off, screaming at the top of his lungs in an embarrassing display of anger. As they faded off into the distance, David turned to Gart.

"Get inside," he rumbled. "If you are not in my solar in a half hour with all manner of explanation as to the heart of this situation, I will have you thrown in the vault. Is this in any way unclear, Forbes?"

Gart simply nodded. David gave him a lingering glare, one of fury and disbelief and understanding, before moving off to assist in collecting the wounded. Gart's gaze lingered on his liege a moment before he went in search of his charger.

He knew he was in trouble. He just wasn't sure how much.

CHAPTER SIXTEEN

THE BLOW FROM David had broken two teeth off at the gum line and the surgeon had to struggle to get the roots out else they would fester. Julian screamed throughout the entire procedure, howling threats at Gart and David when his mouth wasn't full with pliers and other metal implements that were dirty and used.

In the newly built apartments that lined the east wall of the Tower of London, Julian had been issued three luxurious rooms as a guest of the queen. The king had his own women, in some cases the wives of his allies, and didn't give much notice to the company his wife kept. As long as she was available for him when he wanted her, he was mostly unconcerned with her associations.

Therefore, Julian stayed at the castle, living in royal luxury as the lover of the queen. But she had been disinterested in him as of late, ever since a big French mercenary arrived from Bordeaux and caught her eye. Julian could see her attraction to the man and he had worked harder than ever to please her, spending lavishly on her and treating her kindly. He heaped attention on her, telling her how beautiful she was as many times as he could get it out of his mouth. He had a good thing going and he didn't want to lose it.

Which was why the situation with his wife had him brittle and edgy. He had hoped that Emberley's presence at his side would cause Isabella jealousy. Now his wife had vanished and his plans were going awry, the loss of control completely infuriating him. He wasn't worried for Emberley's safety – the thought had never crossed his mind, nor did concern for the children. It was the mere fact she had left him. He knew that Forbes was responsible for Emberley's disappearance no matter what de Lohr said. He didn't trust de Lohr, anyway. Anyone who had been so closely allied with King Richard deserved a measure of distrust.

As the surgeon yanked pieces of broken tooth from his mouth, Julian screamed and slapped at the man. The big, burly surgeon motioned to a couple of Julian's men to hold him while he went to dig for a last portion of broken tooth and Julian tried to fight them off but was unsuccessful. They held him fast as the surgeon probed and Julian yelled.

"Bastards!" Julian yelled, garbled. "I will make them pay, every last one of them. They will all pay!"

The soldier holding Julian's left arm was the same soldier who had led the contingent to Dunster to escort Lady Emberley to London and the same man who had recognized Kevin de Lara. His name was Donnell and he had served Baron Buckland for six years. He was used to the man's moods and rages but he had no particular feelings about the man one way or the other. He was paid for his loyalties and nothing more.

Julian grabbed the man's arm, digging his fingers into his flesh. "We will punish them, will we not?" he asked him. "We will burn Bellham to the ground!"

Donnell was used to his liege's bouts with madness, as predictable as the rising of the sun. "As you say, m'lord."

Julian spit blood out onto his lap, the floor. "I want Forbes," he hissed through swollen lips. "I want you to go and get Forbes."

"He is well protected behind the gates of Bellham, m'lord," Donnell said patiently.

"He cannot stay there forever!"

Donnell sighed faintly. "We can lay in wait for him if you wish, m'lord," he said. "But I am sure he will be on his guard. It could be a long wait."

"I do not care!" Julian spat, spraying blood onto Donnell. "Wait for him! Kill him!"

"If we kill him, then we will never know where your wife went if our only source of information is dead."

Julian growled and grumbled, cursing Gart and de Lohr yet again. The surgeon had him open his mouth one last time to pack in some rags to stop the bleeding but Julian didn't care. He yanked himself away from the surgeon and his soldiers, exhausted and bleeding as he paced the wood floor of his lavish apartment. He was imbalanced even on a good day, now made worse with the beating he had received at the hands of de Lohr. The madness was growing.

"He has her," he grumbled. "He must. He is the only one who would take her. Emberley would not simply run away and take the children with her."

"Are you so sure, m'lord?"

Julian took the question as a challenge and puffed himself up. "You were at Dunster," he hissed. "You saw what Forbes did."

Donnell thought back to that night when there had been a scuffle on the walls of Dunster between Julian and Gart Forbes. He had come in on the tail end of it when men were trying to pull Forbes off of Julian. It had been a chaotic and loud scene with Lady de Moyon weeping in the middle of it. That was all he had witnessed but he had heard several versions of the story well into the night.

"I did not see it, m'lord," he said honestly. "I heard tale."

That didn't seem to deter Julian. "Then if you heard tale, you know that Gart could be the only one responsible for her disappearance. He seduced her and took her away from me."

"But I did not see Gart Forbes at Dunster when I arrived, m'lord," Donnell said. "He was not there but de Lohr's other knight was. I recognized him."

Julian was preparing to rant again but he suddenly stopped and an odd gleam came to his eye. He held up a finger as if a brilliant thought had just occurred to him.

"Perhaps…," he appeared oddly calm, thoughtful. "Perhaps I have accused the wrong knight. You said that you saw my wife at Dunster when you arrived but the next morning, she was missing."

"Aye, m'lord."

"And that knight you recognized was missing also."

"Aye, m'lord. They were all gone, including your children."

Julian threw up his hands. "Then we have focused on the wrong man. That knight took my wife! We want that man!"

"*Want* him, m'lord?"

"Aye!" Julian was nodding vehemently. "We must capture him and force him to tell us where my wife is."

Donnell could see the logic but cornering the knight would not be a simple thing. They had already tried to commandeer Gart Forbes and the situation had gone against them.

"M'lord, if I can make a suggestion," he said. "We failed to capture Forbes and I do not believe it would be wise to try and capture another of de Lohr's men. They are already on their guard. It will be another vicious battle and one we very well may lose. You know how powerful de Lohr is."

Julian was only focused on capturing de Lara. He waved his arms around. "Then what do you suggest? Out with it!"

Donnell put up a hand to ease him so he wouldn't fly out of control. Julian flew out of control quite easily.

"We should find out about the man," he recommended. "Ask around to see if anyone knows him. De Lohr has allies, men that we know and men that are also allied with you. Perhaps other knights know of this man and where he is from."

Julian liked the idea. His dark face lit up. "Of course," he agreed. "Find out what you can about the man. Perhaps he has a home. Perhaps he has kidnapped my wife and taken her there."

"It is as good a start as any, my lord."

Julian was less agitated now that a plan was set, one he considered cunning and true. He would outsmart de Lohr and his arrogant brother. He would win.

"Go, then," he told Donnell. "I will leave this up to you. Decide whom you wish to speak with and take no chances. They must not know our motives."

"Aye, m'lord."

Julian watched Donnell quit the room, feeling a great deal of comfort and happiness at the scheme. Forbes was no longer a suspect but this new knight was. He would track down where this man had taken his wife.

There was no telling what he would do to Emberley once he found her.

☙

"Explain what has happened to me so clearly that there will be no doubt in my mind as to what you have done," David was struggling to keep his patience. "I am waiting, Gart."

Gart stood just inside the door of the solar of Bellham, a lavish room that generations of de Lohr males had made their own. Now it belonged to David and his brother the earl, a pair that was deeply entrenched in the security of England. Gart always thought the room smelled of power, a scent somewhere between leather and smoke and hot steel. Right now, it was a somewhat intimidating smell considering he was here to ask release from his oath. So far, things weren't starting off in his favor.

"With your permission, my lord, I remained at Dunster Castle to become reacquainted with my best friend's sister," Gart began.

"I know that," David snapped softly, leaning against his desk with his arms crossed. His expression was decidedly unfriendly. "Tell me something I do not know."

Gart braced his legs apart, hands clasped behind his back. His manner was professional and non-emotional.

"I spent several weeks with the Lady Emberley de Moyon, my lord," he continued. "I came to know her children as well. In spite of the fact that they attempted to rob anyone who entered the keep at Dunster, they are good boys. They will make fine knights."

"Go on," David urged impatiently.

Gart complied. "Although it was never my intention at the start, during the time I spent with Lady Emberley, I fell in love with the woman," he finally met David's gaze. "She is the most wonderful, kind and beautiful woman in the entire world and I love her with all my heart."

David looked at him, waiting for more of an explanation. When nothing more was forthcoming, he lifted his eyebrows.

"And?" David demanded. "What else?"

Gart wasn't sure what he meant but he continued. "And… and I intend to dissolve, break up or otherwise destroy her marriage to Buckland. The baron is a vile, repulsive excuse for a man and…."

David cut him off. "And his *wife* is pregnant with *your* child."

Gart didn't flinch. "Aye, m'lord."

David just stared at him. Then he clenched his teeth and threw up his hands, pushing himself off the desk.

"You told me that you held no feelings for the woman," he jabbed a finger at the knight. "You lied to me and wove me into your web of deceit."

Gart was shaking his head before David even finished. "Untrue, my lord. I did not love her at the time we last spoke. That came much later."

David grunted and growled, making a fist at Gart as if to punch him in the nose but then drawing back, running the same hand through his cropped blond hair. He was clearly agitated.

"I should, at the very least, turn you over to Buckland," he growled. "It would serve you right for getting yourself into such foolish trouble. What on earth possessed you, Gart? You have always proven yourself to be far wiser than this. I would have never expected this from you, not in a million years."

"If that is true, my lord, why did you send de Lara to Dunster to warn me of Buckland's approach?"

David came to a halt, looking at him as if he truly wanted to punch him. But posturing was all he did, clenching his fists and growling to himself.

"Because I suspected you would still be there," he told him, less bark out of his tone. "In fact, I was sure of it. I suppose all of this is my fault. When you asked me if you could stay at Dunster, I should not have allowed it. You told me that you held no feelings for the woman and I gave you the benefit of the doubt although I guess in hindsight, I did not believe you. I should have made you leave Dunster when I did."

Gart could see that David wasn't truly angry at him, simply at the mess the situation had become. Gart decided to lay it all on the line because at this point, he suspected honesty was the only thing de Lohr would be receptive to.

"Please believe me when I tell you that it was never my intention to do anything immoral or clandestine," he lowered his voice to a beseeching tone. "In fact, even as I say that, it still does not seem wrong or immoral to me. I love the woman with all my heart and soul, as I also love those little ruffians she has raised. I love all of them, so much that I would die or kill a thousand times over for them. Buckland is an abominable, depraved man who flaunts his affair with the queen as if he is doing nothing wrong or immoral himself. He beats his wife senseless when the mood strikes him and has since the day they were married. Why is it wrong for me to love the woman and want to remove her from that hell?"

By this time, David was gazing at him with less anger and more understanding, reluctant though it might be. He sighed heavily.

"It is not as if I do not completely agree with your assessment of Buckland," he said quietly. "But the fact remains that Lady Emberley is his wife. There is nothing you can do about that."

"I can if you will help me."

David's eyebrows lifted. "Help you do what?"

Gart remained calm. "Help me persuade the Church to grant her a divorce."

David looked at him as if he were mad. "That is impossible," he said, "and even if it was possible, the Church would only grant a divorce to her husband and not to the lady. You know that the male is only considered in marital disputes – the wife is property. It would be no better if a horse asked to be given another master."

Gart was struggling not to feel some despondency. "There must be something that can be done for I will never allow her to return to Buckland. Will you please speak with a priest on my behalf and see if anything can be done?"

David could see simply by Gart's expression how serious the man was. He'd never before seen that countenance on Gart's face, the deep longing in his intense eyes. He felt his anger abate completely, replaced by depression. The man had himself in a hell of a predicament. David leaned back against his desk again, folding his arms pensively. After a moment, he simply shook his head.

"My Rock," he eyed Gart, irony in his tone. "I always called you my Rock because when everything around us was deteriorating, you always stood strong and firm. Nothing could crumble you, Gart. You are the strongest man I know. But what you have done… I understand that we cannot control who we fall in love with, but you have certainly created a mess for yourself. I do not know how we can get you out of it."

For the first time since entering the solar, Gart relaxed. All of his defensive posturing left him and he stood there, a lone and weary shell. There was a fine, oak chair off to his right, against the stone wall, and he made his way to it, lowering his bulk onto the seat.

"I never knew that such happiness existed in the world," he said softly. "Every day I spent with Emberley was the happiest day of my life. She is sweet and humorous and wise, and her children remind me of her brother and me as children. Living at Dunster these past few months was like living in a little corner of heaven reserved just for me. It was paradise."

David could hear the adoration in his voice and it surprised him. He had no idea the man was capable of such feeling. But it also deepened his respect for the man, for Gart Forbes had grown in dimension since the last time he saw him. There was breadth and depth to the perfect knight that didn't exist before. The man was learning what was truly important in life.

"Those children still have the money they stole from me," David reminded him quietly, watching Gart grin. "I should take it out of your wages."

Gart merely shrugged. "I will gladly pay it," he said. "Those boys have shown me joy in life that I had forgotten about."

David wriggled his eyebrows as he pushed himself off the desk. "Having a brother of my own, I understand that somewhat, but my wife has three sisters and now I have a daughter, so the womenfolk have the edge in my family. Girls do not rob or try to beat you with a stick."

Gart chuckled softly. "I have hopefully broken them of that."

"It *was* fairly bold for three small boys."

"They are limitless in their courage."

Now considerably calmer than he had been since he first entered the room, David was moving to the seriousness of the situation and what to do about it. Gart was a smart man but his brilliance lay more in tactics and battles. He was a knight and knights followed orders for the most part. Something like this was out of his scope of experience and David realized he had to help Gart or risk losing his best knight. Gart was begging for assistance. His mind began to work quickly.

"Speaking of the boys," David began casually. "You realize that the eldest is Buckland's heir."

"Of course," Gart nodded. "Emberley and I have discussed this at length."

"Even if by some miracle the church should grant her a divorce, Buckland will not let her take the children," David pointed out. "Would the woman leave without her children?"

"She will not, and neither will I," Gart replied, averting his gaze and looking at his hands. It was clear that he was contemplating something. "My father was Viscount Tenbury, heir presumptive to the Earldom of Albemarle. But my father and my uncle, the Earl of Albemarle, had a disagreement and my father left the family and disregarded his titles. But the truth is that the title Viscount Tenbury is rightfully mine, as is Bridgnorth Castle in Shropshire, and I intend to regain my inheritance from my uncle. I will give it all to Buckland if he will divorce Emberley and turn her, and the children, over to me."

David stared at him. "I knew you were related to Albemarle but I did not know how closely." He cleared his throat softly. "You are aware that Albemarle is allied with my brother."

"I am."

"Have you not spoken with your uncle in recent years, Gart?"

Gart shook his head. "There was no reason to. My father severed those ties long ago."

David sighed faintly. For a moment, he appeared at a loss for words.

"Gart, Albemarle has a son," he said quietly. "I have met the lad, perhaps no more than eight years of age. It is the boy that carries the title Viscount Tenbury."

Gart looked up at him, surprised. "I did not even know my uncle had a son. He had three daughters who were grown."

David was trying to be gentle. "The earl's wife died several years ago and he remarried. It is his second wife who gave him the son and the boy carries the title."

"Are you sure?"

"Positive. I saw the boy last year when my brother had a meeting of his allies. Your uncle introduced the lad as the viscount and his heir."

Gart stared at him for a long, painful moment before looking back to his hands. Then he hissed, a long and pensive sigh, and hung his head. His enormous hands ended up on his skull as if to hold his brains in.

"Oh… God," he breathed. "My plans were to mend the rift with my uncle and regain what was mine, providing Emberley and the children with a suitable legacy to replace what they would leaving with Buckland. But with your news, the inheritance I was anticipating is greatly reduced. I still have a small inheritance on my mother side, but I am not entirely sure what it is or how much. I never cared until now. I was counting on my father's inheritance to… now, I have… nothing.…"

David watched the man's lowered head, truly feeling sorry for him. More remarkable than that was the emotion he was exhibiting. Gart Forbes had never been known to exhibit emotion, in any situation, which was one of the aspects that made the man so frightening.

David made his way towards him, unsure how to comfort the man but understanding what it was like to love a woman deeply. He couldn't imagine what would have become of him had he not been able to marry Emilie.

"Do not despair," he told him quietly. "My brother is due here in a few days and we will ask him for advice. Christopher is a powerful man, Gart. If anyone can help you, it is him."

Gart was struggling not to feel completely discouraged. All he could think about at the moment was returning to Trelystan Castle, collecting Emberley and the children, and taking flight to France or the Teutonic countries. Perhaps it was best if they simply fled and be done with it.

"I appreciate your offer, my lord," he said, lifting his head to look at David. "But there is something more I wish to ask of you."

"What is it?"

"I would ask to be released from my oath of fealty."

"Why?"

Gart shrugged. "I should think that is fairly obvious. I am no longer an honorable knight."

David frowned. "That is not true."

"Please release me, my lord."

David regarded him. Then he moved away, thoughtfully, pacing the floor until he reached his desk. He kept glancing back at Gart as if reluctantly considering his request.

"Go and rest now," he told him. "We will speak of this later."

"When?"

"Later."

Gart gazed up at him, stricken at the real possibility that de Lohr would not release him. "But I must return to Emberley," he stood up, weaving wearily. "I cannot remain here much longer."

David could see how exhausted the man was, now mentally weakened with everything that was going on. He moved back in Gart's direction.

"She is safe, is she not?" he asked. "There is nothing to worry over. You do not have to rush...."

Gart put up a hand to interrupt him. "Aye, I do," his gaze was intense, almost imploring. "You do not understand. I cannot stomach to be away from her. Already, I have been gone from her for six days and I can hardly breathe for want of her. My lord, I must be released from my oath because I know that I will never again be an effective knight for you. My thoughts, heart and body are with Lady Emberley and always will be. You would order me to go to France and fight for Buckland but I will not. I cannot. That therefore makes me ineffective and worthless."

David regarded him carefully. "You would disobey me?"

Gart shook his head even before David got the question out of his mouth. "Nay, my lord," he said. "I would kill for you and I would die for you. But I will not go to France and fight for Buckland."

David sighed in resignation and scratched his chin. "You do not have to worry about that," he told him. "I have already withdrawn my support. Buckland was at Bellham today because he came to demand that I turn you over to him. Somehow, he knows you have his wife. He does not know where you have her because, presumably, if he did he would go and retrieve her. So he came here to demand you. I struck him in the face and sent him along his way."

Gart's eyes widened. "You... you struck him?"

"I did."

Gart was taken aback at the predicament David put himself in. "You did this to protect me?"

David rolled his eyes. "Christ, Gart, must we truly revisit this? You saved my life in the France. I have always owed you a debt of gratitude. I am happy to protect you. I will also release you from your oath if that is what you truly want but I am hoping you will reconsider. The de

Lohr war machine will not be the same without you. I need you."

"She needs me more, my lord."

David grinned. "Nay," he said softly. "You need *her* more."

Gart shrugged, nodded, conceding the point. "Please, my lord," he begged softly. "Whatever you can do for us with regards to the state of her marriage… I cannot tell you how grateful I would be. I cannot live without her."

David sighed again, clapping him on a broad shoulder. "You know I will do all that I can," he said, giving him a shove towards the solar door. "You will go and rest now. I will speak with you later."

Gart nodded, hanging his head a moment before speaking. "I am sorry to have disappointed you, my lord."

"You did not disappoint me. But you did surprise me."

Having nothing more to say, Gart wearily quit the room. David's gaze lingered on the doorway even after the man's bootfalls faded away, wondering what he could possibly do to help his knight. Any possibility he could come up with wasn't particularly pleasant. Perhaps his brother would have a better idea when he arrived.

Until then, he did the only thing he could think to do – he sent de Lara into London to summon the same priest who had baptized Christina. Father Jonas St. John was a priest at St. Bartholomew's, well respected and rigidly opposed to the king and his bawdy lifestyle. David had found an odd ally in the priest back in the days when his daughter was newly born. He held a great respect for the man's opinion.

As Kevin rode from the heavily guarded gates of Bellham, David went in search of Gart only to find the man sleeping the sleep of the dead with his mail still on, laying haphazardly across a bed in a room just off of the kitchen. David peered closer and noticed a half-eaten chunk of bread in the man's hand. He had been so exhausted he hadn't even finished it. With a grin, David closed the door and told the cook to let no one disturb him.

Gart would need all of his strength for the biggest battle yet to come.

CHAPTER SEVENTEEN

"HIS NAME IS Kevin de Lara and his father is Viscount Trelystan," Donnell told Julian. "His father is Warden of the Trinity Castles on the Welsh Marches."

Julian's eyebrows lifted. "The Trinity Castles?" he repeated. Then he looked thoughtful. "I have heard of them. De Lara. *De Lara*. Where have I heard that name?"

"Sean de Lara, Kevin's elder brother, is a personal protector to King John."

Julian's expression widened with both surprise and recognition. "The Shadow Lord?"

"The same, m'lord. John's deadliest knight."

Julian nodded his head, stroking his chin thoughtfully as he rose from his chair. It was a bright morning the day after his beating at the hands of David de Lohr, and his face was bruised and tender. He had tried to eat soft foods for breakfast but because of the two broken teeth he had suffered, he was too sore to eat anything. His mood had been foul until Donnell's early morning visit with news obtained on Kevin de Lara.

"Who gave you this information?" Julian wanted to know.

Donnell shifted wearily on his legs. He had been up most of the night finding out what he could about Kevin de Lara. Some of his professional demeanor began to slip.

"I have spent the night moving through taverns known to be patronized by knights from Arundel, Norfolk and other allied barons," he told Julian. "I went to the Pig and Flute over near the docks as well as the Bloody Fist in the Kingsbury District."

Julian nodded, interrupting him. "I know it," he waved a hand, moving to the table laden with food he had not been able to eat. "I have been to both of those establishments."

Donnell eyed him, irritated at having been interrupted. "I found two of Rochester's men at the Fist, knights I have gone to battle with in the past. As a senior sergeant for Buckland, one of the knights recognized me and showed me a measure of respect. We spoke casually for a time and I brought up the subject of de Lohr. It was this knight who told me of Kevin de Lara and how he does not speak to his brother because the man serves the king as his personal bodyguard. De Lara's family was a strong supporter of Richard before his death. The fact that the elder son has given loyalties to the prince does not please them."

Julian was trying to chew on a piece of very soft white bread. "What else did he tell you of Kevin de Lara?"

Donnell shrugged, watching Julian as the man tried to eat. He was hungry, too, along with being exhausted but he knew that Buckland would not offer to share his food. Julian was not a generous man.

"Nothing more than what I have told you," he said. "De Lara's father holds the Trinity Castles on the Marches and his brother is the Shadow Lord."

Julian swallowed a piece of bread and gingerly took another bite. "Find out exactly where the Trinity Castles are," he said with a piece of bread hanging out of his mouth. "I know they are on the Marches but I do not know precisely where. Perhaps de Lara took her there."

Donnell scratched wearily at his head. "It would be as good a place to start as any, I suppose. Even if she is not there, perhaps his father knows something."

"You will find out and you will go there immediately."

"Aye, m'lord. Is there anything else?"

"Nay. Leave me."

Donnell turned on his heel and quit the room, thinking more of sleep and food than of a trip to the Marches. He would find out where the Trinity Castles were located and he would go there to see if he could find the errant Lady Emberley de Moyon. Although he was detached from the situation as much as he could be, a large part of him did not blame the woman for fleeing her husband. He had seen first-hand what Julian could do to his wife. He was a brutal bastard when the mood struck him. Donnell himself had been on the receiving end of a few of Julian's mood swings so he understood Lady de Moyon's pain well.

As he settled down in the bunkhouse of the tower, food in one hand and cheap ale in the other, he was coming to think that maybe he would simply ride in circles for the next few weeks and return to London to tell de Moyon that he could not find his wife. It was a foolish thought but one he entertained. If Donnell thought long and hard about it, he could remember the look of terror on Lady de Moyon's face when he had come for her at Dunster. Donnell was coming to suspect that no knight had a hand in her disappearance – the woman had probably fled on her own out of sheer terror.

More than likely, she was lost to the wilds of Somerset or Cornwall, victim of bandits or fodder for wild animals. It was a better fate than coming to live with her husband in London. Still, Donnell would ride to the Marches to investigate the Trinity Castles for himself, simply because he had been ordered to and not because he had a strong inclination to find the woman. He would do his diligence in a futile effort and be done with it.

Donnell fell asleep without having finished his meal.

೦೩

JONAS ST. JOHN was a tall, thin man, older, with a full head of dark and curly hair. He had been in the clergy for the majority of his life, having grown up as an acolyte at St. Bartholomew the Great Cathedral before working his way up to become a fully consecrated priest. He was a fairly simple man without the vices or addictions his fellow priests indulged in, hiding behind holy robes to mask their deviations. Jonas was an exception to that rule, a truly pious man in a world where such things were increasingly rare.

He had been summoned this day to Bellham Place, home of the mighty de Lohr family, by one of de Lohr's knights. Without question, he went with the man and enjoyed a leisurely ride to the outskirts of London where the great manor houses lay along the Thames like the pearls of an enormous necklace. The day was fine and the birds sang in the great oak trees overhead as Kevin, Jonas and a small escort made haste back to Bellham.

Arriving at the great, white-stoned manor, Jonas greeted David amiably and was kind to Emilie and Christina. David and his wife took the man into the lavish reception room to go through the pleasantries of social graces, providing the priest with food and drink. But when the wine was halfway finished and the food had run out, David politely excused his wife from the room. In her place came an enormous knight with a shaved head and deadly look about him. Gart moved off into the shadows as David closed the door behind Emilie and Christina.

Jonas eyed the massive knight in the corner as David returned to him and reclaimed his seat. His dark eyes moved over the enormous hands, long, thick legs and broad chest. David could see where the priest's attention was and he indicated Gart.

"I would have you meet my most trusted knight, Sir Gart Forbes," he said, noting the apprehensive expression on the priest's face. "He is as deadly as you think he is but I assure you, he is quite docile at the moment. I wanted him to be a part of this conversation, with your permission. It is important."

Jonas agreed, casually, as if the man's deadly countenance didn't matter in the least. He reclaimed his cup.

"It is your home, my lord," he said. "You have the right to demand who stays and who goes. Now, I assume you did not call me from St. Bartholomew's simply for polite conversation."

David shook his head. "I did not," he confirmed. "We seek your counsel."

"We?" the priest looked over at Gart, still standing just inside the door. "You and your knight?"

David nodded, waving Gart over. "Come and sit," he told the knight, looking back to the priest in his woolen robes, dusty from travel. "Gart has some questions that I am hoping you can answer."

Jonas focused expectantly on the big knight as the man assumed a seat across from him. But the knight was perched uncomfortably, stiffly, and Jonas observed the uneasy display. He was coming to feel somewhat sorry for the man, so ill at ease in the comfortable and lovely room.

"Well?" Jonas asked politely. "What is your question, my son?"

Gart cleared his throat, eyeing David as he did so. "I was wondering, Your Grace," he cleared his throat again and coughed for good measure. "What.... What does the Church consider grounds for a divorce?"

Jonas looked rather thoughtful at the question. "The Church is very clear on its stance for divorce," he settled back in his chair. "Only under the most extreme circumstances is it considered, for example, adultery or grievous sins such as heresy. Do you want to divorce your wife, my son?"

Gart shook his head, looking at David for support. Gart was never particularly good with spoken word, especially when he was uncertain on the subject matter. Already he was rattled and struggling not to look like a fool.

"Nay," he assured him. "It is more complex than that."

The priest wasn't following him. "Complex? What do you mean?"

Gart was quickly sliding into embarrassing misery and David came to his aid. "The story is long and complicated," he told the priest. "I will provide you with the details. Gart is in love with a woman whose husband beats her mercilessly. The lady is in love with Gart also and they wish to be together. Gart would like to know if the lady, under extreme circumstances, can divorce her husband."

Jonas tried not to appear shocked as his gaze moved between Gart and David. After a moment, he simply shook his head. "I know of no circumstances that would allow for such an intervention unless the man was proven in the extreme."

"What is extreme?" David pushed.

Jonas was uncomfortable discussing the subject but he obliged. "If the husband was somehow proven to be a follower of Satan or a heretic, the Church might consider a divorce because to remain with such a man would endanger the wife's immortal soul." He looked back at Gart. "But this is not the case. You want the lady to be free of her husband so that you can marry her."

Gart felt like he was already condemned to Hell by the way the man was looking at him. Still, he was not ashamed of his love for Emberley. "Aye, Your Grace."

"How long has this been going on?"

"Months, Your Grace."

"Have you had relations with the woman in the conjugal sense?"

"Aye, Your Grace."

Jonas sighed faintly. "My son, you are committing adultery with this woman. Do you not understand that?"

Gart nodded. "I do," he whispered. "But… her husband beats her regularly and is cruel to her and the children. He is a vile excuse for a man and does not deserve her. Why can she not divorce a man who treats her no better than an animal?"

Jonas could see the vulnerability in the man's eyes. He didn't even know him but he could see that there was longing and concern and compassion there. He began to feel some compassion of his own in spite of himself.

"A husband may do as he pleases with his wife," he said quietly, somewhat gently. "As long as he does not kill her, the Church will not intervene. Beatings alone are not grounds for a divorce."

Gart looked at David with a look of such desolation that David felt the physical impact. He turned to the priest.

"Her husband is the lover of Queen Isabella," he said, his voice low. "The man openly commits adultery with the queen, for Christ's sake. Is that not a violation of God's sanctity of marriage?"

Jonas was beginning to understand more of the situation now. He looked at Gart. "Is this true?"

Gart nodded, struggling against the creeping sense of despair. "It is."

"The man is beyond reprehensible," David put in, more strongly. "Let me tell you about this man and see if the Church approves of the manner in which he obeys God's laws of marriage. Not only has he been the lover of the queen for quite some time, but recently, the queen has started to show interest in another man so her lover, this husband, has sent for his wife and children to join him in London so he can make the queen jealous and remain in her favor. How is it not right for the woman to be granted a divorce from a man who clearly abuses the marriage laws?"

Jonas sighed deeply, obviously given much to think about. Setting his pewter cup onto the table, he rose on his long legs and began to pace the scrubbed wood floor. Gart and David watched him closely as he clasped his hands behind his back, thoughtfully, watching his feet as he moved around the room. He paused by one of the great Norman lancet windows, his gaze moving to the green gardens beyond.

"The Church is very specific about its views on divorce," he said. "I am not entirely sure there is a simple answer to this, at least one that would be acceptable."

"Please," Gart was on his feet, moving towards the priest. "You do not understand, Your Grace. Lady Emberley's brother and I were best friends as children and I grew up knowing the lady and her family. I had not seen her in years until we were reacquainted a couple of months ago, and I subsequently came to know a bright, wonderful and sweet lady who is the epitome of what every woman should be. She has four children that she loves dearly, all offspring of her vile husband, yet there is so much love between the five of them that it is difficult to imagine. I have spent the past two months with them and never have I known so much happiness or peace. Please understand that I will beg, borrow, steal or kill in order to insure she no longer lives in fear and pain from her husband. Even if she did not love me and even if we were never meant to be together, I would still fight to free her from her husband because she deserves far better in life than what she has been dealt."

The priest was watching him from his perch by the window, moved by the man's speech. Slowly, he made his way towards the knight, coming to stand in front of him, inspecting him, dissecting the expression on Gart's face with every ounce of wisdom and intuition he possessed. He could feel the sincerity of the man and it touched him. After a moment, he put his hand on Gart's shoulder.

"Your name is Gart?" he said softly.

Gart nodded. "My name is Gabriel but everyone calls me Gart."

Jonas smiled. "*'And the angel answering said unto him, 'I am Gabriel, that stand in the presence of God; and am sent to speak unto thee, and to shew thee these glad tidings'.*" His smile grew at Gart's confused expression. "Do you not know your Bible, knight? Gabriel was the archangel that announced the birth of John the Baptist and Jesus Christ. He is the bearer of God's secret messages to his chosen ones. He is also the great protector of Mankind."

Gart was torn between interest and embarrassment. "I only wish to protect Emberley and her children, Your Grace, not the entire world."

Jonas chuckled softly. "Even if I knew nothing about you other than the fact that you are a knight, your impassioned plea has shown me that beyond the killing machine lies a man of flesh and blood and heart," he said softly. "You have a compassionate and selfless soul, Sir Gart. That is something not often seen in fighting men."

Gart wasn't sure how to respond. "It is the truth," he said. "I only want to see her happy and would do anything to accomplish this."

Jonas nodded with some resignation, sensing that this simple conversation was the start of a situation that was anything but uncomplicated. Hand still on Gart's shoulder, he looked at David.

"There is another option," he said, "although you may not wish to pursue it. A man can divorce his wife on the grounds of adultery. It has been done. I would assume that the husband knows nothing of the affair?"

Gart shook his head. "He does not, but he will at some point. The lady is pregnant with my child."

Jonas lifted his eyebrows. "Well," he said with some irony. "That will help the husband's case. Perhaps if he were to be told of the affair, it would prompt him to begin proceedings."

David shook his head firmly. "Nay," he said flatly. "It would only give him an excuse to kill his wife. I suspect he would murder her before he would divorce her."

Jonas dropped his hand from Gart's shoulder and sought his chair again, collecting his half-full cup of wine. Gart retrieved the heavy pewter pitcher and filled it to the rim, and Jonas thanked him.

"You would not know this, but the queen comes to St. Bartholomew every Friday for confession," Jonas said. "She has her own priest but she does not trust him to fully absolve her for her sins, so she comes to my church every week to seek forgiveness for a multitude of transgressions. Usually, Father Constantine hears her confession, as head of our order. I have, however, heard her confession twice and with the acts of debauchery she confessions, she cannot do enough penance in a thousand lifetimes to make up for it. God has already turned his back on her."

David held his cup out as Gart poured him more wine. "And she has never confessed the affair with Buckland?"

Jonas looked up from his wine. "So that is who she is having the affair with?" he snorted. "She did mention something about unholy appetites with a man other than her husband but I had no idea it was Baron Buckland."

David scratched as his neck casually. "You are a priest. I do not believe you are supposed to discuss confessions with us."

"You asked."

"I should not have. I will have to ask forgiveness when I next go to

Confession."

Jonas chuckled at the man's quirky humor. "It is not as if everyone in England does not know of her activities. I was not divulging something that was not already common knowledge."

David fought off a grin. "I hope you do not discuss my confessions with anyone or I could be in a good deal of trouble."

Jonas flicked a hand towards the manse entry. "Are hordes of the king's supporters here to burn your home to the ground?"

"Nay."

"And they shall not be, at least not by my lips. Your confessions are safe with me, my lord. I will take them to my grave."

As David and the priest snorted at each other, Gart was still riveted to his information about Isabella's confession. "Do you know of Buckland, Your Grace?"

Jonas nodded and took a long drink of wine. "Again, I am discussing information that is common knowledge. Buckland comes to confession with her. I thought he was simply one of her entourage. I have heard his confession several times and never once has he mentioned a wife."

Gart looked at David as if looking to the man for all of the answers. There had to be some measure of help in all of this information, something they could do that would help Gart's case. David's mind was already working furiously and as an idea began to form, he took the pewter pitcher of wine and topped off the priest's cup. David was naturally aggressive even though he wasn't a natural negotiator. That usually came from his brother. But his brother wasn't here and David had to act.

"I have been going to Confession since I was old enough to speak," David said casually, setting the pitcher back down. "Every time I deliver my admissions, the priest tells me what I must do in order to seek God's forgiveness."

Jonas drank his wine, a very fine, red variety that was delicious. He nodded to David's statement. "Indeed," he replied. "It is our obligation to provide guidance."

David toyed with his cup, watching the priest drink. "You said that Isabella cannot do enough penance for the sins she has committed."

"That is true."

"What if there was something she could do?"

Jonas cocked his head. "What do you mean?"

David was calm and controlled as he spoke. "Perhaps you should hear her confession the next time," he told him. "When it is over, tell her that the only way for her to avoid eternity in hell for all of the misdeeds she has done is to right at least one wrong in her life. As she cavorts with Buckland, she too is committing adultery, a vile sin. If Buckland divorces his wife, it will help Isabella's cause. She will only have to worry about doing penance for her own marriage and not his. She must convince Buckland to divorce his wife."

Jonas lifted his eyebrows, both surprised and intrigued. "Interesting," he said. "I have never heard of such atonement, but it is an interesting thought."

David sat forward, his sky blue eyes glittering. "You will tell Buckland the same thing when he comes for Confession," he lowered his voice. "Make sure he confesses only to you and tell him that he must divorce his wife to erase the sin of adultery. Tell him if he does not, he will face eternal damnation. You will also tell him that if he ever beats his wife again, there is no penitence strong enough to erase his actions and he will spend a thousand years in purgatory. Tell him God is displeased with his actions and hell awaits him if he does not comply with all conditions."

All humor was gone from Jonas' face. "Are you serious?" he hissed. "But it is not...."

David cut him off. "I will pay for a new roof for St. Bartholomew if you will do this. That place has needed a new roof for years and, as I recall, you have been attempting to raise the money. I will provide it if you will do this. Your service will reap my reward. God works in mysterious ways, does he not?"

Jonas stared at him, torn between denial and agreement. He was adamantly opposed to using the confessional as a manipulation tool, especially as it pertained to a sin such as divorce, but on the other hand, priests had been using the confessional for centuries as a springboard for their own desires and agendas. It was nothing new.

As he thought on it, what he was asked to do wasn't meant to be evil in the true sense. The knight was in love with a woman who was abused and his liege was attempting to help him. It was not as if Buckland hadn't violated his marriage vows first.

Jonas set down his chalice of wine, regarding David carefully. He could see how serious the baron was. After a moment, his humor returned.

"I fear that I have stepped into a trap," he grinned.

David relaxed somewhat, sitting back in his chair and reclaiming his wine. "There is no trap," he said. "But we are speaking of two people who do unspeakable wrong on a daily basis. Why protect them with God's laws? Help a poor, defenseless woman break free of the clutches of her evil husband. Buckland is going to hell anyway. A divorce will not make or break his eternal soul."

Jonas sighed heavily, finally looking to Gart who looked both apprehensive and hopeful. He wriggled his eyebrows at the knight.

"Did you tell him to ask this of me?" he demanded lightly.

Gart shook his head. "How could I? I did not know that Buckland and Isabella came to you for confession."

Jonas knew that but he had asked the question anyway. His gaze moved back to David, thinking of the new roof they so desperately needed. He pursed his lips thoughtfully.

"You realize that the entire roof needs repair," he said.

David nodded. "I do."

"It will be quite expensive."

"Gart is a good knight. If you do not do this for him, I will lose him. He will run off with the lady and I will never see him again, and I need him."

Jonas looked at Gart again, who was gazing steadily in return. Weighing the good against the bad, the need against the want, Jonas finally nodded his head. It was a weary, resigned gesture.

"Very well," he said. "I will do it. But this conversation between the three of us must not leave this room. If I am found out, I will lose all credibility at the very least. Is that clear?"

"Perfectly, Your Grace," David stood up, extending a hand to the man. "You have my gratitude."

Jonas stood up, accepting the outstretched hand with some reluctance. "When do we get our new roof?"

"As soon as Buckland makes his appeal for a divorce."

Jonas sighed heavily and shook his head, already feeling guilty for what he had agreed to. "I will probably need to tell him how to go about it so he does not muck up the process. The man is an idiot."

"Aye, he is. I will have Kevin return you to London now."

"Nay," Jonas' attention turned to Gart. "I would have Gabriel escort me back to London. I would come to know this man for whom I am risking my livelihood for."

Gart nodded. "It will be my pleasure, Your Grace."

Jonas eyed Gart for a long moment as if still debating the rightness of what he had agreed to, but in any case, it was too late. He had already done business with the Devil and the bargain was sealed.

On the ride back to St. Bartholomew, Father Jonas and Gart had a very interesting and very long conversation about the moral obligations of a knight. Moral or not, true love seemed to trump everything. It was all Gart could talk about.

CHAPTER EIGHTEEN

Early August
Trelystan Castle

EMBERLEY HEARD LORD de Lara hooting, suspecting one or more of her children was involved with the origination of the sound before she even saw the man. She was scooting down the exterior stairs of Trelystan castle, coming from the enormous keep that was shaped like a giant square box. She had Lacy in her arms, searching for her errant sons who had run off when she was dressing the baby. She had told them not to wander far but, alas, that was too much to ask. Trelystan was a vast place of new discoveries, secret passages and stairs that led to mysterious places and her boys were determined to explore every inch of it.

As she came off the stairs into the vast, muddy bailey, she could hear more hooting and she followed the sounds. It had rained the night before and the ground was slippery as she made her way around the keep and ended up in the stable yards, which were upslope on the hill that Trelystan had been built on. Ahead, she could see her three boys running circles around Lord de Lara, smacking him on the legs and backside with their wooden swords.

"Misfits!" the old man was crying. "You are hooligans and misfits!"

Emberley gathered the skirt of her surcoat as she picked up the pace. Dressed in a coat of faded dark blue that emphasized her voluptuous figure, the gold tasseled belt swung in rhythm to her quick steps as she rushed towards the scene.

"Boys," she called. "Stop this instant. I told you what would happen if you assaulted Lord de Lara again."

The boys came to a confused halt, as did Lord de Lara. Upon closer inspection, the old man was laughing. He was enjoying every minute of the roughhousing.

"'Tis of no issue, Lady de Moyon," he assured her. "The boys are doing no harm."

Emberley lifted an eyebrow at his graceful lie. In her arms, Lacy squirmed to be set down and she set the little girl carefully onto the muddy ground.

"They were swatting you with their swords," she looked at the three little faces staring back at her. "They have been warned. Gart told them to behave and they promised."

"We *are* behaving, Mama," Orin insisted. "We were playing."

Emberley gazed reproachfully at her son. "You were hitting Lord de Lara with your sword," she scolded. "That is *not* playing."

"Truly, Lady de Moyon, it was all in fun," Lord de Lara reiterated. "It has been a long time since children have been at play here at Trelystan and from the way my sons are conducting their lives, who is to say there will ever be children here again? Please do not deny me the joy of it."

She smiled at the old man. "My lord, you have been an incredibly gracious host but I am not sure that includes allowing yourself to be pummeled by your young guests."

Lord de Lara's grin broadened, a vague resemblance to his son. "Kevin and Sean used to rig traps for me to walk in to," he told her. "I would exit a room and run straight into a noose around my foot. I cannot tell you the times that my sons felled me to the ground with one of their traps."

Emberley held her up hands to shush him. "Quiet," she whispered loudly. "If my boys hear that, they will want to make traps, too, and no one will be safe."

Lord de Lara laughed, as did Emberley. Bored with standing around, Romney, Orin and Brendt began fighting each other with their toy swords as Lacy toddled after them, screaming because she wanted to play with their toys also. Emberley stood with Lord de Lara, watching the children play in the muddy yard.

"I want to thank you again for having us at Trelystan," she said, turning to the man. "Your son was extremely gracious to suggest it and you are extremely gracious to allow it. I am not sure how we can ever repay you but rest assured that we will always be in your debt."

Lord de Lara eyed the woman, studying her exquisite profile. She was an exceptionally beautiful woman with a kind manner and warm sense of humor. They had spent some time together intermittently over the past two weeks, and more time together since the departure of Gart Forbes. Lord de Lara knew the story – that the lady was fleeing from her brutal husband who was, in fact, having an affair with Queen Isabella. He felt deeply sorry for the woman, more now that he was coming to know her and her spirited children. Even though he had a long-standing hatred of the king, he still felt strongly compelled to protect them all.

"Your gratitude is sufficient, my lady," he assured her. "I do not consider that you owe me a debt. Your company, and the company of your children, is payment enough. I live a lonely life so the advent of guests is welcome. I will miss all of you when you leave."

She turned to look at him, smiling. "We may be here for quite some time," she teased gently. "You may be quite eager to be rid of us by the time Gart returns."

Lord de Lara snorted softly, shaking his head. "I may beg him to let you stay."

Emberley maintained her smile at the old man, her gaze moving to her children once again when Brendt slipped in the mud and let out a yell. She sighed as she watched the boy try to pick himself up from the slime.

"Gart has been gone for quite some time," she said pensively. "I hope he has not run into trouble."

Even as she said it, she thought on the irony of that statement and felt foolish for voicing her thoughts. The trouble that Gart was facing was monumental and she hung her head a moment, fighting off the depression and loneliness that she felt. Every day since he had been gone had been a struggle for her. She woke in an empty bed, thinking of Gart's warm and powerful body next to hers, missing him more than she could express. She'd never experienced such a thing in her life and was unsure how to gracefully deal with it. Every day without him was like torture.

Emberley forced herself to face the days without him, focused on her children, focused on Gart's return. He had only been gone four days when she began looking for his return, perched in her bower with a view of the southern road that he had taken to London and watching the dusty path day after long day. Sometimes people were traveling upon it and she would wait with bated breath, watching the ant-like figures in the distance as they passed by Trelystan. Always, they passed the castle by, and her depression deepened when she realized another day would pass without him.

As her mind was swamped with thoughts of Gart, Lord de Lara watched her rippling expressions. He was a man unused to womenfolk, as his own wife had died when his sons had been very small, so it was difficult for him to know how to comfort Lady de Moyon during this difficult time. Still, he tried.

"Have faith, my lady," he told her. "I am sure Forbes will return soon."

Emberley glanced at him, a small but grateful smile on her face. Over to their right, the boys were hacking away at each other and all of them had managed to slip down into the mud. Emberley looked at her children, knowing she was going to have a messy group of children to clean up. Even the baby was muddy as she played with Brendt's little, wooden shield, stolen from her brother as he had wallowed on the ground.

Puffing out her cheeks with a heavy sigh, she headed off towards her children with the intention of pulling them out of the mud and back into the keep where she could clean the muck off of them. Although dust, dirt and all things slovenly were a natural part of life and most people didn't worry about the degree of their cleanliness, Emberley didn't like for her children to be dirty. She didn't think it was particularly healthy for them to wallow in dirt like the animals and she had an odd preoccupation with keeping them clean. Like Gart, she wasn't fond of dirty clothing. So she hauled Brendt out of the mud by an arm, listening to him whine when he realized his mother was about to scald him with another bath.

She captured Lacy as well, lifting the little girl onto her hip as she called to Romney and Orin, telling them to follow her into the keep. The older boys complied somewhat but Lord de Lara was still standing there, still a target, and they raced at them with their swords to smack him. De Lara accused them of being vicious and powerful men and begged for mercy, which puffed the boys up with arrogance. Emberley, fighting off a grin, simply shook her head. In her opinion, which she would never voice, Lord de Lara was begging for trouble. Like Gart, he loved it.

As she corralled her errant children, both Emberley and Lord de Lara were oblivious to the group of riders approaching Trelystan's massive gatehouse. They were too busy trying to capture Romney and Orin as the boys ran about like wild animals. Neither boy wanted to go inside the keep and would have kept running had their mother not brought Gart's name into the mix. That seemed to get their attention. As Emberley finally collared the boys with the all-powerful Gart threat, the riders heading in from the southern road reached Trelystan's gatehouse and were admitted.

Emberley had Brendt and Lacy while Romney and Orin followed begrudgingly, crossing the muddy bailey as they headed to the keep. The party of riders that had just entered from the southern road, now a cluster of men and horses in the gatehouse, were required to leave their weapons with the guards and the two groups passed within several feet of each other. Emberley wasn't paying attention to the gatehouse and the men removing their weapons weren't paying particular attention to the activity in the bailey. All was normal and relatively peaceful. That is, until one of the riders in the gatehouse looked up and shouted.

"Lady de Moyon!"

Emberley froze at the base of the stairs that led into the keep, turning to see who had called her name. There was a cluster of men in the dark-stoned gatehouse, men bearing tunics and weapons. Her gaze fell upon a man who served her husband, a sergeant named Donnell, and she felt a jolt of shock when their eyes met. Terror welled in her throat and she could only think of one thing at that moment, an instinctive reaction that fed her sense of horror.

"Run," she told the boys. "Run to your chamber. Hurry! Run!"

Thankfully, Romney and Orin didn't ask questions. They had no idea what had their mother so spooked and were afraid by the tone of her voice. Emberley began to run up the stairs, urging them along with her, and the five of them raced up the slippery stone steps as fast as they could go. Into the dark keep they ran, Emberley's pleading whispers urging them up the stairs.

Bootfalls were suddenly behind them and Emberley shrieked when a big leather glove grabbed her. At a disadvantage with Lacy in her arms, she tried to pull away but she slipped on the steps, dumping the baby onto a stair.

Lacy fell harmlessly on her bum, screaming, as Orin reached down and grabbed his sister to keep her from falling further. Romney rushed to the aid of his mother, whacking the man who had her with his wooden sword. It was chaotic, with men shouting and children screaming. In the midst of the madness, Emberley's beseeching gaze sought out Orin and Brendt.

"Take your sister," she cried as she struggled against Donnell pulling her down the stairs. "Take her to your chamber and bolt the door. Go!"

Orin wanted to help his brother fight off the soldiers but Brendt couldn't manage their baby sister on his own, so he helped Brendt lug

Lacy up the stairs, pulling her away from their mother and Romney as their mother urged them to move faster. Brendt was crying but did as he was told, trying not to fall down the stairs as he pulled Lacy to the upper floors.

It was a painful and frightening scene, made even more painful and frightening when Lord de Lara and several of his soldiers rushed into the keep, armed to the teeth, and began fighting off the men who had captured Lady de Moyon.

Romney was fighting furiously with his wooden sword, banging the man who held his mother. He recognized the man as a soldier who worked for his father, which terrified him. He thought his father was here since his men were and he was angry as well as frightened.

Donnell eventually grew weary of having a wooden sword smacking him around, infuriated when it poked him in the cheek and drew blood. Sweeping his free arm, he caught Romney on the side of the head and knocked the child down six steps. Romney ended up in a heap at the bottom of the staircase.

The skirmish for the lady was quickly turning deadly as the battle intensified. One of de Lara's men was gored in the gut and the man fell to the stone, bleeding heavily. Eager to put an end to the skirmish, Donnell unsheathed a dagger he had hidden in his gauntlet, yanked hard on Lady de Moyon, and ended up with the lady trapped against his chest. The dirk went up against her neck.

"Cease!" he roared. "Cease resistance or she dies!"

Lord de Lara and his men came to a halt, their eyes falling on the soldier who had Lady de Moyon in a very precarious position. Furious at his keep having been breached and his hospitality violated, Lord de Lara dropped his broadsword and approached the soldier.

"Who are you?" he demanded. "How dare you despoil the welcome of Trelystan. You will release the lady immediately."

Donnell's gaze was steady on the old man. "Alas, my lord, I cannot," he said. "I have come on behalf of the lady's husband. I am ordered to bring her to London."

In his grasp, Emberley flinched. "Never!" she screamed. "I am not going to London."

Donnell pressed the dirk against her neck and she gasped as it drew blood. "You do not have a choice, Lady de Moyon," he told her. "Your husband has ordered me to return you to London and I shall."

Emberley struggled not to panic for she knew if she did, all would be lost. "Please," she sounded calmer. "Please do not do this. I do not want to return to Julian. I cannot. Please do not force me."

Donnell's harsh stance wavered. In fact, he was still reeling from having found Lady de Moyon at Trelystan in the first place. It had been a wild stroke of luck. When he had first seen her crossing the bailey with the children, he thought he had been imagining it.

When he had set out to the Marches a week prior, his heart still wasn't in the search. He hadn't truly expected to find anything, perhaps hoping he wouldn't, and was vastly shocked to see that Lady de Moyon was, in fact, at de Lara's holding. Everything Buckland had suspected had been correct, and Kevin de Lara had indeed smuggled Lady de Moyon out of Dunster those weeks ago.

But the fact remained that she was here and Donnell had captured her. It was his duty to return her to her husband no matter how he felt about it. He was a soldier and did as he was told.

"I must do my duty, Lady de Moyon," he told her. "Your husband is expecting you."

Emberley closed her eyes and the tears streamed down her face. Lord de Lara stepped forward, a hand outstretched pleadingly.

"Please," he begged softly. "Do not take her. I will pay you handsomely to forget you ever saw her here."

Donnell looked at the old man. "I will tell Baron Buckland that your son absconded with his wife and that you have been hiding her from her husband," he said. "I am sure he will be extremely displeased. You will forgive me for not accepting your offer."

He moved towards the keep entry, knife still to Emberley's throat as the men from his escort began backing away from de Lara's soldiers. It was clear they had the advantage so no one made a move to stop them, but the tension was thick and brittle. Eyes were riveted to Emberley and Donnell, her miserable face and his serious one. As they reached the doorway, Romney suddenly came around and groaned, pushing himself to his knees. Donnell caught sight of the young boy and nodded to one of his men.

"Bring him," he told him.

The soldier moved to Romney, who hollered and kicked as the man captured him. Lord de Lara followed the escort party as they backed out of his keep.

"Please," he continued to beg. "There must be some manner of agreement we can come to. I will offer you a great deal to leave them here and not tell de Moyon of their location."

Donnell was already on the top step leading down into the bailey, the dirk pressed up against Emberley's neck bringing a small trickle of blood. "Be fortunate that I am not demanding the rest of the children," he told him," but I suspect they are well protected now and I do not have enough men to fight for them. But I have the lady and the heir, and that will have to suffice at the moment."

"I do not want to leave my babies," Emberley wept. She had lost the fight against fear and despair. "Please do not do this. *Please.*"

"Perhaps you should have thought of the consequences when you fled Dunster," Donnell said quietly.

"I fled Dunster to save my life," she spat even as he pulled her down the stairs. "If you take me to Julian, I will never see my children again. He will kill me!"

"I have my orders, Lady de Moyon."

She suddenly came to life, kicking and swinging at him. Donnell wasn't able to pull the dirk away from her before she drove the sharp knife into the side of her neck and blood began to gush. She gasped and stopped fighting, her hands flying to her neck as blood poured down her slender white flesh and onto the top of her shift. Lord de Lara gestured to his men.

"Bandages," he hissed. "Hurry. Before she bleeds to death."

Two of his men disappeared but the rest remained, following Donnell and his escort party as they hauled Emberley and Romney down the stairs. Lord de Lara's men returned with wads of linen bandages and Lord de Lara extended them to Donnell about the time he reached the bottom of the slippery, stone steps.

"Please," he said. "Let me give these to her. She is bleeding all over."

Donnell could see that – her hands and the top of her surcoat were a bloody mess. He nodded shortly and Lord de Lara rushed to Emberley's side, pressing the linen on the wound. She was pale, grasping the wad and holding it fast.

"Thank you," she looked at him, her big, blue eyes glimmering with tears. "Please… tell him…."

Lord de Lara shushed her softly. He didn't want her saying too much because it was apparent that de Moyon's men didn't know Gart was involved in the lady's disappearance. Lord de Lara was happy to be the decoy and allow them to think it was his own son who had abducted Emberley. That way, Gart could have the element of surprise on his side.

"Have no fear, sweetheart," he shushed her again. "He will know everything. Be strong and cooperate. All will be well."

She was beginning to cry. "My babies…."

Lord de Lara had her bloodied hand and he kissed it. "They will be well cared for, spoiled as they have never been spoiled. We will take excellent care of them."

She broke down. One of Donnell's men shoved him away, creating a barrier of swords and men between the lady and Lord de Lara. Donnell pulled the bloodied lady away, surrounded by his men, until they reached their horses tied up just inside the gatehouse.

Some of the gate guards saw the hostage situation and tried to intervene, but Lord de Lara called them off, fearful that Donnell and his men would harm Emberley and Romney. They had already proven that they were bold and fearless, and de Lara wasn't willing to take the chance that the lady or her son would be hurt in a scuffle. He didn't think he could live with the guilt if something happened to them.

Heartsick, Lord de Lara was forced to watch as they mounted Emberley and Romney and tore off through the gatehouse and into the green, rolling hills beyond. He had no idea how de Moyon found his wife and children but the fact remained that the man had somehow tracked them down through common sense or devilry. Either way, Emberley and Romney were headed to London. He felt like a failure and a fool, all rolled into one. It had all happened so fast that he was still processing it.

Turning to his shocked men, he began bellowing orders to mobilize his army. He would gather nine hundred men and follow de Moyon's escort all the way into London, perhaps looking for the opportunity to snatch Lady de Moyon and her son back. He simply couldn't let them go without a fight. Gart had left them in his care. Gart had trusted him.

Lord de Lara's next action was to send a missive to Bellham, telling his messenger to ride harder and faster than de Moyon's escort and arrive before they did. Emberley's only hope was if de Lohr and Forbes were waiting for them on the road to prevent her from ever reaching Julian. It was a weak plan but the only one he had. He sent the fastest man he had.

Not usually a praying man, Lord de Lara prayed a great deal that day.

CHAPTER NINETEEN

THE ARMORY AT Bellham was a busy place at any given time considering the de Lohr war machine and the variety of battles it tended to support. But this evening was different.

The mood was thick with anticipation, with deadly fury, as the knights of David de Lohr's ranks prepared for battle. Silver moonlight streamed in through the lancet windows that allowed a small amount of light and air into the armory, a thickly built room in the lower ground floor of Bellham.

It was a basement, a hole of death, packed with weapons and fighting men. Even the baron was there, his squires strapping the plate armor on his legs and chest, armor of the latest style. As David adjusted the hauberk on his head, standing still as the boys finished with his leg protection, his eyes were focused on Gart.

Gart was near the door that led from the armory and headed up to the rear of the manse. He kept his armor and weapons near the door, always, so he could get to them quickly. Even now, he dressed alone, as was his custom, a man who was adept and faster than most efficient squires at donning his own armor and protection. He dressed silently, his custom mail coat hanging snug and heavy on his broad body, his iron-like expression even harder than usual. In the darkness of the armory, in the shadows of the smoking torches, Gart looked like the Devil himself as he prepared for battle.

David knew how coiled the man was. He hadn't taken his eyes off him since they had received the messenger from Trelystan regarding Lady Emberley's abduction. Although the messenger had been ahead of the escort bearing Lady Emberley and her son, he was sure they were no more than a day behind him, which meant they were probably six hours out of London at the moment. That was, of course, providing they had slowed their pace to accommodate the lady and the boy. There was no guarantee they had. So David had ordered his knights to battle with Gart leading the way. They were going to intercept that escort and retrieve the lady and her son.

Gart hadn't said more than two words since receiving the news. It was as if he were afraid to speak, afraid to let himself go. The "Forbes Wall" was up, surrounding and protecting him, an invincible barrier that would keep Gart in and protected until the *sach*, the madness, was released. David had no doubt they would see a greater madness tonight than they had ever seen before. He was a little leery, truth be told. He wanted to keep a close eye on the man.

When his squires finished adjusting the straps on his leg protection, David gathered his broadsword and scabbard and made his way to Gart across the busy armory chamber. Kevin was standing near Gart, dressing, his gaze locking with David's as the man made his way across the room. Kevin held David's gaze for a moment before guiltily lowering his eyes and returned to securing his scabbard. David's eyes lingered on the man's lowered head, knowing he felt responsible for this mess. Gart hadn't blamed the man in the least, but still, Kevin felt a tremendous amount of guilt.

"Ready?" David asked Gart as he approached the man.

Gart nodded, finished with the strap on his sheath. "Aye, my lord."

David's gaze moved over the man. He was the heart of the de Lohr war machine, invincible, the perfect knight. Standing before him in his mail and loaded down with weapons, he was indeed a fearsome sight.

"It is my feeling that since the escort is returning from the Marches, they are more than likely taking the road that leads from Gloucester through Ealing," he told Gart. "We will take Kew Road through Ealing and meet them upon the main road that leads into London."

Gart nodded shortly, tucking one last dirk into his plate armor where he could get at it. David could feel the tension rising off the man like steam. He knew when Gart shifted into battle mode, for he was the perfect killing machine. No emotion, no mistakes. But he could also be singularly focused and David hastened to remind him of what he already knew. This was no ordinary skirmish they were preparing for.

"Gart," he lowered his voice. "Remember that above all else, we must make sure to remove the lady and the boy without injury. We must be careful and calculated."

Gart looked sharply at him, the intense eyes flickering with confusion, then anger. "Do you think I would blindly attack the escort in a rage, my lord?"

David shook his head. "Nay," he said firmly. "But I believe the best course of action for you would be to target the lady and her son. We will take care of the escort. You must get the lady and the boy free of the fighting."

Gart's gaze flickered again, this time, with resistance. "I will have my vengeance, my lord."

David shook his head again. "Not on an escort party," he said quietly. "They are simply doing as they are ordered. If there is any revenge to be sought, seek it against Buckland when all of this is over. And remember that what we do tonight could jeopardize Father St. John's attempts to convince Buckland and Isabella that Buckland should divorce his wife. We must be very careful."

After a moment, Gart seemed to relax somewhat, seeing David's point of view. He sighed heavily.

"We cannot leave any witnesses, you know this," he muttered. "If we leave anyone alive, they will run back to Buckland and tell him that de Lohr forces attacked them and took the lady. Then Buckland will be back on you like flies to honey."

"We wear no colors. They will not know it is my men."

Gart lifted an eyebrow. "You are in the middle of it, my lord. Unless you want to remain at Bellham and let me lead the raid, I am afraid you have very distinctive armor and a very distinctive sword. The de Lohr hilt is well known."

David scratched his cheek reluctantly, knowing Gart was correct but not entirely sure about the murder raid. His thought was to simply retrieve the lady from the escort party with the least amount of bloodshed possible. But Gart had a point. As David rethought his strategy, a fully-armed soldier suddenly appeared in the armory entry. The man went straight to David.

"My lord," he said briskly. "The Earl is sighted."

David's eyebrows lifted. "My brother? How close is he?"

"They are upon us, my lord."

David passed Gart a long look before bolting from the armory. Gart grabbed his helm and went in pursuit, as did de Lara and the other knights that were donning their gear. Soon the armory was emptied of fighting men, leaving the squires to pick up the remainder of the armor and weapons that had been left behind, but the boys soon began bolting from the chamber as well.

The entire group of knights, squires and soldiers raced to the front of the manse where horses and grooms await, and great torches burned deep into the black of the night. As David came around the front of the building, he could see an army approaching from the great drive that led to the front gates. He could hear the horses making noise and the armor and men grinding and grating after a long ride from Hereford. He hadn't seen his brother in months and it would seem the man had arrived on a most opportune night.

The Earl of Hereford had come.

☙

"THE LONGER WE delay, the more chance there is of Lady de Moyon's escort slipping past us and on into London," David explained patiently. "I have explained the seriousness of the situation to you. I am not sure why you want to discuss it further."

Christopher de Lohr, Earl of Hereford and Worcester, was weary after his five-day ride from his seat, Lioncross Abbey, near the Welsh borders. He was two years older than his brother, an enormous man that was taller than his brother by several inches, with a full head of blond hair and a neatly trimmed beard. He had the same sky blue eyes as David and a square-jawed, excruciatingly handsome appearance. But it was his reputation as a fighting man that all men knew and feared, his brother and Gart no exceptions. They both had a healthy respect for the man and his abilities. He was a hell of a warrior.

In spite of his warring reputation, he was an exceedingly calm and level-headed man. David tended to be the hothead in the family, the rash one, and Christopher was collected and wise. But at the moment, having heard his brother's explanation as to why seventy de Lohr men were mobilized and preparing for battle, his normally-calm demeanor was wavering. He was struggling with his composure.

"Let me make sure I understand this," Christopher dragged a weary hand over his face. "I have brought seven hundred men with me from Lioncross with the intention of supplying Baron Buckland with troops to support his efforts in France only to discover that my alliance with Buckland has been destroyed because Forbes had an illicit affair with Buckland's wife?"

He made the situation sound horrible and despicable. David shook his head strongly.

"You are simplifying the circumstances," he said. "It is much more complex than that. Gart knew Lady de Moyon as a child. They were reacquainted when we went to Dunster Castle, may I remind you, at your request. While we were there, Julian went mad, accusing Gart of seducing his wife. I can vouch that the man did nothing of the sort."

Christopher interrupted him, throwing an arm in the direction of the manse courtyard. "Then why are you mobilizing seventy soldiers to go and rescue Lady de Moyon from a Buckland escort?"

He sounded angry, unusual dynamics between the two brothers. David didn't dare look at Gart, standing strong and silent near the door. He wanted to keep his brother's focus, and his anger, directed at him.

"Because Buckland is insane, unpredictable and dangerous," he maintained his calm. "While we were at Dunster, he struck his wife in front of us. He then proceeded to beat the woman nearly to death. I gave Gart permission, as an old friend of the family, to remain behind after the army left and make sure Lady de Moyon was nursed back to health. Gart is not to blame for succumbing to a woman he had always known and been fond of. She is abused and married to a monster. Naturally, he feels protective of her. He loves her."

Christopher waited for more explanation to come forth but when nothing more was said, he lifted his eyebrows expectantly. "She is married to a baron."

"The man is a beast."

Christopher threw his hands up. "It does not matter and you know it," he insisted. "My alliance with de Moyon is too valuable to lose because your knight cannot control his lust for the man's wife."

David could see that the conversation was only going to get worse. He turned to Gart, still lingering in the shadows.

"Get out," he told him.

Gart didn't hesitate. He quit the solar and shut the door behind him. In fact, he was glad to go, afraid that if he had stayed any longer, his temper would have gotten the better of him and it wouldn't do his cause any good to show disrespect to the earl.

Christopher was usually much more level-headed than his brother but, like David had in the beginning, he didn't understand that this wasn't a simple case of adultery. As Gart had explained it, his relationship with Emberley had never felt like that. It had been a simple matter of a man and woman loving each other deeply. Betrayal didn't even enter into it.

He stood outside the door for several minutes, listening to them argue. The longer Gart stood there, the more frustrated and anxious he became. Every moment they delayed added to the possibility that Emberley and the escort would slip by them and into London.

There, Julian would be waiting for her and he knew for a fact that Julian would not allow her to survive the night. He knew the man would beat her to death for her disobedience. Gart's palms began to sweat and his heart to race. If he had the choice of disobeying his liege or saving Emberley's life, he would choose Emberley every time. He simply couldn't wait any longer.

As the de Lohr brothers argued, Gart slipped off into the night.

CHAPTER TWENTY

THE FIRST ARROW hit Donnell in the ribs, sending the man crashing to the ground. Riding behind him on a small gray mare, Emberley and Romney shrieked as more arrows began to fly out of the trees, hitting four more soldiers and sending them to the ground.

The remaining eight soldiers unsheathed their weapons and began shouting, somewhat disoriented because Donnell, their leader, had been struck down and was incapable of delivering orders. The men of the escort party tried to form a perimeter but more arrows flew out of the dark trees and struck down two more.

The men began screaming to each other and the horses, startled, began to scatter. Panic enveloped the group and the little gray mare bolted off in spite of Romney's attempts to rein it to a halt.

Emberley, seated behind her son on the mare, was tossed off in the ensuing confusion but oddly enough, ended up on her feet. She had literally jumped from the little horse when it bucked and now stood on the muddy, dark road, watching the men around her scatter. Arrows zinged overhead, hitting two more men and she shrieked, squatting down on the road and covering her head with her hands. She had no idea where the arrows were coming from and therefore had no idea where to run. So she stayed put, arms over her head, and called to her son.

"Romney!" she cried. "Come back! Come…!"

Another arrow zinged over her head and she screamed again, ducking down low and trying to roll herself into a ball. Then a wave of horses roared in from the south, shielded by the dark trees. She couldn't see who they were but suddenly, one of them came to an abrupt halt beside her and mud flew up in her face. Sputtering, she tried to stand up and run, but strong arms went around her.

"Kitten, are you all right?"

She recognized the voice. Startled, breathless, her enormous eyes struggled to see the face in the darkness, a face she had never imagined she would see again. Her avenging angel had arrived, the archangel Gabriel, and the hosts of heaven were with him as they went about systematically smiting Julian's evil escort. With a cry, Emberley threw her arms around Gart's neck and began weeping hysterically.

"Gart," she sobbed. "It is you!"

Gart held her tightly, watching his men race off after the remainder of de Moyon's escort. He could hardly speak for the lump in his throat, holding Emberley so tightly that he was surely crushing her.

"Aye, kitten, it is me," he murmured, joyously kissing her cheeks and bumping her with his helm. "Are you well? You have not been injured, have you?"

She shook her head earnestly, and then began to look around frantically. "Romney!" she gasped. "The horse ran off and…!"

"He is well, my lady," de Lara suddenly appeared, walking towards her in the darkness and leading a small gray mare. "I caught him before he could get too far."

Romney, spying Gart, leapt off the horse and ran to the man, throwing his arms around his legs. Gart reached down and picked the little boy up, hugging him tightly even as he held Emberley. He realized, even as he held them in his arms, that he was shaking uncontrollably with relief and happiness. He could hardly believe he had them, alive and warm. They were safe and unharmed. He kissed Romney on the cheek before returning his focus to Emberley.

"Tell me truthfully," he put his enormous hand on her face and forced her to look up at him. "Did they treat you well? Are you…?"

She cut him off. "They treated us as well as they could," she replied. "They made sure we were fed and as comfortable as possible. Romney and I are fine. Romney has been very brave."

Gart gazed into her eyes, haunting things in the shadows of the moonlight, reacquainting himself with her beautiful face. He'd missed her desperately. Then he noticed the gash on her neck and the dark stains around the top of her surcoat. His expression darkened.

"What happened to your neck?" he asked through clenched teeth. "What did they do to you?"

It had been five days since the gash and she'd nearly forgotten about it, as it was healing nicely. Her hands flew to her neck, her fingers flitting nervously over the scab.

"It is nothing," she assured him. "It is healing very well."

"Who did it?"

"I did it."

His brow furrowed. "*You* did it? Emberley, if you think I...."

She cut him off, her arms around his waist and her head against his armored chest. "Please," she begged softly. "No harsh words between us. We have not seen each other in weeks. I do not want our first words to be those of anger."

With a heavy sigh, Gart pulled her back into a tight embrace. He didn't believe her about the gash but in hindsight, it really didn't matter. She was healing and healthy. That was all he cared about.

"The rest of the children are still at Trelystan, correct?" Gart asked softly.

Her head was against his chest and she nodded. "They are," she looked back up at him again. "How did you know we had been taken?"

Gart could see his men coming back through the trees. "Lord de Lara sent a messenger," he replied. "We barely had time to intercept your escort. Thank God we anticipated the road they would take and were here to meet them."

Gart's men began returning from the chase, swarming around them as de Lara turned the gray mare loose, smacking it on the rump so it would run off. Gart pulled Emberley tightly against him so she wouldn't be bumped by the excited horses, moving aside when they came too close.

"Are they all dead?" Gart asked his soldiers.

One man nodded. "Aye, m'lord," he replied. "We killed every one of them."

"Make sure these men lying on the road are dead also," he instructed. "We will leave no survivors to tell de Moyon of the attack."

"Aye, m'lord."

"Make it look like bandits if you can, sloppy."

"Aye, m'lord."

As Gart's men went to the men on the road and began slitting throats for good measure, Gart gathered Emberley by the hand.

"Come along, my lady," he said quietly. "We must get you and your son to safety."

Emberley watched Gart's soldiers ensure the death of the de Moyon escort. There was some disgust and trepidation in her expression as she realized what they were doing.

"Why are your men doing that?" she wanted to know. "Why are they defiling the dead like that?"

Gart put his arm around her, trying to shield her from the sight as he led her back to his charger. "Because we cannot leave any witnesses," he told her. "Julian must not know where you are or who has you."

She gazed up at him. "But he will see your arrows," she said. "I am not a warrior but even I know that each army's arrows are distinctive. Since he is allied with de Lohr, will he not know de Lohr arrows?"

Gart handed over Romney to Kevin as they reached the horses. "We did not use distinctive arrows," he told her. "We used arrows that David had stored in his armory, arrows confiscated off the Welsh."

She eyed him as he lifted her onto his saddle. "Julian will have no way of knowing where we are?"

"Nay."

"But what about my babies?"

"I will send Kevin for them immediately."

Emberley fell into contemplative silence as Gart mounted behind her, relishing the feel of his arms around her, his lips on her ear as he spurred the charger back into the darkness. She felt safe again, so very safe and happy to be with him, but fearful of the future. Even though Gart had saved her from joining Julian in London, it did not eliminate the problem. They still had the same concerns and issues. She was still very apprehensive.

Settling back against Gart as they rode through the night, Emberley's apprehension did not abate. As the lights of Bellham Place came into view, the anxiety only grew worse.

03

LADY EMILIE DE Lohr was as sweet as she could be. She wholly embraced Emberley upon her arrive to Bellham and immediately whisked the lady and her son to a chamber where they could bathe and rest.

The warmth and charm of Bellham welcomed the weary woman and her equally exhausted child, and Emberley was introduced to the Earl of Hereford. David greeted her fondly and she responded in kind, remembering the baron from his visit to Dunster.

After the introductions were finished and Lady Emilie appeared, Emberley panicked when she realized that she would be separated from Gart, but Gart had gently assured her that he would not be far if she needed him. As Gart went with David and Christopher behind closed doors, Emberley and Romney followed Emilie up the stairs.

Bellham was a truly luxurious place with big, spacious rooms and comfortable beds. With Romney in the next room being tended to by a pair of servants, Emilie tended Emberley personally. She helped the lady strip off her bloodied, dirty clothes and climb into a massive copper tub of steaming water.

With the help of a few young maid servants, Emilie proceeded to wash Emberley from head to toe, using valuable and expensive products on her hair and skin. The heady scent of lilac filled the room as Emberley relaxed in the tub, scrubbed and soaped and scraped. She felt better than she had in days, listening to Romney in the next room as he argued with the old female servant about not wanting to get out of the tub. But along with her son's voice, she could hear others.

The chamber they were in was directly above the solar and through the floor she could hear raised male voices. Mostly, she could hear David's voice as if responding to something he didn't much like.

Emberley had been relaxing against the back of the tub but as the voices grew louder, she sat forward in the cooling water, listening to the arguing with increasing trepidation. Someone even said something about arresting Gart – she heard it clearly. Even Emilie, inspecting some of her garments to loan to Lady Emberley, could hear the raised voices and the threats of discipline. She glanced uneasily at Emberley and their eyes met.

"It seems to be a lively discussion," she smiled weakly at Emberley.

Emberley listened as they threw more threats around, hearing Julian's name mentioned more than once.

"They are angry with Gart," she said softly. "They want to punish him."

"Nay," Emilie shook her head. "They would not dare."

But Emberley wasn't convinced. "They are angry that he rescued me."

Emilie wasn't sure what to say to that so she said nothing. Instead, she busied herself and pulled forth a soft lamb's wool sheath and a soft, billowy sleeping robe in shades of yellow. Emberley was taller than she was, rounder of the breasts and bum, and only Emilie's most flowing garments would fit the lady. She also set aside a pair of surcoats that were too big for her but would fit Emberley well. One was a mustard yellow linen and the other was a dashing scarlet, both well-made pieces. Satisfied, Emilie went to the tub to collect the huge piece of drying linen that had been laid before the hearth to warm.

She held up the linen. "Would you like to dry off now?"

The water was rather cool. Still listening to the shouting below, Emberley climbed out of the tub and Emilie wrapped her up in the enormous towel. Emberley moved to the hearth to warm up and dry off as Emilie collected a phial of lilac-scented oil. But as Emberley stood there, drying her tender skin and listening to the raised voices on the floor below, her apprehension bloomed.

The voices were growing angrier. After the harrowing flight of the past few days, compounded by the early pregnancy, Emberley's emotions weren't as strong as they normally were. She couldn't stand the thought of losing Gart to punishment. It was too much to take and she suddenly broke down into great heaving sobs.

"Gart," she was sobbing so hard that Emilie could hardly understand her. "Please... I want Gart. Do... do not let them send him away."

Concerned, Emilie went to the woman to comfort her but Emberley collapsed on the floor in a fit of panic and tears. She was sobbing loudly and Emilie knelt down, hugging her gently.

"He is only downstairs, my lady," she said soothingly. "He will not leave this house, I swear it. He will...."

"Please," Emberley grabbed one of Emilie's hands and squeezed hard. "Please... I want Gart. *Please.*"

Stricken with sorrow and sympathy, Emilie clutched Emberley's hand. "I will bring him to you," she assured her softly. "Please do not cry. I will bring him right away."

Emberley was far gone with tears and panic. As Emilie fled the room, she could hear the angry male voices even from the staircase, descending to the dark first floor and heading towards the solar. The voices grew louder, mostly David's and Christopher's, and she knocked loudly on the heavy chamber door. The voices instantly quieted and, after a long moment, the door creaked opened and David's face appeared.

He was not pleased as he focused on his wife. "What is it?"

Emilie was not pleased in return at his gruff greeting. She gave a shove, pushing the door open, something out of character for the normally docile woman. Her frowning gaze was on her husband.

"I hope you are satisfied," she said in a low tone. "Your shouting, angry voices have been heard all over the house and have greatly upset

Lady Emberley."

David sighed heavily, running a hand through his blond hair. "We did not…."

Emilie cut him off with a sharp wave of her hand, something under normal circumstances she would have never done. But her dander was up and she was bolder than usual. Her eyes found Gart, standing over near the lancet windows. She waved him towards the door.

"Gart," she said softly, firmly. "Go upstairs to Lady Emberley. She is hysterical and has asked for you."

With a look of great concern, Gart pushed himself off the wall and walked towards Emilie. "Is she all right?"

Emilie waved him through the door. "She is exhausted and upset. Go and comfort her." As Gart passed a questioning glance at David, Emilie put up a hand as if to block their view of one another. "Enough of this – Gart, do as I say and go to your lady. David, you and Christopher will continue this conversation at another time when you will not upset the entire house and hold. You are loud and rude with your shouting and I will no longer stand for it. You have upset everyone, including me."

It was as much as a stand as Emilie had ever taken. Surprised, David looked at his normally sedate wife before casting his brother a shocked glance. In no mood to tangle with his lovely bride, David put up his hands in surrender.

"As you say, sweetling," he backed down. "I am sorry if we upset you, I truly am."

Christopher, too, was rather shocked at Emilie's demanding behavior. He would have expected it from his own wife, a spitfire of a beauty he was madly in love with, but Emilie had always been exceedingly submissive and sweet. She was as passive as a woman could be. Realizing they must have indeed been overbearing and loud, he, too, supplicated.

"I am sorry, Emilie," he said softly. "We did not mean to upset everyone."

Emilie was righteously upset, her brow furrowed at both her husband and brother-in-law. She pointed a finger at Christopher.

"She heard you," she told him. "She heard you speaking of arresting Gart. How could you say such a thing?"

Christopher sighed heavily, looking at his brother for assistance. David should be the one to deal with his angry wife because he was better suited for it. Christopher was more geared towards his own wife, a woman who would take a swing at him if she was so inclined. David saw his brother's imploring expression and took the hint.

"He is not going to arrest Gart," he assured her. "Chris simply does not know the situation as you and I do. He does not know what Gart has been through with the lady. I was attempting to explain it to him."

Emilie looked at her brother-in-law. "With all of the yelling you have been doing, have you bothered to stop and listen to what David and Gart have been trying to tell you?" she asked. "Gart is in love with a woman whose husband has beaten her mercilessly since they were married. You know Gart Forbes and you know what kind of man he is. He is strong and virtuous, not given to whims of passion. I have known him for four years and I have never caught wind of the man paying inappropriate attention to a woman. He is not the kind. He is trying to save that woman from hell and all you can do is speak of punishing him because of it. What kind of man are you that you would say such a thing?"

Christopher quickly found himself on the defensive. He held up a calming hand to his lovely sister-in-law. "Emilie, I am not trying to be cruel, but the fact of the matter is that the lady is married and Gart...."

Emilie cut him off strongly. "The fact of the matter is that Gart is trying to do what a truly virtuous man would do. He is trying to save the woman he loves from the clutches of a beast." Now she was beginning to tear up, overcome with the sorrow and strife of Gart's story. "What if Dustin was married to a man who beat her mercilessly? Would you walk away from the woman and consign her to her fate or would you try and do something to help her? Put your wife in Lady

Emberley's position and speak to me again of punishing a man who would save her."

Christopher didn't have an easy answer to that. Inevitably, he thought of his beautiful wife, the Lady Dustin de Lohr, in the clutches of a monster and he could see the situation from Gart's point of view. He sighed once again, looking to his brother and seeing that the man was clearly on his wife's side. As much as he hated to admit it, Emilie made some sense. He knew Gart and knew what kind of man he was. He was the kind of man that most knights aspire to be. Perhaps this wasn't simply a matter of lusting after another man's wife.

Perhaps things weren't so clear-cut after all.

℘

GART TOOK THE stairs two at a time racing to the chamber above the solar where Emberley was. He could hear her weeping as soon as he neared the door. Bolting into the room, he found her collapsed in front of the hearth. He went to her, falling swiftly to his knees.

"I am here, kitten," he threw his arms around her. "I am here. Everything is well."

Emberley wrapped her arms around his neck and held him tightly, sobbing into his neck. "Do not leave me," she begged. "Please do not leave me."

He soothed her gently. "I will never leave you, you know that."

"But… but they are going to arrest you."

He shook his head. "Nay, they are not," he assured her. "We are simply trying to figure out what to do. I will not be arrested."

Emberley's tears were not soothed. Gart picked her up off the floor, wrapped up in the damp linen, and carried her over to the large bed. When he tried to set her down, she refused to let go. In fact, she was holding him so tightly around the neck that she was nearly strangling him. He could feel her trembling in his arms.

"Kitten, let go so I can remove my armor," he said softly, gently. "I swear I will not leave this room. Loosen your arms, sweet."

She shook her head and he tried to gently pry her arms free, but the more he would pry, the tighter she would hold him. He finally gave up and sat down on the bed, pulling her onto his lap and simply holding her. It seemed that she needed that most of all at the moment. The armor was cold and undoubtedly jabbing her, but she never said a word. She simply held tight as her sobs faded. Gart did his best to soothe her, saddened that the shouting downstairs had upset her so much.

As he stroked her damp head, calming her, he glanced over and noticed Romney standing in the door of the adjoining chamber. The boy stood there, wide-eyed as he watched Gart and his mother. Having been through as much as his mother had been over the past few days, he was showing great resilience. Emberley was a wreck, yet Romney was not. Gart smiled weakly at the man-child who was growing up before his very eyes.

"Come in, Rom," he encouraged softly. "Your mother is fine. She is simply exhausted."

Dressed in soft, cotton hose and a long-sleeved, white cotton tunic that was too big for him, Romney came into the room, eyeing his mother. He finally sat down next to Gart, his young face serious with concern.

"Mama?" he said softly. "Are you still sick?"

"Still?" Gart's brow furrowed. "What do you mean still sick?"

Emberley was calmer as she lifted her head from Gart's shoulder, her red-rimmed gaze moving between Romney and Gart.

"Nothing to worry over," she told Gart softly. "My belly has been upset."

Gart looked seriously at her. "Should I send for a physic?"

She leaned into his ear. "My belly always aches when I am with child," she whispered. "Romney does not know that."

Gart cleared his throat softly, almost nervously, hoping Romney had not heard his mother. He smiled at the boy, perhaps a bit too brightly, which looked out of place on his serious face.

"Your mother is fine," he told the lad. "It is time for you to go to bed now. We will speak in the morning."

Romney didn't move. He continued to sit next to Gart, his big, blue eyes moving between the knight and his mother.

"You killed my father's men," he finally said to Gart.

Gart's gaze was steady on the boy. "I had no choice, Rom. They were taking you and your mother to London to be with your father. I did it to save you both."

Romney chewed on that statement, the wheels of thought turning in his smart, young brain. "If I had my sword, I could have helped you."

Gart smiled faintly. "You will be a fine knight someday. I will be proud to serve with you."

Romney blinked. "You will?"

"Of course."

"But you serve someone else, that baron who was with my father when you first came to Dunster."

Gart's smile grew. "That is Sir David de Lohr, Baron Thornden. His brother is the Earl of Hereford and the earl happens to be downstairs at this very moment. The earl is a very powerful man. He was friends with King Richard the Lionheart."

Romney looked interested. "Did he fight the savages in the Holy Land?"

Gart nodded. "Both David and the earl fought in the Holy Land, as did your Uncle Erik and I. That was where we met."

Romney grew excited. "Did you and Uncle Erik know the king?"

"We did," Gart replied. "I will tell you all about it someday."

Romney nodded eagerly. He seemed to be thinking very hard about something, his young brow furrowed in concentration.

He slid off the bed and wandered towards the hearth where the big tub of cold bathwater still sat and the phials of mysterious oils and soaps. He inspected everything, absently, his mind on other things. He had so much to say and wasn't sure how to express himself adequately. All he knew was that there was great turmoil in his young life and all of it centered around his father. When Gart was near, everything was happy and joyful. He loved Gart. But when his father was around, the circumstances were miserable and frightening. He hated his father.

Gart and Emberley watched Romney wander near the hearth, carefully picking up the glass phials of oils and inspecting them carefully. He was, if nothing else, a curious and thorough child. Sufficiently calm now that she was in Gart's embrace, Emberley sighed and laid her head back against his shoulder.

"He has been very brave over the past few days," she whispered. "He never complained once."

Gart watched the boy pick up a bar of soap and smell it. "He is a fine lad," he confirmed. "You have raised him well."

A grin spread across her lips. "That is not what you first thought when he robbed you at Dunster."

He thought back to that day. It seemed so long ago. "I must give credit to a lad who would rob someone three times his size," he smirked. "Did he continue to try and rob Lord de Lara after I left?"

She laughed softly. "I am not going to tell you."

"Why not?"

She sat up, looking at him with a grin. "Because you threatened to tan his buttocks if he continued and I do not think he should be punished."

Gart lifted an eyebrow. "I told him not to rob the viscount."

She curled up on his lap, arms around his neck and stroking his face. "The viscount loved every minute of it, as do you," she said softly. "He is a good boy, clever and happy. You are helping to ensure that. Even in the brief time he has known you, you have taught him much."

She knew how to soften him. He let the subject of Romney's disobedience go, swept up in the warmth and adoration flowing between them as she stroked his face and gently kissed his jaw.

"Can I get out of my armor now?" he asked softly, closing his eyes as she kissed his chin.

Emberley nodded and climbed off his lap, still wrapped up in the enormous linen towel. She wrapped it all around her arms and shoulders, completely covering up as she approached her wandering son, who was now inspecting the finely painted wall with a meadow scene.

"Rom," she said softly. "Go to bed now. We have had a busy day."

Romney turned to his mother, seeing that she seemed much better than she had only minutes earlier. He knew it was because of Gart. He took her outstretched hand and allowed her to lead him towards the adjoining chamber.

"When will Orin and Brendt come here?" he wanted to know.

Gart, over by the bed as he removed his armor, heard the question. "I am sending someone to retrieve them tomorrow," he told the boy. "You need not worry. They will be here soon and we will all be together again."

Romney paused at the door that led into the dark bedchamber beyond. His eyes were on Gart. "And then what will happen?"

Gart peeled off his hauberk and tossed it into the corner. "And then we will be happy. Beyond that, I cannot tell you more."

Romney grew serious. He let go of his mother's hand and went to Gart as the man stripped off his mail coat.

"But what of my father?" he wanted to know. "He sent for us to be with him in London. What will happen when we do not come and he knows we are with you?"

Gart faced the boy, contemplating the question. "I am working on a solution to that problem," he told him honestly. "Baron Thornden and the earl are helping me. That is what we were speaking of downstairs. They are smart and powerful men. They can help us find a solution."

Romney wasn't entirely convinced. "But how can we be with you if my mother and father are married? He will want us with him. He will not let us stay with you and I want to stay with you."

"You will have to trust that everything will work out in the end. Great men are working hard to help us."

"But do they know I do not want to be with my father? I want to be with you."

Before Gart could continue the conversation, Emberley took his hand again and pulled him back towards his bedchamber.

"We will speak more of this tomorrow," she said softly, firmly. "It is time for bed now."

Romney let his mother take him to bed and tuck him in. She kissed him and smiled at him, making sure to leave a small taper lit as she closed the door softly so he wouldn't be in total darkness. He lay still and obedient until she shut the door.

Then, he climbed out of bed. He was a man on a mission.

CHAPTER TWENTY-ONE

WITH ROMNEY IN bed, Emberley moved back into her chamber and made sure to bolt the door that led out to the corridor. The room was lit only by a glowing fire in the hearth, casting dancing shadows on the walls, as she made her way back over to the bed where Gart was stripping off his sweaty, dirty tunic. Lady Emilie had lain out the lamb's wool shift and delicate yellow robe and she fingered them distractedly, thinking on her son.

"He has so many questions," she said quietly. "When I hear him speak to you, I am reminded of the time you told me that he wants very much to become a man. He is trying so hard to grow up."

Gart nodded as he unlaced his breeches and slid them off his big frame. "Indeed he is," he replied. "I told you that you must let the child become a man."

"I am trying."

"I know you are."

As Emberley pushed aside thoughts of her son and began to inspect the quality of the shift, Gart made his way over to the tub. He climbed into the big copper pot and sloshed water over the sides. Emberley gasped when she saw what he was doing.

"The water is cold," she pointed out the obvious. "Do you not want hot water?"

He began splashing water over his head and neck, sputtering when it ran over his mouth. "This will do," he held out a hand. "Will you please give me the soap bar?"

She went over to the table and picked up the lumpy bar that smelled of flowers. "You are going to smell like a woman."

"It is better than smelling like a rotted corpse."

She giggled as she put the soap in his hand. "Very well," she said. "But if men start flirting with you, I will only laugh at your misfortune."

Eyes still closed, he grinned as he lathered up his scalp and neck. "You are a cruel woman."

She giggled as she made her way back to the bed, dropping the big linen towel in favor of the lamb's wool. It fit her snugly but comfortably, and she donned the yellow robe over that. Lady Emilie had left a large bone comb as well as a few other toiletries, and she ran the comb through her hair repeatedly as she watched Gart bathe. Now that he was here, she was fully calm and settled. The situation was feeling normal again, alone in a world with no Julian, only Gart. He was the center of everything.

She took a stool by the hearth and combed her hair to dry it against the heat from the fire. When Gart finished soaping and rinsing, he opened his eyes to find her sitting there, looking like an angel in her yellow dressing gown and silky, blond hair. The glow of the fire behind her gave her a halo appearance, glowing all around her body. Rinsing off the last of the soap, he smiled at her, feeling so incredibly fortunate to have her with him again.

"I have missed you, kitten," he said softly. "Every minute of the days and nights that we were separated were filled with thoughts of you. Have you been well?"

She returned his smile as she combed through her hair, the color returning to her cheeks in the warmth of the blaze. "I have been very well but I have missed you terribly," she replied. "The boys were lonely for you also. They had no one to play with."

He chuckled softly, looking around for the big, linen towel and seeing that it was draped neatly on a chair near the bed. He stood up, water sloshing off his big body and onto the floor as he climbed out of the tub in his quest for the damp towel that Emberley had used.

"You would not tell me what they did to Lord de Lara," he grabbed the towel and began rubbing it across his legs. "I would suspect he served well in my place as an object of their aggression."

She smiled in agreement but that smile soon faded. "I miss my babies," she responded. "They were terribly frightened when Julian's escort came for us."

Gart wasn't going to bring up the subject of the escort just yet, but since she did, he took her lead.

"Do you want to tell me what happened?" he asked gently.

Her smile faded completely. "I am not entirely sure," she said honestly. "I know that Lord de Lara keeps the gates open and people come in and out of Trelystan all of the time. I suppose the escort entered just like any other party. I truly do not know. All I know is that they were suddenly standing there as I crossed through the bailey."

He pondered that explanation a moment. "How is it that only you and Romney managed to go with them?"

She shrugged. "As we ran for the keep, I was captured. Orin and Brendt took Lacy up to our chamber and bolted the door, but Romney stayed behind to protect me. They captured him, too. The only reason they were able to take us from Trelystan was because they held a knife to my throat and threatened to kill me if Lord de Lara showed any resistance."

It all made a great deal of sense to him now. He thought of Romney standing against armed knights, attempting to protect his mother, and it made him proud and sick at the same time. His jaw ticked as he dried off his chest and arms, looking between his task and Emberley's rosy face.

"That is how you got that gash on your neck," he rumbled.

She nodded, hearing the hazard in his tone. "Aye," she admitted. "I tried to fight back and ended up goring myself on the tip of the knife."

He sighed heavily. "But that is the only injury you received? You are well otherwise?"

"I am well."

"And the baby is well?"

She rubbed her belly. "He is."

He tossed the towel aside and went to the bed, yanking back the coverlet. He didn't want to talk about her abduction from Trelystan anymore because he could feel himself growing increasingly upset over it. He didn't want to spend the first night with her in weeks upset over something that was a waste of effort. Focusing on the comfortable mattress before him, he waved her over.

"Come to bed now," he told her. "We will speak more of this tomorrow."

She obediently rose from the stool, feeling that her hair was mostly dry and setting the comb down on the table as she moved to the bed. In silence, she braided her hair into a thick single braid and removed the yellow robe, clad only in the lamb's wool sheath.

Emberley climbed onto the mattress and Gart climbed in after her. He pulled the coverlet up around them, enclosing her within his powerful arms. The moment Emberley felt his flesh against hers, the safety of his embrace, the tears began to come.

She snuggled up against him as close as she could go, settling in, feeling his body envelope her. Gart's hand was against her face, cradling the side of her head, and he could feel the warm tears drip onto his flesh.

"What is wrong, kitten?" he kissed the side of her head. "Why do you weep?"

She shrugged. "I have no idea why," she whispered. "Only that I have missed you terribly and that I am frightened. Frightened that Julian will find where I am, frightened that your liege will arrest you for saving me from Julian's escort, frightened that...."

He cut her off with gentle gruffness, rolling her onto her back and looming over her. "The only thing you should be worrying about is bringing our son safely into the world," he said softly. "You must trust me that everything else will work out. I am depending on that faith. It keeps me strong."

She gazed up into his handsome face, a soft hand coming up to stroke his cheek and watched him kiss the palm of her hand.

"I do have faith," she murmured. "I love you so much, Gart. I dream of the day when you and I can live free from Julian and his terror."

"As do I."

Both hands came up as she gently touched his face. "Tell me where we will live when all of this madness is over."

He kissed her hands when they came close to his mouth. "It seems that things have changed somewhat," he admitted. "It seems that Albemarle has another heir, a young son I was unaware of, so the inheritance I was going to solicit from him is no longer mine. But there is still inheritance on my mother's side. I intend to go to France and seek that as soon as Julian divorces you."

She looked surprised. "Julian divorces me?"

His green eyes twinkled. "It would seem that we have a powerful priest on our side that will help persuade him," he kissed the tip of her nose. "He has heard Julian's confession as well as the queen's, as they attend him regularly. The priest has agreed to tell Julian and Isabella that the penance for their sin of adultery will require Julian to divorce his wife. If everything happens as it should, Julian will come to you very soon with a request for a divorce. As soon as it is granted, you and I will be married."

Emberley was shocked. "Is that why he sent an escort for me? To speak to me of divorce?"

Gart shook his head, feeling the familiar heat of desire fill his veins as he kissed her cheek, her forehead. "Nay," he murmured. "He sent an escort for you because the queen has apparently focused her attention on another man and Julian wants to make her jealous by showing attention to you."

Emberley lay there, struggling to absorb all he was telling her. But then Gart's lips drifted over hers and she responded hungrily, distracted from her thoughts, as his big hands snaked underneath her shift and lifted it over her head. Their hot, nude flesh came together and

Emberley wrapped her arms around his neck, giving herself over to him completely as his big body overwhelmed her.

His mouth was on her neck, her breasts, carefully kneading her flesh and suckling her nipples. He was everywhere, his hands and mouth, tasting her flesh, feeling her heated response against him. As his mouth moved to the pink folds between her legs and he pushed her legs apart, he began to whisper to the child she carried, his mouth against her slightly rounded belly, telling the child how welcome he was. His fingers were inside her, stroking her as if trying to touch the life they had created together.

Emberley listened to his soft whispers, tears of tenderness filling her eyes, loving the man more than words could express. When he finally lifted himself up and thrust into her eager body, the words he whispered in her ear were purely of his love for her.

It had been weeks since he had last felt her against him, around him, and Gart savored every movement, every stroke, listening to Emberley's soft gasps of pleasure. They were like music to his ears. It wasn't long before he felt her powerful release around his throbbing organ, driving him mad as she wept with pleasure.

When he finally took his pleasure deep inside her body, he held her hips firmly, grinding his pelvis against hers and feeling her release around him again and again until she was absolutely exhausted. With one hand to her breast, gently fondling her, he kissed and nuzzled her until he grew hard again and then he resumed making love to her, feeling the wetness he put into her, feeling their bodies as they joined.

They were heavily into lovemaking when a knock on the door startled them both.

CHAPTER TWENTY-TWO

JONAS HAD BEEN hearing confessions since noon. Although he took his job seriously and always had, still, it was rather amusing when the nobility entered the church and made their way to the banks of confessionals against the north wall.

They were dark, little cells built from heavy oak, used mostly by the nobility, as the upper crust of England would not use cells patronized by the poor or lesser classes. These confessionals were meant for high class confessions.

It was just after Lammas Day, a holy holiday celebrating the wheat harvest and usually a holiday where the nobles spent days celebrating with ale and rich foods. It was a festival ripe with debauchery and Jonas was anticipating a host of wild stories as the nobles began to infiltrate the church just after noon. For a man who lived cleanly, there were times when those stories would keep him up at night, wondering what it would be like, just once, to know a woman in the Biblical sense.

Sitting in the confessional bank, in the large confessional at the end where most of the upper crust attended, he could see the light flashing as the door to the church opened and closed. The sunset was glowing, the day growing cool as night set in. He knew it had been a balmy day because he had been outside earlier, enjoying the day and thinking on his conversation with David de Lohr.

Twice, he almost wavered and went back on his word, but the more he thought on the situation, the more he understood that what was considered wrong was, in fact, right. The Queen of England was a wreck of woman, vile and appalling, and any man who would openly cavort with her was surely the same. Perhaps it was a matter of saving Lady de Moyon from her husband's depraved soul. Surely such a man was not a man of God.

That was how he reconciled it in his own mind, at any rate. As he sat in the confessional, mulling over his thoughts, the door to the small booth suddenly opened and a woman slipped in. He could smell the very strong perfume, like cinnamon and cloves. Then a heavily accented voice spoke.

"Forgive me, Father, for I have sinned," she asked softly. "It has been six days since my last confession."

Jonas perked up. He knew that voice. He had heard it before, a few times. Peering through the slats in the confessional wall, he could see a richly robed woman and a flash of a profile.

It was Isabella. He had suspected she might come this day, directly after a holy day and wild feasting. That was usually her pattern, which was why he had taken confessional duty rotation from Father Constantine so the man could focus on other things. Jonas had sat through a morning of insipid confessions from an earl, three barons, and four noblewomen. Now his suspicions had paid off as the grandest lady of all joined him in private.

"Speak, my lady, of sins past and present," he made the sign of the cross against the confessional partition.

Isabella of Angouleme was a mere sixteen years old, a woman who had lived much in her short life. Married to the king at twelve years of age, she appeared much older than her sixteen years. She had not aged well. A small woman with big, brown eyes, she sniffled delicately into her fine silk kerchief.

"I... I have been wicked," she pretended to sniffle but the truth was that it was all an act. "I have drunk to excess and in my drunkenness have allowed men of less reputation to take advantage of me. I am innocent of desire, Your Grace, but my husband does not protect me from those who would prey upon me. I plead forgiveness for being too weak to fight them away."

Jonas listened in silence, contemplating his next move. "These men you speak of," he said softly. "What have they done?"

She pretended to weep, deeply disturbed by the nature of the sin. "They have preyed upon my flesh, taken advantage of...."

He cut her off. "Names, lady. I cannot help you unless I know who has done this to you."

Isabella brought the kerchief to her eyes, wiping them daintily. "I...I do not know their names. They are friends of my husband, men of the court."

He remained steady even though, inside, he was disgusted with her lies. "They are men of the court yet you do not know their names?"

She hesitated. "Perhaps I do know one or two. Why does it matter who they are? It only matters that I be absolved of my sins, sins I did not want to commit."

Jonas was struggling to keep his disgust at bay. So far, she was playing the victim, which enraged him. The woman was no more a victim than Caligula was at an orgy. He tried another angle.

"Man is made fallible by God, my lady," he said softly. "We are made to sin but we are also made to forgive. If you have knowingly given in to temptation, all you need do is admit your trespasses and God will forgive you. In order to name your penitence, I must know who you have sinned with. I will give penitence to you both so that you may be absolved of your sins."

Isabella seemed to perk up, forgetting about the act of remorse she always put on for the priests. She did the same thing every time she went to confession, thinking they would never notice. But they did.

"Is this true?" she asked.

"It is, as long as you are both truly sorry. Who have you sinned with?"

She appeared timid again, looking around the confessional booth to make sure the door wasn't open and no one could hear her. She leaned towards the screen that separated her from the priest.

"Armand de Foix," she whispered.

Jonas sat upright. That wasn't the name he was expecting. A look of supreme confusion crossed his featured and he struggled not to let his confusion show in his words.

"Who is this man?"

She was pressed against the screen. "A man sent by my father," she hissed. "He is a mercenary. I was overcome with desire but I am truly sorry. What is my penance for my sin?"

Jonas was off-balance now. The conversation was not going as expected. "Only de Foix?"

"What do you mean?"

"Is there no one else you have sinned with?"

Against the screen, Isabella's features creased with an angry pout. "There is no one else! Why would you ask such terrible things of me?"

Jonas could see that she was verging on a tantrum and quickly moved to stop it. It would not do to infuriate the young queen, for a myriad of reasons, mostly because he liked his head and neck just where they were.

"You must do one hundred Hail Mary's and pray at the grave of St. Edmund for your penance," he said quickly. "Mention de Foix's name in your prayers and he will be forgiven as well. Go with God, my lady."

Isabella was quickly soothed, crossing herself quickly before leaving the confessional booth. Jonas sat there, watching the flickers of light through the screen, hearing her speak with her women as she wandered from the church.

He left the confessional when she quit the church. There was much on his mind, much that de Lohr needed to know. Making his way to his quarters deep in the bowels of the cathedral, he collected his heavy cloak and his purse. He had to get to Bellham Place and he was sure he was going to have to pay someone to take him there.

The stakes of the situation had changed.

CHAPTER TWENTY-THREE

BELLHAM PLACE WAS very big. Romney discovered this as he made his way down the master staircase, a big thing made out of stone. It was cold on his bare feet. He was supposed to be in bed but he had something he had to do. He was looking for the baron and the earl that Gart had spoken of, men that were trying to help them. He wanted to tell them something.

But Bellham was a big place with scary shadows on the walls. Romney paused at the bottom of the stairs, looking around. He spied two big rooms that were dark and spooky. There were ghosts in there, real ghosts this time. He could hear people moving around but he wasn't sure where the sounds were coming from.

Over to his right, tucked back in a small corridor, there was a door with light emitting from around it. He thought maybe there were people there. Summoning his courage, he came off the steps and headed in that direction.

He stood outside the door, listening to the voices inside. They were considerably softer than they had been earlier and he could hear that they were male voices. Perhaps they were the men he was looking for. Timidly, he knocked on the door. He had to do it three times before someone opened the panel.

A muscular, blond man appeared. He peered into the darkness over Romney's head, looking for an adult, but was shocked when he noticed the child standing in the doorway at his feet. His brow furrowed as he gazed down at the boy, though not unkindly.

"Greetings," he said rather pleasantly. "Who are you?"

Romney swallowed away his nervousness. "My name is Romney de Moyon," he said. "My... my mother and I came here this afternoon."

A faint smile crossed David's lips as he stood back, ushering the boy inside the room and remembering how he and his brothers had robbed him of a pence for each when he last visited Dunster.

"Master Romney," he acknowledged. "Please come in. Do not stand out there in the darkness."

Romney entered the room, his eyes wide with apprehension, noticing a very large man standing over by the softly glowing hearth. That man didn't seem unkind, either. But he did look curious. Romney swallowed again, knowing he should probably speak since he had interrupted these men in conference.

"I...," he swallowed again and almost choked. "I wanted to speak with the baron and the earl."

Christopher came away from the hearth, his focus on the nice-looking, young man in clothes that were far too big for him.

"You have found us," he said. "I am Christopher de Lohr and this is my brother, David. How may be we be of service, Master Romney?"

Romney's mouth popped open as he gazed between the two big men. "Are you really the Earl of Hereford?"

Christopher nodded, his sky blue eyes twinkling in the dim light. "I am," he replied. "How can I help you?"

"And we have already met. You and your brothers robbed me at Dunster recently if you will recall," added David.

Romney was suddenly nervous and excited. He had never met someone so important. He began to shift around on his cold feet.

"Yes, I remember now. Gart said...," he pointed upstairs. "He said that you were trying to help us so we would not have to go to my father."

Christopher's smile faded as he glanced at his brother. "We are discussing many options regarding Gart and your father, young Romney. I would not worry about it if I were you."

Romney sensed the earl wasn't as urgent on the matter as he was.

Realizing that fed his bravery because he wanted the earl to know just how important this was to him. This was his life.

"I wanted to tell you not to send my mother and me to my father," he said sincerely. "My father… he is very mean. He hits my mother until she cannot walk. He makes her bleed and then my brothers and I must tend her because he will not let anyone else help her. Sometimes we cannot help her very much but we try."

All of the humor was gone from Christopher's features. He sighed heavily and crouched down in front of the boy, seriously studying the young features. He could see nothing but truth and honesty there.

"That is very brave of you to help your mother," he said softly. "But you must understand that your mother and father are married. No one can interfere with that, not even me."

Romney began to feel a sense of fear, fearful that all would not be well as Gart said it would be. He had to make the man understand.

"One time, my father pushed my mother down the stairs because he was angry," his eyes started to tear up and he wiped them away furiously with the back of his hand. "She had a baby in her belly and the baby died. I remember that my mother almost died, too, until my father let a physic come and tend her. My mother… I love my mother. She kisses us and gives us treats, and plays games with us. She takes care of us."

Christopher gazed steadily at the boy, his heart just about breaking. The lad was struggling so hard to be brave but his fear, his tears, had the better of him. He put a big hand on the boy's shoulder as he stood up.

"Come over here and sit down, Master Romney," he led the boy over to the hearth where a little chair sat. It was Christina's chair, painted pink, but Romney didn't notice in the dim of the room. Christopher sat in the bigger chair opposite the boy, focused on his distressed young face. "It sounds as if your mother is a wonderful woman."

Romney's lower lip was trembling as he continued to angrily wipe away tears. "She is always afraid when my father is home," he said.

"When he goes away, she is happy again. When Gart came to stay with us, she was happy every day. Gart makes her happy. He is nice to her and buys her nice things, and she... she is not afraid any more. Gart takes care of all of us and he loves us. We love him. That is why I do not want to go back to my father. Please do not make us."

The last sentence was spoken with a sob. The young boy lost his battle against tears and he hung his head, weeping softly. Christopher watched the lowered head a moment before lifting his gaze to his brother.

David stood a few feet away, his features taut with sympathy. He looked as if he were about to cry himself. Christopher put a gentle hand on the boy's lowered head as he stood up and went to his brother.

"Did you send this child in here to try and convince me?" he hissed at his brother.

David rolled his eyes. "Do you truly think I would be so treacherous?"

Christopher pursed his lips irritably at his brother for a moment before looking back to the child. Romney was wiping his face and struggling to stop his tears. Christopher sighed heavily.

"Surely I cannot return the boy and his mother to Buckland now," he whispered. "To hear of the situation from the child's perspective is true and clear."

Romney turned around, hearing the whispers. He focused on the two men. "My father says that the queen is his special friend," he said, wiping at his nose. "Maybe the queen will want him so he will forget about us. Then we can be with Gart and we will be happy again."

Christopher and David passed long glances at each other. "It is not that simple, lad," Christopher said. "We cannot...."

Romney jumped up from the stool, interrupting him. "But my father says he only keeps my mother because she is beautiful and has given him fine sons," he said insistently. "When he tires of her, he will kill her and find another wife. I have heard him say so!"

Christopher went to the boy, gently forcing him back down on the little chair as he sat opposite him. "Romney, I understand your concern," he said gently. "But the fact remains that your father and mother are married. No one can destroy that marriage no matter how terrible your father is."

Romney's brow furrowed as he thought on that, laboring furiously for an answer to all of this. "My father will kill my mother if you take us to him. I do not want my mother to die!"

Christopher patted the boy sympathetically on the arm. "Your father is not going to kill your mother any time soon," he assured him. "You and your mother are going to stay here as my guests for a time."

"How long?" Romney wanted to know.

Christopher shrugged. "Until we can figure out a solution to the situation."

Romney felt a little better, but not much. At least he knew they weren't going to turn them over to his father tomorrow. There was still time. As he sat in brooding silence, Christopher stood up and went to the small service door in the corner of the solar. Opening it, he instructed the servant sleeping in the alcove to bring the boy some warmed milk. Closing the door softly, he went back over to his brother.

"Now what?" he demanded in a whisper. "Since I cannot return the boy and his mother to Buckland, what do you suggest?"

David puffed out his cheeks, looking thoughtful. "It would solve our problem if Buckland went to France and got himself killed fighting Isabella's war," he muttered, half in jest. "Gart could marry Lady de Moyon and we would not have to agonize over this any longer."

Christopher rubbed wearily at his eyes. "Perhaps I should hire an archer myself simply to be done with it. From what you have told me, Buckland has completely lost his mind."

David had to agree. "Who would enter my home and try to slug me in the mouth? De Moyon is an idiot."

Christopher fought off a grin. "I would have liked to have seen you knock his teeth out."

David looked at him with a smirk. "It was purely in self-defense, I assure you."

"I do not believe you."

David started snorting as he and Christopher continued their conversation about Julian and his disturbed behavior. But as they muttered in the darkness, Romney caught most of what they were saying, especially the part about killing Julian.

Although Romney was only seven years old, he was an exceptionally intelligent child. He realized in simple terms that the only way to save his mother and his family was to kill his father. He had been protecting his mother all of his life but now that he was growing older, he could protect her better. Especially from his father.

As he was lost to muddled thoughts, a servant entered through the small door next to the hearth with a big, steaming cup in his hand. Christopher pointed to the boy and the servant handed Romney the cup of warm milk. The servant disappeared as Romney sipped at the milk – it had cinnamon, nutmeg and honey in it, making it sweet and delicious. He tried to gulp it down but it was too hot, so he settled for a steady, loud sip.

At some point, Christopher and David broke from their conference and came to sit near Romney. The earl sat silently in a big oak chair while David sat behind Romney on a chair that was really two built into one, crafted from a giant piece of oak. Romney sipped loudly at his milk, watching the men as they gazed at him.

"Do you have a boy, my lord?" Romney asked Christopher.

The earl smiled at him, mostly because Romney had a huge milk ring around his upper lip. "I do," he replied softly. "I have two daughters and a son who was born to my wife and me last year."

Romney gulped a hot swallow. "Will he be the earl when he grows up?"

Christopher nodded. "God willing," he said. "And I understand you have brothers and a sister, too."

Romney nodded, gulping the last of the cup and dribbling milk onto his tunic. "My brothers are Orin and Brendt," he told him. "My baby sister is Lacy. She likes to kiss everybody."

Christopher's smile grew. "Is that so?"

Finished, Romney set the cup down on the nearest table. "She loves Gart," he told him. "She wraps her arms around his head and kisses his cheek until it is all wet. She slobbers all over him."

Christopher bit his lip to keep from laughing, looking at David to see that the man was silently laughing as well. Neither one of them could imagine the all-powerful Gart Forbes would allow a baby to slobber all over him.

"Well," Christopher wiped a hand over his beard in an attempt to hide the smile. "That sounds delightful."

Romney was feeling more at ease now that he had a belly full of warm milk. "One time, she hugged his head so that he could not see. Her arms were over his eyes and when my mother tried to remove her, Gart told her to let Lacy alone. Lacy hugged his head and licked his scalp."

David couldn't help it. He burst out into soft laughter, quickly looking away when Romney turned around to look at him. David stood up from his chair, struggling with the mental picture of Gart and a licking baby. But it was at that moment that both brothers began to realize the extent of Gart's devotion to Lady de Moyon and her children. An ordinary man would not have tolerated a slobbery baby that was not of his loins, but Gart had. Whatever he was feeling for the family went beyond simple lust for the mother. It went deeper than they could imagine.

Sobering, Christopher stood up also and held out a hand to Romney.

"Perhaps it is time for you to return to bed," he told the boy. "It was an honor to meet you, Master Romney de Moyon."

Romney took the outstretched hand and Christopher shook his little hand kindly.

"Thank you," Romney said. "Are you really going to let my mother and me stay here for a while?"

"I really am."

Romney's relief was visible. He turned around and David was there, holding open the solar door as Christopher and Romney passed through it. The hall outside was dark, the entry hall beyond even darker. Romney wasn't afraid of the ghosts with the big earl walking next to him. As they neared the dark, stone staircase, there was a knock at the front door.

Christopher wasn't concerned because whoever it was would have had to get past the gate guards first. Trouble didn't usually come knocking at the front door. David moved past him to answer it. He threw the big, iron bolt and pulled open the panel.

Jonas was standing in the moonlight, wrapped in his heavy traveling cloak. He looked dark and secretive, his eyes darting to the occupants of the entry hall. His expression was taut with seriousness.

"Father Jonas," David ushered the man inside and out of the cold. "What are you doing here this time of night?"

Jonas pulled the hood off his dark, curly hair. He noticed Christopher on the stairs with a young boy. He had known the earl through his brother, having met the man on a few occasions. He acknowledged him.

"My lord," he bowed slightly at Christopher before turning to David. "We must speak. Is Forbes here?"

David didn't like the tone of the man. Something ominous filled him as he nodded.

"He is here."

"Get him." Jonas began removing his cloak as a servant suddenly appeared with a lighted taper. The priest tossed his cloak at the hovering servant as he turned back to David. "Quickly. Take me someplace private."

David immediately took the priest back into the solar as Christopher escorted Romney up to the sleeping chambers on the second floor. He paused in front of the door where Lady de Moyon was sleeping, knowing that Gart was with her. He rapped heavily on the big oak door.

Christopher and Romney stood there a few moments, waiting, finally looking at each other as they heard movement on the opposite side of the panel. Christopher rapped again and Gart yanked the door open a few moments later.

It was clear that Gart wasn't pleased. Standing in the open doorway, bare-chested and with only his leather breeches on, he was prepared to take someone's head off until he saw it was the earl. Then he saw Romney and he went from angry to concerned, all in a split-second.

"Rom?" he opened the door wider, his gaze on the boy. "What is the matter? You are supposed to be in bed."

Christopher answered before Romney could. "Father Jonas has arrived," he told Gart. "He has asked to speak with you."

Gart stared at Christopher a moment, his features tinted with shock as he tried to gauge, from Christopher's expression, what was going on. There was no good reason he could think of that the priest should be here at this time of night. After a moment, he nodded obediently.

"I shall be down shortly," he said, reaching out for the boy. "Come back to bed, Rom."

Romney turned to Christopher, his big, blue eyes on the man. "Thank you for the milk, my lord."

Christopher smiled faintly at the polite young lad. "You are welcome," he replied. "I look forward to having more conversations with you, young Romney."

Romney nodded, following Gart back into the sleeping chamber. As Christopher retraced his steps back down the staircase, Gart shut the chamber door and went in search of his tunic.

By this time, Emberley was sitting up in the bed, making sure to cover herself up to her neck so her son would not see that she was completely nude. Her eyes were wide on the child.

"Rom?" she asked. "Why were you with the earl?"

Romney continued walking towards the adjoining door that led into his sleeping chamber. "I went to talk to him."

"What about?"

His brow furrowed. "I do not want to tell you," he was grumpy, exhausted and emotional. "I wanted to talk to him and that is all."

Gart found his soiled tunic and pulled it over his head. "That is *not* all," he said. "You will not speak to your mother with disrespect. She has asked you a question and you will answer her."

Romney stood by the adjoining door, frowning. "But it is my business. Why do I have to tell her everything? Maybe it is a secret."

Gart cocked an eyebrow at the stubborn lad and opened his mouth but Emberley stopped him.

"It is all right, Gart," she said softly, her eyes on her son. "He is growing up, as you said. If he does not want to tell me all of his business, that is his choice. But I do want to make sure he did not bother the earl. You are not in trouble, are you?"

When Romney shook his head, Gart spoke up. "You did not try to rob him, did you?"

Romney shook his head more firmly. "I do not have my sword."

Gart grunted, finding his boots and moving to sit on the bed to pull them on. "You did not have a sword and you robbed me quite adequately."

Romney started to make a face at him but thought better of it. "I did not rob him," he repeated, looking to his mother. "May I go to bed now, Mama?"

Emberley nodded. "Sweet dreams, sweetheart."

Romney opened the adjoining door and passed into the dark room beyond, shutting the panel softly behind him. Emberley's gaze lingered on the closed door a moment before turning to Gart.

"What do you suppose he was doing with the earl?" she asked softly.

Gart finished pulling on one boot and moved to pull on the other. "I would not know," he replied, glancing at her over his shoulder. "But with the priest here, I would encourage you to get dressed. I am concerned as to why he has come."

As Gart finished with his boot, Emberley crept up behind him and embraced him from behind, her head on his shoulder and her arms around his waist.

"If it is not good news, promise me that we will run," she whispered. "We will run back to Trelystan to retrieve Orin, Brendt and Lacy, and then we will flee. I care not where we go, Gart, so long as we are together."

He turned to face her, pulling her into his arms. "What about Rom's inheritance?" he asked softly. "You were so concerned that the boy be given his due."

She shook her head, tears in her eyes. "It is more important that we are all together," she whispered. "I put money and power over love and happiness and I should not have. Forgive me. Promise me that if the priest does not bring good news that we will flee tonight."

He kissed her gently, holding her tightly against him. "I swear that we will never be apart," he whispered, kissing her ear. "If that means we must flee tonight, then so be it. I love you, Em. Madly and deeply, I do. I swear I will do what is right and necessary so that we may be together always."

She pulled back, smiling bravely for him as he kissed her once more. Then he released her and stood up.

"Get dressed," he told her. "Come downstairs when you are presentable."

She gazed up at him, hesitant. "Are you certain?"

He nodded. "Aye," he went to the door. "I want the priest to meet you. Letting him see what I am fighting for will only strengthen our case."

She nodded reluctantly, blowing him a kiss as he quit the chamber and quietly shut the door behind him.

Tossing off the coverlets, Emberley leapt out of bed and went in search of the shift Gart had pulled off of her and the surcoats that Lady Emilie had left behind. She tried not to let fear grip her heart, but it was difficult.

If Gart was concerned for the priest's odd-hour visit, she was positively scared to death.

CHAPTER TWENTY-FOUR

"BASTARDS!" JULIAN SCREAMED. "There is no doubt in my mind that de Lohr took my wife. There could be no other explanation!"

The Sheriff of Ealing, Lord Bardwell, stood just inside the door of Julian's lavish apartments at the Tower of London. He had come to deliver the news that several of Baron Buckland's men had been massacred out on Ealing Road, the main drive from Oxford to London. They had found eight men in total, all with their throats slit, men bearing the insignia of Baron Buckland.

So they had come to London to seek Buckland because one of the sheriff's men had heard that Buckland was staying at the tower. The man was a fixture around London and a known companion of the queen, so the sheriff and his men had proceeded to the Tower to let the baron know of his misfortune. The baron, a wily man with a bad smell about him, had exploded.

"My lord, I saw nothing that would indicate the de Lohrs had anything to do with the murder of your men," the sheriff explained. "Your men were set upon by bandits. Their money and anything else of value was missing and the horses gone."

Julian went mad. He began kicking over chairs and trying to wrest legs off tables. The sheriff stood back, well out of the way, as Julian began hurling things towards the hearth. Things were shattering everywhere.

"Where is my wife?" Julian howled.

"We found no trace of a woman, my lord."

Julian roared. "But she was with them," he screamed, staggering to a table near the door and pulling a small piece of vellum off the surface. "This is the missive they sent to me telling me that they had found my wife and were bringing her to London."

The sheriff remained stoic in the face of the vellum being shaken under his nose. "As I said, my lord, there was no trace of any woman. If she was with them, the bandits must have carried her off."

Julian didn't agree with that assessment. He waved the vellum in the man's face a few more times before letting it fall to the ground. "One of my men arrived earlier today with this missive. It clearly says that my wife was at Trelystan and that my men are bringing her to London. And now you tell me that the entire escort has been murdered and there is no sign of my wife?"

"Nay, my lord."

Julian exploded again, kicking over a table that held a lit taper on it. As it fell to the floor and ignited the rushes that were nearby, the sheriff watched the fire gain steam with some concern as Julian continued to rant. Finally, the sheriff moved to the rushes and stamped out the fire, thinking perhaps that it was time for him to leave. He had delivered his message, apparently to a madman, and was eager to be gone.

"He has taken her," Julian seethed. "There is a conspiracy with de Lohr and de Lara to keep my wife from me. I will not have it, do you hear? I will not have it!"

The sheriff was inching back towards the door, silently motioning for his men to quit the chamber. He was very near the door as he spoke.

"Perhaps you should ask the Earl of Hereford personally," he suggested. "The man came through Ealing earlier tonight and brought an entire army with him. Perhaps he took her."

Julian froze mid-rant. "He is here with an army?"

The sheriff nodded. "I saw him myself, my lord."

Julian stared at the man a moment before resuming his madness full-bore. He screamed and fell to his knees, shaking his fists at the sky.

"That is *my* army," he howled. "It is the army for Isabella, for her lands in France. Now he will not give me the manpower I requested because of his stupid brother and… *arrrrrrrgggggggggg*!"

He was off on a serious tangent, tearing into the fine cushions that lined an oak bench and ripping them apart with his bare hands. The sheriff watched him for a few moments before quitting the room. The man was quite mad and he did not want to fall victim to his violence.

Unaware the sheriff had left until he had ripped all of the pillows to shreds, Julian eventually noticed he was alone in the sumptuous chamber. Panting, exhausted, he began to think of all of the things that had gone wrong for him, starting when he had met with Baron Thornden at Dunster those months ago. The day that Gart Forbes had arrived, everything had gone awry.

It was still going awry. Isabella no longer favored him and he knew it was only a matter of time before he was kicked out of his Tower apartments and out of favor completely. His alliance with the de Lohr brothers had collapsed thanks to Gart Forbes' interference. Although he could not link Gart to his wife's presence at Trelystan Castle, he was sure that Forbes had something to do with it as well. The man had invaded his life and stolen his wife, picking away at the very fabric of his existence piece by piece. Julian had to do something before it was gone completely. He had to do something before Forbes destroyed him.

Going to Bellham had not accomplished anything. In fact, it had only made things worse. Now the Earl of Hereford was here, no doubt, being fed lies by his brother and Forbes. Julian knew he could no longer count on the earl's support. But the fact that Julian had promised Isabella manpower for her war in France was nil. If he was out of favor, there were others to provide armies and money to her. She didn't need him any longer.

Gasping, sick, Julian staggered over to the pitcher of wine against the far wall, a lovely pitcher in a pewter container, and drank heavily from the pitcher's rim. Red wine poured down his neck and he sloppily wiped it away. He had to think and think hard on how to retrieve his wife from the de Lohrs and how to beat them at their own game.

That was the trouble – the de Lohrs were one of the most powerful families in England. No one was stronger than they were, except for the king, but he knew that John would never come to his aid. Since Julian had been sleeping with the man's wife, the king had no great love or loyalty towards him. So the matter was in finding someone stronger than the de Lohrs, someone who could force them to turn over Emberley. The strongest man, or strongest army, in all of England would be needed to convince them.

Outside, the church bells rang, signaling the onset of Matins, or pre-dawn prayers. Julian heard the bells, turning in the direction of the sound as a thought came over him. Perhaps he didn't need the strongest man or strongest army to overcome the de Lohrs. Perhaps all he needed was a single man with the army of God behind him, someone who could evoke the holy law of the Church, the law that all men bowed to. Even the de Lohrs would have to obey.

As the bells continued to ring, Julian smiled. Finally, he had his answer.

☙

JONAS COULDN'T DECIDE if he was perturbed or exhausted. Perhaps a little of both. He drank heavily of the wine that was given to him, wiping his mouth on his rough, woolen sleeve.

The low-ceilinged solar was dark but for the fire in the hearth, a foreboding place at the moment. David stood a few feet from Jonas, arms folded over his chest and a concerned expression on his face. He hadn't said a word since taking the priest into the solar and producing a hefty quantity of wine for the man. It seemed as if he needed the fortification. As he stood there and watched him, Christopher entered the solar and quietly shut the door.

"Forbes will be here directly," he told them both. Then he looked at the priest. "What is this about?"

Jonas gazed up at the earl, a man who was well-known throughout England. He was something of a legend, even at his young age. After a moment, the priest sighed heavily and set his chalice of wine on the table.

"I would presume you know what your brother and Gart asked of me," he said.

Christopher cocked an eyebrow. "I do," he crossed his arms, passing a glance at David. The priest's role in Forbes' situation had brought the most heat from Christopher. "I cannot say that I agree with what was asked of you. They were wrong to manipulate you into such a position."

Jonas waved him off. "My lord, surely there have been times in your life when you have bent the rules to your own satisfaction or done something that perhaps you should not have simply because it was the right thing to do." He took another drink of wine. "This is one of those times."

Christopher pursed his lips and shook his head, hanging it in deep thought as he stared at the ground. He wasn't sure what more he could say to that, mostly because he had, in fact, done things in his life that he should not have done simply because he believed they were the right things to do. He didn't want to get into a lengthy discussion about it.

As he stood there in contemplative silence, the door to the solar opened again and Gart appeared. The knight looked rather anxious, unusual for the normally calm man, as he stepped inside and closed the door. He faced the priest expectantly.

"I was told you wanted to speak with me," he said quietly.

Jonas looked at the knight, suddenly feeling a great deal of sorrow for the man. He finally grunted and ran his fingers through his dark hair, feeling the stubble on the bald spot at the top of his scalp. He did not delay in what he had to tell him.

"The queen came to confession today," he said, lowering his voice. "I knew she would come because it is the ending of a holy holiday and she always comes immediately after the cessation of a holiday. It would seem she always has a great deal to confess. I sat in the confessionals for six hours waiting for her to come and when she finally did, she... well, suffice it to say that she did mention a man she had relations with. When I asked his name, she did not say Julian de Moyon. It would seem that our queen has a new lover."

He stopped abruptly and Gart lifted his eyebrows, encouraging the man to continue. "And? What happened? Did you not speak of de Moyon at all?"

Jonas shook his head. "That is what I am trying to tell you," he said. "I cannot tell her to convince Buckland to divorce his wife in penance for their affair because she is apparently no longer giving her affections to the man. To bring up his name on my own would have appeared suspicious. I was unable to make the suggestion at all."

Gart stared at him. "But you said that Buckland comes to you for confession also. You can suggest it to him directly."

Jonas waved him off, weary and disheartened. "He only comes with Isabella and he was not with her today. I doubt he will come on his own. He never has before."

Gart could see that the priest felt they were at an impasse on their plan. He struggled not to become agitated, knowing that would only cause problems. These people were trying to help him and he knew it. After a moment of staring blankly at the priest, he simply turned away and paced into the dark shadows of the room.

"There must be some way to speak with him," he finally said, looking like a phantom in the darkened corner of the room. "He must go to confession somewhere."

"I would not ask of a fellow priest what you have asked of me," Jonas said in a low voice. "Buckland must come to me or this plan will not come to fruition. I will not pull anyone else down into this quagmire of deceit and manipulation you are breeding."

It was a struggle for Gart not to snap at the man, but he did stiffen, a precursor to the *sach* rage that often filled him. As he turned away, laboring for words that would not sound aggressive or angry, there was a knock at the solar door. Christopher was standing the closest and he opened the panel.

Emberley stood in the dim light of the hall, dressed in a ravishing scarlet surcoat that Emilie had loaned her. Her luscious blond hair was plaited into a lovely braid that draped over one shoulder and, in truth, she looked radiant and beautiful, even in the dead of night. She smiled timidly at Christopher when their eyes met.

"Gart asked me to come, my lord," she said softly. "I hope I am not interrupting."

Gart was already moving for the door when he heard her voice as Christopher opened the panel wider to invite her in.

"Not at all, my lady," Christopher said. "We welcome your company."

Her smile turned genuine as she stepped into the room. Gart took her hand immediately, kissing it sweetly and tucking it into the crook of his elbow. As he pulled her deeper into the room, he pulled her towards the seated priest. As the fire in the hearth crackled softly, he faced off against Jonas.

"This," he said pointedly, "is the Lady Emberley de Moyon. This is what I am fighting for, priest. Know that even though you failed in your attempt to aid us, I will find another way. There is always another way. I will not stop until I have her or I will die trying."

Emberley's wide eyes moved between Gart and the priest. At his last few words, she looked rather ill.

"Gart?" she whispered. "What has happened?"

Gart wouldn't look at her. His intense green eyes were focused on the priest. He suddenly let go of Emberley's hand, putting his big palms on her face as if to frame it.

"Look at her," he growled at Jonas. "Look at this face. It is the most beautiful face you have ever seen. Can you look her in the eye and tell her that you will send her back to the husband that beats and humiliates her? Can you tell her that the Church holds no sympathy for her because she is the property of a monster?"

By this time, Emberley was tearing up. Her big eyes were gazing at Gart, seeing a side of him she had never seen before. He was bitter and brutal. Even though it was not directed at her, still, it was disturbing.

Jonas' gaze was on the lady as she looked apprehensively at Gart. She was an exquisite woman, no doubt. He'd never seen finer. He couldn't imagine a man taking his fists to such a fragile creature. After a moment, he simply shook his head.

"Let her go," he told Gart with gruff gentleness, reaching up to take the lady's hand himself. "Sit down, my lady. We must speak. Gart, go stand over there somewhere. Leave us alone for a moment."

Emberley allowed the priest to pull her down into a chair opposite him. He was an older man with a kind face but she was still apprehensive. She knew that Gart was right behind her because she could feel him, like always. She always knew when he was near whether or not she could see him. With anticipation, she sat before the priest, focused intently on him.

Jonas smiled at her, trying to settle the mood down after Gart's outburst.

"I am Father Jonas," he said politely. "My church is St. Bartholomew. Have you heard of it?"

Emberley shook her head. "I am sorry, I have not."

Jonas sat forward, holding her hand. "Did Gart tell you what he has asked of me?"

She nodded hesitantly. "He did."

"What do you think about it?"

She paused, many different thoughts rolling through her head. She suspected he was looking for a righteous answer but she found that she could not give him one. She stared at his hand as it held hers, formulating her thoughts.

"I was raised by parents who were very devout," she began slowly, softly. "I have always believed in God and the laws of the Church. When Julian and I were first introduced, he seemed kind and attentive. He can be quite charming when he wants to be. I was sure I had married a man who was kind and respectful. But on our wedding night, he became ragingly drunk and raped me for most of the night. When he was not raping me, he was beating me."

She looked up from her hands to see Jonas' serious expression. She knew that Gart was behind her, supporting her, and it fed her courage. She cleared her throat softly and continued.

"When I became pregnant with Romney, he told me that he would kill me if it was not a boy," she said. "When Romney was born, I wept with relief because I was sure he would have carried out his threat. I was pregnant again soon after Romney's birth but when I was about five months with child, he pushed me down a flight of stairs and killed the child. He blamed me for the death, of course, and took me out into the countryside where he dumped me in a grove of trees and left me to die. I lay there a day and night, in the rain, until he returned for me. Then I lay ill for months with an infection in my chest that nearly killed me. And all of this was only the first two years we were married."

She could feel Gart's hand on her shoulder, strong and steady, and she turned to see that he had tears in his eyes. She smiled faintly, patting his hand gently, before returning to the priest.

"I suppose the point I will make is that although I believe in God, I surely believe in the Devil because I am married to him," she squeezed the priest's hand. "If you return me to Julian, I have no doubt that he will kill me. I must get away from him any way I can, even if it is by means of a divorce. I think that you are a saint for trying to help me and I think Gart is a saint for asking you to do it. He has been my angel and I love him more than anything else on this earth."

Jonas listened to her story with a heavy heart. He sighed heavily and let go of her hand, sitting back in his chair to contemplate her story. He rubbed at his chin as if the gesture helped him to sort through this mess.

"I was unable to execute our plan," he said. "But in speaking with you, I can say with truth that I no longer have any reserve about the rightness of a divorce from your husband. If even half of what you say is true, then your husband is a beast. But that unfortunately does not change the fact that he is your husband and, by rights, can do as he pleases with you. I am sorry if that is something you do not want to hear, but it is the truth."

The calm expression on Emberley's face vanished. She bolted out of the seat, stumbling, her gaze searching for Gart. He was already heading for her, moving out of the shadows with his arms outstretched. She collapsed in the safety of his embrace.

"I will not go back to him," she hissed.

Gart held her tightly, his gaze moving between Christopher and David and the priest.

"You will not," he said firmly. "I will not allow it."

David, having remained largely silent through the exchange, spoke from his chair near the hearth.

"You worry overly," he told them. "Just because the priest could not tell Isabella to force Buckland into a divorce does not mean that hope is lost. It simply means that we will have to try another avenue."

Jonas could see how upset the lady was. Truth was that he didn't blame her. But facts were facts and he was struggling to think of another avenue to follow, something that would end the lady's suffering as well as her marriage. More than that, he could see in just the few minutes he had spent with Gart and Emberley how much they loved one another. There was genuine concern and adoration between them, and he felt a great deal of pity for them both.

"If de Moyon cannot be convinced to divorce his wife, then what?" Jonas asked.

Gart held Emberley against his chest, his enormous hand on her blond head as he cradled it against his sternum. His intense gaze was even more powerful than usual.

"I will take her and the children and we will flee," he said in a low voice. "We will go someplace safe where no one can find us, least of all Buckland. I will never let her go back to him, not ever."

In the darkness, David and Christopher passed long glances. Gart served David and was essentially telling the man that he would recant his oath and run, with or without his liege's approval. David had known that from the beginning, however, and wasn't particularly upset by it. But he was silently begging his brother for his wisdom in the matter. Christopher knew this, avoiding his brother's pleading gaze until he could avoid it no longer. He sighed heavily, putting his thoughts into words. These thoughts were coming from the heart more than his head.

"When I was in The Levant with Richard, I took a different route home than our king," his voice was barely above a whisper. "My army passed through many different countries and kingdoms and when we were in a particular area called Burgenland, we happened upon a castle under siege. At first we attempted to give the siege a wide berth, but a panicked priest begged for our aid so I complied. It would seem that we aided the Lord of Lockenhaus Castle, *or Burg Lockenhaus* as they called it, and the lord was so grateful that upon his death, he willed the castle to me. It is still mine, with a contingent of soldiers to man it because it sits at the head of a well-traveled valley with mountains as tall as the sky."

By this time, Emberley had stopped weeping and was listening to the earl intently. Christopher held her gaze as he moved away from the door and into the heart of the room, his focus serious.

"I have no doubt that what you have told us is true, my lady," he said quietly. "Your young son told me essentially the same story. I cannot imagine the hell you have endured at the hands of the man who is supposed to protect you. Because I have a wife I adore, I can understand Gart's feelings for you, right or wrong, and will therefore make you this pledge – if Buckland cannot be convinced to divorce you by proper means, then I will send you and Gart to Lockenhaus Castle where you may live your lives free of Buckland's horror. He will never find you there. But the caveat is that Gart will continue to serve me, as my garrison commander. Will this be acceptable?"

Emberley stared at the man in shock. "Ac… acceptable, my lord? Are you serious?"

"Or course."

After a moment of stunned silence, Emberley pulled herself free of

Gart's embrace and went to the earl, gently grasping one of his enormous hands. The look in her eye was beyond the scope of words. It was thanks beyond measure.

"My husband often spoke of you with ill-favor, my lord, stating that he believed you were Richard's trained dog, now forced to do tricks for a new master because John sat upon the throne," she said softly. "It was all I knew of you until yesterday. Now I see that you are a kind and generous man beyond compare, with compassion and understanding that most men do not have. Even as I stand here, I consider myself extremely fortunate to have met you. My thanks is not sufficient for what you have proposed, but please know that you have my undying gratitude."

Christopher smiled at the woman, seeing why Gart loved her so. She was sweet, gentle and gracious. It made him that much more protective over her and her son, more determined than ever to see them to safety with Gart.

Finally, the tides had turned and he was no longer resistant to their quest. Now he was on their side. Christopher squeezed her hand gently before turning to the priest.

"You will seek out Buckland and offer a proposal," he told him. "If he will divorce his wife, I will provide compensation of ten thousand gold marks and Ryton Castle in Worcestershire. Tell him that this offer is non-negotiable and if he does not comply, I will make his life hell until the day he dies. Is this in any way unclear?"

Wide-eyed, Jonas rose from his chair. "It is clear, my lord," he replied. "You will pay the man to divorce his wife?"

"I will compensate him for his loss."

"On what grounds will he base the divorce?"

Christopher looked at the stunned Emberley and the equally stunned Gart. "Adultery," he said softly. Then he shrugged. "The Church would not contest such a thing."

After a long and tense moment, Jonas nodded his head sharply in agreement. With nothing more to be said, David moved out of the shadows, hastily taking the priest by the arm and escorting the man to the door. Jonas passed by Emberley on his way out and his dark eyes fixed on her.

"I will do my best, my lady," he assured her softly. "Have faith that God understands your plight. He will not fail you."

Emberley nodded to his statement, watching the man quit the room with David on his heels. As she stood there with tears in her eyes, saying a thousand silent prayers of thanks to a God that had never particularly listened to her, Gart went over to Christopher.

His handsome face was soft with humility and gratitude. "My lord," he began quietly. "What you have offered for the lady's divorce... I do not have the means to compensate you, but rest assured that I will. I will pay you back every pence."

Christopher was feeling exhausted, satisfied, pleased that he could assist. He clapped Gart on the shoulder.

"The day you saved my brother's life was the day I became indebted to you," he said softly. "No price is too high to pay, Gart, and certainly not ten thousand marks and a broken down castle. You have proved your worth a thousand times over and I am happy to pay you back in any way I can."

Gart smiled modestly. "I am proud to serve the House of de Lohr," he said, eyeing Christopher after a moment. "Will I like Lockenhaus Castle or is my outpost to be in the snowy wilds of the East?"

Christopher snorted. "You will like it fine if you are a mountain goat," he told him. "This castle sits so high on the mountain that God will be your neighbor."

Gart laughed softly, turning to look at Emberley as she moved away from the door to join them. He reached out, stroking her blond head.

"I will have my angel with me," he said softly, his eyes shining with adoration for the woman. "That is all that matters."

Emberley smiled. "And the children as well," she reminded him. "Did you tell Lord Christopher that my boys will ensure that anyone entering his keep will be forced to give tribute? He should be a very rich man in little time."

Christopher looked questioningly at Gart as the man shook his head in resignation.

"She means that her boys rob anyone they come across," he told him. "I fear for our new neighbors. If they come to visit, they will be set upon by bandits within the keep."

Christopher looked at them both in disbelief. "Do you mean to tell me that Master Romney is a thief? I do not believe such slander."

Gart laughed. "I have such stories to tell you that you will fear for your own life from Romney."

He told the earl everything and as Gart had promised, Christopher made his way to his bedchamber later that night, looking over his shoulder for a small boy with a very big stick and demands for coinage.

CHAPTER TWENTY-FIVE

"AND YOU ARE sure your wife is with de Lohr?" the priest asked. Standing in the nave of Westminster Abbey that also served as the baptismal font, Julian nodded submissively to the man who had asked the question.

"I am certain, Your Grace," he said humbly. "My wife has seen fit to run to de Lohr and away from me. He holds her even now, more than likely at Bellham Place. That is the de Lohr residence outside of London."

"Is she his mistress, then?" the priest asked.

Julian tried to look distressed. "I can only surmise," he said. "As I explained to you, I have tried to retrieve her myself but they will not turn her over to me. She is my wife by God and the laws of England, and I need your help to retrieve her. I must take her home where she belongs. Our children need their mother and it is my right to have my wife."

The priest was a mid-level operator in the world of Westminster. It was the most senior man Julian could speak with and he could see his tale was having an impact. The priest called over another priest and the two of them began conferring softly, undoubtedly about how to help Baron Buckland. Julian watched and waited.

Having bypassed several smaller churches near the Tower of London in favor of the grand dame of them all, he thought it best to cultivate the sympathies and services of Westminster simply because it was one of the oldest and most prestigious churches in England.

Having been at the door of the church at sunrise, he had attended

Mass as any other pious parishioner, voicing the right prayers at the right time, pretending to be devoted when the truth was that he had not attended Mass in years. The only time he went to Confession was when Isabella did, and since she would no longer see him, his life was in great disorder. He was focused on retrieving his wife and retreating to Dunster where he would lick his wounds and rethink his strategy. But he needed help.

The two priests finished their conference and motioned for Julian to follow. He did, through the tall columns of the cathedral, across the stone floor that had seen generations of kings walk upon it. The priests left the church proper and headed south, towards the cloisters and other small buildings that dotted the grounds. Julian followed swiftly.

It was becoming a sunny day with the moisture from the Thames heavy upon the air. Julian was swearing beneath his fine tunic and hose, feeling the sweat run down his back as he followed the priests to a stone cottage to the southwest of the cloister block. One priest knocked on the door and was admitted by a servant, instructing the second priest and Julian to remain outside.

Julian stood nervously in the moist air, slapping at the bugs biting his skin and scratching around his neck. The second priest was in heavy, woolen robes so he imagined the man was more miserable even than he was. The man kept scratching at his groin. After an eternity of waiting, the door to the cottage finally opened again and the first priest beckoned Julian inside.

The cottage was small and dimly lit. The floors were uneven as Julian's eyes grew accustomed to the light. To his right near the hearth sat a man in bleached, woolen robes with two servants attending him. One servant was carefully shaving the top of the man's head while the second servant brought food and drink. Julian locked eyes with the man expectantly.

"I am a Canon of Westminster," the man said in a rich, full voice. "My name is Father Mellitus. You are Baron Buckland?"

Julian nodded – now he was getting somewhere. A canon was one of the governing priests of the abbey and he struggled to keep his excitement at bay. Now, he knew he had someone who could help him without dispute.

"I am, Your Grace," he said respectfully. "I am Julian Edward de Moyon, Third Baron Buckland. My seat is Dunster Castle in Somerset. I have come to you with a horrible problem that only you can help me with."

Father Mellitus chewed on a piece of cheese. "My priest has told me," he replied, his dark gaze sizing Julian up. "I have heard the name Buckland. I seem to remember hearing of a concubine of the queen, a man by the name of Buckland. Is that you?"

Julian stared at the man a moment, wondering if he was about to be chastised. If his plan was going to work, he was going to have to project a submissive, victimized state. It never occurred to him that the priests of Westminster would recognize his name as the queen's lover, even though he made sure the rumors about him and the queen flew fast and furious around London. Now, he was hoping the reputation he had taken such pride in wasn't about to sink his hopes.

"It is," he lowered his head dramatically. "Please understand, Your Grace, that I had little choice in the matter. Isabella is the queen, after all, and I must do as she commanded. I was her slave and unable to break free. I prayed daily that she would tire of me and am fortunate that she has. Her attentions are elsewhere."

The priest eyed him, setting the cheese down. It was clear that he did not believe him.

"I see," he muttered. "I am told you have come here involving a matter about your wife."

Julian nodded eagerly, his head coming up. "David de Lohr, Baron Thornden, has taken my wife from me. He will not give her back. I have tried to rescue her but he killed my men in the attempt. Now she is at Bellham Place and I humbly beg for the church's intervention in this matter. I want my wife back and de Lohr will not turn her over to me."

The priest dipped his fingers in a water bowl that a servant brought and wiped them off on an offered piece of linen.

"Thornden cannot keep another man's wife," he said. "What would you have me do?"

Julian was careful to make his wants clear, as if he were begging for their help to restore his marriage.

"I would plead with you to ride for Bellham Place and retrieve my wife under the protection of the Church," he asked urgently. "De Lohr cannot deny the Church's request. He will be forced to turn her over."

The priest stood up from the chair, wiping a linen towel over his freshly shaved head. He eyed Julian, annoyed with the request but understanding he had a duty to the man. If someone was holding his wife hostage, then it was up to the Church to deliver her to her rightful husband. There was no great mystery in that. He tossed the towel aside.

"How long has she been de Lohr's captive?" he asked.

"Weeks, at the very least, Your Grace," Julian said pleadingly. "Please help me, Your Grace. I must return her home. Our children need her."

The priest held out his hands as his servants began shoving on his rings of office.

"I will send a missive to Bellham and ask that the lady be returned to you," he said. "You will deliver the missive yourself."

Julian shook his head. "They will kill me, Your Grace," he said, feigning fear. "I fear they will only release her to a priest when they are forced. I fear that only your divine presence will give me back my wife. Please, Your Grace – will you please help me and go personally?"

The priest sighed heavily, fiddling with his rings once they were on. He turned to Julian, thinking that he simply didn't have time for such nonsense. But the man seemed genuinely distraught so perhaps he needed to do as he was asked simply to get it over with. Otherwise, the situation would drag on and Mellitus would be to blame, especially if the circumstances went from bad to worse.

"Very well," he said, clipped. "I will travel to Bellham Place and retrieve your wife for you."

Julian nearly collapsed with relief. "Thank you, Your Grace," he bowed several times in a gesture of gratitude and respect. "May I ride with you? I want to take my wife home right away."

Mellitus simply nodded, sneezing and wiping at his nose with a linen towel. "We will go before Vespers."

"Today?" Julian asked hopefully.

Mellitus looked at Julian, struggling to keep the impatience off his face. "Aye, today."

Julian left the canon's quarters and took position out in the garden with a clear view of the man's cottage. He remained rooted there until the man was ready to leave for Bellham.

De Lohr would pay now. They would all pay.

CB

GART LET EMBERLEY sleep the next day well into the morning. She was exhausted and pregnant, and after her harrowing adventures, he thought it best simply to let her rest.

Emilie tried to insist that she would take care of Lady Emberley so that Gart could go about his duties, but Gart wasn't going to relinquish the task. It made for a warm, if not odd, standoff as Emilie insisted and Gart politely refused. When Romney finally awoke, Gart saw the opportunity to focus Emilie on the child, which she did so happily. With Christina and Romney in hand, Emilie took delight in tending the children.

Gart did indeed have duties to attend to but he spent most of the morning with Emberley as she slumbered peacefully. Sitting in a chair by the low fire in the hearth, he quietly sharpened his sword against a pumice stone, alternately watching Emberley and paying attention to his blade.

He was content simply sitting with her. She was safe and in his line of sight, and that was all he could ask for in the world. She slept the morning away as he finished sharpening his blade and, finished, quit the chamber with the intention of returning to his possessions for other assorted blades that needed sharpening. He could sit and sharpen, and watch Emberley at the same time.

He took the stairs down to the ground floor, hearing voices from the reception room. He could hear Romney's voice and that of a squealing baby, so he crept to the door and peered inside to see Romney playing with little Christina. The baby was thrilled with Romney, laughing hysterically as he pretended to poke her belly. Emilie sat nearby with sewing in hand, smiling at the antics.

Gart grinned as he watched Romney and the baby, thinking how much he missed Orin, Brendt and Lacy. Those two little ruffians and the slobbery baby had his heart. His plan had been to send Kevin to retrieve the children but David quashed that scheme because he wanted Kevin to remain at Bellham for the time being, especially with Buckland so unpredictable.

With plans changed, Gart intended to send ten of his own men to Trelystan to collect the children, men that the children were already familiar with thanks to their stay at Dunster. It was something he intended to do before the day was out. He wanted the rest of the children with him and Emberley as quickly as possible.

As Gart moved away from the door frame, Romney apparently saw the movement and jumped up, running to the door. He caught sight of Gart just as the man was entering the corridor that led to the kitchens.

"Gart!" he yelled. "May I please come with you?"

Gart paused in the archway, giving the boy a half-grin and waving a big arm at him, indicating for the boy to follow. Romney bolted after him happily.

He followed Gart out into the rear yards behind the kitchen where a staircase led down into the basement armory. It was a warm day, moist, and the summer bugs were thick in the trees overhead.

As Gart descended the stairs to the basement, Romney kicked dirt around, picked up rocks and threw them in the fish pond, and then began throwing rocks at the soldiers on duty. One man was hit in the neck and turned around to yell at Romney until he saw Forbes. The soldier quickly moved the other direction.

Triumphant, Romney followed Gart down into the armory and immediately began touching everything he could get his hands on. As Gart sheathed his broadsword, he noticed Romney and his five hundred hands.

"Leave well enough alone," he told the boy, motioning him over. "Come and help me with this."

Romney went to him obediently, noticing Gart's familiar bags. Be it instinct or habit, he immediately began to rummage through Gart's bags.

"Out," Gart snapped softly when he saw what the boy was doing. "If you do not keep your hands to yourself, I am going to tie you up and hang you from a tree."

Romney grinned but removed his hands. He gazed up at Gart. "What are you doing?"

Gart was in another bag, pulling out small daggers. "You can help me sharpen these."

Romney was eager to do so but yanked his hand away when he reached out to grab one without permission and Gart smacked it. Frowning, he rubbed at his stinging fingers.

"When are Orin and Brendt coming?" he asked.

Gart removed two more small daggers from his bag. "Soon," he told him. "I am sending my men to retrieve them today."

Romney watched Gart carefully set the daggers in a row. "Can you tell your men to bring my sword, too? I left it at Trelystan."

Gart nodded as he inspected a nick on one of the daggers. "I suppose so," he glanced at the boy. "Perhaps we can even have a real one made for you."

Romney's eyes widened. "Truly?" he asked. "Can I have a crossbow, too?"

Gart wriggled his eyebrows. "Your mother has been clear in her decision against the crossbow," he said. "But perhaps we can convince her that a real sword would be in order."

Romney was so excited he could hardly stand it. With an invisible sword in his hand, he began jumping around the armory, fighting mail coats on frames and doing battle with unseen enemies. Gart watched him with a smirk.

"You will be a fearsome knight someday," he told him. "But your new sword will be quite dull until you grow older."

Romney didn't care. All that mattered was that Gart had promised him a real sword. He continued fighting the unseen enemy until he bashed into a mail coat on a frame and tipped the entire thing over. Gart just looked at him and shook his head.

"Pick it up," he commanded softly.

Contrite, Romney tried and tried to heave the frame up but it was far too heavy for him with the mail upon it. Finally, Gart took pity on him and stood the frame up while Romney tried to straighten the mail coat. When he was finished, he looked at Gart with a big eager grin and Gart broke down into snorts of laughter, running his big hand over the boy's blond head affectionately.

On the way out of the armory, Gart carried four daggers and Romney had one in a heavy sheath. Gart was concerned the boy would trip and impale himself so he gave him the weapon with the thickest sheath.

Romney was surprisingly careful, however, carefully taking the steps and then very carefully crossing the kitchen yard. Once inside the manse, he continued to be very careful with the blade as he moved through the corridor and into the entry hall with its big, stone steps.

As they reached the stairs, little Christina spied Romney out in the entry hall and began to squeal for him. Romney didn't want to play with the baby, because he was far too big for that sort of thing, but then he noticed that there was a tray of sweets in the reception hall and that had his attention. Emilie saw the pair as they went to mount the steps.

"Romney," she said happily. "Your mother is awake and will be joining us shortly for a meal. Will you please join us also?"

Romney was lured by the treats but he also wanted to help Gart sharpen the daggers. Gart saw the boy's indecision and pulled the sheathed blade out of his hand.

"Go and enjoy the treats," he told him. "I will save this blade for you."

Romney scratched his head, looking up at Gart. "Are you sure?"

"I am." Gart threw his chin in the direction of the reception room. "Go. I will send your mother down."

Romney skipped off the steps and into the reception room. Gart could hear Christina crowing happily at the boy's appearance, which made him smile. Romney seemed to have that excited effect on children, like a Pied Piper that could lead them all into delirious childhood joy. He had the air of leadership about him, even at such a young age. Mounting the rest of the steps, he knocked softly on Emberley's door.

"Come," she said, muffled behind the panel.

Gart pushed the door open, his gaze falling on Emberley as she secured a linked copper belt around her hips. She was wearing a pale yellow linen surcoat with a square neckline, a garment that enhanced her figure beautifully. Her blond hair was free-flowing, wavy because it had been braided in her sleep, and a pretty shell comb secured the front of her hair off her face. Gart sighed dreamily at the sight of her.

"Good morning, my lady," he greeted softly.

She beamed at him, smoothing down the bodice of the surcoat. "Good morning, Sir Gart," she went over to him, leaning against him and kissing him sweetly. "Did you sleep well, sweetheart?"

He kissed her again, nuzzling her face with his nose. "I always sleep well when you are with me," he murmured. "How do you feel this morning?"

She stood back from him and adjusted the copper belt. "I feel remarkably well."

"No belly ache?"

She shook her head. "Not this morning."

He went over to the table where he had set his pumice stone and set down the collection of daggers in his hand. Then he returned to

Emberley and scooped her up in his enormous embrace. He hugged her tightly as she wrapped her arms around his neck. He just stood there and held her, her feet dangling more than a foot off the ground.

"It is so good to simply feel you in my arms," he whispered against the side of her head. "This reminds me of the days back at Dunster when it was just you and me and the children, without a care in the world."

She held on to him, drowning herself in the man's massive body and warm power.

"We will know those days again," she assured him softly. "Perhaps it will be in Burgenland, high on a mountaintop, but I swear we will know those days again."

He kissed the side of her head and set her carefully to her feet. His green eyes were serious.

"I know that you have already considered this, but if we are forced to flee, we cannot be legally married," he said, his voice low. "But I swear to you, in my heart, mind and body, we will be more married than any two people have ever been on this earth. I will call you my wife regardless."

She smiled at him, holding his big hands in her small warm ones. "And you shall be my husband," she whispered. "Marriage is a foolishly inconsequential thing compared to the love and devotion you and I have. Marriage could not make us any richer."

He returned her smile, kissing her hands gently. "Lady Emilie has a grand meal spread out below for you," he told her. "Rom is already down there, eating everything of noteworthiness, I am sure."

Emberley wriggled her eyebrows. "Perhaps I had better join them before everything is eaten and gone. Will you be joining us?"

He escorted her to the door, opening it for her. "Later," he told her. "I have a few things to attend to now that you are awake."

"What does that have to do with anything?"

He dipped his head in the direction of the table that held the pumice stone and daggers. "I have been sitting with you all morning in case you woke and needed me."

She smiled and shook her head. "I am not a child that needs to be tended every moment, Gart," she pinched his cheek affectionately. "Although I thank you for your sweet devotion, you could have easily gone about your duties as I slept."

He fought off a grin. "I know," he replied, almost defiantly. "But I wanted to watch you sleep. I have not had that privilege in some time."

She laughed softly, touched by his words, as she quit the room. Gart took her hand as they descended the steps. As they neared the bottom of the staircase, talking softly between them, Emilie caught sight of the pair and rose from her chair. She appeared in the door of the reception room, her lovely face alight with a smile.

"Lady Emberley," she greeted. "It is good to see you looking so well this morning."

Emberley smiled at the truly likable woman. "Thank you, Lady de Lohr," she said. "I slept very well in your lovely chamber."

Emilie came towards her, hand outstretched. She was looking at Gart as she spoke. "You have monopolized her enough, Gart," she scolded lightly. "I should like to come to know my new friend. Go now, and do whatever it is knights do these days."

Emberley laughed at Gart's fallen expression as she took Emilie's hand and the two of them looked quite companionable. Gart sighed, putting a hand over his heart.

"You have hurt me deeply, Lady de Lohr," he jested. "I suppose I am being chased away."

"You are," Emilie winked at Emberley. "But we will be right here, have no fear. Your lady will not be far from you."

Before Emilie could pull Emberley away, Gart bent over, cupped her face with one hand, and kissed her cheek sweetly. With a wink and a rather provocative rake of her body with his gaze, he quit the entry hall and disappeared towards the rear of the manse.

Emberley watched him go before turning to Emilie and realizing the woman had been studying the interplay between her and Gart quite intently. Her cheeks flushed a delicate shade of pink.

"He loves you a great deal," Emilie said softly. "I can see it in everything about him."

Emberley was floating on clouds, deliriously in love with the man. "As I love him also," she admitted, not sure what more she could say on the subject. "Have you known Gart long?"

Emilie clutched her hand as they retreated back into the reception room where Romney was stuffing himself with apricot sweets.

"I have known him for four years," she said. "He is a good man. I am so glad he has found happiness with you."

"I have known him most of my life," Emberley replied. "He was my brother's best friend before my brother perished in The Levant."

They reached a pair of comfortable chairs and Emilie indicated for Emberley to sit, which she did. Romney came over to his mother and she pulled the big lad onto her lap. But he didn't want to stay too long, just long enough to be hugged, before slithering off to return to the tray of sweets.

From that point, the conversation was light and gay. Emilie discovered that Emberley was hysterically humorous and the pair laughed uproariously as they enjoyed warmed, watered wine and a variety of foods. The more Emilie came to know of the woman, the more sorrow she began to feel for her plight. She didn't deserve what life had dealt her until she met Gart.

Around midday, Romney was starting to feel like a caged animal as he paced around the reception room while his mother and Lady de Lohr conversed about their respective childhoods.

Emberley could see that her son was restless so she casually suggested that they all go for a walk around the grounds. Emilie agreed quickly, giving sleepy Christina over to a servant as she took her new friends outside to show them the grounds of Bellham Place.

The day was moist and warm, and within a few minutes of being outside, Emberley's face was rosy and damp from the weather. The linen was a cool fabric and kept her relatively comfortable as she and

Emilie began to walk the path to the lovely formal gardens north of the manse. There were massive oak trees lining the path and Romney tried to climb every tree he came across.

Emilie watched the boy try to sprint up a tree. She laughed when he fell off the tree and rolled around in the damp grass.

"Am I to understand that you have three boys, my lady?" she turned to Emberley. "I cannot imagine three boys with such vigor."

Emberley gave her a half-grin. "Truly, you have no concept," she shook her head with feigned resignation. "My boys are full of life and mischief. When Gart first came to Dunster, they robbed him as he entered the keep."

Emilie burst out laughing. "They robbed the great Gart Forbes?"

Emberley giggled along with her. "Do not be so quick to laugh," she told her. "They robbed your husband as well and would have beat him had he not given them a pence each. That was enough to keep the hounds at bay."

Emilie laughed harder. "Say not so," she begged, watching Romney race on ahead. "They are brave young men to attack such powerful knights."

Emberley was forced to agree. She shaded her eyes from the sun, watching Romney pick up rocks and throw them at birds.

"Gart has tried to break them of it," she admitted. "When we went to stay at Trelystan Castle, they robbed the lord of the keep several times before Gart found out about it. He made them return everything but then we found out that Lord de Lara had quite willingly gone along with the robberies. He even let the boys take him hostage and he ransomed himself with the promise of a gold crown each. That was when Gart put a stop to everything."

Emilie was giggling throughout the story. "I hope I get to meet your boys some time," she said. "Do you think they will try to rob me as well?"

Emberley shook her head. "They only rob men, thankfully. But I would still be careful if I were you."

They paused by a fountain that was fed by a stream running across the property. Flowers of all kinds were blooming, foxgloves and hollyhocks reaching to the sky in a riot of color. Romney was throwing rocks at the crows that kept swooping in and Emberley thought it was all quite heavenly but for the absence of her other three children. She tried not to think of Orin and Brendt and Lacy because it only brought her to tears. She knew that Lord de Lara was spoiling them rotten and that they were well tended. Still, she missed them.

Emilie was watching Romney, oblivious to Emberley's longing for her other children. She pointed to the boy.

"He has good aim with his rocks, my lady," she observed. "He will make a fine marksman."

Emberley turned to her. "Please call me Emberley," she said. "It seems odd to be so formal with someone who has very nearly saved your life."

Emilie smiled broadly. "You will call me Emilie," she insisted. "Or Em. I will answer to either."

Emberley lifted an eyebrow. "I am called Em, also. We very nearly have the same name."

Emilie giggled. "The same name and the same blond hair, but that is where the similarities end."

Emberley cocked her head. "Why do you say that?"

Emilie looked rather hesitant to speak, her gaze drifting over Emberley's delicious figure, something that had not gone unnoticed by her or by the men at Bellham. She began to make hand gestures around her waist and bosom.

"Well," she said. "You have... you are much better endowed than I am and... well, you are quite attractive."

Emberley could see what she meant as she held her hands over her breasts like great cups and she burst out laughing.

"It is the pregnancy, I assure you," she said. "My breasts grow enormous as the child grows."

Emilie grinned in return. "As I recall, mine did as well. I look forward to that day again and, I am sure, so does my husband. He was quite... pleased."

The two of them giggled like girls as the sounds of thunder caught their attention. Turning to the south, they could see a pair of chargers approach from the rear of the manse where the stable block was located.

Emberley recognized Gart's black and white charger as he roared towards them. It was then that she noticed that Gart was leading a cream-colored pony with a black mane and tail. Romney saw Gart coming and he was nearly run over as he ran out to meet him.

Gart had to settle his charger down as the horse reared up, having been abruptly prevented from stomping on Romney. Kevin was beside Gart astride his silver charger, having brought up the rear.

"Gart!" Romney was jumping up and down, his focus completely on the pony. "Can I ride him? Can I please?"

Gart was dressed casually in a heavy tunic, breeches, big boots and a mail coat. On his hands were enormous leather gloves. He grinned down at the excited child.

"Lord de Lohr said you could ride him while you are at Bellham," he handed the pony over to Kevin as he dismounted his charger. "What do you think of him?"

Romney was beside himself with excitement. "He is strong and fine," the child gleefully ran up to the pony and began stroking his face. "What is his name?"

Gart looked over at Emberley, winking at her smiling face. "His name is George," he replied, moving to the boy and lifting him up into the saddle. He put the boy's feet into the stirrups and took the reins from Kevin, handing them over to Romney. "Do you think you can ride him?"

Romney nodded eagerly, kicking the pony in the sides to get him going. As the adults watched, Romney directed the pony straight through the flower garden, knocking over a tall stalk of hollyhocks. Emberley winced.

"Rom!" she called. "Take the pony out of the garden!"

Romney steered the pony out of the garden but not before tramping over several other bushes. Emberley sighed heavily, looking apologetically to Emilie.

"I am sorry," she said. "He has not ridden by himself very much. I will make sure he stays out of the garden."

Emilie waved her off. "No need," she assured her. "He is welcome anywhere, even in the garden."

Emberley chuckled softly, turning to Gart as the man stood there, watching Romney trot around on the pony. She greeted Kevin amiably as she made her way over to Gart.

"That was sweet of you to bring him a pony," she said. "He has been pacing the floors endlessly all morning. This will give him something to do."

Gart smiled at her, wrapping an enormous arm around her shoulders and pulling her against his torso.

"I could see this morning that he needed something to occupy his time," he replied. "Without Orin and Brendt, there is no one for him to play with."

Emberley nodded, watching Romney bounce around in the saddle as the pony trotted. "Have you sent your men for the other children yet?"

Gart nodded. "They left about an hour ago," he told her. "They have strict instructions to ride hard to Trelystan, collect the children, and return as quickly as they can without causing the children undue stress."

Emberley sighed. "Thank you," she said sincerely. "I miss my babies. It will be so good to have them in my arms again."

"It will be good to have all five of you back in mine."

They grinned at each other and Gart kissed her forehead. As they turned back to watch Romney, the boy kicked the pony a little too hard and the little beast bucked, sending Romney flying off onto his arse.

As Emberley flinched, Gart let her go and made his way over to the boy, who was picking himself off the dirt and rubbing his bum. Kevin spurred his charger after the runaway pony, corralling the animal near the main gates of Bellham and leading him back over to the little boy with the bruised pride.

"Are you well?" Gart looked Romney over, brushing the dirt off the boy's back. "No broken bones?"

Romney shook his head, looking rather sheepish. "I... I was not holding on tightly," he told him. Any excuse was better than the truth that the horse had managed to throw him because he was inexperienced. "I will hold on tighter next time."

Gart simply nodded, unwilling to damage the boy's pride further, as Kevin brought the pony back around again. As Gart instructed Romney how to mount the pony from a standing position, they began to hear dogs barking upon the wall. Bellham Place had several dogs, in fact, some roaming around the grounds in packs while others were used by the sentries. Three or four dogs stood at the closed front gates, barking through the iron grate.

Gart didn't give any thought to the dogs as he helped Romney mount the pony again. Even Kevin wasn't paying any attention. Emberley strolled upon her son, watching him adjust himself in the saddle and commenting on his proud stance on horseback. She suspected his pride needed some mending after the fall so she made a good attempt.

Romney made a second attempt to ride the pony, reining it in the direction of the open lawn area to the east of the garden. Gart took Emberley's hand, pulling her out of the way as Romney tried to direct the stubborn little pony.

Emilie eventually joined them. As the four adults watched Romney take another try at riding horseback, a sentry from the gates came jogging over to their group. Gart heard the mail grating and turned just as the soldier was upon them.

"My lord," he saluted Gart. "A party approaches the gates."

"Who?" Gart asked.

"Papal standards, my lord," the guard replied. "Blue, red and yellow."

Gart stared at the man a moment before looking to Kevin. "Westminster?" he cocked his head, confused. "Those are his standards. Do we know any other papal standards that bear those colors?"

Kevin shook his head. "I do not know of any," he replied. "Westminster is only four or five miles to the west. It must be them."

Gart's confusion was growing. "Why would they come here?"

Kevin sat straight in the saddle and reined his charger for the gates. "I shall find out their business."

Gart watched the man trot away, still relatively unconcerned at the visitors. He took Emberley by the hand and directed her towards the manse.

"I am not entirely sure who this is or what they want, so it would be best if you and Emilie retreated to the house for now," he told her, a kiss to the temple. "Lady Emilie, I shall inform your husband we have guests."

The ladies were unconcerned, doing as they were told. "What about Rom?" Emberley asked.

Gart turned in Romney's direction, emitting a piercing whistle between his teeth and waving the boy over when the child turned to look at him.

"I will collect him," he told her. "Go inside now and prepare for visitors. I will be in shortly."

Arm in arm, Emilie and Emberley headed for the manse. Gart watched them go before turning to make sure Romney was on his way. The boy was heading in his general direction even though the pony was trying its hardest not to cooperate.

Gart turned one last time to make sure Emberley and Emilie were near the manse, which they were. They were just entering the door. Returning his attention to Romney as the child directed the stubborn pony towards him, he was startled when Kevin suddenly roared up next to him. Dirt and rocks hit Gart in the legs as Kevin came to abrupt stop.

"It is Westminster," he said, sounding breathless. "Get Emberley upstairs and lock her someplace safe, Gart. We have trouble."

Gart's brow furrowed with concern. "What kind of trouble?"

Kevin's handsome face was deadly serious, an expression that Gart would never forget as long as he lived.

"Buckland is with him."

CHAPTER TWENTY-SIX

AT THE MOMENT, Gart's main concern was Emberley. Seated in her borrowed bedchamber with the door bolted and a chair pushed up against it, she had only just stopped sobbing hysterically.

Gart sat on the bed with her in his arms as Emilie forced a cup of wine down her throat, floating with a palmful of crushed chamomile flowers to calm her nerves.

He rocked her gently, her head cradled against his chest, as Emilie forced her to drink every few seconds. Emberley would sob, breathe, and drink. It went on that way for what seemed like hours but the truth was that it was only minutes. It was agonizing.

"Why… why….?" Emberley sobbed.

"Shhhh," Emilie put the cup to her lips again and forced her to sip the contents. "Quiet, now. Be still and calm yourself."

As Emilie tended Emberley, she glanced at Gart. The knight was stone-faced as usual but oddly pale. She struggled over her own fear and shock, swept with pity for the pair. She fought back tears herself, unwilling to show weakness because Emberley was so upset. She was focused on calming her friend.

"Drink, sweetheart," she whispered, holding the cup to Emberley's lips again, watching the woman drink and sputter. "That's a good girl. Everything will be all right."

Emberley calmed to the point where she was no longer sobbing hysterically, but she lay with her head against Gart's chest, eyes closed and tears streaming down her face. Emilie set the cup down and collected a kerchief from the wardrobe positioned against the wall near the door. She returned to the bed, gently wiping off Emberley's cheeks. When she looked up, Gart was gazing at her.

She smiled weakly at the man, knowing he was more than likely crazed to go downstairs to find out why Buckland was here with a supporting army from Westminster. But his priority had been Emberley and he would not leave until he was sure she was in a better state. Emilie deeply admired his devotion.

"I will sit with her for a while," she told him. "I am sure you would like to go downstairs and find out what is transpiring."

Gart nodded but the second he moved, Emberley exploded into hysterics again.

"Nay!" she shrieked, throwing her arms around him. "Do not leave me. Please do not leave me!"

Gart didn't want to leave her but he was increasingly eager to find out why Buckland was downstairs. He forced himself to take a stand, putting his big hands on Emberley's face and forcing her to look at him.

"Kitten," he said softly, firmly. "You must listen to me. Stop your weeping and listen. Please. It is important."

Emberley gazed back at him with wide, terrified eyes. Her lower lip trembled and her eyes watered over with tears.

"Please," she begged. "Do not go down there. Let us leave, now, run far and fast so they can never catch us."

He kissed her wet cheeks. "What about Orin, Brendt and Lacy?" he asked. "We cannot leave now. We cannot leave them behind."

She closed her eyes, a sob escaping her lips as she nodded. "Nay, we cannot."

Gart sighed heavily, kissing her cheeks again. "I am going to go downstairs and find out why Buckland is here," he told her firmly but gently. "It is very important to me that you compose yourself. I cannot think if I know you are hysterical because all I will be thinking of is comforting you. If I know you are strong, I will be strong. Do you understand?"

Emberley swallowed hard, meeting his gaze. "A-aye," she hiccupped. "I am... am sorry to weep so. It is simply that... Julian is here and...."

He kissed her soft mouth, cutting her off before she could start crying again.

"I know," he said softly. "I intend to find out why but I need for you to be calm and composed. It will help me immensely. Agreed?"

She nodded unsteadily, wiping at her nose as she labored to stop the tears. "I will calm," she said with more bravery than she felt. "I will do my best."

He smiled at her, cupped her face and kissed her one last time.

"Good girl," he cooed. Then he stood up, peeling her hands from his arms and handing her over to Emilie. "I will be back as soon as I can, I swear it. But you stay here with the door bolted. You will not open it for anyone but me or David or the earl. Is that clear?"

Emberley nodded obediently. "It is, Gart."

He winked at her as he moved to the door, noticing Romney standing in the corner, looking terrified. His heart softened as he gazed at the frightened boy, extending a hand to him. Romney emerged from the corner and went to him.

Gart took a knee in front of the boy so he could speak to him at his level. He was serious but gentle.

"I need you to watch over your mother until I return," he put a big hand on the boy's shoulder. "Can you do this?"

Romney nodded solemnly. "Aye, Gart."

Gart patted his shoulder and stood up. "Good lad," he glanced back at Emberley and gave her a smile. "I will return shortly."

Gart pulled the chair away and unlatched the bolt, quitting the room. Once he was gone, Romney rushed up and threw the bolt, shoving the chair up against the door again. He kicked it for good measure just to make sure it was solid.

Turning to look at his mother, he could see that she was still crying, now quietly into her hand. Lady Emilie was trying her best to comfort her. Confused, frightened, Romney wandered back over to the corner where he had been standing, lost to his own young and turbulent thoughts.

His father was at Bellham, invading a place that had been full of joy and comfort for Romney and his mother. He even had a pony to ride. Now his father had ruined everything, like he always did. How many times had Romney wanted to protect his mother from his father's brutal beatings, to comfort her and make her smile. He'd never been able to help her very much, but that was before. Now he was older, bigger, and Gart had taught him much about weapons and fighting. Well, for the most part. A wooden sword wasn't an effective weapon but a real sword would be.

As Romney wandered over to the darkened corner, he brushed by the table where Gart had been sharpening his sword. The pumice stone still lay there as did the five daggers Gart had brought up from the armory.

As his mother sat on the bed and wept, Romney eyed the daggers. Glancing over his shoulder to make sure his mother wasn't looking, he shoved one of them into his tunic.

He had to protect her.

☙

OUTSIDE ON THE landing, Gart heard the door shut behind him and the bolt thrown. He stood there a moment, struggling to push his last vision of Emberley's face out of his mind – terrified and pale. He heard the bolt engage behind him, taking a deep breath to compose himself before heading downstairs.

The moment he put a foot on the staircase, he saw David standing at the base of the steps. Quickly, he took the stairs to join him.

"How is she?" David asked softly.

Gart nodded, rubbing the back of his neck as if to rub away the stress. "Understandably upset," he said. "But she is calming. Emilie is with her."

David nodded. "Good," he muttered, pulling Gart in the direction of the solar. "You and I must speak."

Gart looked around as David pulled him aside. "Where is Buckland?"

David didn't say anything until he pulled him into the solar and quietly shut the door. When he faced Gart, his expression was serious.

"He is in the reception hall with Father Mellitus, a canon at Westminster." David ran a hand through his blond hair in a nervous gesture. "Gart, we have sent for Father Jonas. I believe we may need him."

Gart didn't like the sound of that at all. "Why?"

David lifted his shoulders, unsure where to start the sordid tale he was coming to understand.

"Because somewhere, somehow, Buckland has become a cunning opponent," he replied. "He knew that all of the posturing and aggression in the world would not force us to turn Emberley over to him. Somehow, he figured out that I was involved in the ambush on his escort. I am not sure how he knew, but he did. You said that you left no trace? No survivors?"

Gart shook his head. "Nothing at all. We killed all of the witnesses and stripped the area of any identification. There is no way he could have known I was involved."

David shook his head. "It is not you at all," he said. "He believes that I am involved solely, assisted by de Lara. Your name has not even entered into the conversation yet, but I am sure it will at some point, especially when Father Jonas arrives."

Gart was increasingly apprehensive, a big, hollow weight in the pit of his belly that was causing him to feel ill. "How does he know Emberley is here?"

"Call it a historical assumption. He may be an idiot, but he is not a fool. Somehow, he figured it out for himself."

"But he has not seen her yet. Perhaps there is still time to escape unseen."

David shook his head. "Papal guards are all over the grounds. There would be no way to remove her unseen."

Gart couldn't imagine how the man knew Emberley was at Bellham but that didn't matter. All that mattered was why he had come.

"You still have not told me why Buckland is here with a Westminster canon," he said quietly.

David sighed heavily, turning to look at him but fearful of what he would see when he explained their purpose.

"Because Julian has gone to the Church to demand his wife returned to him," he said after a moment. "Father Mellitus is here to take possession of Emberley and return her to her husband. You know as well as I do that we cannot refuse the Church – to do so would have unfathomable consequences."

Gart stared at him, shocked. "Surely you cannot be serious."

David cocked an eyebrow. "I am afraid I am."

Gart continued staring at him, shocked. He needed to clarify to make sure he heard correctly.

"Buckland has asked the Church to intervene?" he finally rasped.

David nodded slowly, feeling so very sorry for Gart. "He has," he replied quietly. "I have asked for a delay until Father Jonas arrives to mediate."

"Mediate?" Gart repeated, incredulous. "What is he to mediate? There is no question that Emberley will not go with Buckland. She stays with me, Church or no."

David sighed heavily. "Gart, do not make this more difficult than it already is," he said. "If the Church demands Emberley, we cannot refuse."

Gart began to feel the warmth of rage starting in his feet, moving its way up his legs, causing his palms to sweat as the heat entered his chest before moving to his head. Sweat popped out on his brow and, as David watched apprehensively, Gart began to work his massive fists. David knew that gesture, having seen it many times before. It was the catalyst to an explosion of epic proportions.

"They cannot have her," he growled. "I will not let them take her."

David put up his hands, trying to soothe the rage before it exploded.

"That is why I have sent for Father Jonas," he said. "If anyone can help us work through this, he can. Until he arrives, you and I will remain here in this room while my brother watches over Julian and Westminster. We are going to stay right here until Jonas arrives."

"Father Jonas be damned!" Gart roared. "I will kill Buckland before I let him take her!"

David moved to him, putting his hands on the man to ease him.

"Gart, you must control yourself," he pleaded. "You must stay calm if there is any hope of allowing Emberley to remain with you. If you fly into a rage, the Church will see you as a madman and remove Emberley for her own safety. Do you understand me?"

Gart was struggling to control himself, more than he ever had in his life. He knew David was right about maintaining his control. He didn't want to appear insane, as much as that reputation had been to his advantage in the past. This is one time it would not work in his favor.

Frustrated, filled with rage, he turned away from David and paced the room until he ended up nearly walking into a wall. He leaned forward, bracing his big arms against the wall, struggling to calm down and realizing he was trembling.

"What can be done, David?" Gart asked in an extreme breach of etiquette. He had never before called the man by his forename but somehow, he felt entitled to. It was no longer knight to liege. It was friend to friend. "Please help me. What can be done?"

David wasn't offended by the breach. It seemed natural to him as well.

"I do not know," he said honestly, feeling the man's pain. "I could give you some horses and see how far you can get, but you would be traveling with a young boy and a pregnant woman. How well do you think they would travel under such difficult conditions?"

Gart thought of Emberley and how hard she would try to be brave. She was a strong woman but he doubted she could survive a harried flight. Moreover, there were the children to worry about, children she would not leave behind under any circumstances. Nor would Gart – although her children were not of his flesh, it didn't matter. He loved them as if they were. He could not leave them behind, either.

Sighing heavily, he hung his head, struggling not to feel the despair that was gripping him. The desolation he was feeling was nothing he had ever experienced before. He turned to David.

"I am going upstairs to Emberley," he muttered, pushing past David as he headed for the door. "I will wait with her until Jonas arrives."

David grabbed him by the arm. "That may not be wise," he said. "She will see how upset you are and you will undoubtedly tell her why. If I were you, I would not tell her anything until Father Jonas arrives and we know more of the situation."

Gart held up a hand to the man, understanding his words yet inherently disagreeing with them.

"You just told me that the Church has come to take Emberley from me," he hissed. "If this is true and Father Jonas cannot work a miracle in our favor, you will not be offended when I say I would rather spend this time with Emberley and not you."

David didn't argue with him. He let him go, although he followed him out into the entry hall just to make sure he wasn't going to run into the reception room and tear Buckland apart.

David stood at the base of the stairs, watching Gart mount each step with weariness to his movements that he had never seen before. It was Gart Forbes facing a life sentence, all of the joy drained out of him at the prospect of losing the only thing in his life that mattered.

Heartbroken, David stood at the base of the steps and didn't move until Father Jonas arrived.

CHAPTER TWENTY-SEVEN

KEVIN DE LARA had informed Father Jonas of the circumstances currently embracing Bellham and the priest, with a full de Lohr escort, made all haste to the gray-stoned manse that sat along the River Thames. He honestly wasn't sure what he would find once he arrived and was pleased to see that there was no blood or carnage, and that the place was still intact. Everything seemed peaceful for the most part as softly glowing light emitted from the windows of the big structure.

Dismounting his horse in the yard in front of the house, he was met by David. The fair, young lord was tense as he approached.

"Where is Forbes?" Jonas asked before any greeting could be given.

David came to a halt. "With Lady Emberley," he told him. "I have kept him away from Buckland. He has not seen or spoken to the man."

Jonas removed his gloves. "Excellent," he replied, eyeing David. "De Lara has told me what has happened."

David nodded, his manner laced with anxiety. "You were supposed to offer Buckland a ransom in return for his cooperation in a divorce," he pointed out what he had been wondering most of the day. "What happened?"

Jonas faced David with some anger. "I could not locate the man," he hissed. "I have spent the better part of the day sending out missives, looking for him. He was not at the Tower and no one seemed to know where to find him. Now I see that he has been at Westminster all along. There was no way I could have possibly known that."

"So you have not been able to propose the divorce at all?"

"Nay."

David sighed, turning to look at the house with the softly glowing light emitting from the reception room windows.

"He is here with Father Mellitus from Westminster," he said as they started to walk towards the house. "The canon from Westminster has demanded we turn Lady Emberley over to the custody of the Church so she can be returned to her husband."

Jonas seemed to harden, pausing just before they went inside. He faced David seriously.

"I have heard of Father Mellitus and from all accounts, he is a fair and just man," he said in a low voice. "But if there is any chance of swaying the man's mind, I must go in there and hit hard and furious. I will attack Buckland with his foul reputation and horrific deeds, and it may be necessary to have Lady Emberley corroborate my assertions. Perhaps if we can prove the lady is in mortal danger, then Mellitus will not demand she be returned to her husband pending further investigation. Do you believe the lady is capable of defending herself?"

David lifted an eyebrow. "She will have to be," he said, opening the door. "It is not her I am worried about. It is Gart."

Jonas moved through the door. "Bind him if you have to," he muttered. "The man must remain in control while we settle this."

The warm entry hall of Bellham greeted them and Father Jonas removed his cloak, handing his things over to a hovering servant. Followed by de Lara, David took Jonas into the reception room.

An odd looking standoff unfolded before them. Father Mellitus was sitting in the center of the room, looking impatient and bored as Julian sat several feet away near the hearth.

Christopher was standing next to Julian, practically hovering over the man like a great, powerful sentinel. Two Westminster guards stood by the door and two other priests were over near the lancet windows.

In spite of all of the people in the room, it was as silent as a grave. The mood was cold and uncertain. Jonas walked in, eyed the occupants of the room, and headed straight for Father Mellitus.

"I am Father Jonas of St. Bartholomew," he introduced himself to the gray-haired canon. "You are Father Mellitus?"

Mellitus stood up, nodding his head. "I am," he said. "We have been waiting for you for several hours. What connection do you have to this issue?"

"I am an advisor to the earl and his brother," Jonas replied, sensing Mellitus' impatience. "I am here to speak on behalf of Lady Emberley de Moyon."

Julian suddenly bolted up from his chair. "Who are you that you would speak for my wife? I do not know you."

As Jonas focused in on Julian, David sent Kevin for Gart. As the knight fled, David watched Jonas stalk Julian as a hunter would stalk prey. He could sense that things were about to get interesting.

"But I know you, my lord," Jonas was cool as he approached Julian, sizing up the man he had heard so many horrible things about. "I thought the queen's lover would be a big man of handsome countenance but I see I was mistaken. You are not the mighty hero I expected. What of your relationship with the queen, Baron Buckland? What will she think of your attempt to regain the wife you forsook when you sated your lust with the queen's flesh?"

He was bending down, whispering his vile words in Julian's face. Julian, having entered the room as the properly desperate and anxious husband, immediately found himself on the defensive.

"You have no right to involve yourself in matters that do not concern you," he snarled. "Who are you that you would spout such slander?"

Jonas cocked an eyebrow. "I am Father Jonas St. John and I have heard the queen's confession many a time," he replied, knowing he was divulging privileged information but also knowing he had to attack Julian's character immediately if they were to have any chance of succeeding. "I have heard of her exploits with you many a time."

By this time, Mellitus was on his feet. "You may not speak of what was delivered in confessional," he said strongly. "You may not speak of...."

Jonas swung around, cutting him off. "I realize that Your Grace, but I am seriously wondering if you know the character of the man you are representing." He moved towards Mellitus, lifting his eyebrows when he saw the confusion on the man's face. "No? Then allow me to educate you. This man you are advocating, Baron Buckland, has been the queen's lover for almost a year. He has a wife and four children, yet he has openly cavorted with our most gracious and virtuous queen. Did you not know this?"

Jonas was bordering on mocking as he spoke, watching Mellitus' expression carefully. He continued. "I see by your face that you are perhaps confused by my words," he went to the canon in a companionable manner, wanting to pull the man to his side. "Baron Buckland is something of a monster, Your Grace. He has beaten his wife to the point of death many times. He has been cruel beyond measure to her. He abuses her in every way possible, this fragile woman that God has created as one of his most beautiful creatures. To further cement his beastly behavior, he has taken up with the queen in a lustful and sinful affair, humiliating his wife and openly defying God's sacred laws of marriage. And you have come here to retrieve this woman so he can continue his appalling treatment of her? Does this seem fair or just to you, Your Grace?"

By this time, Mellitus was looking at Julian with a great deal of contempt. Jonas, completely in control of the situation, turned his smug expression in Julian's direction to see that Buckland was red in the face. The man's jaw worked angrily, his entire body twitching with contempt.

"Is this true, Buckland?" Mellitus asked with veiled patience. "Tell me the truth or I walk from this room."

"She is my wife!" Julian burst, moving towards the priests and tripping when his careless foot caught the edge of a chair. "She is my property to do as I please and you cannot take her from me. *She is my wife.*"

Mellitus gazed at the man for a long moment before turning to

Jonas.

"A man is held accountable only to God for his marriage," he said frankly. "Whether or not any of this is true is not of issue. The fact remains that the lady is indeed his wife and, as his property, will be returned to him."

Jonas was unmoved. He turned back to Buckland. "What do you want with the woman, baron? Why do you want her returned to you if you are the lover of the queen?"

Julian was so red in the face that he began frothing at the mouth. "She is mine," he growled. "You cannot keep my wife from me."

"Divorce her," Jonas snapped before Julian could finish his sentence. "Did you hear me? Divorce her. She has been committing adultery and you have every right to divorce her. I would if I were you. Rid yourself of your unfaithful wife and find yourself another bride who will tolerate your hideous behavior. Find someone else you can beat to death."

Mellitus looked at Jonas as if the man were insane. "Divorce?" he repeated, incredulous. "What manner of madness is this?"

Jonas looked at him. "No madness at all, I assure you," he said frankly. "Lady de Moyon has committed adultery. She is pregnant with another man's child. Baron Buckland must divorce her to save his honor. The Church would not refuse his request under these circumstances."

The rapid-fire exchange of conversation was overwhelming everyone in the room, Julian included. His eyes bugged at the shocking information.

"She is… she is *pregnant*?" he gasped. Suddenly, he looked to David and his entire face tightened with rage. "You bastard! You stole my wife and compromised her!"

David, standing by the door, remained cool. "I did nothing of the sort," he said evenly. "But I can promise you that if you accuse me of deceit again, I will call you out and you will lose. Is this in any way unclear?"

Julian was mad with shock and rage. With a throaty growl, he turned his back on the occupants of the room, grabbing the nearest piece of furniture he could find, which happened to be a small cherry-wood table, and began banging it against the floor. Jonas and Mellitus watched him closely, watching the building rage, as Jonas returned his attention to Mellitus.

"He is unstable and unsuitable," Jonas said to the canon, his tone low. "He will kill the lady if we return her to him and we would be responsible for her death. I cannot, in good conscience, support any manner of reunion between the baron and his wife."

Mellitus looked at him. "I agree with you but we cannot dispute the law of marriage," he ran a hand over his gray head, an indecisive gesture. "What more can we do?"

Jonas had been waiting for that question all night. He was prepared.

"We can take the lady into custody as a ward of the Church," he replied. "She will be removed from her lover as well as her husband. Until we can decide what is to be done in regards to the dissolution of the marriage, I do not see where we have a choice."

"We cannot dissolve the marriage."

"We can if Buckland appeals for a divorce on the grounds of adultery. Meanwhile, we will hold the lady in protective custody."

Mellitus was starting to think like Jonas. He turned to watch Buckland as the man pulled a small table apart as if he were peeling a lemon. He was talking to the table as he destroyed it. As the two priests contemplated their next course of action, they caught movement over near the reception hall door.

Gart entered the room, looking strong and composed. David and Christopher immediately moved towards him to both support and restrain the man if necessary. The emotions of the room were volatile to the point of madness and the introduction of Gart would only heighten that explosion.

But Gart was calm. As he moved through the door, it was apparent he had hold of someone. Gently, he pulled Emberley through the door behind him, whispering encouraging words to the woman who had the look of a hunted animal on her face. She hovered near the door, not entirely into the room yet able to see the entire chamber from where she stood. And she was fully able to see Julian.

Christopher was surprised to see the woman but David was not. He had sent Kevin for both Gart and Emberley. David wanted Father Mellitus to see the source of all of the contention, the sweet lady who had caused all of the trouble. If the canon was going to insist that the lady be returned to her husband, then David wanted the man to see the flesh and blood woman he would be condemning. It was a calculated risk he felt necessary to take.

"My lady," David went to her, taking her other arm. Between Gart and David, they were able to pull her into the room. "I am glad you have come. I want the priest from Westminster to meet you. It is important."

Emberley's gaze never left Julian. His back was to the room as he ripped apart a table. She took a few unsteady steps into the chamber as Gart and David gently pulled, but then she came to a halt and refused to move any further. She was in as far as she wanted to go.

Gart looked at David over her blond head, shaking his head faintly at the man. Then he put his arm around her shoulders gently.

"No worries, kitten," he murmured. "You do not have to go any further."

Emberley stood there and trembled, her eyes never moving from Julian. Truth was, Gart was surprised she had come this far. It had taken some convincing but when he made it clear that it was important for her to face the Church as well as Julian, she understood. Her fate was being decided and she needed to be a part of it. Her bravery held up as long as Gart was next to her but even now, with the man pressed up against her, it wasn't enough to chase off the terror entirely. The sight of Julian had her reeling.

David, standing on her left, suddenly felt something brush up behind him. He turned to see Romney behind his mother, straining to catch a glimpse of his father, so David stepped aside and directed the boy up beside his mother so he could see.

David thought that having the boy there could only bolster their case. The Church, that institution of laws and absolute rules, needed to see the face of terror that a marriage had brought a family. They needed to see all of it.

"Father Mellitus," David said. "This is the Lady Emberley de Moyon and her eldest son, Romney. Perhaps they can help you determine...."

Hearing Emberley's name, Julian whirled around, his expression wide with shock. He had pieces of the table in his hands, holding them up above his head as if they were trophies. He stared at Emberley, spittle dripping from his mouth, coiled like a man gone completely insane.

"Emberley!" he gasped. "You *bitch!* How could you humiliate me like this? How could you do it?"

Emberley was trembling so violently that she was having trouble standing. Even though she was surrounded by men who would not let Julian hurt her, still, she was beyond terrified. She was in the realm of panic, an insanity that made it difficult to think rationally. All she could see was Julian standing before her, screaming at her as he had screamed so many times. All she could feel at that moment was complete, utter hatred.

"Because...," she sputtered. "Because I hate you. I have hated you since the day of our marriage when you beat me so badly that both eyes swelled shut and I could not sit up or eat for two days. I have hated you since the day Romney was born and to celebrate the birth of your heir, you became ragingly drunk and raped me within hours of his birth. I have hated you since you killed the daughter I carried and blamed me for your actions. I have hated everything about you every day of my life, praying that God would strike you down and end your evil ways. But still you lived, tormenting me, and my hatred for you has only grown. I hope you rot in hell, you vile bastard."

Every man in the room looked at her, startled by her brutal and honest speech. Gart had his arm around her shoulders, squeezing her gently to let her know that he was in full support of her words. He could feel her composure returning, proud of the woman who had been so utterly terrified only moments earlier. She was beginning to show her strength, the strength he knew she had.

Julian, however, had a decidedly different reaction. He threw the wood in his hands and it sailed across the room, missing everyone by a wide margin but the message was obvious. He screamed like a madman.

"You cannot speak to me that way," he howled. "I will punish you severely, do you hear me? Not de Lohr nor his guard dogs nor the holy church will be able to spare you from my wrath for your insolence!"

He was yelling but he wasn't moving towards her, which fed Emberley's bravery. It was the first time she had spoken her mind to the man and the sensation was liberating. She took a deep breath, swallowing hard as her composure gained strength.

"You will not touch me again," she told him, sounding more in control of herself. "I will not allow it and neither will Gart. Julian, you have no use for me. Why do you want me returned to you so badly?"

Julian was verging on another tantrum but steeled himself. Something in her softly uttered sentence had his attention.

"Gart?" he repeated, looking at Forbes with his arm around Emberley. He didn't know why he hadn't noticed that before except that Emberley had held his complete focus. Oddly, he seemed to relax. "Of course. I should have known this. It was not de Lohr at all but Forbes. Fleeing to Trelystan and then safe haven here at Bellham has all been a cover for Forbes."

Emberley was feeling much more confident than she had been only moments earlier. Gart's presence and the fact that she knew Julian wasn't going to run at her and grab her helped her to regain her composure. She looked at Father Mellitus.

"I am the Lady Emberley, Your Grace," she sounded much more in control of herself. "I would be happy to answer any questions you would have for me regarding my marriage to Baron Buckland."

Everyone in the room was looking at her as the focus of the entire situation, the key to hell or peace in so many ways. Father Mellitus cleared his throat softly.

"My lady," he greeted. "Your husband has asked me to intervene on his behalf so that you may return to him as his wife."

Emberley took a few steps towards the priest, patting Gart's arm reassuringly when he tried to follow her. She wasn't going far and she realized that this was something she had to do on her own. Gart, David, Christopher and a host of other men had supported her and made her feel strong. Now, she could finally handle her fear of Julian. But the rest she had to do on her own.

"My husband has made it clear that he does not wish to be married to me," she said frankly. "He has spent the past year bedding the queen. He would not bed me because he said it was immoral for him to do so because he was in love with another woman. Now he suddenly wants me returned to him like a stray dog that has run away? I find it astonishing that the Church should support his request."

Mellitus sighed heavily, passing a long look at Julian. "The fact remains that he is your husband and it is his right to have his wife," he told her. "Father Jonas and I have discussed taking you into protective custody at this time."

Emberley was close enough to the man that he could grab her if he reached out his arm and she quickly stepped away from him, feeling her calm stance waver.

"I will not go," she asserted. "I will never go back to him. I love Gart and he loves me and we will be together, whatever comes. I will never go back to that hell of a marriage and face certain death."

"Forbes," Julian hissed. "He has turned her against me."

"You did that yourself," Gart growled, knowing he should keep his mouth shut but unable to restrain himself. "Your own actions have cost you your wife and family."

David grabbed Gart to hush him and also to prevent him from trying to move against Julian as Emberley focused on her husband.

"You have no use for me," she repeated, almost pleadingly. "Your focus is with the queen and if not the queen, I am sure there are any number of noblewomen who can occupy your time and your bed. You never wanted me, Julian. You agreed to a marriage because my father supplied me with a large dowry. It certainly was not because you loved or needed me. You are incapable of such feelings. Let me go. Please."

Julian was grinding his teeth so hard that he bit his lip, and the frothy saliva around his mouth began to turn pink.

"You are my wife," he snarled. "I will never let you go. I will take you back to Dunster and I will erase all of this madness from your mind as I erase the touch of Gart Forbes from your body. I will exorcise you as one would exorcise a demon. I will purge you until there is nothing left to purge."

He was shouting by the time he was finished and David was having a devil of a time hanging on to Gart. As Julian shouted and Emberley began to back away fearfully, Romney suddenly ran forward.

"You leave my mother alone!" he shouted. "You are a bad man and I do not want you to be my father anymore. You hurt my mother and make her cry. I hate you!"

Emberley grabbed the boy before he could rush on his father and possibly get hurt. Julian was so coiled there was no telling who he would lash out at. Emberley picked up Romney, her big boy, cradling him against her.

"Please, Julian," she begged softly. "A divorce...."

"No divorce!"

"If you do not divorce me, I shall run with Gart and you will never find me or the children, not ever. Do you understand me? We will run away and never look back. That will be more shameful to you than a divorce would." A sob caught in her throat as she spoke beseechingly. "I am willing to be labeled an adulteress so you can save your honor. Is that not worth considering?"

Julian almost charged her but thought better of it. Forbes was too close and his colossal hands were working furiously, Julian was sure, in waiting for the opportunity to wrap around Julian's neck. Julian may have been bordering on madness but he was not a fool.

As he gazed at Emberley, holding Romney, he knew what he had to do. He had to get the woman alone. Then, no one could stop him from doing as he must. This had to end.

He had to kill her.

CHAPTER TWENTY-EIGHT

"Very well," Julian suddenly seemed very resigned. His mercurial fury had tempered and he ran his hands through his dark hair, laboring for control. "Very well, then. If we must speak of divorce, then I will speak only to you. I want to talk to you alone. Everyone else must leave this room."

"Never," Gart roared. "You will never be alone with her, Buckland, not if God himself stood before me and demanded it. I will kill you before I allow you to be alone with her."

He started to move forward but Christopher rushed over and grabbed him, holding him at bay along with David. Even with the two of them and their considerable strength, it was still a struggle. It was like trying to stop a raging bull.

Julian was clever and knew how to play the game. He could play it very well when his temper didn't have the best of him. He looked Gart in the eye.

"Then you shall not have your divorce," he said frankly. "If you want it badly enough, you will have to make allowances. I want to speak with my wife alone without interference from anyone. Those are my terms or no divorce."

Stricken, Emberley looked at Gart. He was barely holding himself in check, trapped between David and Christopher, and she knew that the entire situation rested on her shoulders. She was the only one that could convince Gart of what needed to be done. Setting Romney to his feet, she went to Gart.

Pressed up against his heaving chest, she put her hands on his shoulders.

"Gart, please," she whispered. "If there is a chance he will do as we asked, then I am willing to concede to this demand."

Gart was so angry that he was trembling, straining against David and Christopher.

"Nay," he rumbled. "I will not permit it."

"*Please*," she begged softly. "Nothing will happen. You will be right on the other side of the door, listening to everything. If you hear trouble, you can come right in and save me. Please, Gart. We must do as he asks if there is the slightest chance I can obtain my divorce."

Gart didn't like it – God knew, he didn't like it in the least. He was as resistant to the idea as he had ever been, hating Julian for the manipulative suggestion and more than eager to wrap his hands around the man's throat and squeeze.

He tried to ignore the idea that Emberley might be correct, too fearful to allow her to be alone with the man. For the past several hours, it had been Emberley who had been afraid to even be near Julian. Now, she was begging to be alone with him. If only for the opportunity to discuss divorce, she was willing to try. Gart should be willing, too.

Trembling, struggling, he gazed into her pleading face and began to relent. An expression of extreme pain crossed his face.

"Kitten…," he whispered.

She smiled bravely at him. "'Twill be all right," she assured him softly. "You will be right outside the door. Nothing can happen. But if he is willing to discuss a divorce to me alone, then we must take the chance."

He gritted his teeth. "*Nay*."

"Do you have a better idea, then?"

He didn't. It was then he began to realize that he might have to allow her to do as Julian had asked. Gart hated the idea. He really did. As Emberley caressed his shoulders gently, encouragingly, he finally surrendered and hated himself for it.

"Very well." He felt as if all of the air had been sucked out of him, weak with defeat. He looked over at Julian, standing smug and expectant. "You may speak with her alone but rest assured I will be right outside the door. If I hear any sounds other than civil conversation, I will come in here and I will kill you. Do you comprehend?"

Julian smiled thinly, nearly setting Gart off, and Emberley threw her arms around his neck, squeezing him tightly. It was enough to distract him from his fury and he wrapped his arms around her. The feel of her, the smell of her, settled and calmed him. Face against the side of her head, he inhaled deeply of her sweet, musky fragrance.

"Go," Emberley whispered. "Take Romney with you."

"Nay!" Romney heard his name, crying out. "I want to stay with you!"

Emberley released Gart and bent down to her son. "You must go with Gart. I will not be long."

Romney shook his head furiously, holding on to his mother's arm as if afraid Gart was going to drag him away. He turned to his father.

"I want to stay with Mama," he told Julian.

Julian waved him off. "You may stay."

Now Gart was worried about the boy as well as Emberley but he allowed Christopher and David to turn him around and steer him towards the chamber door. Emberley put her hands on his back, helping the baron and the earl remove him. Gart was a very big man and he wasn't moving easily.

Mellitus began to follow, motioning to the papal guards, but Jonas hesitated.

"I would like to stay," he looked at Julian. "As a neutral witness and for safety's sake, I would like to remain."

"I would agree with that suggestion," Christopher almost had Gart through the door as he spoke. "I am sure it would make the lady feel comforted."

Julian simply shrugged his shoulders as he moved towards the hearth, pretending to inspect the enormous and elaborate mantel. He ran his hands along the wood, ignoring those exiting the room. He was focused on what he was about to do, what he must accomplish, and it would not work to his advantage to either be too eager or too resistant to the priest's presence. The man would not get in his way.

Gart's gaze lingered on Julian, seemingly interested in the hearth, before looking to Emberley one last time. She smiled at him and blew him a kiss, and he couldn't help but smile in return. But that was his last glimpse of her as David and Christopher managed to get him out the door, followed by Father Mellitus and the papal guards. One of the guards shut the door softly behind him.

Gart stood right next to the door. He wasn't going to budge and no one would force him. No one seemed to be moving from the entry hall, in fact, most of them clustered near the door as well. Only the papal guards moved off into the shadows.

Gart found a comfortable position next to the door, his ears peaked, listening for any movement or any words beyond the panel. For the moment, it remained silent. He didn't hear a thing until from the other side of the heavy oak door, there was distinct sound of the bolt being thrown.

It was a final, sickening sound. Gart immediately grabbed the latch, seeing that it was indeed locked. David moved up beside him.

"What happened?" he jiggled the frozen lock himself. "Who locked the damn door?"

Gart knew the answer to that. Dear God, he knew the answer. He began pounding on the door.

"Buckland!" he hollered. "Open the door or I will break it down!"

Christopher, seeing the commotion, tried the lock as if he didn't believe Gart and David. Shoving Gart aside, he lashed out a massive boot and kicked the door. The old panel shuddered but didn't break. Panicked, Gart began ramming his big shoulder into the door jamb.

"Emberley?" he hollered. "Can you hear me? Open the door!"

He heard Emberley scream his name and he froze, a look of such horror on his face that it was difficult to fathom. He looked at David, and then Christopher, before going wild and trying to kick the door in.

But the heavy, well-built door stood strong.

"Emberley!" he bellowed. "I hear you, kitten! I am coming!"

David bolted to the kitchens, racing outside and shouting across the yard toward the troop house that was down near the stables. As he roused the soldiers, Christopher and Gart continued to try to break the door down. They could hear screaming and things breaking from the other side.

Gart was beside himself with terror. He was ramming into the door so hard that he'd managed to strike his head against it, drawing blood.

"Is there another way in?" he demanded.

Christopher shook his head. "Only this door," he told him. "The exterior windows are too narrow to enter. The house was built so that each room can act autonomously if the manse is breached. This door can withstand almost anything."

That wasn't the answer Gart wanted to hear. He could hear more screaming and objects breaking and he was crazed with fear.

"We need something to break the door down with," he grabbed the earl with his bloodied knuckles. "We cannot break this door down without assistance."

David came barreling back into the entry hall at that moment. He had a battle axe in his hands.

"Here," he tossed it to Gart. "Breach the door."

Gart deftly caught the axe, planted his feet, and swung the pike-end of it at the door. Pieces of wood flew off but it was going to take time. Gart began swinging with all his might.

"I have more men coming," David told them, breathing heavily from having run to the yard and then to the armory. "They are bringing axes and weapons."

"She will be dead before they get here," Gart grunted, hacking away at the junction just above the bolt. "If I can just make a hole in the door, I can get my arm in and unlock it."

Above their heads on the staircase landing, they heard weeping. Gart didn't bother to look up, but David and Christopher did. Emilie was standing there, sobbing with fear.

"What has happened?" she wept. "Where is Emberley?"

David raced up the stairs to his wife, taking her in his arms. He didn't quite know how to explain that they had been duped by a madman, feeling sick and ashamed.

"It is all right, sweetling," he held her close. "We will get to her."

"But... she is screaming!" Emilie wept. "He is killing her! Oh, please, hurry!"

"Gart is moving as fast as he can," David was wrought with terror, too. He knew they were all listening to a murder taking place. "He will save her."

Even as he spoke the words, a great screaming arose from the room. Not only could they hear Emberley's screams but Romney's cries as well, his high-pitched howls joining his mother's. It was a harrowing sound, pitiful and panicked. They were speaking as they were screaming, shrieking words that no one could understand.

Everyone in the entry hall was filled with anguish at the sounds, but no one more than Gart. He continued to swing away at the door, tears streaming down his face. He swung so hard that his arms nearly fell off but nothing was going to prevent him from getting through that door to Emberley and Romney. He could hear their combined screaming, the sounds filled with terror. It was destroying him.

And then... silence.

CB

EMBERLEY HAD BEEN moving to one of the chairs with Romney while Julian meandered over near the hearth. As she sat in the chair, she looked up in time to see Julian throw the bolt on the reception room door. Before she could react, Julian suddenly brought up the fire poker he had picked up from his inspection of the hearth and brought it down on Father Jonas' skull.

The priest never had a chance. He had been facing Emberley and Romney and never saw it coming. He fell to the floor, his skull split, and Emberley screamed with terror. Julian was suddenly running at her with the poker and she bolted up from the chair, running for her life.

"Gart!" she screamed.

Julian swung the poker at her, missing her by a wide margin and slamming it into a chair.

"He cannot help you," he snarled. "You foolish bitch – did you truly think I would grant you a divorce? Did you truly believe I would reward you for shaming and disobeying me?"

Emberley was in a panic, struggling to keep her wits about her as Julian chased her around the room, swinging the poker and smashing valuable and expensive pieces as he went. They could hear banging on the door and men shouting, trying to break in, but the old, oak door, built to withstand a siege should the enemy break into the house, held fast.

"Julian, stop!" she begged. "Please stop!"

He wasn't listening to her. He was fully committed to smashing her skull with the poker just as he had smashed the priest's and the more he chased her, the more excited he became.

"You have always been disobedient and insolent," he seethed, swinging at her again as she neared one of the lancet windows and getting the poker tangled up in a tapestry that hung there. "I should have killed you long ago but you were beautiful and gave me three strong sons, so I allowed you to live. Now I hear that you are pregnant with Forbes' child? I shall kill you for it!"

Emberley screamed as he came close and narrowly missed clipping her in the back. She raced across the room, dodging fallen chairs and the broken table that Julian had so willfully smashed. More banging filled the room as shouts and threats emitted from the other side of the locked door but still, the sturdy oak and iron held fast. No one could budge it.

"Gart!" she screamed again. "Help!"

Julian crowed with laughter as he cornered her by the edge of the room and a table. Emberley tried to dodge the flying poker but this time, it caught her in the arm. She shrieked with pain, grabbing hold of the gash he had inflicted.

"Forbes cannot help you," Julian was fed by the bloodlust, an almost spiritual experience for him. "Come now, wife. Do not make me chase you any longer. Come to me like a good girl and face your punishment."

Emberley was racing all around the room, trying to avoid Julian and his swinging poker. She could see Romney in the corner of the chamber, absolutely terrified as his mother fought for her life. But she couldn't focus on the boy too long, afraid that Julian would catch up to her if she did. She had to stay alive.

Julian was growing weary of swinging. He tried to leap over a chair to get to Emberley but she dodged him and he ended up falling, twisting his wrist. Furious, he fell back, holding his wrist, suddenly noticing Romney cowering against the wall. He reached out and grabbed the boy by the hair. Romney screamed and swung his fists.

"Nay!" Emberley cried. "Leave him alone!"

Julian cocked a confident eyebrow. "Come here and I shall."

Emberley was cringing on the other side of the room, tears on her face as she watched Julian hurt Romney. She knew she could not allow the man to harm her child no matter what the consequences. She thought of Gart, of Orin and Brendt and Lacy, and of the child she carried in her belly. So many people depended on her, people she loved with all her heart and soul. She had so much to live for. But none of that mattered if she let just one of those precious souls sacrifice themselves when she could prevent it.

"I will," she swallowed her tears, pushing down the terror for Romney's sake. "Let him go and I will come to you."

Julian yanked the boy by the hair again. "Come to me now or I will not let him go."

Emberley didn't hesitate. She went to Julian and he lashed out a fist, catching her in the jaw and sending her to the ground.

As Emberley fell, Romney yanked himself from his father's grasp and ran away, all the way to the other end of the room. He wanted to run further but he couldn't. He knew what was going to happen and he knew he had to stop it. He had to protect his mother.

Fumbling around in his tunic, he pulled out Gart's dagger that he had stolen from the table in his mother's bedchamber. The moment he had feared had finally come and he wondered if he was brave enough to do as he must. For his mother's sake, he had to. He began to move towards his father.

Julian had his back to Romney as he stalked Emberley, now struggling to pick herself off the floor. He lifted the poker over his head, getting a good grip on the iron pole as he prepared to do his worst.

"I should have done away with you years ago," Julian hissed. "Now you shall know what it means to be punished. You are a foolish, wicked woman, Emberley. For the humiliation you have caused me, you shall feel my wrath."

Emberley was only half-conscious, hearing his words but having no idea where he was. She could hardly see for the spinning room and she struggled to move away, in any direction, hoping that it would be away from Julian and his madness. She knew he meant to kill her and she labored to collect her wits enough to run again, but she couldn't seem to manage it. The blow to the head had her reeling and she was fumbling in the dark.

She couldn't even manage to be terrified at the moment. All she could feel was desperation to get away, to survive, to continue to fight. Rolling onto her back, she saw that Julian was right on top of her, the poker held high. She lifted her left arm to block the blow, hoping it would be enough.

As Julian drew the poker back with the intention of smashing it downward into her head, the man suddenly howled with pain and the poker fell to the floor.

Julian grabbed his back and thrashed, falling to the floor in fits. Emberley screamed as the man came down on top of her legs, blood gushing from a dagger rammed into the small of his back. Looking up, she saw Romney standing behind his father, a look of shock and terror across his young face. There was blood on his hands.

Romney's eyes met with his mother's and the boy suddenly burst into loud, terrified sobs. Panicked, he reached down and picked up the fallen poker, slamming it into Julian's back and legs again and again.

He was screaming louder and louder as he continued to beat his father, hearing his mother scream his name but not acknowledging her. Romney was in a world of such terror that he had to kill the source of it, the only thing he knew to do, stamping out the source of his fear. He had to beat it until it was dead.

Sobbing heavily, he struck Julian one more time, weakly, before dropping the poker to the floor. Emberley was shrieking with fright, with horror, and Romney was sobbing as if his heart were breaking. He could hear men yelling from the opposite side of the closed reception room door, and someone was ramming into it heavily, attempting to dislodge the lock.

With bloody hands, wiping at his tear-stained face, Romney went to open the door.

CHAPTER TWENTY-NINE

GART COULDN'T THINK about the silence beyond the door. He couldn't let the deafening roar of nothingness fill his brain because it would shatter him. He blocked it out and kept swinging. He had to get to Emberley. It was the only thought that kept him going.

He was about to bring the axe down again, widening a small hole he had made, when the bolt suddenly twitched. He came to a grinding halt, panting with exertion, holding the axe aloft because he was sure Julian was about to step through the door and he was going to cave the man's skull in. He waited, coiled, as the bolt was removed.

Christopher had retrieved his broadsword and stood next to Gart. Once the axe came down on Julian's skull, Christopher intended to gut the man. They were all feeling furious and full of sorrow.

Christopher glanced at Gart as the iron bolt rattled, seeing tears streaming down the man's face and feeling an enormous sense of anguish. It was sorrowful, the results of this day, and he deeply pitied Gart. He didn't even know what to say to the man. He did the only thing he could – he stood there with his sword at the ready, preparing to help.

The door shifted, rattled again, as someone tried to open it. With the bolt thrown, the panel was unlocked and Gart kicked out a massive boot to shove the door open wide. With the axe raised, he saw movement in the doorway and blindly moved to bring the axe down. He was startled when Christopher threw up his broadsword and blocked him.

"Nay!" Christopher snapped. "Look!"

Gart did. Romney stood in the doorway, rubbing his eyes with bloodied hands. Gart stared at the boy and, with a cry of anguish, dropped the axe. He reached out and grabbed the child.

"Rom?" his voice cracked. "What happened? Are you injured?"

Romney shook his head. "Nay," he wept. "But… my mother…."

He couldn't finish, sobbing, and Gart picked him up and stepped into the room to view the carnage. He held the weeping boy tightly against him, trembling with horror as his gaze moved over the chamber. There were bodies everywhere.

"Oh, my dear God," Gart breathed.

Father Jonas lay on the ground with a bloodied head wound, his brains spilling out onto the wooden floor. Gart's gaze searched frantically for Emberley, spying her over in the corner with Julian lying across her legs. There was blood all over the two of them.

With a strangled cry, Gart set Romney down and raced to Emberley. She was sitting up, holding her head, weeping uncontrollably. Gart didn't even bother to look at Julian – he shoved the man off her legs and swooped in to pick her up.

"Kitten," he breathed. "Where are you injured?"

Emberley was weeping heavily. She threw her arms around his neck, holding him tightly. She was hysterical and battered, but she was alive. Gart's warmth in her arms confirmed that. Nothing in her life had ever felt as wonderful as holding Gart at that very moment. It was relief beyond description.

"I am not injured," she gasped, her face pressed into the crook of his neck. "He tried but he did not hurt me. But Romney… Romney killed him!"

A look of shock, then disbelief, washed over Gart's face as he pulled back to look her in the face as if attempting to determine the validity of her statement. He simply couldn't believe it. Still holding Emberley, his gaze sought out Romney. The boy was standing a few feet away, still rubbing his eyes and weeping. Gart held out a hand to the boy.

"Rom," he said softly. "Come here, lad. Come here and tell me what happened."

Romney went to Gart, falling against the man as he wept. Gart sat on his knees, Emberley in one arm and Romney in the other. Knowing they were both relatively unharmed, he was able to push aside his own terror to comfort them both.

"Calm down, lad," he rubbed Romney's back gently. "Tell me what happened."

Romney sniffled, wiping his face with his bloodied hands. "He... he tried to kill my mother," he said. "I could not let him do it. He was going to hit her with the poker and I could not let him. So... so I stabbed him. I had to stop him."

Gart listened to the halting explanation, his heart aching for what the young man had to do but also feeling a great deal of pride and gratitude. He shifted, managing to get a look at Julian lying crumpled on his side. He could see the hilt of a dirk sticking out from his back and peering closer, he realized that he recognized the blade.

"Where did you get that dirk, Rom?" he asked, astonished.

Romney, his tears easing, pulled his face from Gart's shoulder and looked at him. "It was upstairs. It was the one you were going to let me sharpen. I stole it. I am sorry."

Gart shook his head, kissing the boy's temple. He sighed heavily in understanding, in relief. Even if Gart had not been able to save Emberley, still, he had been there in spirit in the palm of Romney's hand. It was all so incredibly ironic and incredible appropriate. He still couldn't believe it.

"No need, lad," he finally murmured. "You did me proud. It seems that you finally stole something worth stealing. You saved your mother when I could not."

Romney didn't seem so upset with Gart's reassuring words. He looked at the knight, the man who had come to mean the world to him, and wiped the last of his tears from his face.

"I did not want to kill my father," he said quietly.

"I know."

"I had to."

"I understand."

"You are not angry with me?"

Gart smiled at the boy, shaking his head. "You did what you had to do," he said quietly. "I do not know many young lads who would have had the presence of mind to do what you did. I am very proud that you saved your mother's life."

Romney smiled timidly and Gart ruffled his blond head affectionately. Gart then turned to Emberley, who had her head against his shoulder, watching the interaction between Gart and Romney. Gart kissed her forehead.

"Are you sure you are well?" he asked softly.

She nodded. "I am," she murmured. "My angel saved me."

Gart turned his affectionate eye back to Romney. "He certainly did."

Emberley put her hand on Gart's chin, forcing him to look at her. Her gaze was filled with adoration, with respect. She ran a gentle finger over his lips. Gart forgot about his terror as he met her gaze, feeling only the great love he felt for her.

"Nay," she whispered. "I did not mean him. I meant Gabriel."

EPILOGUE

Dunster Castle
June, 1210 A.D.

"LADY FORBES?" KEVIN de Lara called down from the battlements. "I finally see them. They are approaching."

Emberley gazed up at the knight, high on the walls of Dunster, shielding her eyes from the nooning sun. It was a cool but bright day, a snappy breeze blowing in from the sea. She couldn't help the smile from her face.

"Are you sure?" she called back.

Kevin nodded. "I can see the banners," he told her. "Baron Buckland returns."

Her grin broadened and she turned to the children around her.

"Lacy," she called to her daughter. "Bring the children. Your brothers are home."

Lacy de Moyon, now eight years of age and an exquisite blond beauty like her mother, squealed with delight. "Is Dada with them?"

Emberley nodded. "Of course, sweetheart," she replied. "Did you think he would not return with them? He went to collect them from Lioncross Abbey, after all."

Lacy shrugged. "Sometimes the earl makes him stay because he needs his war counsel."

Emberley stroked her daughter's soft hair. "Not this time," she said softly. "He has returned to you, I promise. Now, please help me round up the children so we may greet the returning heroes properly."

Lacy promptly hustled to capture her younger siblings. Five-year-old Brydon was fairly easy to capture because he was more obedient than the rest, a calm and intelligent boy who resembled his father a great deal in both appearance and demeanor. He was a proud Forbes son.

The bigger problem were the twins, Elizabeth and Emmaline – at nearly three years of age, they were blond, bright, beautiful and extremely aggressive. They were very vocal about their wants and dislikes, and they greatly disliked being corralled by their older sister. Lacy held her baby sisters' hands, attempting to pacify them as they cried.

Emberley watched the scene, bending over to soothe her unhappy daughters but stopping short of picking them up to comfort them. At nine months pregnant with a very large child, the physic had forbidden her from lifting anything, including her children, for fear that she would harm herself and the babe she carried.

So she bent over to whisper sweetly to her children, even as the great gates of Dunster began to open and welcome the first members of the Buckland party. As more riders entered and the bailey became loud and busy, she stood straight, rubbing furiously at her back to ease the strained muscles as she spied two of her three returning sons.

She waved happily at Brendt and Orin, now ten and twelve years respectively, who were heading straight for their mother astride the new warmblood geldings that their father had given them.

Romney, now thirteen and six feet tall, came roaring in behind them aboard the new charger he had received for his last birthday. It was a big animal the color of chalk and rumor had it that Romney loved the beast so much that he slept with it in its stall at Lioncross Abbey Castle. At least, that was the story that Gart had told her between giggles.

Emberley's heart swelled with happiness as her three oldest children approached. Brendt jumped off his horse and ran to his mother, hugging her tightly. Orin was directly behind him, both boys hugging their mother and overwhelming her. Even though they were growing up now, older boys who were learning to be knights, they still were not beyond showing their mother affection. Emberley hugged them gleefully until a loud, deep voice interrupted their reunion.

"Gently, young men, gently," Gart was pointing at them as he rode up on his dancing charger. In full armor, he looked terrifying and imposing. "If you squash the woman, you will have me to deal with."

The boys grinned while the younger children began to squeal and jump with excitement. Gart flipped up the visor on his helm, a smile on his face as he viewed his entire family, together for the first time in months. With the older boys off to foster with the Earl of Hereford, times like this were few and far between. He relished the moment with great joy.

He dismounted his black and white destrier and handed him over to a groom. He hadn't taken two steps when the little ones rushed at him, screaming his name. He grunted as they ran into him, pretending to teeter off balance.

"Good Christ," he grunted again as Brydon jumped up and latched on to him. He picked the boy up, his first born son, and hugged the lad tightly. "Brydon, you have grown by a head since last I saw you. Are you ready to go and foster with your brothers?"

Brydon had his little arms wrapped around his father's neck, grinning.

"I am ready, Dada," he said confidently.

As Gart kissed the boy's cheek again and set him to the ground, the twins were howling at his feet and he scooped them up, one little girl in each arm. Kissing rosy cheeks, he approached his wife and bent down, kissing her sweetly on the lips.

"Greetings, kitten," he murmured, kissing her again. "How are you feeling?"

Emberley smiled at him, cupping his face between her two hands. "Very well," she said, kissing him yet again because she was so glad to see him. "But I will admit that I am ready for this child to be born."

"Is everything all right?"

"Everything is fine. I am simply ready to be done with it."

He nodded in sympathy, watching as Romney approached his mother. Emberley embraced young Baron Buckland, having inherited his title from his father and Dunster Castle along with it. Romney had grown up tall and handsome, favoring his mother's blond attractiveness tremendously.

At thirteen years of age, he was wise beyond his years and although he remembered his real father, he considered Gart the only father he had ever had. He and Gart were inordinately close and Gart could not have been prouder of the boy. With Gart's guidance and calm, fair manner, all three of Julian's boys were growing into fine, strong, young men. To them, Julian was just a bad memory.

"Greetings, Mother," Romney kissed his mother on the cheek. "It is good to be home."

Emberley smiled. He was growing up, sounding so formal in greeting. "It is good to have you home again," she said. "Lacy and the children have missed you."

As if on cue, Brydon jumped on his older brother and Romney grunted as the child hit him in the gut. He picked the little boy up and swung him around in circles, listening to him giggle. Then Brendt and Orin jumped in, tickling the little boy, and Brydon squealed with delight as his three older brothers gently teased him.

Gart and Emberley watched as the four boys dashed for the keep, setting Brydon to his feet and encouraging the boy to chase them. Brydon did so happily, following them up the stone steps into the enormous keep of Dunster.

Emberley shook her head at the humor of the scene, turning to look at Gart just as the boys disappeared into the keep.

"Poor Brydon has been so lonely without them," she said, wrapping her hands around her husband's elbow. "He has only had girls to play with."

Gart had his daughters in his arms, sweet, little faces that reminded him so much of his wife, and he kissed them again as they hugged their father in tandem. He then noticed Lacy standing beside him and he set Emmaline to her feet so he could hug his oldest daughter.

"I rather like girls," Gart said as he kissed Lacy on the top of the head. "I have missed mine."

Emberley smiled up at him. "We have missed you as well," she said, taking Emmaline by the hand and moving towards the keep in the wake of the loud boys. "Now, tell me all of the news from Lioncross and mind you, do not leave anything out."

Gart took her command seriously. "The earl's wife just had another baby, a boy," he dutifully told her. "His name is Henry and he has blond hair and big blue eyes just like the rest of the earl's brood."

Emberley lifted her eyebrows. "That makes four boys now, does it not?"

Gart nodded. "Emilie is also due to give birth very soon, just as you are," he told her. "David is convinced it is a son."

Emberley giggled softly. "After three girls, the man is desperate for a son. He told me that if Emilie has another girl, he may try to trade the baby for one of our boys."

Gart grinned as they reached the stone steps leading up to the keep. "He cannot have any of them," he said flatly, setting Elizabeth to her feet so she could take the stairs by herself. "I will keep my sons. He will have to produce his own."

Emberley chuckled softly, falling in to the rear as the three girls mounted the steps. Gart had Emberley by the arm to make sure she was steady while simultaneously shepherding the toddlers up the stone. He didn't want anyone slipping and falling.

By the time they reached the entry with the squirrely little girls, he puffed out his cheeks wearily and came to a halt. Lacy took the twins inside as Emberley paused beside her husband.

"Exhausted?" she asked, a twinkle in her eye.

He shrugged. "A little," he admitted, reaching out to take her hand. "We rode hard to make it home as quickly as we could. Three weeks is too long to be away from you and the children."

"It *was* long, but now you are here," she said softly, reaching up to touch his face and watching him kiss her palm. "In fact, the girls have planned a special meal for your return. Shall we go inside and enjoy it?"

Gart turned towards the darkened entry, started to move, and then abruptly came to a halt. He turned to Emberley with a smirk on his face.

"You would not want to go in first, would you?" he asked.

She burst out into soft laughter. "Not a chance," she told him. "Go inside. Show your courage, Forbes."

He shook his head. "The odds are not in my favor."

"You will survive."

He knew what was waiting for him in the darkened entry. "Do you suppose they could resist just this once?"

"Nay."

Gart took a deep breath, puffed out his cheeks again, and forged ahead into the darkened entry. Emberley followed, standing in the doorway to watch Brydon, Orin and Brendt attack Gart and try to put him to the ground. The boys were yelling encouragement at each other, having no real luck at toppling Gart until Romney emerged from underneath the spiral stairs and took him out by the knees.

Gart went down with four boys on top of him, Brydon making the demands for money at the prompting of Brendt and Orin. Gart refused and they tried to strip him of his helm and anything else of value he had strapped to his body. Gart got the upper hand before they could strip him completely and tried to get away, up the stairs, but the four of them latched on to him again and pulled him down to his knees.

There was laughing and giggles going on, which led Emberley to believe that it was not a real robbery. Moreover, Gart could get away if he really wanted to. She stood there and chuckled, watching the thievery without thought to stopping it. It reminded her of the first time she ever saw Gart at Dunster, being robbed by three young boys and not realizing what impact he was about to have on a family that very much needed a miracle.

The Archangel Gabriel had heard their prayers. He'd given them everything. He'd given them heaven.

ଓଃ THE END ଃ୦

AUTHOR NOTE

Archangel is, first and foremost, a deeply passionate love story. The feelings that Gart and Emberley have for each other are obvious from the onset and the question of adultery is presented – how wrong is it given the circumstances? And how sacred is the institution of marriage when it is an unhealthy and volatile contract? Gart and Emberley wrestle with those questions, but not for long. The love they have for one another transcends all.

Once again, we meet the powerful Brothers de Lohr in this novel. Christopher de Lohr was one of my original "Epic" heroes back when I started writing, the main character in a book called "The Defender". His brother, David, was also in the book and went on to star in his own novel called "Steel Heart" centering on how he met and married Emilie. Good stuff. Both brothers also appeared again in "Spectre of the Sword". They are my favorite go-to guys and I adore them. Writing about them is like seeing old friends again.

Also introduced is Kevin de Lara, brother of Sean de Lara, hero in the novel "Lord of the Shadows". Sean mentions Kevin once in the novel, stating that "my brother and I do not speak much". That is because Sean, in this novel, has only recently crossed over to the dark side with King John and his family is at odds with him. Sean de Lara knew the true meaning of self-sacrifice, since he was a spy and his entire cover was working for the king. But no one knew that, not even his brother.

Lastly, when Gart is speculating of somewhere to take Emberley and the children where Julian can't find them, he mentions that he has a friend at Prudhoe Castle. The friend Gart refers to is none other than Creed de Reyne, the hero of "Guardian of Darkness". I can only be speculated if Gart had traveled north and met up with Creed, what an adventure they would have had! So, yes, to varying degrees, Kathryn Le Veque's novels have cross-characters in nearly every book. They're all one big, happy family!

The de Lohr Dynasty series also contains the following novels:

Rise of the Defender

Novels where the same name or cross-over characters appear:

Unending Love

Netherworld

Bonus Chapters of the exciting Medieval Romance **SPECTRE OF THE SWORD** to follow.

1203 A.D. – The Lady Elizabeau Treveighan is the illegitimate daughter of Geoffrey, Duke of Brittany. Elizabeau was sent to foster at a very young age, her identity known only to herself and the earl who fostered her. When her half-brother Prince Arthur is murdered and rumors begin to fly that the opposition to King John intends to marry her to a Teutonic prince and supplant her and her new husband as the rulers of England, she suddenly becomes a very hot, and very dangerous, commodity.

Sir Rhys du Bois is charged with keeping Elizabeau safe until her arranged marriage can occur, but the task turns into one of monumental proportions. It's one harrowing flight after another as Rhys tries to keep Elizabeau from harm's way. Somewhere in the process, they fall madly in love with each other and the knight finds himself battling duty and love in order to stay on task. Torn, but with a tremendous sense of duty, he cannot escape the feelings that are swamping him, and Elizabeau does not make it easy for him. Her love for him supersedes her loyalty to her country, and to a family name that has only meant heartache for her.

When Elizabeau is finally captured by the king's men and slated for execution under the charge of treason, Rhys will risk everything to save her from the executioner's sword. However, Rhys is betrayed by another knight and soon, he too is slated for the executioner's axe. As Rhys and Elizabeau face death together, allies come together for a covert operation that will save their lives. It's a race against time before King John's men can execute the last legitimate heiress to the throne and her protector turned lover.

CHAPTER ONE

Year of our Lord 1203 A.D., November
Hyde House, London

"Take her, du Bois." The command was a staccato hiss. "Even as we speak, there are assassins on her tail. You should have been out of here an hour ago."

A massive knight with brilliant blue eyes was in motion before the command left the old man's lips. In the dark corridors of the manor house with its mossy walls and cracked floors, he took the small lady by the arm and pulled her towards the stairs. Behind him, the old man who had issued the orders followed on their heels.

"You must leave London this night," he went on, almost tripping as he took the steps too fast. "I've arranged a safe haven for you in Ealing at Courtenay's lodgings, but that is of course providing you can even make it there."

They reached the bottom of the steps, continuing back into the bowels of the neglected old house. There was a sense of urgency in the air, bordering on panic. The knight felt it, even without the elderly man shuffling along behind him or the snarling lady in his grip. But he was a professional, a knight born and bred. He would not allow the fear or panic to touch him. He had a job to do.

"I can make it to Ealing, my lord," he assured the old man in a tone that suggested no counter comment. "But your men must buy me some time. Just enough time to get her out of London is all I need."

"No promises, du Bois. Be on your way."

The old man followed the pair into the kitchen; the hollow chamber would have been pitch black had it not been for the torch the old man was carrying. As the knight grasped the iron latch that would lead into the kitchen yard where his charger waited, the old man reached out to grab him.

"Rhys, listen to me," the man's eyes, yellowed with age, bore into him. "I realize this is sudden and I further realize that until a few hours ago, you had no knowledge of the political upheaval transpiring. But hear me and hear me well; this is a mission in which you must not fail. If you do not get this lady to safety, much will be lost. England will be lost."

Rhys du Bois gazed into the elderly man's eyes as they reflected the torchlight. Hubert de Burgh was an old man now, having served his share of Plantagenet kings. He was the Chief Justiciar of England, wielding as much power as the king himself and this mission was no folly. As Rhys opened his mouth to reply, the front door to the manor house swung open, spilling forth a collection of men in wet armor. They brought torches with them and more weapons.

Rhys' first instinct was to go for his broadsword until he realized that he recognized the men. The group headed towards him, splattering rain on the floor and walls.

"Rhys," the big man in the lead spoke. "Why have you not left yet? We've already had two groups of assassins killed within a half mile of this place. You'd better leave right away and we'll do what we can to cover your retreat."

"We were just leaving, my lord," Rhys assured his liege. "The lady had a bit of a… delay."

The group of knights came to a halt. Two or three ran up the stairs with weapons drawn as a couple ran past Rhys and Hubert and the lady, throwing open the door and entering the soaked kitchen yard. Lightening flashed, showing their heavy broadswords poised and ready. They were looking for a fight, waiting.

The big knight flipped up his visor, his sky blue eyes fixed on Rhys. "What delay?" he demanded softly. "This is no time for foolishness, du Bois. You must remove the lady immediately."

De Burgh cleared his throat softly, eyeing both Rhys and the cloak-covered lady. "It was not du Bois' fault, Chris," he said quietly. "They lady was... well, she was...."

A portion of the cloak suddenly flew back and the figure beneath was revealed. Luscious golden-red hair was bunched up around her slender shoulders, the face of an angel evident in the weak light. She would have been an exquisitely beautiful creature had the countenance of her face not been so dark. Her dark green eyes flashed furiously.

"I was locked in the closet," she announced. "If those murdering blackhearts want to kill me, let them try. They shall have to get to me first. I was perfectly safe until de Burgh and his guard dog wrested me from my place of safety. And now they want to take me out into this horrific weather where all manner of creature can take aim to kill me? 'Tis lunacy!"

Christopher de Lohr, Earl of Worcester and Hereford, gazed at the angry little woman before him. He tried to keep his cool, knowing time was of the essence. Besides, having a wife with much the same flaming disposition gave him the practice of keeping his calm when faced with a furious female. Still, it was a struggle.

"Lady Elizabeau Treveighan," he greeted her calmly. "Allow me to explain the situation to you. You are in serious jeopardy. As the daughter of Geoffrey of Brittany and now the only surviving child that is not in captivity with the passing of your half-brother Arthur, you are the target of your Uncle John's madness because you have been declared Arthur's successor to the throne. Do you understand this, my lady?"

Even angry, she was a delectable little doll. Her sweet face was scrunched with rage. "I do not want to be his heir," she snapped. "What of Eleanor? She is Arthur's older sister. Give her the throne; I do not want it."

"What you want is of no matter," de Lohr replied evenly. "Eleanor of Brittany is, even now, a captive at Corfe Castle. If we do not remove you to safety, you too shall be either murdered or captured."

There was more fear in her features than true anger. "But Eleanor is the true heiress."

De Lohr sighed patiently. "But you are free. Eleanor cannot be Richard's successor while she is bottled up in Corfe's dungeons." He took another step in her direction, an enormous man with an intimidating manner. "By virtue of the fact that you are not captive or prisoner and by virtue of the fact that you are Geoffrey's sole remaining living child, you have been named successor. You must accept this and I promise that we shall all get along much better."

She wasn't happy in the least; her expression said so. "I would know who made this decision that I should take Arthur's place and not Eleanor. Who on earth has the power to make this so?"

De Burgh interjected. "I did, my lady," he said softly. "While John lives, only madness shall rule in England. The country will not survive. We need a true and noble ruler, my lady. We need you."

The anger faded from her features, replaced by some trepidation. "But I am not a true royal," she insisted, more softly this time. "I have not been groomed for this duty."

"You will be."

The way de Burgh said it made the statement sound as if there was no argument. Even de Lohr looked at him as he spoke the words; there was power and decision in them. They all knew the stakes. They were the opposition to the crown; this was treason of the highest order.

Elizabeau knew it too and the more she thought on it, the more frightened she became. But she refused to let them see her fear. "If that is so, then why are you sending me out into the dead of night with only one man for protection?" she asked. "Every man under John's belt is out to carve a piece of me."

De Lohr cocked a blond eyebrow. "You have been pledged to a nephew of Emperor Otto the Fourth, a marriage which will solidify the unity between The Holy Roman Empire and England. France will be boxed in from both sides with The Holy Roman Empire to the east and England to the West. The emperor's troops will help us secure your throne once the marriage has taken place. Phillip's power will be seriously limited and your Uncle John will be neutralized."

Elizabeau gritted her teeth impatiently. "I know all of that. But you still have not answered my question."

"And what is that, my lady?"

"Why are you sending me into the dark with a lone knight for protection?"

De Lohr, who had once been the right hand of Richard the Lion Heart and the man known throughout the realm as the King's Champion, cast a long glance at Rhys. *The man is in for one hell of an experience with this one*, he thought dryly.

"This isn't simply a lone knight, my lady," he said after a moment. "The man holding you within his grasp is one of my very best. Make no mistake; he is a man of great experience and strength."

"He is a mere knight. How dare you trust my life to someone so… so simple."

De Lohr held up a finger. "Ah, that is where you are grossly mistaken, my lady," his reply had an edge of sharpness. "The knight you have just insulted is the fourth son of the Duke of Navarre. He has lineage and nobility to match your own. If I were you, I would have a little more respect."

Elizabeau inevitably looked up at the man holding her arm; he was in full armor, a broad bear of a man made more enormous by the protection he wore. All she could see, and all she had ever seen of him since they had been introduced a scarce half-hour earlier, were his eyes, nose and part of a mouth beneath the mail and three-point helm. Everything else was covered with well-used armor or buried under layers of dirks and weaponry.

She locked gazes with him, eyes of the most brilliant blue she had ever seen. They were so bright that they glowed. There was a strange jolt to the moment, as if something was buzzing inside her head, and she quickly tore her gaze away. The brilliant blue eyes of the knight were unnerving. In fact, the entire evening had been unnerving and she was struggling with her equilibrium.

"Then I apologize," she said, though it was not directed at anyone in particular. "But I simply do not understand why I am not kept here, under guard. Surely it will be much more difficult to kill me if I am locked up in a fortress."

De Lohr was finished discussing the subject. He snapped his fingers at Rhys, who began walking again. "I will meet you in Ealing," he told du Bois, eyeing more knights racing from the front of the house and through the kitchens. "For now, I will hold back the pursuers. But I cannot guarantee that you will not be followed. You will have to be vigilant."

Rhys nodded sharply. "Understood, my lord."

Elizabeau opened her mouth to protest but Rhys jerked her through the kitchen door and silenced whatever words she had been preparing to spout. De Burgh and de Lohr followed.

It was pouring rain as he led the lady out into the elements. The kitchen yard was full of mud, horses and armed men as Rhys leaned over and swept the lady into his arms, lifting her up onto his destrier. He did not handle her gently and she glared at him as he roughly settled her. But he ignored her as he mounted behind her, adjusting his stirrups to account for his altered position in the saddle. The lady tightened her cloak against the weather.

"Lady Elizabeau," de Burgh was standing next to her left leg, watching her fuss with her hood. "Please understand that we are doing this for your own good. You must make your rendezvous with your betrothed and du Bois is ordered to escort you there. This marriage must take place if England is to survive. *You* must survive."

Most of the fire went out of Elizabeau. The concept was still mind-boggling; she hadn't known of her brother Arthur's death until two days ago and was subsequently informed that she had been named his heir. But that was providing she marry the prince of the Holy Roman Empire, a man with a name she didn't even know. All of this to create an alliance that her Uncle John and his ally Phillip could never break. It was a maelstrom of politics and she was caught up in the eye of the storm.

Gazing down into the faces of the most powerful men in England, she knew it was a destiny that she could not refuse, as much as she wanted to.

Du Bois dug his spurs into his charger just as the high-pitched screech of an arrow penetrated the muffled noise of the rain. De Lohr and du Burgh scattered, the earl finding cover behind a kitchen wall as the old justiciar scampered back into the house. Rhys put his massive arm over Elizabeau, pulling her into a crushing embrace against his armored chest as they fled the confines of the yard. She could hear the sounds of more arrows behind her, of de Lohr's men shouting and scrambling.

They were the sounds of war.

CHAPTER TWO

THE DESTRIER WAS so exhausted that huge flecks of foam kept flying back and smacking her on the arm or in the chest, and Elizabeau had to turn her head on more than one occasion to keep from being hit in the face. But the big black beast pounded onward into the torrential night, sheets of water pouring from the sky and entire cities of lightning filling the clouds.

Rhys had taken them away from the main road almost immediately. They had entered woods so black that she could scarcely see a foot in front of her face, never mind the terrain. After the first few harrowing minutes, Elizabeau finally closed her eyes and lowered her head, praying fervently that she wasn't about to break her neck when the horse made a bad step and threw her off. But so far, the charger remained surefooted and Rhys directed the horse through the black grove of trees.

There was a small row of homes and an equally small avenue once they exited the woods. Rhys plowed through someone's side yard, into the avenue, and back out through another row of thatched-roof huts. There was a field on the other side and the horse raced wildly into it, leaping over a stream and continuing on into the next cluster of trees.

They rode for hours the same way. Eventually, the small villages surrounding London came to an end and they found themselves in open territory. Twice Rhys had backtracked and crossed his own path so if there was anyone following, the tracks would be muddled. With his clever path, and the continuing rain, he was confident he could lose anyone in pursuit that had managed to escape de Lohr's defenses.

But it was exhausting work. The horse was hearty and responded eagerly to Rhys' commands, but even the beast would eventually have to rest. Elizabeau simply held on to the pommel of the saddle and kept her mouth shut, miserable with the circumstances but knowing this was being done to save her life.

The rocky road was swamped with water and mud that flew from the charger's hooves as the animal grunted down the path. The land around them was pounding with rain. Though wrapped tightly in an oiled cloth cloak, her feet had been uncovered by the wind and wild ride and were soaked through. Yet she did not complain; at this point, her exhaustion had set in and the fight had momentarily left her. She was simply looking forward to the point when the horse would stop and she would be able to sit on something that wasn't moving.

Through the sheets of driving rain, lights became evident in the distance. Du Bois increased his pace, entering the small berg of Ealing and heading for the fortified manor to the north and west of the town that belonged to Thomas Courtenay, Earl of Osterley and strong supporter of the John's opposition. Even through the rain and wind, he could see it in the distance as he passed through the main street of the town, though he made sure to keep his attention on his surroundings in case dangers lurked. As they approached the manse, he unstrapped his double-barrel Welsh crossbow and perched the weapon on his left knee as he switched the reins to his right hand. Being left-handed, he was deadly accurate within several dozen yards.

Courtenay's manor was separated from the main part of town, secluded behind enormous walls that were manned by sentries. Rhys could see them as he approached. When a man on the wall lifted his hand to Rhys in greeting, Rhys lifted his crossbow and neatly shot the man off the wall.

He dug his spurs into the charger's sides, prompting the exhausted animal on again at a harried pace. Elizabeau grabbed hold of the saddle lest she slide to the ground.

"What's wrong?" she cried.

Rhys tried to hold on to her, his crossbow and the reins at the same time. He didn't answer her as he drove the horse into the nearest bank of trees. Behind him, he could hear shouting over the driving of the rain.

"Sir knight," Elizabeau ducked as a small branch came at her head; it missed her but struck du Bois and did nothing more than glance off. "What's wrong? I thought we were…?"

"It would seem that Courtenay's house is occupied," he replied, somewhat wryly. "We will have to find alternate quarters for the night."

She almost slipped off as the charger made a sharp turn in the bramble. "What do you mean? How do you know this?"

Rhys grunted when another branch caught him heavily in the shoulder. "Be still. If we're being pursued, they'll hear your voice."

Elizabeau gripped the saddle with white knuckles. The horse took another sharp turn in the darkness and she suddenly lost her grip, sliding off the wet saddle before Rhys could grab her. She fell heavily, landing in the muck.

Du Bois turned his weary horse about in a flash. To their left was a heavy cluster of trees and overgrowth and he plowed the horse into it as far as the beast would go. Dismounting swiftly, he secured the horse and raced to where Elizabeau was picking herself up. Grabbing the woman by the arms, he yanked her into the brush.

"Are you injured?" he asked with quiet urgency.

She shook her head, a bit dazed. "I… I do not think so."

"Then stay here and be quiet."

It was not a request. Elizabeau looked at him with wide eyes but she did as he commanded. Rushing back to the area where she fell, du Bois used a fallen branch to sweep their tracks clean. Even though the rain would very shortly wash away any evidence, still, he wanted to make sure they were not detected. Dropping the branch, he raced back to their hiding place and made sure the horse was adequately concealed.

He dropped to his knees, taking Elizabeau down with him. His brilliant blue eyes scanned the forest, ears attuned to any sound. But the rain continued to fall around them and the trees remained relatively silent. After several long, tense minutes, he let out a sigh and turned to the lady beside him.

"Are you sure you did not hurt yourself when you fell?" he whispered.

She looked at him, his features barely visible in the dark night. "I am sure," she breathed. "What happened back there that we had to flee? Were we being chased?"

His gaze lingered on her a moment before returning to the forest beyond. "Not chased."

"Then what?"

He paused a moment before replying. "The sentry."

"What about the sentry?"

"No sentry would have lifted his hand to me in greeting. He would have demanded my name before ever showing me a measure of welcome." When she opened her mouth to question him further, he cut her off. "Be quiet now. Your voice carries a mile and I'll not have you give our position away."

It was an insult, but he was probably correct. In fact, she couldn't get too angry over it so she plopped on her rump and tried to huddle under the oiled cloak, which was now completely covered with mud. It was freezing, wet and miserable but, contrary to her nature, she didn't open her mouth to complain. She wouldn't give du Bois the satisfaction of commanding her to be quiet again. He seemed to like it too much.

The charger swung its big head, knocking her on the side of the face with his foamy lips. Features contorted with disgust, she wiped the saliva from her cheeks and spread it on the leaves beside her. She looked up to see du Bois watching her. His gaze lingered on her a moment before turning back to the dark forest beyond. There was no compassion in his expression at all. He only wanted to make sure she wasn't going to make a sound; he could have cared less about her comfort. Tired, wet, and disgusted, Elizabeau scooted away from the horse but du Bois stopped her.

"Nay, lady," he rumbled softly. "Stay where you are."

She was prepared to snap at him but again decided to keep her mouth shut. Du Bois could bully her all he wanted and she wouldn't say a word. Turning her head away from him, she laid her left cheek on her up-bent knees and closed her eyes, struggling to keep the tears at bay. Her exhaustion had them very close to the surface.

But her eyes flew open and her head came up as the sounds of hooves suddenly intermingled with the rain. Shouting filled the air and soon there were horses and men tramping in the distance, several of them with torches. They were heading for the cluster of trees that shielded them.

Eyes wide with fear, Elizabeau slid back in du Bois' direction until she brushed up against him. The closer the men came, the more terrified she grew.

"They're coming closer," she hissed. "We must run."

He shook his head steadily. "They would only chase us down."

"But they will find us," she pressed. "We must flee!"

He turned to look at her, then. "My horse is bordering on exhaustion, my lady," he replied quietly. "He would not get much farther before collapsing and that would not be a good thing on open ground. At least here, we have cover."

"But they will find us. There is nowhere to go should we become boxed in."

Rhys' brilliant blue gaze remained on her a moment before his eyes suddenly traveled upwards into the trees surrounding them. An idea occurred to him as he reached out to finger one of the yearlings. "Can you climb a tree?"

She could see where he was leading and her gaze snapped to the canopy above. "These trees will never hold you," she hissed.

"I am not concerned with me. I am only concerned with you. Can you climb a tree?"

He was deadly serious. They stared at each other a moment and she felt that odd buzzing sensation again in her head as their eyes met. Though distracted by it, she nodded. "Aye."

"Good. Then get ready to climb. I'll push you up as far as I can, but the rest is up to you. And you will stay there and not make a sound no matter what you see or hear. Is that clear?"

She nodded, wide-eyed, before returning her gaze to the approaching group. It seemed as if there were dozens of men, carrying both torches and weapons. They were spread out in a search pattern, searching for tracks on the ground. Just as they entered the edge of the trees, a rumble sounded off to the east. Elizabeau and Rhys turned their attention to the new sound, seeing a large party of men on horseback approach. They, too, had torches and swords drawn. Beside her, Rhys suddenly stood up and moved to his charger.

He removed his double-sheath and two broadswords from where they were lashed to the saddle. The swords were almost as long as Elizabeau was tall, enormous weapons that Rhys slung over his back and secured in a harness that wrapped around both shoulders and across his narrow waist. All he had to do was reach over either shoulder to unsheathe a weapon, or even both at the same time, making him twice as deadly an adversary than the normal knight. He then took his shield in one hand and the re-loaded cross bow in the other. He was preparing for battle. Elizabeau watched him anxiously.

"Where do you go?" she demanded.

His brilliant blue eyes watched the approaching party in the distance. "De Lohr approaches," he replied. "I must be ready to defend you if the fighting grows close."

She turned to see the large contingent of men closing in on the group that was near the edge of the trees. In fact, the group near the edge of the trees was scattering as de Lohr's forces closed in. Soon, the clash of metal filled the air as the battle commenced.

Rhys stood beside Elizabeau as they watched de Lohr and his knights engage the others. Elizabeau recognized de Lohr himself in the middle of it; he was a very large man and there was no mistaking his size or strength. The sound of men struggling for their lives was amplified in the rain, which was now pounding with epic proportions. The wind howled through the trees, whipping branches about and creating spray. Elizabeau watched the battle, pulling her cloak more tightly about her slender body. It was an awesome sight.

Suddenly, a pair of knights burst into the trees near them, locked in mortal combat. Rhys and Elizabeau watched as the men fought ravenously, hacking away with skill and power. One knight's charger slipped in the mud and the beast fell to its knees, allowing the opposing knight the upper hand. Off balance, the knight on the compromised horse was at a distinct disadvantage.

In a flash, Rhys lifted his crossbow and fired at the dominant knight, striking him squarely in the ribs when he lifted his right arm to deliver what could have been a mortal blow. The knight grunted, dropped his sword, and fell to the ground shortly thereafter.

Rhys emerged from their shielding haven, approaching the knight whose charger was righting itself. The horse was muddy, but unharmed. The knight saw Rhys approach and tossed up his visor.

"Du Bois!" he threw a leg over the saddle and plunged to the ground. "Thanks for the help, man. We were wondering where you had gone."

Rhys propped the crossbow against his hip, holding on to the hilt. "Only as far as the trees once I figured out that Courtenay's fortress was compromised. But my charger is about to collapse." He nodded his head in the direction of the bulk of the fighting. "How did you know they would be here?"

"Chris interrogated one of the fools who attacked us back at Hyde House," the knight replied; he was handsome and blue eyed. "He managed to wrest some interesting information from him, mostly that John was aware you were taking the lady to Courtenay's Ealing manor. His men were waiting for you. We tried to catch up with you and could only hope we made it in time."

Rhys scratched his damp forehead underneath the mail hauberk. "How would he know?"

The knight shrugged his shoulders. "Spies abound everywhere, Rhys. You've been at court long enough to know that."

Rhys shook his head. "I cannot believe there would be a spy in our midst, David. The earl's men have been with him for years. There's no way it would be one of them."

David de Lohr lifted his broad shoulders. "Probably not, but it's not the first time we have run into betrayal. The informant could be one of the soldiers or servants. Or it could be another knight; we simply do not know. We must watch what we say in front of those we do not know intimately."

The fighting was growing weaker; some were running off as de Lohr's men chased them. Rhys and David watched as the group began to scatter, fleeing into the pounding storm. David finally turned back to Rhys.

"Where is the lady?" he asked.

Rhys turned towards the shielding foliage just as Elizabeau emerged; she had been listening to their conversation. Soaked to the skin and very cold, her pert little nose was bright red beneath the folds of the cloak.

"Where do I go now?" she asked snappishly. "Courtenay's manor is obviously compromised. Or do you plan to run with me night and day until we all drop from exhaustion?"

Rhys didn't react other than to indicate David. "My lady, this is Sir David de Lohr, brother of the earl."

Elizabeau studied the man as he dipped his head at her in greeting; he wasn't nearly as big as the earl, but she could tell just by looking at him that he had the trained, muscular body of a warrior. He was very handsome with pale blue eyes and a square jaw.

"My lady," David acknowledged. Then he looked back at Rhys. "There's an inn at Hanwell. Chris says to take her there and stay there until he comes."

Rhys nodded sharply and turned for the lady, taking her by the arm and leading her silently back towards their hovel of bushes. But Elizabeau wouldn't be led away so easily. She fixed on David.

"So is this your cunning plan?" she asked, belligerence in her tone.

"One step to the next, hoping to avoid trouble with no real strategy in mind? I'll not be dragged all over England like common baggage. Where on earth are you taking me?"

David removed his helm, pulling his mail hood back to reveal cropped blond hair. He scratched his scalp furiously. It was evident he was taking his time in answering her.

"We are doing what we must to save your life," he fixed on her, his blue eyes hard. "If you have a better plan, then by all means, take your own life in your hands and try to stay one step ahead of your uncle. He's already killed your brother and now he wants you. If the lords of Brittany were unable to protect Arthur, then what makes you think you alone will be able to save yourself?" He walked towards her, stalking, anger in his manner evident. "All you need do is command us to leave you, Lady Elizabeau. 'Tis you who hold the power; not us. We are your servants. Command us away and we shall obey."

By this time, he was standing in front of her, drilling holes into her with his piercing gaze. Elizabeau tried not to appear too intimidated.

"'Tis not that I do not appreciate your devotion, Sir David," she was considerably softer. "But it would seem to me that there should be a definitive plan in place, safe houses where you will take me until I can be united with my betrothed. Surely the emperor is sending men at this very moment to aid us in our endeavor. This marriage means as much to him as to us."

David had lost none of his harsh stance. "My brother is a brilliant tactician. He would not be the King's Champion where this not so. You must trust him, my lady. He will do what he feels best for you. It would make it much easier for all of us, especially du Bois, were you to simply comply with what we ask without question or resistance."

Elizabeau dared to look up at Rhys; he stood beside her, more than a foot and a half taller, gazing steadily at her with his brilliant blue eyes. He hadn't said a word, nor had he changed expression. She was suddenly coming to feel the least bit guilty for her difficult behavior. A powerful chill raced through her and she pulled the cloak about her as tightly as it would go, averting her gaze at the same time.

"It is not my intention to be difficult," she said quietly. "This... this has all been a bit overwhelming for me. I've never had men try to kill me before. I never knew I was going to be a queen before."

David's manner softened somewhat. He glanced at Rhys, who was looking at the lady's lowered head. David cleared his throat quietly.

"We want you to be queen, else we would not be risking our lives so," he said. "We are trying to help you achieve this, for all of England. Do you not understand this?"

"I do."

"Then it would help our cause considerably if you would simply cooperate."

She looked at him, then. After a moment, she sighed heavily and lowered her eyes again. "As you say."

David simply nodded; he didn't believe her for a moment but would not contradict her. Like his brother, he knew women somewhat, having a spirited wife of his own and her two equally spirited sisters that lived with them. He knew what it meant to contradict a woman when one was attempting to gain her compliance. He would have a battle on his hands.

He turned back to Rhys. "Get her to Hanwell. The inn is on the outskirts, called the Blond Gazelle. We'll meet you there."

With that, he pulled his mail hood back on and turned for his charger, now munching on wet grass. Rhys took the lady by the elbow again and led her back to their leafy haven.

His charger had cooled somewhat and was nibbling on the bushes he was tethered to. Rhys secured his shield and his crossbow and led the horse out of the foliage. He mounted Elizabeau without a word and leapt on behind her.

"Sir knight?" Elizabeau's voice was soft.

"My lady?"

She turned slightly, gazing up into his strong face. "I do apologize if I have made this a miserable trek for you. It was not my intention."

Rhys had been largely silent since the beginning of the foray. It was what it was, and she was the way she was. He accepted it.

"It is of no matter, my lady," he said honestly.

"But it is," she insisted. "I never meant to imply that I was ungrateful for your loyalty. It's just that I have lived my entire life in relative peace, with a relatively normal routine, and suddenly two days ago I am told I am heir to the throne of England and my uncle, whom I have only met twice in my life, is out to murder me. It is all so difficult to believe."

Rhys' professional persona was wavering slightly. He wasn't used to emotion or apologies, in any form, especially from a woman. In fact, he'd made it a practice in life to stay clear of women in general. They could topple a man faster than the mightiest enemy. He'd seen it before.

Now the firebrand was banking her heat and he had no idea how to deal with it. But he knew, instinctively, that he did not trust her. There had to be an ulterior motive to her kindness.

"Understood, my lady," he said.

"I would wager that if I could only speak with my uncle, I am sure we could settle this issue. Perhaps this is all some horrible misunderstanding."

"Impossible, my lady. It is my duty to keep you safe and I shall do so with my last breath."

It wasn't much of an answer. In fact, it was the generic knightly rhetoric. With a resigned wriggle of well-arched brows, Elizabeau returned her attention to the landscape before them. Even as he spurred the charger forward, her mind lingered on a final thought; what if these knights attempting to supplant John and place her on the throne were wrong? What if they were all wrong?

She wondered.

CHAPTER THREE

HANWELL WAS A town inundated by the driving rain. The streets were flooded and so were some of the houses. As Rhys and Elizabeau entered the outskirts of the berg, some of the residents were bailing water out of their homes. Doors were open and buckets were flying. Rhys steered his charger clear of more flying water as they made their way down Argyle Street toward the northwestern edge of town.

The Blond Gazelle wasn't hard to find. It was a brightly lit place with several drunken patrons lingering by the open door, soaked to the skin but not caring. They were having a marvelous time. Rhys pulled the charger to a halt when he came to within several yards of the place, watching the activity for a moment before proceeding. He wanted to make sure there were no obvious signs of John's assassins.

Quietly, he directed his charger behind the inn and lowered Elizabeau into a huge puddle of horse piss and rain. She sloshed her way out of it miserably as Rhys dismounted behind her and collected his weapons and saddlebags. A sleepy lad emerged from the small stable, rubbing his eyes and taking hold of the charger. Rhys gave the boy a few coins to care for the charger. Collecting the lady by the elbow, he took her around front and into the warm, loud establishment.

It was crowded inside. Rhys scanned the room for foe and ally alike before directing the lady towards the smoking fire. Elizabeau was so cold that her lips were blue and it took Rhys a few moments to realize that she was nearly frozen. Before this moment, he'd been so consumed with scouting threats that he hadn't noticed. He suddenly felt somewhat guilty that he had not paid closer attention to his charge as he watched the blue lips quiver and the teeth chatter.

There was a man, probably a merchant, in a fur-lined cloak seated near the fire and enjoying a large meal. With the lady in hand, Rhys went to the man and ripped the cloak from his shoulders, pulling him to the floor in the process. The man coughed and bellowed, looking up to see a knight of enormous proportions hovering over him. Before the man could utter a word of protest, Rhys grabbed him by the neck and tossed him halfway across the room.

"The lady requires your seat," he said as the man skidded across the floor.

Elizabeau watched with surprise as the wealthy merchant tumbled into a heap. But she did not have time to comment as Rhys literally picked her up and set her down in the chair the merchant had occupied. She was suddenly very close to the fire and any thoughts of the merchant died in her throat as the searing warmth enveloped her.

"You're freezing," Rhys said as he pulled the wet oilcloth off of her and replaced it with the merchant's dry, fur-lined cloak. "Sit here and warm yourself. I shall return."

He was gone, off across the crowded room and heading for the barkeep. Chilled, hungry, Elizabeau turned back to the fire and held her hands over it, feeling the heat like a thousand pin-pricks against her flesh. It was delightful. She closed her eyes, feeling the warmth on her face, thawing her. She'd not felt such comfort in days. Not since men from Hubert de Burgh's ranks came to her mother's home in South London and forcibly escorted her from its walls.

She opened her eyes, her mood growing somber as she thought of the turn her life had taken over the past two days. Until then, she had been blessed with a relatively privileged existence. Being the niece of the king, though illegitimate, had brought her that honor. In truth, she had seen her father only five times in her life and her Uncle John only twice. The royal family, for the most part, had left her alone as the bastard of Geoffrey. But that life of obscurity was apparently no longer.

Gloomy thoughts rolled through her head as she stared into the fire with deep green orbs. There was sensuality to her eyes and unearthly beauty to her face, something no Plantagenet possessed. She was an exquisite example of female beauty from her mother's side, the bloodlines of the fair-skinned Norsemen running strong in her veins. She didn't know if she was equipped for this life that was about to be thrust upon her. She'd never prepared for it. She wasn't sure her sense of duty was that strong.

There was food at her elbow, a cooling knuckle of beef left by the merchant. She was hungry and took a bite. A second bite quickly followed and then a third. She hadn't realized how ravenous she was until the moment the meat touched her lips. When Rhys returned with a tray loaded with food, she was already well into the knuckle.

He tried to remove the food to replace it with the hot meal but she refused, holding fast to the beef she was enjoying. He simply shrugged his shoulders and sat the hot tray next to the cooling one.

"This meat is fresh, my lady," he pointed out. "Perhaps you would enjoy this more."

She shook her head, wiping at the juice on her chin. "This is fine."

Rhys didn't say anything; he just watched her stuff her mouth, thinking yet again he had been very negligent of her state as they had traveled. He set a cup of ale beside her right hand and then took a long, healthy drink from the second cup he had procured for himself. Smacking his lips, he took a moment to remove his helm and set it at his feet. The crossbow went next to it. Then he peeled his mail hauberk off his damp head and went to work on his own knuckle of beef.

Elizabeau looked up from her meal to see a man she didn't recognize sitting across from her. She'd not yet seen du Bois without his helm or mail hood and, for a moment, she stopped chewing as she stared at him; he had black hair, short and stiff with moisture. But that wasn't all; she could see his entire face, now unobstructed by the helm, and it was a striking vision. He had black eyebrows, arched over his brilliant blue eyes, a square jaw with a huge dimple in his chin. Dark stubble covered his cheeks and she watched the movements of his features as he chewed heartily on the beef. Her eyes raked over him, seeing the man in a different light, wondering why her heart pounded so strangely at the sight of him. Confused over her reaction, she went back to her meat and hoped it would pass.

Rhys was done with his beef before she was, tossing the bone to the floor and watching the dogs fight over it. He glanced over at Elizabeau to see how she was faring and noticed she was only picking at her bread. She didn't seem as hungry as she had earlier and his concern returned.

"Is something amiss, my lady?" he asked. "Is the bread not to your liking?"

She looked at him as if startled by his question. Quickly, she shook her head and lowered her gaze.

"It is fine," she said.

Rhys looked at her as if he did not believe her. She seemed depressed and remote, not at all like the woman he had taken from Hyde House earlier in the evening. That woman had been full of confidence, spit and fire. He swallowed the bite in his mouth, trying to ascertain her disposition.

"Are you feeling poorly?" he probed politely. "It is well after midnight. We might be able to spare a few hours for you to sleep."

Her head snapped up, the deep green eyes fixing on him. He could see the wheels of thought turning. "You are a duke's son," she said after a moment. "Why do you serve de Lohr as a common knight?"

He lifted a dark eyebrow at her. "I am not sure what you mean, my lady."

"I mean that you are born to privilege. If your father is the Duke of Navarre, then he must be related to Philippe Auguste."

Rhys' gaze lingered on her. "He is the king's cousin. His mother and the king's father were cousins."

"Then Phillip is your cousin."

"Aye."

She stared at him. Then she put the bread down. "Yet you serve an English earl? This makes no sense."

"Why not?"

Her eyebrows flew up. "Why not? Well… well, just look at you. You're a big knight with big weapons. You should be in France serving your father or ruling over your own lands."

He sat back in his chair; for some reason, he was enjoying her confusion. A smile played on his smooth lips.

"Yet I am not. Who I serve, and why I serve, should be of no concern to you, my lady. You have greater problems of your own to think about."

Elizabeau looked at him, realizing he was keeping a definitive wall up. He did not want her to know anything about him; that much was clear. He had been nothing but professional and calculating since she had met him. He was her escort and nothing more. Not that it mattered to her, but the man could at least show some measure of friendliness and answer her question. She was puzzled why the son of a duke should serve a mere English earl.

She returned her gaze to her bread, hunting for a knife and possibly some butter. If he did not want to speak of himself, so be it.

Rhys watched her as she busied herself with more food. He wasn't hungry any longer, more interested in studying the lady at the moment. He'd not allowed himself to give her any regard other than professional treatment up until this moment; there hadn't been the time or the focus. He had been trying to keep her alive. But now, at least for the time being, the situation was calm. The ale was relaxing his body as well as his tongue.

"I am not in succession for the duke's title," he said quietly, watching her look up from buttering her bread. "My mother was a lady in waiting for the duchess."

She stopped buttering. "You're a bastard?"

"Like you."

Elizabeau began to understand his position somewhat. "Is that why you do not carry the duke's name?"

He nodded. "De Foix is for the family of Navarre. I carry my grandmother's surname on my father's side."

"Why do you not carry your mother's name?"

He toyed with the cup in his hand, the brilliant blue eyes with their guard down for the first time since they'd met. He and the lady had common ground, something they both understood clearly being illegitimate offspring. He felt no humiliation in telling her.

"Because my father would not hear of it," he said quietly. "Yet he did not want me to bear his name, either. So I am named after his mother's side of the family."

Elizabeau watched him play with the cup, finally pouring himself more ale. "But I bear my mother's name," she said.

"That was not possible in my case," he replied. "Although my mother is of minor Welsh nobility, my father would not permit me to carry a Welsh name. It simply was not an option."

Her lovely arched eyebrows lifted. "I should have seen it in you. You carry the darkness of the Welsh."

He smiled wryly, the first such gesture she had ever seen from him. He had massive dimples carving through each cheek. "And you carry the fairness of the Norsemen."

She blinked. "How would you know that?"

"I have served de Lohr for many years. There is not much I do not know about you or the rest of the Plantagenets."

Elizabeau met his brilliant blue eyes a moment longer before returning to her buttered bread. She felt strangely akin to him, knowing they had a common lineage. Somehow, in their brief conversation, she did not feel quite so overwhelmed or unbalanced by her situation. She was with a knight who understood her background because his was the same. It was difficult to explain why she felt more relaxed now, but she did.

Rhys watched her lowered head, the way the firelight played off her golden red hair. She seemed curious and intelligent. He wondered what kind of queen she would make. Given their choice of monarchs at the moment, anything would be better than what they had. But he would never voice his opinion. He was a knight and knights did as they were told.

He drained his cup for the third time and decided that he'd had enough ale for the night. His face felt warm, a sure indication that he had imbibed enough. Any more would find him growing drunk. As he turned to look for the serving wench to order something more that would not dull his senses, the door to the inn suddenly slammed back on its hinges and the merchant he had thrown from the table bolted inside. He was followed by four soldiers, the thunder from the storm punctuating their arrival.

It was as if a door from Hell had opened wide and the noise and clashing associated with such a place poured through. The merchant's gaze fell on Rhys and he jabbed a finger at him, pointing out the target to his men. The implication was obvious.

The room began to scatter with panic. Rhys stood up and moved away from the table; he did not want any fighting in the proximity of the lady. The four soldiers advanced on him, spreading out in a pattern of attack. Rhys noted the movement, understanding in that tactical move that they were experienced. They would not be caught in a bunch, instead, choosing to stalk their victim and maximize their advantage.

But Rhys was ready for them. He was calm, collected, as he unsheathed both of the swords still strapped to his back. He swung them with deadly precision, in concert, displaying not only his skill but his control. The metal sang through the warm, stale air with a chilling hum. As his senses reached out, tracking the movements of the men closest to him, Elizabeau was suddenly in his line of sight.

"My lord," she was addressing the insulted merchant loudly. "Please call off your men. There is no need for fighting."

Some of Rhys' calm faltered; she was too close should any fighting start and he did not want her in the line of fire.

"My lady," he hissed at her. "You will remove yourself at once."

She held out a quelling hand to him, banking on the fact that the men threatening him would not lash out at a defenseless lady. She continued to move towards the merchant, passing in front of Rhys as she did so. A soft, white hand came to rest on his right wrist, gentle pressure requesting that he lower his weapons. Though her flesh was cold, it felt like a branding iron against his skin; Rhys almost forgot all else but her tender hand against him. It was difficult to stay focused.

"Please, my lord," she was still in front of Rhys, still with a hand on his wrist. But her focus was on the merchant. "My… husband had but one thought, and that was to place me next to a warm fire. You see, we've been traveling all night and I am very wet, as you can see. Unfortunately, you happened to be in the way. He did not mean to insult to you; he only meant to help me. Will you please call your men off now?"

She sounded very calm, very rational, and very wise. Rhys looked at her; she did not seem like the same lady he had met only a few hours ago, the spitfire who complained at every turn. She was serene and relaxed as she attempted to diffuse the situation. But the merchant was still rightly upset.

"He should not have thrown me from my meal," he said petulantly. "There were other tables."

"But yours was the closest." Elizabeau's grip tightened on Rhys' wrist and she gently, firmly, forced him to lower his weapons. "You are correct, my lord; he should not have thrown you from your table. It was a mistake, but he was only acting in my best interest. He was not attempting to deliberately insult you. Please call off your men and I shall happily pay for your meal and for your men's meal. Will you not accept my offer?"

The merchant looked uncertain, then dubious. He looked to his men, who were now looking at him for further instructions. They could fight or not; it was all the same to them. They were paid to do what they were told. But the fact remained that the merchant had been insulted. He jabbed a fat finger at Rhys.

"Your husband should show more manners," he said to Elizabeau.

Elizabeau nodded patiently. "Indeed he should." She turned to Rhys, smiling sweetly, which caught him completely off-guard. "Lower your weapons, darling, and apologize to this man. Yours was an impetuous, rude act."

He stared at her for a moment. But in a flash, both swords were sheathed. Elizabeau continued to smile at him, wrapping her small, cold hands around his right arm.

"Apologize, Rhys," she repeated softly.

He almost didn't know what to say. He was so off-balance by her sweet voice and lovely smile that the words simply wouldn't come. But when she nodded her head at him encouragingly, he cleared his throat softly and focused on the merchant.

"My apologies, my lord," he said in a low, deep voice. "My only thoughts at the moment were of my... my wife. She was cold and I would do whatever necessary to warm her."

The merchant gave in without another word. He waved a hand at his men, who backed away and sheathed their weapons without protest.

"If she's that cold, then go put her in a warm tub and a warm bed," he was already walking past them, heading for his former table. "In fact, make love to her all night. That will warm her blood quick enough."

He laughed at his bawdy suggestion, resuming his seat at the table as the room gradually returned to normal. Those who fled were slowly returning to their seats, righting chairs and tables as they went. Rhys and Elizabeau stood in the middle of the room, watching the activity slowly resume. When Rhys finally looked at Elizabeau, she was staring up at him intently. He gave her a wry twist of the lips.

"Well, my lady, it seems that you managed to negotiate my way out of a battle," he said quietly. "But next time, you will not jeopardize yourself like that. You could have been gravely injured, or worse."

"And so I was not," she shot back softly. "If I can negotiate you out of a battle, I will gladly do so. We've come this far. I would hate to see something happen to you after you have fought so hard to preserve my life."

He cocked an eyebrow, watching two of the soldiers who had been intent on attacking him quit the inn. The other two remained, just inside the door. His gaze returned to her. "Husband, am I?" he muttered. "What possessed you to make a foolish claim like that?"

Her brow furrowed. "Because we are traveling alone together, you and I. What else would you have preferred I said? That you were my lover? My brother? Husband came to mind the quickest, so husband is what I said. It makes the most sense."

He was forced to agree. He turned back towards their table, now crowded with the merchant, taking her hand in his own in the process. He hissed when his big palm closed over her fingers.

"Christ," he breathed. "Your fingers are like ice. Come over here by the fire before you freeze to death."

Elizabeau allowed him to lead her back over to their table by the fire, where the merchant was now eating heartily of their dinner. Rhys propped her right up against the flames, taking the chair opposite the merchant and eyeing the man as he noisily slurped his food. The merchant glanced up, seeing the two of them. He gestured at Elizabeau.

"The fire will do her no good," he said, mouth full. "You must get her into dry clothes. She's soaking."

Rhys glanced over his shoulder at her, noting that the merchant was correct. He was coming to think he was the most unobservant man on the face of the planet; other than her lovely face and her sweet voice, he'd noticed little more about her. He felt like an idiot.

"I fear that most of her clothing is wet," he said, pouring himself another cup of ale in spite of his earlier vow not to do so. "The fire is the best I can do for her right now."

The merchant was slopping and burping as he ate. "I have something for her to wear," he said. "I'll send one of my men outside to my wagon. It will cost you, though."

Rhys looked at Elizabeau again; she was looking at the merchant. "How much?" she asked.

The man noisily drank his ale. "Depends," he wiped his mouth with his sleeve. "I am returning from a trip to Paris. I have all manner of premade surcoats and shifts to sell in Gloucester and the Marches. My goods are the latest rage of fashion, you know. I have some your size if you wish to see them."

"I do," Elizabeau agreed readily. "What is your name, my lord? I fear we should become acquainted on more pleasant circumstances."

"Robinson Marchant," the man replied without missing a beat, gnawing on his beef.

Elizabeau waited for Rhys to introduce them, but he made no move to do so and she tapped him on the back so he got the hint. Rhys was very careful, and very reluctant, with any information he might give. But he had to say something.

"Rhys de Foix," he said softly, glancing over his shoulder at the lady behind him. "And my lady wife, Elizabeau."

Robinson's gaze moved between them. "She's a lovely woman," he said to Rhys. "Such beauty is very rare. And she seems intelligent as well. Is her disposition as lovely?"

Rhys lifted an eyebrow. When he didn't answer right away, Elizabeau pinched him on the exposed hand that held the ale cup. It smarted and Rhys winced.

"Of course," he said dryly. "Can you not tell? She is an angel."

Robinson snorted. Then he laughed out loud. "I like her," he announced, slurping his ale again. "She has spirit."

"Is that what it's called?"

Robinson was grinning, watching Elizabeau's lovely profile in the firelight. "And she is very protective of you, I can tell. A truly loyal woman is hard to find."

Elizabeau looked strangely at Robinson before quickly looking away. She had no idea what to say to that statement, wondering if she had indeed come across as the fiercely loyal wife. All she had meant to do was diffuse the approaching battle. Anything else that was conveyed was incidental.

"Where are you two traveling to?" Robinson asked as he crunched into a turnip.

Unaware of Elizabeau's reaction to the merchant's faithful wife statement, Rhys replied to the question. "To the Marches."

Robinson wiped at his chin. "As I said, I am traveling that direction. I should like it if you two would travel with me. I am bored with only my stupid men to keep me company. They are horrific conversation. But with the two of you, we could keep each other entertained on a tedious journey."

Before Rhys could reply, Robinson turned to his two remaining men standing by the inn door and bellowed at them to bring in two of the trunks for the lady's review. Rhys watched the men disappear into the howling night, suddenly realizing he was sitting on the fur cloak he had ripped from Robinson's shoulders. He stood up, picked up the cloak, and held it out to the man.

"I believe this is yours," he said.

Robinson waved him off, still eating. "Your wife needs it more. In fact, if I were you, I'd take my advice. Order her a hot bath and get her into a warm bed. And then we shall leave at daybreak for the Marches."

Rhys looked at Elizabeau, standing damp by the fire and trying desperately to warm her frozen hands. He wasn't sure they had time for a hot bath and a warm bed; he wasn't sure when de Lohr would be upon them. But it was evident that she needed something to bring her some comfort. He'd been insensitive to her long enough.

He snapped to the nearest serving wench and the girl went running for the barkeep, who hurried over to Rhys across the crowded room. The man didn't have a room to spare, but he offered up his daughter's simple chamber in the rear yard attached to the stable. Rhys didn't argue with him for a better room; he simply paid the man and watched the flurry of activity as he set about bellowing for the big copper tub. When the wheels were in motion, one of the serving women came to escort Elizabeau to her waiting room.

"Go with your wife," Robinson told Rhys. "When my men bring the garments in, I'll shall come and find you. We'll find her something warm and dry to wear."

Rhys wasn't about to let Elizabeau out of his sight, but accompanying her to her bath was an entirely different situation. Still, they'd backed themselves into a mistruth of stories and he had no choice but to go with her. A husband would have, after all. He only hoped de Lohr would understand.

Without a word, he rose and followed Elizabeau and the serving wench back through the kitchen and out into the yard. The rain and wind were howling as they crossed the muddy yard and entered a small room adjoining the stable. It wasn't particularly comfortable or clean, but it was warm and dry. Rhys stood aside, pulling Elizabeau with him, as a burly old man brought in the massive copper tub.

It wasn't so much a tub as it was a giant cooking pot used for baths and sometimes to feed the livestock. The young serving girl even mentioned they used it to boil down bones. The wench fled back into the stormy night and the burly old man reappeared with buckets of steaming water. The girl returned, too, carrying a linen sheet, some manner of soap and a scrub brush. She had also been thoughtful enough to bring Rhys more wine, which he took from her and moved to the corner of the room near the door. He poured himself a cup as he sat down, watching the burly old man with the long hair full the copper pot to the rim.

The old man finally gathered his buckets and shut the door to the room quietly behind him. The serving wench moved to help Elizabeau from her wet clothes, confused by her mistress's extreme reluctance. Elizabeau wasn't about to budge until Rhys turned his back, which he did by discreetly adjusting his chair and facing the window.

Rhys drank his wine as Elizabeau quickly stripped her wet clothing from her body and plunged into the pot. It was deliciously hot and she sighed with contentment as her flesh began to warm. But just as relaxation set in, the wench picked up the soap and the brush and went to work. Within minutes, Elizabeau was positive the woman meant to strip the skin from her bones and she found herself gripping the side of the pot for support. From the top of her golden red hair to the bottom of her small feet, the wench did an admirable job of scrubbing her silly.

When the woman's job was done and Elizabeau was struggling against the heat of the pot and the near-beating she had just received, the wench looked about for something to dress the lady in but shortly realized that the couple had no baggage. There was nothing to clothe the woman in but the damp dress recently stripped off of her. Slightly confused but resourceful, the wench asked for the lady's patience and fled the room.

The room was abruptly quiet with the wench gone and the activity quelled. Elizabeau sat in the warm pot, watching the back of Rhys' dark head and listening to the storm outside. Realizing they were very much alone, and she was naked in a tub to boot, made her vastly uneasy. Not that she didn't trust the man, but she was rather vulnerable.

"Feeling better, my lady?" Rhys' baritone voice broke the silence.

Elizabeau started at the sound of it. "Aye," she replied quickly, nervously. "But I will feel better still when I have my clothes back on."

Still facing the window, Rhys grinned and held up a hand. "I swear that I shall not turn from this window until you are appropriately dressed. But it would have looked rather odd had I not accompanied you to your bath, as your husband, though I do apologize for the uncomfortable situation."

The corners of her mouth twitched. "Why should you apologize? Is this not your duty? To hound my every move until I can be safely delivered to my betrothed?"

Rhys' grin faded as he thought of the perils that surely lay ahead; tonight had only been a foretaste. "Indeed," he replied quietly, draining his cup. He'd had far too much wine but picked up the pitcher again. "Would you like some wine, my lady?"

"I am not sure how you can hand it to me without turning away from the window."

"True enough."

Elizabeau watched him as he set the pitcher down, and the cup, and settled back in his chair, gazing at the storm outside. She was seeing him through slightly different eyes, more so as the hours passed, coming to know a man with whom she had a great deal in common. He was respectful, intelligent, and wildly handsome. Her gaze moved over his impossibly wide shoulders and to the enormous arms still covered with mail and armor. Her thoughts lingered heavily on the man with the royal sire and Welsh mother.

"Rhys?" she leaned forward in the pot, her chin resting on the edge.

"My lady?"

"Are you married?"

"Why do you ask?"

She shrugged, her fingers toying with the edge of the pot. "No particular reason other than… other than I was just wondering what it was like, that's all."

"How do you mean?"

She shrugged again, moving away from the edge of the pot and flicking away at the soapy bubbles that lingered on the surface of the water. "I mean just that. What is it like? How do you behave with someone you are married to? Are you and your wife friendly to each other or do you simply tolerate one another? If you make a decision, does she support you? Or do you simply make a decision with no care to what she might think?"

Rhys turned his head slightly; he was no longer looking out of the window but staring at the door; Elizabeau could see his perfect profile. "You are assuming that I am married, my lady," he said quietly.

"I was not assuming anything; I guess my question was simply a general query. I am thinking aloud, I suppose."

He was silent a moment, still gazing at the darkened door. "It is different for everyone, I would think," he said quietly. "I was married, once. My wife and I had known each other for a short time and were already acquainted upon our marriage. I was not home enough to truly be a part of any decision making process; she ran the household as she saw fit."

Elizabeau's big eyes were upon him. "I do not understand. You were married once?"

He nodded his head faintly. "She died a few years ago giving birth to my son."

Elizabeau closed her eyes briefly, with sorrow. "I am sorry, Rhys. I did not mean to pry. Please accept my sympathies."

He shook his head as if snapping himself out of that particular train of thought. Rising swiftly, he moved to the hearth where the linen sheet lay warming before the fire. He held it up to her.

"Get out," he commanded softly. "You'll catch chill if you're in there any longer."

Elizabeau gazed up at him, realizing their line of conversation had taken him back to the cold, walled-up knight she had known for the bulk of their association. She further realized she was very sorry; he had proven something of a good conversationalist and she was disappointed that her line of questioning had shut him off again.

"Rhys," she said softly, sincerely. "I am very sorry if I upset you with my question about your wife. I did not mean to stir up sorrowful memories."

"You did not, my lady," he said, though his tone was cold. He shook the sheet slightly. "Come along, now. Get out of the tub and dry yourself."

It was apparent he had no intention of either delving into anything more about his wife or accepting her apology. With a heavy sigh, Elizabeau reached out and pulled the sheet from his hand.

"Turn around," she instructed him. "You promised not to look and I see that you have already partially broken that promise."

She had meant it in jest, one last hope that he would loosen to her humor. But he turned away without a word and went back to the window. Elizabeau watched his stiff back a moment before climbing from the tub and wrapping herself tightly in the sheet. There was a small stool next to the hearth; she pulled it away from the wall and sat directly in front of the fire to warm up and dry out.

She wasn't surprised when he quit the room without a word and disappeared into the stormy night.

☙

ELIZABEAU WASN'T SURE how long she'd been asleep on the small, lumpy bed. The fire in the hearth had died somewhat and the room was chilly when she heard the door open again. Startled, she rolled over to see Rhys locking the door behind him. She also noticed that he had an armful of material.

Rubbing her eyes, she sat up with the linen sheet still wrapped tightly around her body. It was dark in the room and difficult to see just what, exactly, he had.

"What have you got there?" she demanded sleepily. "Where did you go?"

He moved to the bed with some kind of garment in his hands. He held it up to her, nearly striking her in the face with it.

"I went to see our fat friend," he said. "I hope you don't mind that I selected your garments. You were in no condition to select them yourself, being that you only had a sheet to wear, so I selected them for you. I hope you are pleased."

"Good lord," she muttered, eyeing him in the weak light. But she dutifully fingered the garment he was offering to her, inspecting it as she tried to blink the sleep from her eyes. Upon closer inspection, it was a lovely wine-colored damask with exquisite craftsmanship.

She took the garment from him and padded over to the hearth where the light was better. It was a finely made surcoat of a ruby-rich fabric, lined in soft pink wool, with a square neckline and long, draping sleeves. The sleeves from the elbow down were made from the same colored brocade, giving the garment a delightfully detailed look. It was, in fact, very beautiful. Curiosity made her wander over to the chair where he had draped the other garments and she inspected her way through surcoats of cloud-soft yellow lamb's wool, light blue *Perse* fabric that was similar to very soft linen, and pale green broadcloth. Upon further notice, she came across a soft leather girdle, two delicate shifts, a pair of soft woolen hose, a pair of doeskin gloves, a bleached wool cloak and a pair of bright red silk pantalets.

The pantalets were at the bottom of the pile and she held them up to Rhys, almost accusingly.

"Why on earth did you buy these?" she demanded, peering at him from around the garment. "They're... they're...."

"The latest from Paris," Rhys told her helpfully. "The merchant says that he cannot keep them in stock. All finely dressed women demand them."

She cocked an eyebrow at him before returning her dubious eyes to the pantalets. She fingered them; they were very soft. She imagined they would feel nice against her skin. With a shrug, she laid them back with the other garments and turned to him.

"I cannot pay you for these at the moment," she said with some embarrassment. "I am afraid that my coinage is in London. We left so quickly that..."

He waved her off. "De Burgh supplied me with more than enough to cover expenses. You needn't worry."

He seemed to be in a better humor than he had when he had left the room earlier. It was a curious mood, as if he had blown off his depression in the past hour and then returned to her without a grudge. Not wanting to upset him again, she took a deep breath and forced a smile.

"Then I would thank you for being so thoughtful," she said. "You have been a chivalrous and kind escort and I thank you very much for your foresight in all matters. And I am very sorry that I called you simple back at Hyde House; it is clear that you are not a simple man at all."

He almost looked embarrassed; he chewed his lip briefly, displaying the deep dimples that carved through his cheeks like canyons. The brilliant blue eyes never left her. After a moment, he turned back to the chair where the pile of clothes lay and dug into the very bottom of the chair. There was a small bag there that she had missed; he picked it up and tossed it to her.

"More items from the merchant that I thought you might need," he said quietly. "Soap, a comb, some hair things," he made funny jabbing gestures at his head, "and some manner of cosmetics. I do not know what they are; the merchant told me that women in Paris use them so I told him just to include them."

She lifted an eyebrow at him before pulling open the bag and digging inside; there was indeed sweet-smelling soap, a tortoise shell comb, several decorative hair pins, two glass phials of perfumed oil, an ointment for softening the skin and a tiny alabaster pot of red ointment for the lips. Very feminine, foolish things, but she was deeply grateful. And deeply touched. With a twinkle in her eye, she sought his gaze.

"I cannot possibly thank you enough," she said sincerely. "It was very thoughtful and very sweet of you to procure all of this for me."

He dipped his head. "A genuine pleasure, my lady. Now I shall wait outside while you dress." He pointed at her. "You're still running about in that sheet."

She grinned, shrugging her shoulders in agreement. "Rhys," she said hesitantly. "I am truly sorry if I upset you with talk of your wife earlier. Please believe me when I say that I did not mean to. You have been very kind to me and I would do nothing to intentionally upset you."

His gaze lingered on her. "I know, my lady."

"Then you are not upset with me?"

"It is of no matter, my lady."

"But it is to me," she insisted. "Your feelings matter very much and I am truly sorry."

He almost dismissed her again; they could both see it coming. But after a moment, he simply shook his head. "It is kind of you to be concerned for my feelings. But I truly have none in the matter. And you did not upset me."

She wasn't quite sure it was the truth but she let it go. Rhys' attention lingered on her a moment longer before he quit the room, moving out into the night that now seemed to be clearing. Even after the door softly shut, she stood there, her thoughts lingering on the massive bear of a man who had been both very cold and very kind to her. The paradox was baffling. But those thoughts vanished in favor of thoughts of her new garments, and within little time she was clad in a new shift, the red pantalets, the woolen hose and the soft yellow lamb's wool surcoat that hugged every curve of her delicious torso.

She pinned her considerable mane into a neat bun at the nape of her neck and wrapped herself up in the new bleached woolen cloak, a magnificent garment that was lined with gray rabbit. She also pulled on the gloves. Wrapped in her new clothes, she felt so warm, so cozy, that the heat invited sleep and before she realized it, she was back on the bed. Her intention had been to doze until Rhys came back for her, but she quickly fell into a deep sleep as the sun began to rise. For the first time in a day, she was at peace.

The next sensation that infiltrated her sleep-hazed mind was that of a hand being clamped over her mouth.

Read the rest of **SPECTRE OF THE SWORD**
in eBook or in paperback.

About Kathryn Le Veque

Medieval Just Got Real.

KATHRYN LE VEQUE is a USA TODAY Bestselling author, an Amazon All-Star author, and a #1 bestselling, award-winning, multi-published author in Medieval Historical Romance and Historical Fiction. She has been featured in the NEW YORK TIMES and on USA TODAY's HEA blog. In March 2015, Kathryn was the featured cover story for the March issue of InD'Tale Magazine, the premier Indie author magazine. She was also a quadruple nominee (a record!) for the prestigious RONE awards for 2015.

Kathryn's Medieval Romance novels have been called 'detailed', 'highly romantic', and 'character-rich'. She crafts great adventures of love, battles, passion, and romance in the High Middle Ages. More than that, she writes for both women AND men – an unusual crossover for a romance author – and Kathryn has many male readers who enjoy her stories because of the male perspective, the action, and the adventure.

On October 29, 2015, Amazon launched Kathryn's Kindle Worlds Fan Fiction site WORLD OF DE WOLFE PACK. Please visit Kindle Worlds for Kathryn Le Veque's World of de Wolfe Pack and find many action-packed adventures written by some of the top authors in their genre using Kathryn's characters from the de Wolfe Pack series. As Kindle World's FIRST Historical Romance fan fiction world, Kathryn Le Veque's World of de Wolfe Pack will contain all of the great storytelling you have come to expect.

Kathryn loves to hear from her readers. Please find Kathryn on Facebook at Kathryn Le Veque, Author, or join her on Twitter @kathrynleveque, and don't forget to visit her website and sign up for her blog at www.kathrynleveque.com.

www.ingramcontent.com/pod-product-compliance
Lightning Source LLC
LaVergne TN
LVHW012029071225
827201LV00035B/388